Angela
MARSONS
DEAD
MEMORIES

bookouture

Published by Bookouture in 2019

An imprint of StoryFire Ltd.

Carmelite House
50 Victoria Embankment
London EC4Y 0DZ

www.bookouture.com

ISBN: 978-1-78681-772-3
eBook ISBN: 978-1-78681-771-6

This book is dedicated to Maureen King who, although gone, will never be forgotten.

PROLOGUE

Amy Wilde's eyes closed as the liquid gold entered her vein and travelled around her body. She could visualise the trail of white hot beauty hurtling towards her brain.

The effects were almost immediate. The pleasure suffused every inch of her being, almost painful in its intensity. The euphoria transported her to another planet, another world, somewhere undiscovered. Nothing in her life had ever felt so good. Elation pumped through her body. Wave after wave of ecstasy surged through her skin, muscles, tendons – right through to the centre of her bones. She tried to hang on to it as it weakened in strength.

Don't go. I love you. I need you. Don't go, her mind screamed, pleaded, begged, desperate to hang on to the sensation for as long as she could.

As the last tremors of happiness faded away she turned her head to her left to share that secret smile with Mark, her lover, her friend, her soulmate as she always did after a shared hit of heroin.

But Mark didn't look okay, she realised, through the fatigue that was pulling her into the welcoming dark oblivion that always followed the hit.

She knew they were sitting on the floor in an unfamiliar room. She knew the radiator was warming her through the denim jacket.

She knew there were handcuffs around her wrist but she didn't care. Nothing mattered after a hit like that.

She tried to say Mark's name but the word wouldn't crawl out of her mouth.

Something was wrong with Mark.

His eyes were not closed, already succumbed to the warm drowsiness. They were wide: staring, unblinking, at a spot on the ceiling.

Amy wanted to reach across and touch him, shake him awake. She wanted to share that smile before she gave in to the dark.

But she couldn't move a muscle.

This wasn't normal. The usual heaviness that soaked into her bones made her feel lethargic and weighted down but she could always muster enough energy to turn and snuggle Mark.

The exhaustion was trying to take her, pulling at her eyelids, willing her to sleep, but she had to try and touch Mark.

Through the descending fog she tried with all her might to move a single finger, but there was no response. The message was not making it out of her brain.

She tried to fight the creeping drowsiness, but it was like a blanket being pulled up over her head.

She felt helpless, weak, unable to shoo away the blackness, but she knew that Mark needed her.

It was no use. She couldn't outrun the shadows that chased her.

Her eyes began to droop as she heard the door to the flat slam shut.

CHAPTER 1

Kim felt her jaws clench at the incessant tapping sound niggling her left ear.

A moth had entered her garage space through the open shutter that was capturing little breeze from the storm-heavy June air. The insect was launching itself repeatedly against the 60 watt bulb.

But that wasn't the tapping that was annoying her.

'If you're bored, piss off,' she said, as a few flecks of rust dislodged from the wheel spokes and landed on her jeans.

'I'm not bored, I'm thinking,' Gemma said, tipping her head and looking up at the moth, who was giving himself an aneurism.

'Convince me,' Kim said, drily.

'I'm trying to decide whether to take the flowers with me or arrange them in a vase at home.'

'Hmm…' Kim offered, helpfully, as she continued to scrape.

She knew that Bryant and many other people questioned her relationship with the teenager who had been sent to kill her, manipulated and used by Kim's nemesis, Doctor Alexandra Thorne.

Bryant's view was that the girl should be locked up at Drake Hall prison, where her mother was currently residing and where the girl had come into contact with the sociopathic psychiatrist who had made it her life's work to torment Kim at every opportunity since she had put an end to her sick experiments on her vulnerable patients.

As far as Bryant was concerned there were no circumstances under which you could befriend a person who had wanted you dead. It was simple. Except it wasn't. Because Kim understood two things perfectly: how skilled Alexandra Thorne was in manipulating every weakness or vulnerability a person had – the ones they knew about and even the ones they didn't. And that the girl had suffered a shit childhood through no fault of her own.

She wasn't being facetious in not responding to the girl's comment. It just wasn't something she could see happening.

Gemma's mother had been in and out of prison all the kid's life, palming her child off onto any relative who'd have her, until no one would take the child. Gemma had resorted to selling her body in order to eat. Yet, for some reason, the kid had maintained regular contact with her mother and visited at every opportunity.

The woman was due for release the following week but somehow she always managed to get herself into some further trouble that extended her sentence.

Kim had offered Gemma a loose invitation that whenever she was in need of a meal to come round, instead of heading for the streets, and while she couldn't offer a gourmet meal she could throw in some oven chips or a pizza.

And Gemma had taken her up on the offer, even after she'd secured a job a month ago working part-time at Dudley Library.

'So, how's work?' Kim asked, avoiding the subject of her mother completely.

Gemma blew a raspberry, and Kim laughed.

There were days Gemma was an old eighteen-year-old hardened by choices and what life had thrown at her already and other times she was just eighteen.

And Kim hadn't minded the unexpected company today. Of all days.

'Look, Gem, it might not be brain—'

'Numbing,' she cut in. 'It's brain numbing,' she said, pulling a face.

'I check books out; I check books back in. I put 'em back on the shelves. In the evening before we close I get the coveted job of wiping over the keyboards of the communal computers.'

Kim hid her smile. It was much more entertaining hearing Gemma complain about her job than moaning she couldn't get one.

'Oh, and yesterday I had this lovely old dear approach me,' she said, standing. She hunched her back and pretended to walk with a cane across the space. '"Excuse me, love, but could you show me how to send these photos to my son in New Zealand?" she asked thrusting her ancient digital camera at me. I swear…'

'Hang on,' Kim said, as her phone began to ring.

'Stone,' she answered, brushing rust off her jeans.

'Sorry to disturb you, Marm, but something happening over at Hollytree. A bit garbled. Got an address and one word,' said a voice from dispatch.

'Give me the address,' she said, getting to her feet.

'Chaucer block, flat 4B,' he said.

Her stomach turned. Same block, three floors lower. Today, of all fucking days.

'Okay, I'm on my way. Get Bryant en route too.'

'Will do, Marm.'

'And the word?' she asked. 'What was it?'

'It was "dead", Marm. The word was "dead".'

CHAPTER 2

Kim negotiated the maze of streets, dead ends and shortcuts with ease on the Ninja, drawing curious glances from the groups of people congregating on the pavements wearing as little clothing as possible in an effort to catch the night-time breeze.

The sun had set fifteen minutes earlier leaving a red marble sky and a temperature still in the high teens. It was going to be another long, sticky night.

She wound the bike around the bin stores and headed for Chaucer House, the middle block of flats at the bulging belly of the sprawling Hollytree housing estate.

Chaucer was known for being the roughest of the tower blocks, home to the worst that society had to offer.

It had also been home for the first six years of her life. Normally, she was able to keep that thought pinned to the noticeboard at the back of her mind. But not today. Right now, it was front and centre.

She eased the bike through two police cars, an ambulance and a first responder bike and parked behind Bryant's Astra Estate. He lived a couple of miles closer and it had taken her a few minutes to shepherd Gemma out of her house. The girl had been wide-eyed with curious questions about what she'd been called to.

Not that Kim would have told her but she hadn't known herself.

'Oi, pig on a bike,' shouted a voice from the crowd as she removed her helmet.

She ran a hand through her short black hair, freeing it from her scalp, while shaking her head. Yeah, she hadn't heard that insult for at least, oh, three days or so.

The crowd around the voice laughed, which Kim ignored as she headed for the entrance to the tower block.

She'd passed an outer cordon, an inner cordon and then met a wall of constables at the lifts and staircase.

The lift on the right had dropped below floor level and its doors gaped open, obviously out of order.

'Evening, Marm,' said a WPC stepping forward. 'One working lift,' she said, pointing to the display which told her it was currently on floor five. 'We're clearing the floor above and the floor below, Marm.'

Kim nodded her understanding. The stairs were being kept free for police use, while the lift was being kept as a means of access for the residents.

Evacuating the whole building for an incident on one floor was not an option, so the situation had to be managed.

She headed for the stairs and began the ascent to the fourth floor.

Thank goodness her left leg was now in a stronger state to deal with it, following the fracture she'd sustained after falling from the roof of a two-storey building in a previous case three months ago.

Officers were stationed at each floor to ensure no one tried to get closer to the incident. One of the officers at the fourth floor smiled and held open the door into the lobby.

She approached the open doorway.

Inspector Plant blocked her way.

'What the?...'

'If you can just hang on?' he said, looking behind him.

She gave him a hard stare. She knew this guy well, had worked with him a few times. What the hell was he playing at?

'Plant, if you don't move yourself from that—'

'Your colleague, Bryant,' he said, uncomfortably. 'He doesn't want you in there.'

'What the fuck are you on?' she raged. It was a crime scene, she was the SIO and she wanted access.

'I don't give a shit what…'

Her words trailed away as Bryant came into view behind the inspector, who moved out of the way.

His face was ashen and drawn, his eyes full of horror. He hadn't looked as bad as this when he'd been lying on the floor with her hand in his stomach to stop the blood that was oozing out of him on their last major case. If he wasn't known to the constables as a detective sergeant someone would be wrapping him in a foil blanket.

'Bryant, what the?…'

'Don't go in there, guv,' he said, quietly.

Kim tried to understand what was going on here.

Together they had witnessed the worst that mankind could do to each other. They'd viewed bodies where the stench of blood clung to the air. They'd seen corpses in the worst state of decay, alive with maggots and flies. Together they had unearthed the bodies of innocent teenage girls. He knew her stomach could handle just about anything, so why was he trying to stand in her way now?

He ushered her to the side. 'Kim, I'm asking as a friend. Don't go in there.'

Never before had he used her first name on the job. Not once.

What the hell had he just seen?

She took a deep breath and fixed him with a stare.

'Bryant, get out of my way. Now.'

CHAPTER 3

Kim weaved her way through the personnel that were providing a guiding tunnel towards the crime scene. No one gave her a second glance. She was expected so what the hell was Bryant's problem? she wondered, feeling his presence behind.

Bloody drama queen.

A wall of uniforms parted, and she froze.

For just a few seconds every sound around her was muted, every movement not seen, as her eyes registered the scene before her.

The saliva dried in her mouth as she wondered if she was going to pass out. She felt Bryant's hand on her elbow, steadying her.

She turned to look at him. His expression was fearful, concerned. And she got it. She knew why he'd tried to protect her.

She swallowed down the nausea and turned back, trying to shake off the slow-motion feel to her actions.

An emaciated black-haired male in his late teens sat with his back against the radiator. His dead, glossy eyes stared straight ahead, his head lolled to the left. His bony legs were lost inside the jeans that covered them. Milky white arms, little wider than a snooker cue, hung out of the short-sleeved tee shirt.

Undeniably dead, his body began to move, to shudder rhythmically. Kim followed the line of his right arm, slightly extended from his body, to his wrist and the handcuff that was still attached to the radiator and the wrist of the girl on whom the paramedics were still working, causing the awkward, jerky movements that rippled across.

Events around her began to filter back in as though someone was gradually removing headphones from her ears.

'I think we gotta move her, Geoff,' said one of the paramedics. 'We got her back twice, next time…'

His words trailed away, no need for a full explanation.

She moved aside as they lifted her effortlessly onto the stretcher. The preservation of life over the preservation of evidence.

No one got to investigate anything while paramedics were working.

There were no grunts of effort as they lay her down.

The girl was even thinner than the dead boy beside her. Her bones appeared to be barely covered by the thin layer of skin that hung loosely in places. Her young face was gaunt, cheekbones and chin sharp against her skin. Dark rings circled her eyes and sores littered her skin.

A low moan sounded from her mouth as they headed towards the door.

The second paramedic kicked something as he passed by. It landed at her feet.

She heard Bryant's sharp intake of breath as he looked down at the empty Coca Cola bottle.

Kim tried to maintain her composure as she looked around. She expected all eyes to be on her. Waiting for some kind of reaction. A reaction that every cell of her being wanted to scream.

No one was looking her way. Of course, they weren't. They didn't know.

A boy and a girl chained to a radiator. A Coke bottle. This same flat a few floors up.

The sweltering heat outside. The boy dead, the girl alive.

They didn't know this was a recreation of the most traumatic event of her life.

Bryant did and yet there was something even he wasn't aware of.

Today marked the thirty-year anniversary.

CHAPTER 4

It was almost eleven when Kim parked the Ninja outside Halesowen Police Station.

And whether or not the weariness that had taken over her body had wanted to propel her straight home, she hadn't been surprised to see the message from Woody on her phone instructing her to return to the station upon leaving the scene, whatever the time.

And she had been only too pleased to get away from Bryant who had asked her a hundred times if she was okay while his eyes had searched hers to see how she was feeling.

She had convinced him that she was fine and now it was time to convince Woody.

'Sir,' she said, putting her head around the door. She entered and left the door open. Subtle, she thought.

'Close it,' he said.

Not subtle enough.

She stood behind the chair opposite his desk.

Still here at this time of night and his only concession to the hour was a loosening of the tie and a few crumples in his brilliant white shirt.

'Saw the report, so tell me more about the crime scene.'

'Not sure there is a crime yet,' she answered. 'Two teenagers, drugs, one overdosed and one pretty close. I'll attend the post-mortem of the male tomorrow but I think it'll turn up as accidental overdose.'

'That's it?' he asked, his face hardening.

She opened her arms expressively, unsure what he wanted to hear. 'Err… Bryant got there before—'

'And appeared to remain alone judging by the level of detail you've just given me.'

'I'm not sure what?…'

His gaze intensified in line with his irritation. 'Were the needles used for the hit present? Was the tourniquet on the male's arm and were you even there?'

Kim thought for a moment, before speaking.

'I arrived at the scene and entered the larger of the two bedrooms, which was approximately ten feet by ten. On my right were two police constables and a female sergeant. One of the officers was blonde and two were brunette; one had an eagle tattoo on his left forearm; and the blonde guy had a beard.'

'Stone, I think…'

'On my left was a third constable standing over two paramedics who were on the ground trying to keep the female alive, who had died twice, incidentally, before I got there. One of the paramedics was wearing—'

'Stone, shut up,' he snapped.

'Yes, sir,' she said.

'What about the handcuffs, chained to the radiator?'

'Yes, sir,' she answered, pushing the vision from her mind.

'You didn't think to mention this to…'

'Coincidence,' she finished for him, totally convinced that's what it was.

'You don't believe in coincidence,' he responded, shrewdly.

'In all honesty, I'm thinking it's some kind of sex game gone wrong. Perhaps some type of I'll inject you and you inject me thing that got out of hand. I'm sure the drug paraphernalia is there somewhere and Forensics will have it bagged and analysed.'

'So, you don't draw any comparisons at all?' he asked.

'To what?' she replied, being deliberately vague as though the thought had never occurred to her.

If she was honest, the second she'd walked into that room a few floors below her own home for six years, she had immediately been transported back thirty years and saw her dead brother lying against the radiator, but as her working brain had kicked in she'd realised that it was purely coincidental and had no link to her own childhood. Sad as it was, these kids were drug addicts and had died by the sword.

The loss of the young man's life, although tragic, had no link to her or Mikey.

She should have guessed that Woody would remember the salient facts from her personnel file and, although they'd never spoken about it, she was well aware that he knew things she had shared with very few people. Even Bryant only knew the barest of bones.

'So, Stone, I repeat my question: you're convinced there is absolutely no tie to you at all?'

She didn't hesitate. 'Completely, sir,' she said, and meant it. Almost.

CHAPTER 5

By 7 a.m. on Tuesday morning Kim had drunk a pot of coffee back home, walked and fed Barney, her unsociable, spirited Border Collie, got into work and prepared herself for Bryant's early entrance.

'Morning, guv. You—'

'I'm fine and there's no reason why I shouldn't be. Got it?'

'So, how'd you sleep?' he said, asking her the exact same question but with different words.

'I slept fine,' she answered, pouring her fourth coffee of the day. And that was a blatant lie.

After her late-night walk with Barney she had crawled into bed and instantly felt wide awake. She'd stared into the darkness, playing back the scene in her mind, and pushing away the memories that were trying to force open the lid of the box within which they were stored.

She'd employed all her old habits to trick her mind into shutting out the intrusive thoughts. She picked one of her favourite biking routes: up through Stourton to the Bridgnorth Road, past Six Ashes and through villages like Enville and Morville.

She tried to imagine herself handling the Ninja, dipping and leaning into the bends, opening up the engine, working hard to control the bike on the route she knew all too well. Normally she'd feel her mind react to the need for concentration, her body tensing and adjusting until she fell asleep, her mind distracted for just long enough to escape the thoughts.

But not last night. In her mind, she'd crashed the bike four times as her brain had refused to join in the exercise that was her version of counting sheep.

All she could picture was that young man's body slumped lifelessly against the radiator and lying in the dark silence of her bedroom had not helped rid her of that vision.

And so she'd risen, made coffee, and worked on the bike for a couple of hours before commencing her morning routine, which had been dangerously close to her night-time routine.

'Ooh, is that a caffeine twitch or are you just pleased to see me?' he joked.

'Yeah, splitting my sides at that.'

He glanced sideways at her. 'You trying to be funny?' he asked, glancing down at his own left-hand side which had been split with a five-inch blade a month earlier.

'Jeez, Bryant, I didn't mean—'

'Morning,' Penn said, saving her from continuing.

He placed the Tupperware box on the spare desk before removing his man-bag and throwing it beneath his desk.

'Sorry I'm late, boss,' Stacey said, rushing in and throwing herself into the seat that had once belonged to Kevin Dawson.

Kim knew they all missed him every day, sometimes still expected him to breeze in with some kind of smart-arse comment. But not as often as the early days. Their acceptance was coming with time.

'Okey dokey, folks,' Kim said. 'Update on cases from yesterday?'

'Didn't you get called out last night, boss?' Stacey asked, frowning.

Normally a call-out late at night was a precursor to their next big case meaning other cases had to be resolved quickly, where possible, or handed over to another team.

Normally one of them would be at the board, writing the name of the victim, underlining it, stating the priority of uncovering the reason for the person's demise.

Normally, there would be an air of anticipation, a crackle, invisible but electric, an energy that only came at the beginning. Bryant would compare it to the beginning of a four-course meal at his favourite restaurant. She would liken it to starting a new build of a classic motorcycle in her garage, bits and pieces strewn all over the concrete floor. Each with their own purpose waiting to be put together, attached to the next component which eventually formed the whole.

Except this case had no mysteries to unravel and, as tragic as the scene had been, it had not been murder and it had no link to her.

'Double overdose, Stace,' Kim explained. 'Just waiting on a call from Mitch to confirm scene findings and it'll all be closed.'

'Oh, okay,' she said, trying not to let the disappointment show.

People outside the profession might think the response cold to the death of one young person and the near-death of another but Kim understood it. Every detective she knew had signed up to stop bad people getting away with bad acts. Stacey was not unfeeling towards the person who had died. She was only disappointed at not being able to track and find the person responsible. And normally Kim would agree with her. Only this time she wanted to get as far away from this scene as she could so the vision and the memory could fade from her mind.

The sooner the better.

'So, Penn, where are you at?'

'Three witnesses left to interview, boss, but not enthusiastically confident about the outcome.'

She nodded. Two thirteen-year-old kids passing the entrance to Hollytree had been beaten up by three older kids, and despite decent descriptions no one on the estate was talking.

'Keep at it,' she said, feeling a 'we did everything we could do' chat coming on with the parents. It happened rarely but sometimes there was just nowhere left to go.

But when she did have that conversation she wanted to be sure that they actually had done everything they could.

'Stace?' Kim asked.

'Final interview with Lisa Stiles today and should be ready to present tonight.'

'Good work,' Kim said.

Lisa Stiles was a woman in her early thirties with two young boys. She'd been the victim of spousal abuse for a decade and had said nothing. She'd accepted the behaviour from her husband thinking she'd been protecting her children from the truth. Until a month earlier when her youngest child had punched her in the mouth 'Like Daddy did'.

The realisation that she could be raising two small boys to believe this was normal behaviour had terrified the life out of her.

It was Stacey who had taken the initial report and continued to guide her through the process gently, efficiently and with sensitivity.

She had built a strong, solid case that would be presented to the CPS.

'Penn, you know what's coming,' Kim said, nodding towards his desk.

He pulled a face. 'Really?'

Kim nodded.

'So, when you said Betty was my "welcome to the team present"…'

'Yeah, it was loose, so hand it over. Stacey gets the plant.'

Stacey offered him a triumphant look as she stroked the green leaves.

'Work harder, Penn and you'll get her—'

She stopped speaking as her phone rang. 'Just gonna take this call from Mitch,' she said, walking towards her office, signalling they could continue with their own work.

'Hey,' she said, throwing herself into her seat.

Bryant appeared and propped up her door frame.

'Morning, Inspector. Trust you're well after your late-night outing,' he offered.

She'd missed him at the scene but there'd been no reason to stay.

'I'll send over a full inventory by lunchtime but thought you'd want a summary of our initial findings.'

'Go ahead,' she said, twirling a pen between her fingers.

'Loose change fallen from male's jeans pocket totalling £1.72. A tissue in his front pocket, an empty wallet, a faded receipt from B&M and very little else.'

By the time he'd finished speaking she'd worked out there were seventeen blue stripes on Bryant's tie.

'And…' she said, waiting for the most important thing. The thing that would rule this some kind of suicide pact or accidental death.

'Err… and isn't it a beautiful morning?'

'Needles,' she said, shaking her head at Bryant. Sometimes Mitch was excellent at his job and other times not so much.

'Sorry, no needles,' he said, definitely.

'But, the paramedics… the officers…'

'Definitely no needles,' he said, with finality.

Make them up, she wanted to scream. Lie to me.

'So, the full report—'

'Thanks, Mitch,' she said, ending the call.

Bryant viewed her questioningly.

'No needles at the scene,' she said quietly.

His expression reflected the horror she was feeling at the realisation.

Those kids hadn't injected themselves.

CHAPTER 6

'Post-mortem starts in about five minutes,' Bryant said, as she strode into Russells Hall Hospital and headed in the opposite direction of the morgue. Kim was still unable to walk these halls without remembering the stab wound her partner had sustained during their last major case.

'On the dead victim,' she retorted. 'And last I heard we still had a live one.'

'Fair point,' he said, following her to the main reception, which was in the process of opening.

Kim smiled in what she hoped was an apologetic manner as she passed the two people already waiting in line.

Bryant's whispers of 'Sorry' behind her told her she hadn't been all that successful.

'Detective Inspector Stone,' she said, showing her ID to the woman who was about to explain to her the queuing system.

'A girl was brought in last night: late teens, suspected drug overdose.'

The woman turned to her computer. 'Name?'

Kim was tempted to say that had she known that it would have been the first thing she'd said, but stopped herself. Co-operation from this woman could prevent her trawling around countless wards searching for the girl.

'Unidentified,' she answered.

The woman's lips pursed slightly as she tapped a few more keys.

She paused to reach to her right and switch on a small desk fan.

'High Dependency Unit,' she said, finally granting a half smile. 'Do you need…'

'No, thanks. We know where it is.'

Bryant followed as she headed past the café at speed.

'So, guv, about last night…' he said, catching up with her.

'Bryant, I didn't want to talk about it then and I don't want to talk about it now. Yes, there was a vague similarity to an incident in my past but it's purely coincidental and nothing I'd like to analyse further. Okay?'

'Yeah, good to know, but I was only gonna apologise for overreacting.'

'Oh, apology accepted,' she said, taken aback.

'Although, you have to admit—'

'Bryant, shut it and press the button,' she said, as they arrived at the ward.

He did both.

Kim held up her ID to the woman, who flashed her a beginning-of-shift smile.

'May I help you?'

'A teenage girl was brought in last night. Suspected overdose. I need to speak to—'

'I'm sorry, I can't help you,' she said, shaking her head.

Kim's patience was wearing thin. 'But the receptionist said she'd been—'

'I can't help you, Inspector, because the girl you're after died. Not more than fifteen minutes ago.'

CHAPTER 7

Austin Penn sat in his Ford Fiesta at the entrance to the Hollytree estate.

He'd always known about the place, even when he was at school. It had always been rough and had featured on the news most nights. Back then and even when he'd been a trainee the estate had been known for violence, antisocial behaviour and drugs, but only in the last ten years had the gang mentality come to the fore.

West Mercia had had its share of similar estates. He'd been called to Westlands in Droitwich more times than he could count but it hadn't come close to the sheer hopelessness that pervaded every inch of Hollytree.

Frustratingly, no one snitched, no one talked but it wasn't anything to do with community. Most people on Hollytree were there because they couldn't exist within a community. They didn't talk for two reasons. Firstly, because they hated the police and secondly because they were scared of the Hollytree gang. It was difficult enough to combat one of those problems but both was near impossible. But if he could just find someone who wasn't quite as scared of the gang.

He glanced towards the abandoned row of shops, all boarded up except for two.

Douglas Mason and Kelvin Smart had ventured onto Hollytree two nights ago, got no further than the row of shops before receiving six broken bones and an unenviable collection of cuts and bruises between them.

When interviewed they had both claimed they thought there was a chippy on the corner.

Penn had said nothing to the kids' parents but he hadn't believed them.

After asking around he had established that many local kids from decent, hard-working backgrounds dared each other onto Hollytree to see how far in they could get. Well, these two hadn't got very far at all. But no matter whether or not it was a game, the kids had been bothering no one and certainly hadn't deserved that.

They were both back home now being cosseted and likely spoilt by parents who were waiting for justice. And he suspected they were going to be disappointed.

He had seen the look on the boss's face when he'd revealed his progress on the case. He didn't relish the conversation with the parents either.

How can they have been beaten black and blue in broad day light without anyone seeing a thing? they would ask.

His response of 'this is Hollytree' would not suffice. Understandably.

Equally, that expression on his boss's face was not something he enjoyed. He knew her disappointment wasn't at him personally but at the situation.

'Damn it,' he said banging his hands on the steering wheel.

If only he could find one person prepared to talk to him.

'Fuck me, mate,' he said out loud as an oversize vehicle passed by his parking spot leaving only a hair's breadth of space between them. Penn's car shook with the impact.

'I'll bloody report...' his words trailed away as he read the words on the back of the truck.

He smiled, started the car and followed the van.

CHAPTER 8

Keats paused his Dictaphone as Kim and Bryant entered.

'Well, how lovely to see you, Bryant,' he said, glancing her way. 'And I see you brought your bulldog.'

'Don't bait her, Keats. She is not in a good mood,' Bryant said, wearily.

'Discernible how?' Keats asked.

'Certainly not enhanced by you two clowns acting as though I'm not here,' she snapped.

'Ooh, tetchy, Inspector,' he said, unruffled. 'So, who stole your favourite toy?'

'The girl died,' she said, flatly, heaving herself up onto the metal work surface.

'Aah yes, I heard she was in a bad way. I understand the paramedics already saved her.'

'Twice,' Kim confirmed. 'But she slipped into a coma and died half an hour ago.'

Keats sighed. 'If help had come sooner, who knows? Heroin overdose can be prevented if caught in time.'

'Really?' Bryant asked. 'I'd have thought too much of that poison running round your body would just be game over.'

Keats shook his head. 'Heroin is an opioid as you know. It enters the brain and is converted back into morphine which binds to the opioid receptors throughout the central nervous system. Dopamine floods the system giving a rush of pleasure much higher than you could ever hope to experience naturally.'

'And that's what keeps them addicted,' Bryant observed.

'Actually, no,' Keats replied. 'The feelings of euphoria are short-lived. The feeling dissipates and then disappears altogether as the user builds tolerance to the drug. Most seasoned users continue to use to avoid the withdrawal but the high they originally felt is a distant memory.'

'But an overdose can be reversed?' Kim asked, surprised.

Keats nodded. 'There are chemicals that bind to the same receptors temporarily displacing the heroin, but these chemicals have a shorter life than heroin and won't stay in the body for long. It's not perfect but it can be done.'

'Not for our girl, unfortunately,' Bryant said.

'Poor child,' Keats said, shaking his head. 'It would seem I'll be meeting her properly later.'

Kim checked her watch. 'Thought you were doing matey boy at nine?'

All three sunken dishes were empty.

'He is done,' Keats said with a smile. 'When Mitch told me there were no needles at the scene I had this strange premonition, accurately as it happens, of you storming in here first thing this morning, demanding answers.'

'Hardly a shot in the dark, was it?' she asked.

He ignored her and read from his clipboard. '"The unidentified male is five feet seven inches with curly black hair. Weighs one hundred and seventeen pounds", which is four pounds below the lowest figure for his height. You don't need to be told he had needle marks from injecting heroin. "Historically he has four broken bones from childhood".'

'Either clumsy or beaten,' Bryant said.

Keats nodded. 'No way to tell for sure but his bones tell me he wasn't taken care of during childhood. All major organs in reasonably good shape, although he was a bit of a drinker too. Minor liver damage.

'In the absence of any other clear method it is my opinion that this male died of a heroin overdose. Now how that heroin got into him is your job, Inspector.'

'Anything to help us identify him?'

Boy how she hated thinking of victims without a name. She needed to know who she was fighting for.

'Opinions or fact?' he asked.

'You don't normally ask before you share either,' she observed.

'And, she's back in the room,' Keats said, peering over his glasses.

'In my opinion he is late teens, early twenties, and is homeless. His nails and teeth don't reflect someone with easy or regular access to hygiene facilities. He has a Celtic band tattoo around his upper left arm.'

Keats paused while Bryant took out his notepad.

'A piercing in his right ear which has been left to heal over. All samples have been sent to the lab and I'll have results for you in the next couple of days.'

Kim jumped down from the counter lighter than when she'd jumped up. Clearly there was no link to her or her past, and although two people had lost their lives in a similar way to how her mother had tried to kill her and Mikey, there was no connection. It really was coincidence and she could attack this murder like every other she'd been tasked to investigate. Everything that had linked them was nothing but coincidence, which for once she was prepared to consider. The Coca Cola bottle could have been left there at any time, but a vital part of the scene was missing and that was all she needed to know to rule out any connection. Woody had instructed her to return if there were any further developments.

'Phew,' Bryant said, as they reached the doors. 'I can see you're relieved there's no link, so no need to head back to the—'

'Just one more thing, Inspector,' Keats said.

Her stomach turned. Of course there was.

She turned to face him as the tension seeped into her jaw.

'There were barely any stomach contents but he must have fancied some kind of snack not long before he died.'

'What do you mean?' she asked, as her mouth began to dry.

'I'm being facetious about the snack but there was a tiny bit of paper in his throat. Deep. I mean somehow it was wedged deep down in there; it looks like it's from some kind of cracker.'

Kim turned to her colleague and held his questioning glance. 'Take me back to the station. Now.'

CHAPTER 9

'Sir, we need to talk,' Kim said, walking into Woody's office.

His slight flare of the nostrils and tense jaw told her she'd forgotten to knock. Again.

He held up a hand as he continued listening to the voice on the other end of the phone.

'Understood, sir. I agree. I'll keep you updated,' he said, ending the call.

He linked his fingers and placed them beneath his chin.

'And what's so urgent you barge into my office without knocking?'

'A development,' she said, taking a seat.

Woody's frown deepened, not because he hadn't invited her to sit but because she never did if she could help it. In fact, given the choice she communicated from the doorway.

'What kind of development?' he asked, before turning to his computer. 'I understand it's no longer the cut and dried drug overdose you thought it was, that it's now a double murder. It's barely 10 a.m. and you're telling me there's even more.'

She nodded. 'Afraid so,' she said, taking a deep breath. What she was about to say could change everything.

'Sir, there might be a link.'

'To what?'

'Me,' she answered. 'Something was found in the throat of the male victim.' Her voice lowered. 'A portion of a cracker packet.'

'Oh,' he said, and then repeated as the finer detail of her personnel file made its way to the front of his mind.

He was silent for a full five seconds. 'So, we…'

'Sir, I don't want you to take me off this case,' she blurted out. 'I understand your position, but if this case is linked to me I'm the best person to head the investigation and if it isn't linked to me I'm still the best person.'

He offered her a brief smile. 'And modest too.'

She knew what was coming. Given what she'd told him he had no choice but to pull her from the case, bring in a new DI or even pass it along to another team entirely.

'Do you know the victims?' he asked.

'Both still unidentified but they are not familiar to me at all.'

'So, we have two unknown heroin addicts murdered in a flat close to where you used to live and one had paper in his throat?'

'Yes, sir, but it was—'

'Stone,' he snapped. 'Have I yet said anything that is incorrect?' She shook her head.

'Then I suggest you shut up for a minute.'

'But sir, I just think—'

'That's the problem, Stone. It matters not one iota what you think and the only important opinion in this instance is mine.'

CHAPTER 10

'Okay, guys, drop what you're doing,' Kim said, walking back into the squad room.

Everyone looked surprised but Penn looked positively crestfallen. 'Really, boss?'

'Well your case is hardly pressing, is it?' she asked. She was sure the parents of the two teenage boys could wait just a few more hours to learn they'd been unable to make a case for prosecution.

'Got a witness to the assault of the boys, boss,' Penn said.

She frowned. 'How?'

She'd only been gone a couple of hours.

'Mrs Mowbray from number 9 Church Court. Outside her maisonette when three youths, all named and shamed, passed by laughing and bragging about what they'd done.'

Kim regarded him suspiciously. 'How'd that happen?'

'She's moving out. Had enough. Going to live with her sister on Anglesey. She's not frightened to speak out any more.'

Kim was impressed. 'Stace, give Betty back to Penn.'

'But boss…'

'The man deserves his plant back,' she instructed.

Stacey begrudgingly pushed it back across the desk, into Penn's waiting hands.

'Okay, guys, someone get the board.'

Bryant stood.

'Okay, someone who isn't Bryant get the board,' she said. His handwriting was atrocious.

Stacey stood and grabbed the marker pen.

As ever it had taken her a few seconds to catch up to Woody's thought process. He had encouraged her to stop speaking for a reason. It was his call whether or not she should be removed from a case, so it didn't matter right now if she thought there was a link to her past. It mattered if *he* thought there was a link to her past. And right now he was calling the cracker wrapper coincidence.

'Before we start, Woody has insisted on some assistance for us on this one. Not sure who or why but it's a condition.' And one she'd been unable to argue against. 'And even more upsetting is that none of us is allowed to speak to, interact with, or engage the press in any way shape or form. That will be handled from above.' A condition she'd been happy not to argue against.

'That must have upset you, guv,' Bryant observed.

'Gutted,' she answered.

Stacey stood poised at the board.

'Okay, unknown female on one board and unknown male on the other.' It irked her that she had no names but she hoped to change that as quickly as possible.

'Beneath the male, add tattoo of Celtic band, homeless and biscuit wrapper.'

'Huh?' Stacey asked, turning.

'In his throat,' Kim said, keeping her voice even. She'd decided that thinking of it as a biscuit wrapper helped her objectivity, and distance.

'Jesus, what's that all about?' Penn asked.

Kim shrugged.

Her team would know as little as possible.

Hopefully, they could find the sick bastard responsible before she had to tell them anything.

'Okay, Penn, I want you on CCTV and Stace I want you on victim identification and the anonymous call to the police.'

'And what about us, guv? What are we doing?' Bryant asked.

She took a breath. 'We, Bryant, are going back to the scene of the crime.'

CHAPTER 11

'You really think it's a good idea to say nothing to them?' Bryant asked, as they headed out of the building.

'What would you have me do, copy my personnel file and circulate it around the station?' she snapped.

'You don't think you're tying their hands a bit?'

'Bryant, we've had this case approximately two hours and I've barely had a chance to tie my laces never mind their hands. They have the facts of the case and that's all they need.'

'So, who is this person coming to help us and what exactly are they going to be doing?' he asked, deftly changing the subject.

'I have no idea and I have no idea,' she answered, as he pulled out of the station.

'So, it was a condition of keeping the case?' he asked, shrewdly.

'I know, let's pretend we have a double murder to solve and have us a conversation about that, shall we?'

'Ah, I thought so,' he said, knowingly. 'But fair enough. I do have some questions about that. Who are these kids? How were they killed? How were they lured to the flat or are they squatters? Who made the anonymous call to the police? Was it intentionally planned for your on-call? Why the handcuffs? Why the wrapper in the mouth? How did...'

'Jesus, Bryant, give it a rest and answer just one simple question for me.'

'Which is?'

'Are we bloody there yet?'

CHAPTER 12

'Go on then, I'll have another,' Stacey said, reaching into the Tupperware box for a chocolate chip cookie.

'Don't remember offering,' Penn said, without looking away from the screen.

'Compensation for losing Betty so soon,' she said, taking a bite and dropping crumbs onto her desk.

'You snooze, you lose,' he said, reaching for the headphones.

Stacey had learned by now that was Penn's not so subtle way of saying he wanted total immersion in the job at hand. And that was fine by her. She could respect that.

'So, what do you make of this case?' she asked.

He shrugged. 'I've worked a double murder before,' he said.

'Yeah, yeah, yeah, haven't we all, but isn't something a bit off? Boss attends and it's not a murder, next day it is and now we've got some help coming.'

Penn thought for a minute. 'You know, responding to any of that is not gonna help me trawl through the CCTV any quicker,' he said, putting on the headphones.

She'd already sent emails to every shelter and community centre in a 20-mile radius with a description of the unidentified victims and was waiting on a response. Mispers had turned up nothing so far.

Penn was tapping away furiously, and Stacey couldn't help the smile that landed on her lips. She was done being subtle with her colleague.

'We have nothing on Hollytree, so you're wasting your time,' she said, loudly.

'And I'll take your advice over the boss's direct instructions, shall I?'

'She'd expect you to work it out and spend your time productively,' Stacey offered.

'Yeah, yeah. You do know I'm not really new any more?' he asked, lifting up one earphone.

She shrugged, happy that she'd tried to help. He should know by now there were times when you followed the boss's instructions to the letter and times when you worked it out for yourself. Knowing which was which was a perilous journey and shouldn't be attempted without safety equipment.

'Hmm…' Penn said, removing his earphones completely.

Stacey peered around her computer.

'Ah, so now you want me?' she asked.

'Anonymous call came in at 10.03 p.m. and Keats has time of death of the male at around 9 p.m.'

'And?' Stacey asked.

'Well, we know officers had to force entry, so the call could only have come from the killer.'

Stacey nodded. They had listened to the recording countless times and could not establish the age or gender of the caller through the words 'Chaucer 4B, dead'.

Penn continued. 'So, the killer was in the room and must have known the girl was still alive.'

Stacey was beginning to understand why the boss insisted on early identification. She hated hearing The boy, The Girl, The Male, The Female. It depersonalised them. Put distance between the victim and the investigation.

'Go on,' she urged.

'Well, wouldn't you want to make sure they were both dead?'

'Could have been disturbed,' Stacey reasoned.

'And then go call the police?' he asked, doubtfully. 'Especially if you'd been disturbed. Wouldn't you want to just get as far away from the scene as possible?'

'Penn, your attention to detail…'

'But why not make sure the girl is dead before leaving or even just do it and go and leave them to be found whenever. Why the call to the police?'

Stacey took a second cookie, but paused before taking a bite.

'No violence, no struggle, no bruises or defensive wounds. It's like they both walked into that flat, sat down quietly and obediently and just waited to die.'

He nodded. 'There's a word that keeps going through my mind but it's not very nice. I keep thinking they were inconsequential, that they don't matter, do you know what I mean?' he asked, appearing puzzled at his own feelings.

'I think I do,' she said, following his train of thought.

'It's like this murder wasn't even anything to do with them. It was all to do with something else. They were a part of the set, a prop.'

Stacey could understand his view but she'd never worked a case where the victim or victims were not the focus of the investigation, so wondered if Penn was barking up the wrong tree completely.

She was about to voice her thoughts as her inbox dinged the receipt of a message from the community centre in Stourbridge.

She read it and then turned to Penn.

'Well, whether or not Mark and Amy mattered to our killer, let's make sure they matter to us.'

CHAPTER 13

Kim took a few deep breaths before ducking below the crime scene tape. It was harder to enter now than it had been the night before.

Fourteen hours earlier every available space had been filled with paramedics, police officers, potential witnesses and onlookers jostling for position even though they could see nothing four floors up.

Last night the area had borne no resemblance to the flat a few floors higher but today things were different. The crowds had dispersed from the cordon tape, having gone back to normal daily life after the previous night's entertainment. The barrier was being patrolled by two constables already feeling every gram of the 3 kg stab vest in twenty-degree heat before lunchtime.

Beyond them one officer milled around the front entrance. She couldn't pass any one of them without a small jolt of sympathy. This was not the dream of being a police officer; standing on a cordon. Guarding the entrance to a block of flats did not get you out of bed each morning.

The officers had been removed from the other floors, allowing most residents to go about their business, except for the fourth floor which had officers stationed on the lift and the stairs.

With less people, reduced activity and more open space Kim could see the detail of the property. She could see the narrow, windowless entrance hall that led all the way to the front room. A door to the kitchen and one bedroom on the right and the second bedroom and bathroom on the left. And that was the way she turned, into the room with a south-facing window, ideal for attracting the heat of the sun and turning the room into a space that could cook pottery.

Normally spaces seemed smaller as you grew older but this one seemed bigger than Kim recalled although she knew it was the exact same size in the flat on the seventh floor.

Of course in that flat the two single beds wedged together had completely dominated the room, leaving space only for a battered dresser that had easily held their meagre collection of clothes.

Kim shook herself back to this room, in this flat where a white-suited Mitch and his colleague were putting the carpet back down. Her eyes fell onto the radiator, her mind replaying the images from the previous night.

'Hey, Inspector,' Mitch said, removing his blue gloves and face mask. 'What brings you back?'

She shrugged and moved away, stepping towards the window. 'Just wanted to get a feel for the place,' she said, almost adding 'again'.

The logical, adult police officer knew this wasn't the same room and yet she could picture Mikey sleeping peacefully in the left-hand bed. She could see him wrapping himself like a sausage roll in the grey, coarse blankets and shouting 'come and find me' and herself pretending to look for him.

She could see clearly the fear in his face as their mother had pinned him to the bed, holding a bread knife to his chest swearing she would cut the devil right out of him if she had to.

But clearest of all was the image of his small frame resting against her as his weakened, sickly body had finally betrayed them both. And even then the six-year-old girl had thought that if they were found soon enough her brother could be brought back to life.

Help had come eventually. At first she'd thought the banging sound was from the radiator to which she was tied. Twice a day,

8 a.m. and 8 p.m., the heating system had kicked in to keep a supply of hot water to each flat, sending a loud shudder from the roof through the ancient pipes. Initially, she'd tried to count the rumbles to keep track of time but she'd become confused.

Only when the banging had continued and punctured her semi-conscious state had she understood that help had arrived. But it had been way too late for her twin. Just as it had been for the male who had sat in the exact same position the night before. And yet they'd reached the girl in time – not to save her, but she'd been alive, just as Kim herself had been thirty years earlier. Malnourished, weak and frail but with enough energy to fight the police officers who had tried to separate her from her brother.

She couldn't help draw the comparisons like a list in her mind.

Location – check.
Radiator – check.
Handcuffs – check.
Boy dead – check.
Girl alive – check.
Cracker packet – check.
Coke bottle – check.

She understood that Woody was choosing to ignore the blatant connection so that he could keep her on the case after she'd assured him that she could handle it.

And she could.

She was sure of it.

CHAPTER 14

Kim returned Stacey's missed call and put the phone on hands-free.

'Jeez, Bryant, your air con broke?' she asked right before the constable answered.

He shook his head, started the car and switched on the air conditioning. The cool air hit her face immediately with a blast of freshness.

'We have names,' Stacey said before Kim had chance to speak.

'Go on,' Kim said, feeling something tense within her body. She realised she was waiting for names she recognised.

'Mark Johnson and Amy Wilde, boyfriend and girlfriend who hung around a couple of shelters and community centres but mainly Stourbridge. The guy there talked to the pair quite a bit.'

'Great work, Stace, and where can I find this guy?' she asked, motioning for Bryant to turn the air con down. Her right ear was getting frostbite.

'Langley Road, at the back of the bus station.'

'And his name?' Kim asked, motioning again to Bryant, who turned the dial up once more.

'His name is Harry—'

'Hang on,' Kim interrupted. She turned to her colleague. 'Down, Bryant, not up,' she said.

'Sorry, my mistake,' he said with an expression that said it wasn't a mistake at all. Damn his little victories.

'Go on, Stace.'

'Harry Jenks manages the centre.'

'Got it. Thanks, Stace. Good—'

'Boss, Penn and I were talking and we think there's something a bit weird going on here. It's a bit like the murder of these kids wasn't about them at all. I mean—'

'Thanks, Stace, talk later,' Kim said, ending the call.

Damn it, this wasn't going to be as easy as she'd thought.

CHAPTER 15

'Yeah, not sure that's a line of enquiry the boss wants us to follow,' Stacey said, stunned by the silence in her ear.

Adjusting to the boss's operational levels of brusque had taken some fine-tuning on her part over the years.

In person, she registered as chilly but with the benefit of facial expressions and body language. Over the phone she normally dropped a few degrees once the body language had been lost, but that response had been positively arctic. Most unlike the boss to refuse to even listen. Normally she heard people out and then said no.

'Guess it's back to the CCTV for me then,' Penn said, as his phone began to ring.

He answered it, frowned, wrote something down, said okay and ended the call.

'Dobbie's Salvage, Brierley Hill, some hysterical woman on the phone,' he said, standing. 'Officers en route but want CID to pop along, just in case. You coming?'

Stacey shook her head, still smarting from the boss's attitude. 'Sounds like a waste of time. I'll get on to the CCTV close to Hollytree and you can join me when you get back.'

He nodded and left.

Stacey sat back and sighed heavily. Her own instinct had been echoed by Penn, but the boss had told her to leave well alone.

There was something off with these two victims but the boss wasn't interested.

The question was, should she continue to pursue it anyway?

CHAPTER 16

Kim took an instant dislike to Harry Jenks but wasn't sure why.

She could forgive the hair dye that coloured his hair an unnatural black. She could forgive the sweaty palm, the memory of which wouldn't leave her until she'd nicked one of Bryant's antiseptic wipes back in the glove box of the car, but what she couldn't forgive was the bling.

The watch on his left wrist was expensive and showy. On the other wrist was a thick chunky belcher chain that matched the one around his neck. She'd never been a fan of jewellery on men but, even her own prejudices aside, it was the context. In her mind, you didn't come to work in all your finery when you were dealing with people who didn't know how they were going to get their next meal.

The people that frequented the community centre didn't do it out of choice. It wasn't found on any 'places to visit' website, like TripAdvisor, or listed as a desirable destination. The people who came here were at rock bottom, homeless, street workers, unemployed. All of them in need of help. The man was doing nothing wrong but it just struck her as a little cold and insensitive.

'I understand you're familiar with a couple that go by the names of Amy Wilde and Mark Johnson,' she said nodding an acknowledgment towards a woman sitting at a desk on the other side of the room.

On the far-left wall was a row of blank screens. Kim thought about the one-room centre on Hollytree that was run by volunteers who opened for just a few hours each week and the place was rammed from the second they opened the door. They had one computer that had been thrown out by the dinosaurs with less memory than a smartphone but it was constantly in use.

'Yes, your girl sent out an email asking.'

'Yes, my detective constable was attempting to make an identification,' Kim said, coolly.

She saw a smile tug at the mouth of the woman although her typing fingers never paused.

'And you knew them?' Kim clarified.

He hesitated. 'As well as I know any of the people that come here. We don't get emotionally involved with our customers,' he added, narrowing his eyes. 'But I'd like to know exactly what they've done, officer.'

She didn't appreciate the immediate assumption that they'd done something wrong.

'They died, Mr Jenks,' she said, aware that the victims' names had not been included in any news reports. She'd only known their names for half an hour herself.

The fingers to the right of her stopped tapping but the woman didn't turn.

'How?… I mean…' His words trailed away as he put it together. 'The news last night. It was Amy and Mark – the couple that overdosed?'

'What can you tell me about them?' she asked, answering nothing.

The tapping to her right had resumed but slower.

He took a moment to think.

'They were a strange couple. From very different backgrounds. Amy had a stable family, Mark was shunted around the care system and has never had a proper home, so they were very different characters.'

'Any enemies you know of?'

The typing stopped.

Kim turned to her colleague.

'Bryant, mind taking a couple of notes?'

His expression asked if she'd lost her mind but he took out his notebook anyway.

Harry Jenks licked his lips and shook his head.

'No one they pissed off at all?' she repeated. 'Took one too many needles, ate an extra portion from the soup kitchen?'

He shook his head.

The typing resumed slowly but Kim could see a set expression on the woman's face. Kim found it ironic that she was learning more from the person in the room that wasn't speaking.

'And when was the last time you saw then?' she asked.

He consulted something on his computer screen. 'They last signed in three weeks ago. They took condoms, needles and ate cottage pie.'

'And that's the last time you saw them?'

'Absolutely,' he answered.

The woman pursed her lips.

Kim held out her hand for Bryant's notebook.

'Just making sure you've got everything,' she said, opening it up.

She read the single line that he'd written: '*The Guv has lost the plot!!!*'

Kim hid her smile.

'Yes, I think that's everything,' she said, standing. 'Thank you for your time, Mr Jenks, and I'm sure we'll be back to talk again once we know more.'

She motioned for Bryant to go ahead as she passed by the woman's desk. She caught her eye and nodded before continuing to the door.

She closed it behind her before Bryant raised an irate eyebrow.

'What the hell was that all about? I'm not bloody senile and I can recall basic facts, especially when we've just learned a total of bugger all,' he ranted, striding to the car.

She stayed silent while he vented. Sometimes it was a welfare concession on her part. The poor bloke was stuck with her day in, day out. He needed to vent now and again.

'And where's my pocket notebook?' he asked, holding out his hand.

'Ah, well, about that…'

'Officer, wait, you dropped this,' said the typing woman holding out Bryant's notebook.

'Devious, guv,' Bryant whispered before the woman reached them.

Kim pretended to check herself and then shook her head.

'Oh, I'm sorry. Thank you, Miss?…'

'Mrs Tallon, Emma. I'm the Assistant Manager.'

'Oh, so, you'd have known Amy and Mark too?' she asked, conversationally.

Mrs Tallon hesitated before nodding. 'I don't do much of the evening work, kids you know, but I was here that last night any of us saw Amy and Mark.'

'And did something happen that night?' Kim asked, knowing there was something this woman wanted to say.

'Yes, Inspector, it was the night Mark Johnson punched Harry Jenks in the mouth.'

CHAPTER 17

Penn had seen aerial shots of the scrapyard but he'd never set foot in it.

From above he could picture the strip of land a quarter mile long containing row upon row of cars, some stacked three vehicles high.

He parked behind two squad cars and headed towards the building he knew lay at the centre of the property.

As he approached there was no sign of staff or police officers. Walking around reminded him of the public library when he'd been at school. The shelves of books had towered above him just as the broken cars did right now. Had they been in tidy rows he may have been able to see to the end of the site.

He suddenly remembered going to the Great Worcester Maze at Broadfields when he was a kid. His father had been working and his mother was heavily pregnant with Jasper.

She hadn't been up to doing the maze with him but she'd given him instructions on what to do if he couldn't find his way back.

He smiled and hoped someone else had been lucky enough to have such a pragmatic mother and he followed her instructions now just as he had back then.

He put two fingers into his mouth, curled his tongue and blew.

Three seconds later came a response and a direction of travel.

He travelled to the eastern edge, close to the canal bridge that led over to the Waterfront Office and Leisure Complex.

Finally, he heard voices and turned out of a car alley into an open space that held the crane and the vehicle crusher.

He appraised the scene quickly and ignored the 'new boy' glances that passed amongst a couple of the constables.

The crane operator was smoking a cigarette and shaking his head; a woman he assumed to be the hysterical caller was sitting away from everyone still sobbing. An overweight man with a tee shirt that stopped shy of his waistband attempted to comfort her with a hand on her shoulder.

'You the owner?' Penn asked the big guy, wondering if there'd been some kind of accident. There were no ambulances present.

'Warren Dobbie, third generation,' he said.

'And this is?…'

'My wife, Debbie,' he said.

Penn tried in earnest not to put the two names together in his mind.

'And you called the police?' he asked the trembling woman.

She nodded and sobbed again.

He turned back to third generation Dobbie. 'Is someone hurt?' he asked, still unsure of the reason for his presence.

'Well, no, not so much hurt…' he said. 'Just… well… here, tek a look for yerself.'

Penn followed him through the milling police officers to the object of their attention.

A cube.

Penn knew that the compactors used at junkyards flattened the metal using hydraulically powered plates and a baling press that compressed from several directions until it resembled a large cube. And on first inspection there was nothing spectacular about the perfect cube of metal around which they all stood. He looked around at the police officers and then looked again with fresh eyes.

And that's when he saw the human hand.

CHAPTER 18

Kim arrived at Dobbie's at the same time as Mitch and his team.

The revelation from Mrs Tallon had been on her mind the whole time she'd been driving.

She had wondered if the woman was telling them the whole truth when she'd said she didn't know the reason for the violent outburst from Mark Johnson. But Harry Jenks had chosen not to report the assault to the police and she couldn't help but question why not. But they now knew that Mark Johnson had a temper. Who else had he upset? Although she was struggling to convict him in her mind for smacking Jenks in the face. Unfair or not there was something about him that made her want to smack him too.

And then the call had come from Penn to get to Dobbie's straight away.

'Hey, Mitch, I hear you've got your work cut out with this one,' Kim said, as she and Bryant joined him at the cordoned entrance.

'Did I hear right that there's a body part in the metal?' he asked, as they passed Keats's van.

'Apparently,' Kim said, as they followed the line of officers to the location Penn had explained to her.

She knew it well. She'd spent many Saturday mornings trawling the place looking for bike parts that were thrown haphazardly into piles at the end of car rows like the special offer displays at the aisle end in a supermarket.

She spied Penn up ahead who came walking towards her.

'Pathologist is here, boss,' he said. 'But seems at a bit of a loss.'

She nodded and followed him to the crusher.

'So, what happened?' she asked as she walked.

'Guy operating the crane removed the cube from the press and saw the hand as he lowered it to the ground. Got out and touched it and hasn't stopped shaking since.'

Yes, it was a discovery that would stay with him for some time.

'Hey, Keats,' she said to the pathologist who stood on the other side of the cube.

'Well, this is a puzzle, isn't it?' he asked, stroking his bearded chin.

'Not sure your rectal probe's gonna help on this one,' she said, bending down to take a better look.

The hand itself looked in reasonable condition but icy cold to her touch despite the heat of the day. The skin was smooth and she suspected the hand was male.

'Has it been moved?' Kim asked.

Penn shook his head as Kim began to walk around it.

'Is it just a hand?' Bryant asked as Mitch took out a large plastic sheet and began to unfold it.

Keats shook his head. 'There appears to be a foot on that side and an elbow on that side and some hair on the top.'

Kim moved aside as two techies began taking photographs from all angles.

'So, you reckon we've got the whole body in there?' Kim asked.

'Definitely possible given the body parts we can see, but separating them from the mangled metal is not going to be an easy task.'

Kim had a sudden thought. 'So, who gets him, you or Mitch?'

Were they looking at a body or clues? How could Keats perform any kind of post-mortem and how could Mitch take the metal apart while trying to preserve the body parts, because one thing was for certain: suicide it was not.

'I'm pretty sure this is going to be a joint project,' Keats said as the photographers stepped back from the cube.

'Okay, guys, lets tip it,' Mitch said.

Mitch's team gathered around the cube, and Keats stepped forward to observe. Mitch gave the instructions and the cube was eased over onto the plastic sheet exposing the side that had been on the ground.

'Oh shit,' Kim said, when she saw that the whole underneath was stained with blood.

CHAPTER 19

Kim ended the call as Keats headed out of the yard closely followed by Mitch, who were both following the low-loader that had been ordered to transfer the cube to the lab. Neither vehicle had been equipped for transportation, so Mitch had simply wrapped it in plastic to preserve evidence.

A second team of Forensics had arrived and under instruction from Mitch would focus on the area the vehicle had been stored prior to crushing, while the initial team would focus on the crusher.

Penn had been dispatched back to the office to start searching the missing persons reports and identifying possibilities.

'So, how you doing, Dob?' Kim asked, entering the office building at the centre of the site. The afternoon sun was beating down on the felt roof and the south-facing windows making the space stuffy and unbearable. A three-speed fan did nothing to cool the air and only threw up dust particles into the rays of sunlight.

'I'm all right but the missus is still shitting bricks,' he said, although Kim could see the slight tremble to his hand as he moved a paperweight to the pile of papers closest to the fan.

'Understandable,' she acknowledged.

He used the back of his hand to wipe a line of sweat that had formed between his nose and upper lip.

'Look, I dow mean to be insensitive…'

'Then don't be,' Kim said simply. 'You can have your equipment back when we're finished but until then, you're closed, matey.'

His mouth opened and his eyes rolled all at the same time as though he was using every body part he could think of to communicate his displeasure.

'I gotta pay guys to just sit around until…'

'You could always get 'em in here for a spring clean,' she said, lifting up a folder to reveal another pile of papers hiding underneath. 'Talking of which, I need the make, model and registration number of the vehicle, the name and address of the person who brought it in and on what date.'

'Toyota Corolla,' he answered.

She waited.

Nothing.

'Okay, that was two answers of the six I want and to be fair they're the least helpful two answers you could have given me,' she said, glowering at him.

He shrugged and motioned to the desk that looked as though two printing presses had made babies. 'It's on a bit of paper. It's 'ere somewhere.'

'Bookkeeper took a holiday?' Bryant queried, taking a look over the desk.

'Yeah since the last bloody recession when folks stopped buying new cars,' he said.

Kim tipped her head. 'You're not suffering too bad, Dob,' she said, nodding outside to the rows and stack of cars. It wasn't like he had a lot of room.

'Tell that to the bank manager or even better tell it to the wife,' he moaned.

'You gotta have a system of some kind,' she said. Dobbie had been in business too long for this level of stupidity.

'Yeah, I write shit down on a piece of paper until I get time to do the books,' he said, rubbing a dirty wrist across his forehead.

'So, you don't put cars in any area based on the day they came in or?—'

'Is that really a serious question?' he asked, looking to Bryant for a clue.

Her colleague nodded.

'Yeah, I operate under the "wherever there's fucking space" system and it's worked all right for me for—'

'Well, not really because the undisputed facts are that there was a person in that car when you put it in the crusher. So, how the hell did he get there?'

'Hey, we ay done—'

'Was the car on ground level?' Kim asked.

Dobbie nodded.

'So, we could be looking at some homeless guy who wandered in, fancied a comfy seat in one of the cars, fell asleep, went unnoticed and got more than—'

'You think he was alive?'

Kim shrugged. 'Dunno, Dobbie, that's what we're going to have to find out but hang on,' she said, frowning. She remembered a TV programme she'd recently seen. 'Don't you strip these cars of everything but the paint before they go in the crusher?'

'Hell, yeah, that's where we make our money. Seats, pedals, wiring, the lot comes out.'

'So, when was that done?'

'Fuck me, Inspector, I can't remember…'

'So, the boot might not have been checked?'

'Should have been if these lazy bastards were doing their job. There's carpet and sometimes spare tyres been left in there.'

'Well, our victim had to have been in the car somewhere,' she said. 'And I'm assuming your guys didn't move him aside to take the seats out, and put him back again.'

He donned an expression that said it wouldn't surprise him.

She couldn't yet rule out that a vagrant hadn't wandered in unnoticed and got into the car and that they were dealing with some kind of tragic accident. What she needed were the owner or car details.

'Okay, Dob, when you gonna have that information for me?' she asked, looking at her watch to underline she was talking hours.

'Soon as the lazy bastard who was supposed to strip the car gets this place tidied up.'

Kim nodded her begrudging acceptance and stepped out of the office.

'Well, Rubik's a bit of a puzzle, isn't he?' Bryant asked as they headed towards the car.

She paused with her hand on the car door.

'Bryant, please tell me you didn't just call our guy in the cube Rubik?'

He nodded. 'I considered Ice but I think this name we'll remember.'

She shook her head as she got into the car.

'Where to?' he asked, starting the engine.

'Russells Hall,' she said. 'Wanna see how the boys are getting on with Rubik and see if the present I ordered for them has arrived.'

'Present?' he queried.

'Oh, yes, I've ordered something that I think they're going to need very much.'

CHAPTER 20

It was almost four when Kim pushed the button to access the morgue area. She headed for the end of the corridor, just before the fridge, to a room she'd only seen used once before, when Keats hadn't had enough space for a two-car accident. Seven people had been burnt beyond recognition. The charred bodies of four adults and three children had been lined up against the wall. She shuddered at the memory as she entered for the second time.

'Hey, guys, how's it going?' Kim asked, standing between them as they pondered opposite sides of the cube.

Mitch held a saw and Keats held a scalpel.

'We have to try and loosen some of the metal,' Mitch said.

'You'll destroy valuable evidence,' Keats said with exasperation. 'We need the tissues intact for testing and for clues.'

'We're on the same side with that one, Keats, but we can't get bits of him out until we've loosened some of the crumpled metal.'

Kim looked from one to the other as the exchange continued.

'Inspector, your thoughts?' Mitch asked, as Keats rolled his eyes. He didn't much care for her opinion.

She shrugged. 'Personally, I'd get the chainsaw on it but what do I know?' she said as they both shot her a horrified glance.

Kim did not envy either one of them. Ultimately, they wanted the same thing: to preserve the body to get information. Keats's medical training steered him in one direction and Mitch's efficiency dictated that the sooner they opened up the metal the sooner they could both get answers.

Kim stepped back to the edge of the room, stood next to Bryant and folded her arms.

'It's like two kids who've been given a present to share at Christmas and can't decide how to open it.'

'Yeah, one could almost forget there's a person in there who has lost their life,' Bryant said, quietly.

'Said the man who has named him Rubik,' she noted.

'Well, he's certainly puzzling the life out of these two,' he noted as they continued to move around the cube observing at every angle.

'Yeah, amusing, isn't it?' she asked.

'Definitely, but not gonna yield us answers any time soon.'

'Oh, Bryant, chill out.'

'The irony is astounding,' he said, and then turned to her. 'Hang on, you should be stamping your feet by now and issuing them with threats of violence. I find your calmness disconcerting.'

She offered him a smile. 'Be patient.'

'Didn't you say you'd ordered something that could help?'

Kim hesitated as she heard the whoosh of the automatic doors at the end of the suite.

'Yep, and I think it's just arrived.'

Keats and Mitch were still in heated debate when a diminutive blonde figure appeared in the doorway.

'Good afternoon, gentlemen. Doctor A at your service. Now how much have you missed me?'

Kim smiled and stepped forward as she heard the collective groan of three grown men.

CHAPTER 21

'Doctor A,' Kim said, moving towards the woman with her hand outstretched. 'Thank you for coming. I think we could do with a little help.'

Doctor A returned the handshake warmly while looking around her to the metal cube taking centre stage.

'I don't think…' Mitch said.

'I'm sure we'll be…' Keats said.

'Shush, men,' she said, moving towards it.

Keats shot daggers her way, and Kim smiled in return.

Doctor A was a Forensic Anthropologist that Kim had worked with on a number of occasions and trusted implicitly. Hailing from Macedonia, she herself simplified her long and complicated name to Doctor A. Many people were put off by the woman's direct no-nonsense manner but it only made Kim warm to her more.

It had occurred to her at the scrapyard that they needed someone who was used to searching for clues with speed and accuracy. Someone who understood the need for preserving the evidence while also digging around for it.

'Is that a hand?' she asked, taking an elastic band and tying back her long hair.

'Yes,' Kim answered.

Doctor A turned on her. 'You didn't tell me you had metal Michael here.'

'Mickey,' Mitch corrected. 'Metal Mickey.'

'Is what I said,' she snapped, continuing to walk around the cube making no sound on the plastic with her trademark Doctor Marten boots.

'You think male?' she asked, turning to Kim.

Kim nodded. 'The size of the hand,' she explained.

'And do you think he is all there?'

Kim shrugged. 'Not sure but there's a possibility it's a vagrant who fancied a comfy sleep in a warm car.'

She continued looking and glanced at Mitch's saw before giving him a filthy look, and laughed out loud at Keats's scalpel.

'It is a good job I am here.'

'Can you offer some advice on the best way in?' Kim asked, diplomatically.

Doctor A shook her head. 'I'm afraid I can not.'

Kim tried to hide her disappointment while three others almost danced with relief.

'This metal box is no different to the ground. You develop a method and a rhythm as you go. The material begins to open up to you, to guide you, advise you. This is not something I can do from afar. I can not supervise from on top.'

'Above,' Kim corrected, quickly.

'I will stay and work it,' she said, decisively. 'I shall bring tools of my own but I will be in charge.'

'Done,' Kim said, offering her hand and turning on her heel before Keats or Mitch managed to catch her eye.

For the briefest of seconds when the two men's antagonism had been deafening she had wondered if she'd made the right call.

But right now, the Macedonian scientist was kneeling on the floor stroking the single hand.

'Do not worry, my friend, we will have you out of there in a jif, I promise.'

Nope, Kim thought, heading away from the morgue.

She hadn't made a mistake at all.

CHAPTER 22

'Okay, Stace, what you got?' Kim asked, sitting on the spare desk.

The evening sun had moved around the building and a breeze was winding its way around the coffee pot and cooling the room.

Content that everything possible was being done with the man in the cube, the priority was the murder of two young people.

'Mark Johnson was twenty-one years old, born to a prostitute who tried for seven months to keep him and then gave him up. No father registered. Over the years he got harder to handle, meaning he spent the majority of his life at a place called Fairview.'

Kim hid the churning of her stomach in reaction to the mention of the place she'd spent most of her childhood too.

She simply nodded and fair play to Bryant, he didn't react at all either.

'Not sure when he first got on to drugs but he completed a thirty-day programme a year ago and didn't stay clean for very long. I've got no registered address for him since then and surprisingly he has no criminal record.'

Kim had a clear picture in her mind now about Mark Johnson. Never been in serious trouble, had tried to get clean. He'd entered the programme but more importantly had stayed in it. That was someone who wanted to change their life.

But he had been thrown back into the world drug free, with no home, probably no friends, no job and no way to make the changes stick. He'd fallen back into the same crowd, same surroundings, same life. His return to drugs had been inevitable.

Kim tried to ignore the pang that shot through her. In many ways, she knew him or at least felt like she did.

'Amy Wilde was an only child who just turned twenty. Normal kid moved around a fair bit as her dad was military until he was killed by an IED five years ago in Afghanistan. No clue how the two of them met but seem to have been together for a couple of years. Her mum lives on the Lakeside estate in Stourbridge.'

'Give—'

Kim closed her mouth. Stacey was already passing the address to Bryant.

Her watch told her it was almost six and the day had been full-on.

'Okay, guys, that's enough. Let's call it a day.'

'So soon, Inspector, but I only just got here,' said a voice from the doorway.

Kim turned, groaned and dropped her head to the desk.

CHAPTER 23

Kim stayed in that position for a good ten seconds.

She was sure that if she waited long enough it wouldn't be Dr Alison Lowe who was standing there.

'May I come in?' she asked, confirming to Kim that her shrewd denial plan hadn't worked.

She lifted her head as Penn turned and shook her hand, introducing himself.

Kim dragged herself to her feet and nodded towards the spare desk. 'Nice to see you again,' she said, moving to the top of the squad room.

'Completely insincere but appreciate the effort,' Alison said without breaking a smile.

Kim noted that she hadn't changed a bit. Still wearing the tight black power suits with the stiletto heels as though she'd travelled back to the Eighties to watch films like *Working Girl* on a loop.

Her straw-coloured hair had obeyed her instruction to stay neat and tidy for the whole day.

'Penn, this is Alison Lowe who assisted us on the kidnapping of two little girls a couple of years ago as a profiler and behaviourist. She gave us some great insights into the mind frame of the perpetrators.'

But she hadn't identified that the person behind it all had been right under their noses the whole time. The more reasonable part of her added that none of them had worked that out but she chose to ignore that fact.

Alison placed her briefcase on the desk.

'So, I hear you had a crime scene that bears simi—'

'Time to go, guys,' Kim cut in, offering Alison a withering glance.

Penn got to his feet, took off the bandana, grabbed his man-bag, bid them good night and left the office. Stacey appeared to be taking her time.

'Good work today, Stace, on the background of the two kids.'

'Cheers, boss,' Stacey said but there was no smile in her eyes. Just suspicion.

She nodded her goodbyes around the room and left.

Kim waited a good couple of minutes before turning on Alison. 'Well, that was bloody tactful,' she snapped.

Alison appeared unapologetic. 'You have a problem with someone stating the obvious?'

'In front of my whole team, yes.'

Alison's left eyebrow lifted. 'Wait a minute, you've got half of your team blindly working a double murder case that bears some resemblance to a traumatic event in your own childhood which may or may not be linked directly to you.'

'We think not,' Kim said.

'Your boss is choosing to think not so he can keep you on the case, but you're keeping your team in the dark and asking them to work this case to the best of their ability with both their hands and feet tied behind their backs?'

'I don't want them to know,' she said, stubbornly.

'And I will say, for the first of many times I'm sure, that you are making a terrible mistake.'

CHAPTER 24

'How very fucking dare she?' Kim blustered as they got into the car.

She offered a filthy look up to the squad room window for good measure.

'You're angry with her for telling the truth?'

'Bryant,' she protested. He was supposed to be on her side.

'Sorry, guv, but I'm not going to pretend to disagree for your sake when she's right. The guys need to know what they might be dealing with. They're both bloody good officers who have the ability to think outside the box and to join the dots but they're pretty stuck if you're only giving them half the picture. And that's before we even get to the trust issue. Both of them, but especially Stacey, will be hurt that you've not trusted her enough to give her the whole story.'

She shook her head. 'Not happening.'

'I know what's stopping you,' he said quietly.

'Leave it, Bryant.'

'You can't stand the thought of being weakened in their eyes. You think they'll view you differently, lose respect and—'

'Oh, Bryant, you have it so wrong,' she said, looking out of the window.

'You're gonna live to regret it,' he warned.

And wasn't that just the story of her life.

CHAPTER 25

'You know when I was a kid anyone who lived on Lakeside was posh,' Bryant observed as he slowed down to negotiate the speed bumps on the main spine road of the estate.

The Lakeside housing development of approximately two thousand homes built in the 1980s and 90s and often called Withymoor Village after the opencast colliery upon which it was built.

Kim's understanding was that the average property sold for around £350k, so the area wasn't exactly chopped liver now.

'Ah, down here,' Bryant said taking a left past three successive driveways containing camper vehicles.

He pulled alongside the kerb in front of a home without a recreation vehicle but with a four-year-old BMW.

The small front garden was awash with summer colour. Flowers tumbled out of hanging baskets either side of the door. The ground popped with pinks, purples and vivid yellows, so much that the eyes couldn't take it all in.

This household had never heard the phrase less is more.

The door was opened by a woman Kim guessed to be mid-sixties and instantly reminded her of Judi Dench.

'Mrs Wilde?' Kim asked, unsure.

She shook her head. 'I'm her mother,' she explained, waiting.

Bryant took out his identification, and the woman stood aside.

Kim stepped into a small hallway that didn't match the perception of space alluded to from outside.

The woman pointed to the right, and Kim followed her direction into an airy open-plan kitchen diner with patio doors out onto the small but colourful garden.

A woman sat at the breakfast bar looking out.

'Mrs Wilde?' Kim said.

She turned to reveal reddened eyes and a dumbfounded expression. Kim couldn't quite relate to the loss of a child but she did understand the realisation that someone you loved was never coming back.

Bryant offered their condolences and moved forward to offer his hand.

Mrs Wilde uncurled it from the mug of something and returned it limply.

'Tea?' asked Mrs Wilde's mother from behind the breakfast bar.

Both Kim and Bryant refused as they took a seat.

'Lovely photos,' Kim said of the collection of formal posed pictures on the fireplace wall.

'Andrew loved getting them done,' she said, glancing over. 'And he always looked so handsome in his uniform.'

He certainly did, Kim agreed, and although she wasn't a fan of formal photos there was something about this collection that got her attention.

Despite different poses and different backgrounds, one thing stayed the same. On each photo there was a brightness. The smiles were open and honest, eyes bright with enjoyment. Almost like one of them had said something funny just a nanosecond before the camera took the shot. This had been a happy family.

'Mrs Wilde, I know it's painful but may we ask you some questions about Amy?'

Kim couldn't help glancing at the latest photo on the wall where Amy appeared to be about 15 years old with braces and nicely rounded cheeks. Her long hair had been cut and thinned from previous photos.

The kid bore no resemblance to the girl Kim had seen fighting for her life the other night.

'Of course, but I haven't seen her for a while, officer. Five months to be exact. She came to see me in hospital.'

'And, how was she?' Kim asked, wondering if anything five months earlier offered any significance or insight into her daughter's death.

'High,' she answered. 'I could see it in her eyes and she couldn't keep still for two minutes. She shouted at the woman in the next bed for snoring after surgery and closed everyone's curtains laughing her head off. The nurses asked her to leave.'

Kim couldn't help glancing at the photo on the wall.

'Did she say anything at all, any trouble she was having with anyone?'

Mrs Wilde dabbed at her eyes. 'Told me she was fantastic and hashtag loving life, whatever that means. I hadn't seen her for about six months prior to that, around the time I refused to give her any more money to put that shit into her arm. I always thought she'd come back in her own time, that something would happen to make her realise what she was doing to herself.'

And she might have done, Kim thought. But that choice had been taken away from her.

'I'd have been waiting, you know,' she said, as a sob broke out of her. 'If she'd have given me any encouragement I would have supported her through getting off it. And now she'll always be known as the druggie who overdosed while chained to a radiator.'

Kim could offer no response because it was true.

'Mrs Wilde, may I ask how the two of them met. They don't seem a likely couple. Mark's background…'

'Oh, I know all about his background,' Mrs Wilde said, her face and voice turning hard at the same time. 'Amy told me all about it while trying to persuade me to let him move in.' She shook her head. 'And I probably should have let him, because that's the day she left.'

'Because you wouldn't let him live here?' Bryant asked.

With a daughter not long out of her teens Kim could hear the outrage in his voice.

'Yes, she'd been seeing him for a few months by then. Fell over his bag of *Big Issues* as she left Tesco's in Cradley Heath. Helped him pick them back up and that was that. Next day she went back to talk to him again and the next, and the next until she couldn't bear to be parted from him for even a minute.'

Kim heard a sniff from behind her. The grandmother had turned her back.

Kim saw Mrs Wilde's wish to comfort her mother but she looked away. Her own pain was just too great to take on anyone else's.

Due to the time of estrangement between mother and daughter Kim was not convinced there was any more to be gained.

The girl could have made countless enemies, been involved in a dozen different situations that her mother would have known nothing about.

Kim had a sudden thought and wanted to offer the woman some comfort before she left.

'At least she came to see you in hospital.'

'Not so sure about that, officer. Probably came to see if her plan had worked.'

Kim was genuinely perplexed. 'Sorry, I'm not sure…'

'I was in hospital, Inspector, because I was mugged and beaten and I'm pretty sure it was Amy and Mark behind it.'

CHAPTER 26

It was almost seven when Kim handed Bryant the keys back to his own car outside the station.

'Okay, get off home now,' she said.

He glanced up at the squad room window. 'Want me to come up?'

She shook her head. 'Nah, we gotta have this conversation before she can start profiling this killer and be some use to us.'

'Okay, but if you want a chat later…'

'I'll give your missis a call cos I like her more than I like you.'

He thought for a minute. 'Yeah, can't say I blame you,' he replied, before getting in the car.

She headed inside, nodded at Jack on the desk and took the stairs to the second floor.

Kim had made no secret of her disdain for profiling, behavioural analysis and other hocus pocus when Alison had joined them on the kidnapping case. Kim firmly believed that people were individuals and couldn't be generalised by the actions of people in the past and assuming that they could was dangerous.

Kim liked to profile a murderer based on the clues and events of a crime. If a victim received twenty or so stab wounds it was safe to say the murderer was angry, enraged, but it was less safe to say he was a twenty-seven-year-old male who had been bullied at school and still lived with his domineering mother while working some dead-end job.

Because everyone had access to anger. Anyone could feel enraged by a person, a situation, a circumstance. And everyone had the ability to just snap.

And yet Kim had to admit that Alison had offered some valuable insights into the mind of a killer when they had worked together before.

So, she appreciated the help of the woman but knew they would need a conversation first.

'All caught up?' Kim asked, entering the squad room.

Alison nodded and stood, heading over to the percolator.

Kim was amused to see her walking in her stockinged feet with her high heels discarded beneath the desk.

'Hey, don't judge me. They've been on my feet for almost twelve hours.'

Kim held up her hands in a non-judgemental way. 'Hey, I wear biker boots an inch high so, trust me, I'm not judging,' Kim said as Alison sat back down.

Kim took Bryant's chair opposite. 'So, what do you think we're looking at?' she asked trying to bypass the inevitable.

'Easy tiger, cool your heels. First things first. Obviously, DCI Woodward has given me the general outline but I'd like to hear more from you,' she said, taking out a black spiral notebook. 'So, tell me the similarities to the events in your childhood. All of them.'

'Boy and a girl,' she said.

'Hmm, hmm, 'Alison replied, motioning for her to continue.

'Flat three floors beneath where I lived.'

'Yep.'

'Boy dead, girl not,' she said.

Alison looked up. 'But I just read…'

'Not dead when help arrived. Paramedics worked on her for hours.'

'Got it. Next.'

'Chained to a radiator with handcuffs.'

'Yes.'

'Coke bottle.'

'Yep.'

'Cracker packet lodged in the throat of Mark Johnson.'

'Anything else?' Alison asked, raising her head.

'Isn't that a fucking nuff?' she snapped.

'What's your problem?'

Kim said nothing.

Alison sat back in her chair and shook her head. 'There's no pleasing you. You expected an emotional response from me and you got none. You're annoyed at my coldness and yet that's exactly what you want. You don't want understanding, empathy, sympathy otherwise you'd have told your team by now.'

'Oh, please continue,' Kim growled when Alison paused. After the day she'd had this was exactly what she needed right now.

'I intend to. Do I think your past is horrific? Absolutely. Do you gain anything by me telling you so? Not at all because you were there and, quite frankly, I've interviewed people so twisted and broken by past events that make yours look like a trip to the bouncy castle followed by ice cream.'

'I'm not in any fucking competition for shittest childhood of the century.'

'You'd lose by a mile, so please tell me if there has been anything else,' Alison said, meeting her gaze, calmly.

'Fairview. Mark Johnson spent much of his childhood there, just like me but I think that's just coincidence.'

'And you're sure that's it?'

Kim nodded. 'So, when can you help out and give us your observations on the killer?'

Kim read genuine confusion in the eyes of the woman opposite.

'Detective Inspector Stone, there appears to be some kind of miscommunication. My brief and instruction has nothing to do with the killer. I'm here to observe you.'

CHAPTER 27

Alison tried to shake the feeling of doing something wrong as she entered the front foyer of Worcestershire Royal Hospital. She told herself that visiting a sick person was not a crime.

She was well aware that Inspector Stone had wanted more of an explanation. She had wanted the entire brief, word for word, as to her role in the case. And much as she would have loved to stay and fend her off she'd known she had a twenty-mile drive down the M5 to the hospital to make it before visiting hours ended.

Alison knew they weren't as strict on the timings in ICU if you were visiting alone and made no fuss. In the silent cloistered environment of the gravely ill any cough or chair scrape was magnified as though in church or a library. Nurses moved around soundlessly in foam-bottomed shoes or crocs amongst the low beeps and tings of life-preserving equipment.

'How is she?' Alison asked Valerie, the ward sister, as she entered.

'Same,' she said, with a kindly smile.

'Thank you,' she said, heading over to the bed at the end. She removed her jacket and sat before taking a good look at the woman in the bed.

The bruises had barely faded in the six days since Alison had first seen Beverly lying here. Her face was still stained purple and yellow, with an occasional inch of pale cream flesh peeking out from beneath. And the marks didn't stop there. The plum-coloured skin continued over her body where she'd been kicked and punched both before and after the vicious rape.

Alison shuddered as she thought about what this woman had endured.

She brought her gaze back to Beverly's face; the stretched, shiny skin that had ballooned over her left eye. The shaved head bearing the scars of major surgery to reduce the swelling and bleeding on the brain.

Alison took the cool, smooth hand and stroked the thumb rhythmically.

'I'm so sorry,' she whispered.

'You have nothing to be sorry for,' said Valerie, startling her. She hadn't heard the ward sister approach. Damn those crocs. 'You didn't do this to her.'

Oh, but I did, Alison almost said, but managed to stop herself just in time.

'I know,' she said, recovering quickly. 'But I was away on business and I can't help but think if I'd been—'

'Shh now,' she said, kindly, straightening the sheet around Beverly's shoulders. 'That's not the kind of talk she needs to hear. You need to tell her all the things you're going to do once she's better.'

Alison appreciated the optimism that didn't match the prognosis, which was little more than a shrug of your shoulders and wait-and-see assessment.

'Talk to her about shopping trips,' Valerie said, squeezing her shoulder gently. 'Talk to her about a weekend at a spa or a trip to the theatre. I'm sure that's what your sister wants to hear.'

Alison nodded and fought away the reason for her own uneasiness and feeling of wrongdoing.

This woman was not her sister.

Alison was an only child.

CHAPTER 28

Kim tried to keep her face neutral as Alison entered the squad room for the morning briefing and sat at the spare desk.

She'd put in a call to Woody immediately following their conversation the previous night to be told he was giving some kind of speech at an awards ceremony. She'd been sitting outside his office at 6 a.m. but he hadn't shown. A cynical person might have thought he was actively avoiding her. Realistically she knew he wasn't. Woody always had the courage of his convictions and would never back down in the face of her anger, but that didn't stop her wanting to question it.

She'd spent the night pacing and raging wondering why the hell he felt she needed babysitting to this degree. And she wanted to tell him he was wrong.

And if he was avoiding her it wasn't going to last for long.

'Okay, guys, what we got on the CCTV for Amy and Mark around Hollytree?'

'Very little so far, boss,' Penn said, tapping on his keyboard. 'Got this one snatch of 'em coming out of Brierley Hill Asda at around 4 p.m. on Sunday from the car park camera. The footage is grainy at best and Amy's carrying something, but still waiting on Asda for footage around the store. They head down Little Cottage Lane and disappear.'

'Keep on it, Penn,' Kim said.

Any footage of them on that final day might help.

'Stace, I know you were doing background and we got some ourselves from Amy's mother,' Kim said. 'Apparently, Amy fell for Mark, literally right outside Tesco. Not exactly a fairy-tale beginning but one has to wonder if part of the charm for Amy was in trying to save him and then got hooked on the stuff herself.'

'Typical rescuer syndrome,' Alison interjected. 'Mainly females who focus on and worry about their partner more than themselves. Normally drawn to people with depression, anxieties or addictions. Love equates to work and suffering instead of a healthy, balanced relationship.'

'Precisely, anyway,' Kim continued, 'Amy's mother was mugged and beaten a few months ago and feels Amy and Mark were behind it after she refused to give her daughter money. Apparently, the woman had tried everything, even getting her friends to try and talk sense into her but nothing worked; she even came to the hospital high and was thrown off the ward.'

'Visiting her own mother?' Stacey asked, with disgust.

Kim understood Stacey's disgust. The constable was very close to her parents and could never picture herself disrespecting her mum in such a way, but Kim understood what drugs could do to someone. They eroded the person you were, attacked and destroyed the feelings you had for other people so that it became the most important thing in your life. Getting high the only priority: above family, love, feelings. It destroyed everything. The accusation from Mrs Wilde about her daughter being involved in the vicious attack was not beyond the realms of possibility despite how unpalatable it was.

'Stace, there was some kind of altercation between Mark Johnson and Harry Jenks at Stourbridge Community Centre. Not mentioned to us by Jenks himself but by a co-worker. I'd like to know what it was about but, more importantly, why Jenks is hiding it.'

Stacey nodded and made a note.

'And as you know, we have an unknown victim found within a junked car. Keats, Mitch and Doctor A are all working to extract Rubik from his cube.'

She saw the look of disapproval pass over Alison's face and turned her way.

'What?'

'It's disrespectful,' Alison said.

'You think?'

She nodded.

Kim took a breath. She nodded to the photos of the cube already on the board. 'You think he gives a shit what we call him?' she asked, not waiting for an answer. 'As you well know there are coping strategies for what we deal with every day and humour is one of them. It keeps us sane.' She glanced across at Bryant. 'Well, most of us anyway. It helps us cope and function and I make no apology for that,' she said, feeling her phone vibrate in her pocket but she didn't need to look to see what it was.

'You mention the word disrespectful, but we have to find a way to personalise every victim that comes our way. Once we have a name the victim becomes a person, a life, a soul.'

Kim headed for the door and paused. 'Or we could scrub out his new name and replace it with "unknown subject"; now in my opinion that would be disrespectful.'

As she took the stairs two at a time Kim couldn't help wondering if the two of them could make it to the end of this case alive.

CHAPTER 29

'Ah, Stone, here already,' Woody observed, switching on his computer.

Oh yes, she'd bribed Jack on the desk with his favourite apple pie from the canteen to let her know the minute he arrived.

'Sir, I respectfully—'

'There's a contradiction,' he said, pointing to the chair.

She ignored it.

He pointed again and narrowed his eyes.

She sat.

'Sir, I don't need Alison bloody Lowe babysitting me on this case and watching my every move.'

'Continue,' he instructed.

'With what?'

'You've probably come up with a whole litany of reasons to toss at me and I'd like to give you the opportunity to voice them all so that your time wasn't completely wasted.'

She took a breath and exhaled loudly. 'You're not going to budge, are you?'

'No,' he answered.

'But why her?' she insisted. 'We don't work well together.'

He lifted his head from rummaging in his top drawer. 'Are you being serious, Stone? You honestly think I have the time to find someone you would work well with? I'll settle for tolerance and at least Alison has the backbone to fight back.'

'But you never said…'

'I said you needed help but I didn't specify the type or package in which it would come.'

'I just wish you'd have told—'

'Stone,' he said, quietly. 'Last night I attended a ceremony to award the George Medal posthumously to a female police officer killed by an exploding car bomb seven months ago. The award was presented to a grieving husband who didn't let go of his two-year-old child the whole night and accepted the medal in front of an oversize photo of his dead wife. So, right now, if your feelings are a little bit hurt, I couldn't care less.'

Kim had no response to offer.

There had been so much that she'd wanted to say, had felt entitled to say, and right now the words would not come.

She had reached the door before he spoke again.

'You know, Stone, for someone so intelligent there are times when you really can be a bit dense.'

'Sir?' she said, turning. Had her boss really just called her dense?

'My apologies for the terminology, so let me put this another way. A few years before my wife died she bought me a letter opener. Beautiful it was. Carved wooden handle inscribed with my name. Shiny, thin blade in a leather presentation box. Thing is I'd managed to open envelopes perfectly well without one for forty years but it was the best damn backscratcher I ever had. Got that spot right between your shoulder blades. Not its purpose but...'

'I get it,' she said, allowing a brief smile to touch her lips.

'Stone, this killer managed to get two young people into a block of flats and murder them without being noticed. We're either looking at two killers or one very clever one and you need every resource to make sure this doesn't happen again.'

'Agreed,' she said, opening the door.

'And one more thing,' he said.

Kim was beginning to feel like the headline act at a concert being called back for one more encore.

'Go easy on her, eh? She's not as tough as she thinks she is.'

Kim nodded and finally left the room, her interest piqued. What the hell was that all about?

CHAPTER 30

Kim read the text message that had beeped its arrival as Woody had finally finished with her.

She frowned, followed its instructions and headed down to the cafeteria.

She found Alison and Bryant sitting in the corner nearest the kitchen. Alison had clearly missed breakfast and had opted for toast and orange juice, Bryant a mug of tea, and a large coffee appeared to be waiting for her.

She wound her way through the tables occupied with officers tucking into full English breakfasts. Other healthier options were available and would disappear from the chiller cabinet throughout the day, but right now it was all about the protein.

'Feel better now, Inspector?' Alison asked, taking notebooks from her briefcase.

'About what?' she asked, sitting down. Woody may have given Alison access to her case but she wasn't getting access to her mind.

'Well I assume that you've waited all night to speak to DCI Woodward after what I told you last night and you've been to see him at the earliest opportunity to have it out with him, and although nothing has changed you have lodged your objection; so I'm asking if you now feel better about my involvement in this case?'

'S'pose so but what are we doing down here?' she asked, as a cool breeze of air from the air con unit above travelled down her back. Not that she was complaining.

'I assume, knowing you, that you haven't changed your mind about involving your team since we last spoke?'

Kim shook her head.

'Given that I felt it better to have this conversation in private, I have no interest in being distracted by efforts to identify the unknown subject in the metal.'

Kim admired her refusal to call him Rubik.

'So, it's best we do this away from the others.'

Kim looked to Bryant who shrugged.

'What exactly are we doing?'

'Right now, your team is looking for independent leads and clues, finding grudges, links, people they may have upset in the past, family and—'

'Yes, it's called police work and is something Bryant and I would like to be getting—'

'So, we need to be looking at the other possibility,' Alison said, completely ignoring her, causing Kim to wonder what the hell Woody had been talking about. There was not one vulnerable bone in this woman's body.

'Inspector, this double murder may somehow be linked to you, and as we can't do that as a full team we're going to have to do it away from the others.'

'And how exactly do you propose we do this?' Kim asked, crossing her arms.

'We start by making a list,' she answered, pushing a spare notebook and pen towards her and Bryant. 'We make a long list of everyone you've managed to piss off.'

Bryant shook his head and pushed the pad back towards Alison. 'Sorry, but I can't be a party to this,' he said, seriously.

Alison frowned. 'Why not?'

Kim also looked to him for an answer.

'Cos I've only got seven years until retirement.'

CHAPTER 31

'Why the cafeteria?' Stacey asked, looking around her computer screen. 'When have you ever known the boss take a meeting in the bloody cafeteria?'

Penn removed his headphones. 'Well, never but I've only been here for—'

'Never is the correct answer,' she said. 'And why is that woman here at all?'

'If you're gonna keep asking me questions I can't answer I'm going back to my own work,' he said, picking the headphones back up.

'You know the boss is keeping something from us, right? I mean, *even you* know that,' Stacey said, drumming her fingers on the desk.

'Not sure what you're inferring with the "even you" thing but of course I know she's not telling us everything, so I'm guessing she has her reasons and will share when—'

'Penn, do you have any normal emotional responses at all?' she asked.

'Yes, when necessary,' he said. 'But now you're just narked that I don't feel the same way as you.'

Yes, she had to admit there was an element of truth to that. She wanted him to feel as pissed off as she was feeling at being left out in the cold.

'Look, she's given us work to do so we'd best just get cracking on the things she wants.'

'Okay, what do you make of Rubik?' she asked.

'Jesus Christ,' he muttered with frustration. 'Tell me what you want me to think, I'll think it, and then hopefully you'll let me get back to work.'

'Strange death, don't you think?' she asked, trying to picture the man's entire body squashed amongst the metal.

'Not really. There have been plenty of stranger deaths. There was a Brazilian guy who was killed when a cow fell through his roof. A nineteenth-century US lawyer accidentally shot himself demonstrating that a supposed victim could have shot themselves. A Canadian lawyer died throwing himself against a glass panel on the twenty-fourth floor of an office building. Glass didn't break but it popped out and he fell to his death. Another—'

'Penn, where do you keep all this unnecessary information?'

He shrugged, retrieved his headphones and this time she let him. But her brain hadn't stopped working.

Yes, the person inside her was hurt that she was being kept in the dark, but the investigator in her wanted to know what it was and why.

She knew the boss wanted her to investigate Mark Johnson's altercation with Harry Jenks at the community centre and she would, but something suddenly came back to her. When Alison had arrived the previous evening, she'd been about to say something when the boss had cut her off.

She tried to remember it word for word: *So, I hear you had a crime scene that bore sim—*

Stacey wrote it down on a Post-it note and studied it for a minute.

She had no idea what that could mean but she made the decision she was going to do her best to find out.

CHAPTER 32

'Seriously, though,' Bryant said reaching to take the notebook back. 'How are we gonna narrow it down to the hundreds?'

Kim knew he had a point.

Alison turned her way. 'Okay, if this has anything to do with you it's not as simple as pissing someone off. No one is going to do this because you pissed them off,' she explained. 'This is going to be a life ruined; someone who holds so much rage towards you that they're prepared to kill people to make their point.'

'That may have cut it by a third,' Bryant said, starting to write names on the notepad.

'Nina Croft?' Kim questioned, looking across at his pad.

'Who is she?' Alison asked, also noting down the name.

'The wife of a local councillor on one of our earliest major investigations into a children's home called Crestwood.'

'And?'

'It's fair to say that the things we uncovered pretty much ruined her life,' Bryant said. 'It's also accurate to say she hated the guv with a passion.'

'Put her on the list,' Alison said.

Kim found it doubtful that Nina Croft would have held on to her hatred for such a long time. It had been over three years but Bryant was right that there had been a deep hatred from the woman and Nina had held her personally responsible.

'Symes,' Bryant said, writing down the name.

Alison nodded her agreement. It was the kidnapping case they had worked together and she had worked with them and knew these perpetrators well.

'Symes is a possibility. He hates you enough.'

'But he's in prison,' she said, shuddering, as she recalled that the only thing that mattered to the man was causing pain, and the younger his victim the better.

'Some people are angry enough and powerful enough to exact revenge from behind bars,' Alison said. 'Put him on the list.'

Oh yes, she'd had experience of people tampering with her life from behind bars.

Bryant appeared to be following her thought process.

'You don't think Alex?…'

'No,' Kim said. 'She had her shot and failed. She doesn't repeat herself.'

'Care to explain?' Alison asked.

Kim opened her mouth but Bryant cut in.

'Doctor Alexandra Thorne is a sociopathic psychiatrist who used and abused her patients for her own sick experiment; a game resulting in countless deaths.

'During the investigation, she got particularly fascinated with the guv and tried to tear her apart. She failed but tried again from behind bars to bring her to her knees, psychologically, by toying with her weakest points and had someone ready and waiting to kill her if that didn't work.'

'Put her on the list,' Alison said.

'Take her off,' Kim replied.

'Inspector, I know sociopaths,' Alison shot.

'And I know Alex. It isn't her, now take her off the list.'

Bryant looked between the two of them and scrubbed out her name.

Alison did not.

'Okay, what was your next major investigation?' Alison asked.

'Female victims at a body farm,' Kim said.

'Anything there?'

'Don't hate me enough,' Kim said.

Bryant nodded his agreement.

Alison's pen hovered above her pad. 'Next.'

'Next of kin murders,' Kim said, remembering finding Woody almost unconscious on the floor of his holiday home in Wales.

'Not powerful enough.'

Again, Bryant agreed with her.

'Next,' she asked.

'Hate crimes case,' Bryant said. 'Our DC, Stacey, almost lost her life.'

'Anyone?'

Kim began to shake her head and then stopped.

'Powerful enough?' Alison asked.

Kim nodded.

'Hates you enough?'

'Very probably,' Kim answered, as Bryant added the name Dale Preece to his list. Because of her the man had lost everything. Now that one she agreed with.

'Next?'

'Prostitution Murders,' Kim said. 'And no, that person doesn't hate me enough even though they think they probably do.'

'Next?' Alison said.

Kim swallowed. 'The Heathcrest Investigation.'

She would never be able to say those words without thinking of Detective Sergeant Kevin Dawson.

'Anyone?' Alison asked, quietly.

'During the investigation we uncovered a secret society with members in high and powerful places. They don't like me very much but they've had a few months now to come get me and they haven't, and the family most affected by that investigation hate each other more than they hate me.'

'You must get great comfort from that,' Alison said, drily.

'And our last major investigation centred on one of the doctors linked to Heathcrest who I had tried to charge with carrying out illegal abortions.'

'Family?' Alison asked.

Kim shook her head after giving it some thought. 'Luke was pretty hostile at the beginning but he'd warmed slightly by the time the case was over.'

'How hostile?' Alison asked.

Kim remembered him stepping towards her with both his face and fists filled with rage.

'Substantially,' Bryant said, obviously recalling the same memory.

'On the list,' all three of them said, together.

'Anything current?' Alison asked.

Kim shook her head.

'So, we have Nina Croft, Symes, Alexandra Thorne, my list not yours, Dale Preece and Luke Cordell.'

'Yep,' Kim said.

'And that covers the last three years only,' Bryant said. 'We've barely scratched the surface yet.'

Alison looked at the list. 'I think we've found a pretty good place to start.'

CHAPTER 33

Penn wondered if his colleague realised she was holding a permanent scowl on her face as she tapped away on her computer.

He had mixed feelings about her concerns regarding the boss's secrecy.

He had come from a team where the head of the department had often shared stuff on a need-to-know basis so this wasn't new for him, but his colleague was taking it seriously and definitely personally. If there was stuff that wasn't for sharing he would respect that.

'Got anything?' the boss asked as she entered the squad room ahead of Bryant and Alison Lowe.

He removed his headphones. 'Got all the footage from Asda. They were in there for almost an hour and for folks with no money that's quite a long time, so I'm trying to trace their steps from when they entered to when they left.'

The boss nodded in his direction, which he had come to understand meant carry on.

'Stace?'

'Nothing on Harry Jenks yet, not a sniff of scandal and perfectly qualified for his job.'

Penn detected a note in Stacey's voice indicating that she felt she wasn't only barking up the wrong tree but that she was in a completely different forest.

If the boss noticed she didn't show it.

Penn turned back to his screen.

'Bryant and I will be out following fresh leads and—'

'What fresh leads?' Stacey asked, raising her head.

'We'll let you know if anything comes up, Stace.'

'And I'm going to make a few calls to Drake Hall,' Alison said.

'In there,' the boss said, nodding towards The Bowl.

Alison gathered up her belongings and moved to the office.

He saw Stacey watching proceedings with interest while saying nothing, but something on the screen had caught his attention. He went back and played it again.

'One sec,' he said, raising his hand.

'Penn, you really don't have to raise your hand.'

'Sorry, boss,' he said, bringing his hand back to his keyboard. It was force of habit. On a bigger team, it had been necessary so the guv could see who was speaking straight away.

'What is it?'

'Watch this,' he said, pressing the play icon.

They both watched as Amy Wilde stopped walking around the vegetable section and reached into her back pocket.

Despite the poor image quality, it was clear she was putting her hand to her ear. Mark, who had continued walking, stepped back and stood beside her.

'She had a phone,' the boss said. 'But not on her at the crime scene.'

'Someone stole her phone?' Bryant asked.

'Either it was stolen between this Asda visit and the murder or the killer took it.'

'And the killer would only do that if there was something on the phone to incriminate him,' Penn observed.

'Which means?' the boss asked.

'However loosely, Amy Wilde knew her killer,' Bryant said.

Penn felt a tap on the shoulder.

'Good work, Penn, but now I want more. I want to know their every movement around that shop from the minute they entered to the minute they left.'

Penn knew there was no point approaching the mobile networks. Without a current address or number they wouldn't have a chance and it was unlikely the phone was contract, anyway.

'Got it, boss,' he said, assessing the job before him. With the volume of footage sent to him by the supermarket that was gonna be most of his day, but he got it. This was the only CCTV they had of the couple in the hours leading up to their deaths. If there were no further clues here, they were stuffed.

So, he thought, glancing across the desk at his colleague, Alison had moved office to work on something secret, the boss and Bryant had left the office to work on something else and he wondered if Stacey realised she'd been scowling the whole time.

CHAPTER 34

'You do know she knows you're not being truthful?' Bryant said once they were in the car.

Kim ignored him.

'And you do know she's pissed off?'

'Really?' she answered, sarcastically. 'And here was me having worked with Stacey for three years and being totally clueless in reading her. So grateful to have you—'

'Point taken, guv, but there are other considerations.'

'Like what?' she asked.

'Division of labour, using appropriate resources for the—'

'Hang on, you're getting narked because you had to do a bit of data mining?'

It hadn't been that difficult for him to find out what Nina Croft was up to these days.

'You know me and the computer are not besties but my point is that things like that take either of them about a third of the time it takes me, or you for that matter. It's not efficient.'

'Neither is having this conversation time and time again. I'm not budging.'

She firmly believed they could solve this double murder without her having to give a personal history lesson.

'So, what do we know about Nina Croft?'

'Not a lot,' he said, honestly. 'In the time given I managed to establish she runs her own practice from an office in Cradley Heath High Street.'

'Hmm…'

She probably could have found out that much herself. Like her, Bryant's IT skills stretched to typing a name into Google and then scrolling to the most promising-looking hit. Given the same amount of time Stacey would probably have found the school her kids attended and if Nina had any contact with her husband in prison. She'd probably have been able to tell them what the woman had eaten for breakfast, but that was neither here nor there.

'Wonder if she's happier now?' Kim said, as Bryant headed towards Colley Gate.

'Yeah, I'm sure she is. Probably gonna give you a big bunch of flowers, invite you over for—'

'Okay, enough,' she said, as he headed across Lyde Green and into Cradley Heath. 'Might not even remember me; I'm not even sure she should be on the list,' she said as the car came to a stop outside a carpet shop that Kim remembered from her childhood.

'What are we doing… ooh,' she said when she saw the name-plate to the right of the carpet store entrance.

She got out of the car and followed Bryant up the narrow stairway to a closed, single door at the top.

'You know, she might even thank me for uncovering exactly what her husband had been up to,' she said as the door began to open.

The almost-smile dropped as the dark eyes filled with hate.

She looked Kim up and down with disbelief. When she spoke, venom dripped from every word.

'What the fuck do you want?'

CHAPTER 35

Alison knocked on the door and waited to be called in.

'Take a seat,' DCI Woodward said, pointing to the chair she had occupied for less than five minutes the day before.

'Sorry we didn't have chance for a proper discussion yesterday but thank you for assisting on short notice,' he said.

She acknowledged his words choosing not to point out she was hardly rushed off her feet right now.

'And how have the team reacted to your presence?'

'Don't you mean how did your DI react?' she asked. 'And I would think you had a better idea of that than me given that she's already been banging your door down,' she said.

'Well, initially, I'd like to know about the whole team. They've been through a lot in the last few months.'

Yes, she had read about Dawson's death in the newspaper and been saddened but not wholly surprised. When she'd worked with the team on the kidnapping case she had watched him closely, fascinated by his impetuous energy and the efforts he employed to stifle it.

'The team is doing okay,' she answered. 'Penn is a pretty open book. Stacey is wary and suspicious and Bryant is fiercely protective.'

'And Stone?' he asked.

'I've not seen that much of her,' Alison admitted. 'But seems to be handling it at the minute.'

Alison didn't mention that she was still getting familiar with the DI's body language and making notes. She'd been difficult to read three years ago and hadn't improved since. Alison also chose not to reveal that she was looking forward to the challenge, but some people were much easier to read than others.

She remembered when she was nine years old and at gymnastics practice after school. As ever she had found herself people watching and looking round at the other girls. Naomi, a superb athlete a year younger than herself had been told she was focussing on the beam. She had nodded enthusiastically but Alison had noticed her toes curl underneath. She worked on the beam and fell off, constantly. A few weeks later the exact same thing happened. Toes curled, she fell off.

A month after that while competing in regional championships the beam star, Kaisha, had been taken ill with tummy cramps and the gym coach had chosen Naomi to take her place. Alison had seen the toes curl and had fearfully told the gym teacher that Naomi was going to fall. She hadn't listened and said Naomi was perfectly capable.

Naomi had taken to the beam and during the routine had fallen and sprained her wrist. Alison had later come to understand that although capable of mastering the beam she had developed a mental block that had made her fearful of the apparatus and that fear had manifested itself as a toe curl of which the girl herself had been unaware. From that moment Alison had been fascinated with understanding people's behaviour. What they were aware of and what they weren't.

'I'd also like to talk to you about the other business.'

She nodded and forced herself not to swallow, revealing her own concession to nerves.

She had already realised that the 'other business' would somehow be invisibly attached to her CV for the rest of her career, that the 'other business' would overshadow any of her previous triumphs and anything she might achieve in the future. She would never outrun or escape the 'other business' and the proof of it was lying silently in a hospital bed.

'It has no bearing on what you've been brought here to do.'

'Thank you,' she said revealing nothing.

'We all make mistakes,' he said, meeting her gaze.

She returned his stare unflinchingly while appreciating the kindly way he'd addressed the mistake she made.

Except one small problem remained. She wasn't totally convinced it had been a mistake at all.

CHAPTER 36

The room was poky, dark and filled with folders. Kim was reminded of TV private eye offices.

'I wouldn't invite you to sit even if I had more chairs,' Nina said, standing beside the desk.

Kim was relieved to see that the woman still dressed well in a fitted, straight navy dress that ended just below the knees. The designer wasn't obvious to her but she looked smart and functional. The dark brown hair was an inch longer than she remembered. Possibly the result of fewer salon visits, Kim wondered.

'So, how've you been?' she asked, taking the single seat.

Colour flooded into Nina's face. 'Are you serious?' she exploded. 'What the hell are you doing here?'

Kim shrugged, 'Just passing.'

'Liar,' she spat. 'Now unless this is an official call about one of my clients you can—'

'Who are?' Kim asked. 'I mean, who are your clients these days?'

The hatred bubbled behind her eyes. 'None of your fucking business. Nothing here concerns you. You're not welcome either here or at my—'

'Where is that, now?' Kim asked, unable to resist needling her. This was guiltless, calorie-free fun, especially when she remembered the dog that had died a painful death after she'd fed it antifreeze to warn her off the investigation into the Crestwood children's home. 'You still living in that nice big house in…'

'Don't be so bloody ridiculous. You know full well I had no chance of keeping my home, or my children in private education, you fucking bitch. I live in a terraced house in Old Hill and my boys attend the local comprehensive because of you and—'

'Oh, Nina, please,' Kim said, losing patience with the holier-than-thou attitude. 'Your husband deserved everything he got and I'm sorry you lost everything you had. I'm sorry you lost your high-paying job in Birmingham, I'm sorry you missed out on your imminent promotion to partner. I'm sorry you lost your home and that your boys have had to be uprooted to new schools. And all because of what your husband did.'

Kim could see the clenched fists were trembling by her sides.

'Except I'm not sorry at all, Nina, because you knew everything he'd done and you never told anyone. You speaking out could have saved lives, so I couldn't really give a shit about—'

'Leave,' she barked, pointing at the door. 'The very sight of you is offensive to me and I don't have to tolerate—'

'Not to mention what you did to that dog,' Kim said, shaking her head. 'I mean, that was low.'

'Get out,' Nina cried.

'And obstructing the course of the investigation to protect your own—'

'Inspector, I'm warning you. Get out.'

'Where were you Sunday night, Nina?' Kim asked, calmly, wrong-footing her.

'At home with my boys,' she shot back without thinking. Too caught up in the rage to consider not answering.

'Thanks for your time,' Kim said, jumping up from the seat. 'Been lovely to catch up,' she said, following Bryant out of the office.

She wasn't surprised to hear something crash against the wooden door as it closed.

'What do you think?' she asked Bryant as they reached the bottom of the stairs.

'Not sure,' he answered. 'But I can tell you that if she wasn't angry enough to hurt you before, she sure is now.'

CHAPTER 37

Penn glanced down at the timeline he was painstakingly building for the boss detailing the journey of Amy and Mark around the supermarket on Sunday afternoon.

3.09 p.m. – A+M enter Asda
3.14 p.m. – Look at Sandwich fridge
3.18 p.m. – Peruse fruit and veg
3.20 p.m. – Pick up apple and put back
3.26 p.m. – Wander up and down chilled meats aisle
3.30 p.m. – Take telephone call (3 mins)
3.33 p.m. – Chat beside fresh bread aisle
3.34 p.m. – Look at wrist
3.37 p.m. – Peruse toiletries aisle
3.40 p.m. – Slip something into pocket
3.42 p.m. – Go into toilets

And that was where he was right now waiting for either or both of them to come out of the toilets. He'd seen a cleaner come and go, countless shoppers rush in and rush out, but the two of them had been in around seven minutes.

'Coffee?' he heard through his headphones.

He paused and glanced at his colleague. She never touched the stuff and rarely made it. He normally had one or two in the morning and then laid off. Much more and he was like a freed bumblebee on a summer day.

He shook his head but watched from the corner of his eye as she glanced a few times towards Alison, making calls in The Bowl.

He resumed the recording and saw both Amy and Mark exit the toilets at 3.52 p.m., just eight minutes before the store closed.

He switched to the camera covering the entrance and exit doors and waited: 3.53; 3.54; 3.55, nothing.

Where had they gone? It took less than ten seconds to get from the toilets to the door.

He backtracked to the camera covering the cigarette kiosk, the only thing between the toilets and the doors.

He caught them, deep in conversation behind the newspaper stand. Amy walked away first and Mark followed, but he knew they hadn't reached the doors.

He sat up in his chair tapping away furiously, switching from one camera to another to pick them back up.

Finally, he found them again and watched as they perused, chose and finally made a purchase.

He noted the entry on the timeline but, by goodness, he hadn't expected that.

CHAPTER 38

Kim couldn't recall the last time she'd visited Winson Green prison but it hadn't been long enough.

Now referred to as HMP Birmingham it would always be Winson Green to her. She remembered the occasional trips with Erica and Keith into Birmingham on the train. Each time Keith would warn her that a view of the imposing building was coming up and each time she had been compelled to look. And then regret it. The sight of the Victorian exterior had both frightened and fascinated her. She had feared its stark, harsh, unforgiving shell but also wondered about the bad men that it contained.

Well, right now 1,450 bad men were held within its Category B walls: a mixture of adult and remand prisoners, and she'd been instrumental in putting a fair few of them in there.

They approached the iconic police blue columns and entered. Bryant had called ahead and their first visitation was being set up in a private room with a heavy security presence. Not at Kim's request but Bryant and the director had been in agreement. This visit would not take place over the road at the visitor's centre.

A man in his thirties with black hair and a tidy moustache moved forward to greet them.

'Team Leader Gennard. I'll be supervising your visit here today,' he said, showing her his customer service training.

A part of her objected to the emblem on his shirt of the private security company. The privatisation of prisons which began in 1992 did not sit well with her. Her mind could not reconcile the idea of the protection of the public from dangerous criminals as a profit-making business. The potential consequences of cost-cutting and penny-pinching could be disastrous.

But that wasn't this man's fault, she thought, as Bryant shook his hand and thanked him.

'ID please,' he said, pleasantly, with an expression that said: *No one bypasses that rule.*

They both held up their identification. He produced a basket and nodded towards it. 'Everything in here,' he said. 'It'll all be returned.'

'Everything?' Kim questioned.

'The improvised weapons would make your toes curl,' he said. 'I've seen knives made from toothbrushes, razor whips. We even have to monitor water usage,' he said, pleasantly as though still trying to make their visit a positive experience.

'Water's pretty harmless, isn't it?' Bryant asked and even she was wondering what the most ingenious minds could make of that.

'Ha, don't be fooled into thinking anything is harmless around a devious criminal mind. Water seems safe enough until you fill a plastic bag with it and drop it from a great height on someone's head. Then it's a water bomb with the ability to kill.'

She was sure of it.

'Okay, all set?' he asked, as though they were taking some kind of day trip.

'Almost,' she said, turning to her colleague. 'Bryant, stay here.'

His expression said, *not bloody likely*, but it was important for what she was about to do.

'Guv, I don't think…'

'I'll be fine,' she said, decisively before turning away.

'Harris, Iqbal, with me,' Gennard called to a group of white-shirted officers.

The two biggest stepped forward and followed them through the key-coded door and remained silent until Gennard stopped short at a heavy metal door.

He key-coded his number and opened it.

Iqbal stepped in before them and took a place in the left-hand corner. Harris moved in behind.

Kim appraised the muscly, shaven-headed man with a scar where his left eye should have been. Kim felt no remorse that she'd been responsible. She was looking at the most evil, twisted man she had ever met whose thirst for inflicting physical pain knew no bounds. The hatred in his eyes travelled the space between them.

She smiled right through it as she said, 'Hey, Symes, are you pleased to see me?'

CHAPTER 39

'Settle down, settle down,' Gennard said, as Symes tried to wrench his handcuffs from the security bar that confined him to the table.

There were no chairs on this side of the table. Evidently, his feelings for her had not softened since they'd last seen each other and she had embedded glass in his eye. She was exceptionally proud of the scarring she'd given this man as a permanent reminder that he'd failed in his efforts.

'So, how've you been, Symes?' she asked as Gennard came to stand beside her.

'What the fuck you want, bitch?' he asked, as his nostrils flared.

'Just a welfare check. See if you're behaving yourself.'

'I swear if I could—'

'Symes,' Gennard warned.

'You been making friends and playing nice in here?' she asked.

'The fuck it's your business,' he spat.

'Ahhh, nobody wants to play, eh? Good to see the guys in here have standards.'

Kim could feel Gennard stiffening beside her at the lazy, taunting tone but it was necessary, calculated and intentional. And that's why she had wanted Bryant out of the room. He would have tried to stop her.

'I mean, even these guys can't stand cowards that hurt children,' she said, staring into his one good eye.

'Just one hand around your fucking throat and—'

'And they don't much care for failures, do they? I suppose they know you were stopped by a woman, which must do your credibility zero good,' she said, making the figure o with her thumb and finger.

'Gennard, you wanna get this?…'

'And I'm sure you'll be happy to know that those little girls are happy, fit and healthy and they give you no thought at all,' she added with a smile.

'I'll wring your—'

'So, come on, who you been taking needlework classes with, anyone interesting?' she asked, noting how the rage was travelling all the way to his white clenched knuckles but for once he remained silent.

'So, you been thinking about me much?' she asked.

Symes suddenly sat back and regarded her coolly.

'Somebody got it in for you, bitch?' he asked.

Kim realised that throughout their exchange he had not looked at anyone else in the room once and neither had she.

'Answer the question, Symes,' she said.

'You really think I'm after you?' he asked.

'Answer the question,' she said again.

'You know, Stone, your face keeps me awake every fucking night. I picture you underneath me struggling and screaming while I rape the fuck out of—'

'Symes,' Gennard warned.

Kim held up her hand. 'Let him speak freely,' she said. She was here to learn the depth of his hatred for her and whether he could be responsible, remotely, for the murder of Amy and Mark. She had goaded him into brutal honesty and now she had to listen.

'I picture you screaming for mercy as I fucking break you in half with my cock. And when my dick is done I lamp the living daylights out of you. One broken bone after another until I'm kicking around a bag of skin with every internal organ smashed.'

Kim could see the veil of ecstasy dropping into his eyes as he spoke. This man had only ever lived for violence but now he only lived for violence inflicted on her.

She had no doubt what would happen if this man ever got free.

She hid the sensation of the cold finger travelling up her spine.

'Yeah, whatever, now are you gonna answer the question?' she pushed.

'If somebody's rattling your cage then they have my fucking vote, but one thing you should already know about me, you fucking bitch, slut, whore.'

'Which is?'

'If it was me that was after you, you'd already be dead.'

CHAPTER 40

Symes closed his palm around his flaccid dick and started to pump.

Yesterday, after a visit from Deana – the dirty slag – he'd had the pleasure of whacking off in the visitor's toilets after telling Gennard he couldn't hold himself back to the wing.

There was something satisfying about having a wank in the visitor's toilets. The clean floors with well-stocked bog roll and a smell that wasn't four-day-old piss and shit.

But not today. Today he hadn't even been taken to the visitor's room. Not safe for the visitor, they'd said and they'd been fucking right to chain him to the damn table because if his hands had been free…

His hand moved back and forth trying to expel the poison the bitch had put right into his balls. The rage that, always present, had been fanned and needed to fire out of him in order for him to think straight.

He thought back to Deana's visit the previous day, her big tits straining against the cheap tee shirt two sizes too small. Her wobbling flesh had done nothing for him but the slut knew what he liked. Her right hand had hovered over the milky white skin before pinching her own flesh, gently at first, teasing him and then harder until red patches had started to appear. His arousal had begun as the marks had deepened, when the discomfort had showed on her face. She'd grabbed the flesh harder, twisting it roughly, digging in her talon-like nails until she'd cried out with the pain.

He'd thought he was gonna come there and then.

He pumped harder trying to hold on to the image of her discomfort, her bruises, her pain.

But his dick hung loosely in his hand.

He returned his mind to the one memory that always got his juices flowing, used sparingly in case he ever wore it out.

He pictured Kim fucking Stone on the floor of the basement, placing herself between him and the nine-year-old girl whose life he'd been promised.

He remembered the feeling of kicking her hard in the knee to bring her to the ground. The groan of pain that had escaped from her mouth.

There it is, he thought to himself, as his dick began to wake up.

He pictured himself on top of her, his fist smashing into the side of her face.

Oh yes, oh yes, oh yes, he thought, as his hand worked harder.

Her face flinching against the pain he was inflicting.

This was more like it, he thought, as the heat surged through his hand.

'Come on, Symes, we ain't got all day,' Gennard called from outside.

'Fuck off,' he shouted back at the intrusion.

But it was too late. Gennard's voice prompted the reminder of why the guard was with him anyway. Because of that bitch's visit.

And the new vision now came to haunt him, replacing the old, treasured memory kept safe for his own pleasure.

The bitch, fit and healthy, pain-free and without injury. Her smug, victorious face mocking him from the other side of the room.

His dick turned limp in his hands and he knew that he would never get that precious memory back.

And now he hated the bitch even more.

CHAPTER 41

Alison watched as Stacey approached and knocked before entering The Bowl.

'Coffee?' she asked.

Alison shook her head.

'Tea, water?'

Alison held up a silver flask containing a smoothie prepared at home. 'I'm good, thanks.'

'Anything I can help with?' she asked, pleasantly. 'Data mining isn't everyone's cup of tea and—'

'Stacey, it doesn't matter if you creep around the subject all day or ask me outright, it'll be the same answer, which is, I can't tell you what I'm working on.'

'But she's hiding stuff from us, isn't she? You can at least tell me that.'

Alison hesitated for just a second before nodding.

'I'm sorry to say, Stacey, that she's definitely doing that.'

Alison watched as the constable retook her seat in the general office. Regardless of whether or not she agreed with Stone's secrecy she had to respect it.

Despite the DI's insistence on Alexandra Thorne she had placed a call to the warden of Drake Hall to ring her back to establish any changes in the woman's pattern of behaviour. Any new visitors on the scene? Any new alliances in the prison? If the psychiatrist truly was a sociopath she was a contender whether or not she was in prison. Bryant's comments led her to believe that Thorne's efforts had already taken place from behind bars, which only increased Alison's suspicions. And unlike Stone, her own experience of sociopaths was that they rarely gave up after one attempt.

But after her meeting with DCI Woodward her mind was still on Beverly Wright, lying in a hospital bed and the mistake she'd made which had put her there.

She wondered whether it was her own arrogance that refused to accept the outcome of the West Mercia Police investigation. She knew that was a possibility. No one ever wanted to admit they were wrong, especially when the error had led to an innocent female being brutally beaten and raped.

Alison was unable to stop herself opening the folder on her laptop, asking herself for the hundredth time why she hadn't archived it or let it go.

And it was because she couldn't understand her mistake. She needed to know where she'd gone wrong. How could she do her job here with this team or any team in the future if she didn't understand where she'd messed up?

It was almost four months ago that she'd been called in to assist on the brutal rape and murder of a twenty-nine-year-old woman in Malvern due to a lack of physical clues left at the scene.

She had known immediately that the task was challenging, given that a fundamental aspect of profiling was that multiple crimes could be linked to a specific offender, and that the profile could be used to predict the offender's future actions.

With only one crime she'd had no choice but to work on the premise that behaviour reflects personality.

With multiple crimes she would have been able to use linkage analysis to find similar cases with little evidence and link them through similarities, but the brutal rape and murder of Jennifer Townes was like nothing she'd ever seen before.

She'd studied every piece of information, reading it over and over again, extracting typologies – categorising the crime scene and by extension the offender's personality.

And eventually she had given them a profile of the offender, by which time the team had decided on a prime suspect, but she had insisted they were wrong.

They had fancied an ex-boyfriend of Jennifer, a wannabe musician who toured the pubs and clubs of Worcester gigging and sniffing after his big break. Alison had insisted they were wrong. Curtis Swayne was a creative, unstable drifter who lived in someone's spare room. Their interest was all because he'd demonstrated violent tendencies after a pub fight at a bar where Jennifer had worked part-time.

They had listened initially and had focussed the investigation on people they'd interviewed that did match the profile. Two suspects in particular.

Gerard Batham, a twenty-eight-year-old junior partner at the law firm where Jennifer worked during the day. His ambition, ruthlessness, drive and organisation along with his good looks had made him a possible suspect.

The other was Tom Drury, the owner of Elite bar in Kidderminster, where Curtis played and Jennifer worked.

And then Beverly had been attacked on a night she'd been at Elite and Curtis had been playing, and Tom had been behind the bar.

Tom had an alibi and Curtis couldn't even remember where he'd gone once he'd finished his set.

Within two days of Beverly's attack Curtis had been arrested and charged and she'd been shown the door.

To add insult to injury the chief super, during a press conference, had made a public, damning statement about the use of 'hocus-pocus' methods of detection instead of solid police work.

She had hidden in her house for two days, surrounded by tissues and fast-food containers.

She'd watched every news report on the murders, streaming *Sky News* continually for any further update. She had watched as Beverly Wright had been identified as a prostitute and her name had slowly faded from the news.

And Beverly was the one she was interested in, whatever her profession. Jennifer had been dead when she'd been seconded to the case but the attack on Beverly was the one she could have, should have, been able to prevent.

She'd eventually plucked up the courage to call the hospital and had been mortified to learn that hers had been the only call.

And she'd visited the girl every night ever since.

For the last five days she'd pored over every detail of the two cases and tried to marry either one of them to Curtis and she just couldn't do it. Not without going against everything she'd ever learned.

Since being removed from the case she'd also been frozen out by everyone she'd worked with, her reputation and career in tatters, which bothered her but not nearly as much as the sickness in her stomach that refused to go away every time she sat beside the figure of Beverly Wright.

She looked over the names of the men who had been questioned in connection with Jennifer's murder.

Her eyes continually returned to two names on the list. And one in particular.

She sighed heavily. Only one question really mattered.

What was she going to do about it?

CHAPTER 42

Kim wouldn't have minded a nice hot shower after leaving Symes in the holding cell.

'Phew, that was a bit intense,' Gennard said, waving away the other two officers. 'Won't be needed for your next guy but I'd rather you left your belongings in here for now.'

Kim nodded her understanding as Bryant joined them.

'Rules are rules,' he elaborated, unnecessarily.

'So, where will we find Dale Preece?' she asked.

He nodded towards the visitor centre across the road. 'Halfway through afternoon visiting. His mum's normally here.'

She didn't relish the idea of seeing either of them again.

She took a breath and headed across the street.

The room was about half-full of prisoners and visitors sitting on plastic seats at fixed wooden tables holding cardboard coffee cups and sandwich wrappers.

Dale Preece had changed very little, she thought, as she got a second to appraise him.

His black hair was short and looked smart. He appeared to have dropped a few pounds making his cheekbones more pronounced.

She wasn't surprised to see him holding his mother's hand across the table. There were only the two of them left.

She took a step forward, and Dale looked her way.

For the briefest of seconds, they were back in that farmhouse and Dale was pointing a rifle straight at her.

His face hardened as he appeared to travel through the same memories of the horror that took place that night.

Sensing his distraction Mallory Preece turned her head too.

There was no joy contained in her expression of surprise. But Kim wasn't interested in Mallory Preece who had shown herself to be a limp, ineffectual woman dominated by her racist father who had destroyed the lives and relationship of both his grandsons. And she didn't believe that Mallory had known nothing.

'What do you want?' they said together.

'Just a word,' she said, looking only at Dale. His dark eyes were unreadable but the set jaw gave away his displeasure at her presence.

Mallory Preece glanced at her watch. 'I'll go, sweetheart,' she said quietly to her son. 'I'll see you tomorrow.'

He nodded and squeezed her hand before she stood.

Mallory offered her a filthy look as she clutched her handbag and left the room.

'She visit every day?' Kim asked, taking a seat.

He nodded. 'Pretty much.'

Kim suspected she'd got little else to do without her despicable father to take care of.

'She's on her own now,' he said, and although there was no accusation in his tone, she could hear the control he exercised to keep it that way. Dale Preece had always managed to keep control. 'She's had to learn to take care of herself.'

Kim almost said she was lucky to be free of the ruthless, evil bastard but just remembered that Dale and his grandfather had been very close.

'So, how is it in here?' she asked.

'What do you want?' he asked again , coolly, meeting her gaze. Not surprisingly he had no interest in exchanging pleasantries with her.

Her aim had been to gauge emotional responses and levels of hatred. With Symes it had been a piece of cake, but Dale was not going to be as easy. He was a man who kept his emotions hidden well behind the dark, handsome exterior.

That night in the farmhouse he had chosen to save her life and had probably regretted it ever since. Instead he had lost both his grandfather and his brother, which was not something she could find herself sorry about.

'Welfare check to see…' her words trailed away. No, this wasn't going to work. 'Dale, someone may be out to get me and I'm here to see if it's you.'

A shot of surprise did register in his emotionless eyes. It was quickly hidden and his face reverted to neutral.

'You seem shocked?'

He shook his head. 'Not that someone may be out to get you but that you chose to come and see me. What could I do from in here?'

No denial she noted.

'You'd be surprised,' she answered honestly.

'But why me? Surely, there are people who hate you more than I do.'

Kim could only marvel at the lack of emotion attached to such a line. A sentence where he'd admitted he hated her. Somehow that chilled her even more than the man with one eye.

'Like Symes,' he added.

'You know Symes?' she asked, her turn to be surprised. Yes, they were in the same prison but the men couldn't be more different. They wouldn't have met at knitting club.

Dale nodded. 'He sought me out when I first got here.' He paused. 'To be honest he approaches anyone who is in here because of you. It's his own personal Hate Club.'

Kim frowned. This really was something that prison intel should have picked up on.

'Okay, thanks, Dale,' she said, standing.

'And for what it's worth, his cellmate, another member of the club, recently got out.'

CHAPTER 43

Kim was ready to get updates from her team at the station by six o'clock.

'Stace, what you got on Jenks?'

Stacey shook her head. 'Nothing yet, boss.'

'Sorry?' Kim asked. She and Bryant had been gone the whole day and Stacey had nothing to show for her time.

'Trying all the normal channels. No red flags. He's qualified for the job and—'

'I could tell that from the wall behind him, Stace. He wears it like a badge.'

'Sorry, boss, but—'

'Office, Stace,' Kim said, heading for The Bowl.

Stacey closed the door behind her.

'Look, boss, I've—'

'Not interested, Stace,' Kim said, taking out her phone. She dialled a number and put it on hands-free.

The call was answered on the second ring.

'Hey.'

'Hey, Gem, know anything about that community centre in Stourbridge, behind the bus station?'

Gemma blew a raspberry.

'Meaning?'

'Place is okay, got loads of stuff in there but head honcho is a bit of a sleaze, by all accounts.'

'Go on,' Kim said, glaring at her colleague.

'Most girls I know won't go there, cos that guy, Jenkins—'

'Jenks,' Kim corrected.

'Yeah, him. Apparently, he offers the girls money and help with stuff for a blow job. Never experienced it but it's what I heard.'

'Got it, thanks,' she said, ending the call.

Kim waited.

Stacey nodded to the phone. 'I don't know—'

'I'm aware you don't know Gemma but you have your own sources, your own contacts, people you've met over the years. You tried official channels and got nothing, so you try them again and see if they change their mind or look elsewhere. Bloody hell, Stace. A whole day?'

Stacey had the good grace to look mortified but her own anger was not dissipating quite so easily.

'Whatever's niggling you, park it,' she said, striding over to the door and opening it.

She knew what Stacey's problem was and she wasn't dealing with it now.

Stacey followed her out of the office back into the squad room. All eyes looked away, even Alison.

'Stace?'

'Yes, boss.'

'Start looking at the name John Duggar, recent inmate of Winson Green.'

'On it,' she shot back.

'Alison?'

The woman shook her head. 'The lead I was following came to nothing. I think you might be right about Alexandra Thorne.'

Kim didn't hide her smile of triumph.

Alex didn't play the same game twice. She bored too easily and Kim had known she wasn't involved, but sometimes you just had to give people a little bit of rope.

From Alison's set expression Kim guessed Alison didn't enjoy being proven wrong.

'Penn?' she asked, praying he'd got something.

He took out a piece of paper and passed it to her. It was a full timeline for the period Amy and Mark had been in the supermarket.

'After the phone call Amy slips something into her pocket. It was in the toiletry aisle, so I'm guessing a roll-on deodorant or something like that.'

Kim nodded her agreement.

'But that's not the interesting bit,' Penn said, turning his screen towards her.

Kim watched the montage of footage taken from different cameras and pieced together by Penn.

She saw Amy and Mark exit the toilets, pass the cigarette kiosk, the newspaper stand, the security kiosk and then stop.

Kim frowned as she continued to watch. The footage ended.

'Play it again,' Kim said, scratching her chin.

She watched once more.

'So, a couple of homeless drug addicts go into the supermarket, stare longingly at the food, get a phone call, steal deodorant but spend what little money they have on flowers?'

Penn nodded. 'Exactly.'

'So, who the hell was on the phone and what did they promise these kids?'

CHAPTER 44

'Saved herself a bit with that one, eh?' Bryant said, as they reached the car.

Stacey had pulled out all the stops to get a current address for John Duggar, Symes's recently released cellmate. She still didn't recall his name from any major investigation but she'd worry about that when she met him.

'Yeah well, she needed to,' Kim said.

'If you'd just—'

'Shut up and drive,' Kim said, looking out of the window. There was still no definitive proof that the murders of Amy and Mark were anything to do with her. The call she'd made to Gemma had also highlighted Harry Jenks. She suspected he had offered Amy money for sex and Mark had found out, leading to the altercation. Which also explained Jenks's failure to reveal the incident at all or report it.

She was looking forward to her next conversation with him and doubted she'd be quite so polite.

'So, you know where this guy lives?' she asked Bryant as he negotiated the Shenstone traffic island.

'Yeah, just behind The Civic in Old Hill.'

'Jeez, Bryant, where's that?'

'You don't know The Civic?' he asked, aghast.

'No, and now you're making me feel as though I'm really missing out.'

'Called The Civic for decades even after being renamed The Regis. Built early Fifties and hosted everything: weddings, works parties, the lot. Six hundred capacity ballroom. Supposed to be posh and if you'd been invited to a—'

'Bryant, shut up,' Kim snapped.

'Well, you asked…'

'Shush,' she repeated.

She turned up Bryant's handheld station radio that accompanied them everywhere.

'Shit, sounds serious,' Bryant said as voices filled the car.

'Fire at Dudley Wood,' Kim said, trying to piece together the details through the crackling and disjointed voices.

Bryant slowed down as he approached a line of traffic through the centre of Old Hill.

'Did he say car fire?' he asked.

'I heard the word occupied,' she answered, turning up the radio.

'I just heard speedway,' Bryant said.

Kim swallowed deeply as that cool finger was back on her spine.

'Bryant, take us there. Now.'

CHAPTER 45

Bryant got them as close as he could before they had to abandon the car outside the Kawasaki bike shop and run.

The scene was mayhem. A build-up of traffic, sirens, police cars trying to get through and the unmistakable sound of water gushing from the fire hoses.

As they turned the corner Kim saw the plume of smoke reaching into the sky, the acrid smell wafting straight into her lungs.

Four police cars and two fire engines were right in front of what used to be the entrance to the speedway, which was now a housing estate.

A third fire engine was trying to get through the traffic that was clogging Dudley Wood Road.

A cordon had already been established and uniformed officers were assembling in high-vis vests to redirect traffic away from the scene.

Both Kim and Bryant showed their ID before ducking under the cordon tape.

Kim could now see that the chaos was organised and although frenetic every person there was engaged in either tackling the fire or protecting the people that were.

'Hey,' Kim said to the first officer she recognised. Sergeant Bowyer operated out of Brierley Hill.

He frowned. 'I was expecting an Inspector but not CID,' he said.

'We were close,' she explained, trying to get a look around the sergeant.

'Forget it, they won't let us any closer than this. Trust me, I've got one hero that tried,' he said nodding towards an officer on the cordon with an angry red graze on his left elbow.

'Guys'll throw you out the way if they need to.'

'So, what did hero do?'

'Tried to get to the folks inside.'

'Definitely occupied?' she asked.

He shrugged. 'I couldn't see anything through the flames but the fucking heat…'

'And your officer tried to get close?'

'Yeah, he didn't think. Fire guy tackled him to the ground and said even if they were still alive they probably wouldn't thank him.'

Although horrific Kim could understand the statement.

A fireman's first priority upon arrival at a scene was the likelihood of preserving life but they could only do so much and risking the life of other people in the process was never a good idea.

Even if the occupant had been alive he or she may well have suffered such extensive burns that rescuing them would only have fated them to a much longer and more torturous death.

'Anything we can do?' Bryant asked.

The sergeant shook his head as a constable approached.

'Got it, Sarge,' he said, handing over a piece of paper.

'Thanks, Ash,' he said, reading the note.

'Victim?' Kim asked.

The sergeant nodded. 'Car is registered to Bill Phelps. Aged fifty-four and lives in Hagley with fifty-two-year-old wife, Helen.'

He took out his phone and called a number. He waited and waited and then ended the call.

'And no one appears to be home.'

'You think they're both in that car?' she asked.

'Looking likely.'

Kim took a step away to regulate her breathing.

'You used to come here with Keith and Erica?' Bryant asked, standing so that she could not be seen.

'Here and Dudley Castle were our favourite places,' she whispered.

Bryant leaned in to hear her above the noise.

She sighed heavily as she processed all she'd learned in a few short minutes.

A middle-aged couple in a car fire outside what used to be the speedway.

The nausea bubbled in her stomach.

She turned to her colleague.

'Okay, Bryant, it's time to talk to the team.'

CHAPTER 46

Stacey had barely finished the last bite of the lasagne when the text message dinged to her phone.

And she wasn't sure how she felt about it.

If this was the boss wanting to tear another strip off her she was sure it could wait until the morning.

Yeah, she accepted that she'd been bollocked in private but it wasn't like the rest of the team didn't know why she'd been hauled into The Bowl anyway.

'Was she right though, babe?' Devon asked, removing her empty plate.

She had already recounted the story to her partner.

'That's not the point,' Stacey protested. Jeez, if she ever expected an easy ride with this woman, she could think again.

'Dee, can you just be on my side?'

Devon chuckled. 'Of course, if you're in the right or I've had my full frontal lobotomy. Was your boss right? Were you sulking because she's holding something back from you?'

Stacey sighed. 'Not what you'd call sulking really…'

'So, you were sulking but thought you were hiding it?'

'Oh, come on, Dee, now you're just—'

'Three weeks ago, when I booked a meal out for your birthday and took you to The Chateau with romantic lighting, soft music and the best table in the place, it was clear to me that I'd messed up.'

Stacey was surprised. 'It was a lovely restaurant with—'

'And you'd have been happier at the Brewers Wharf at the Waterfront because you love their food.'

'But I didn't say—'

'You didn't need to, babe,' Devon said, turning to face her in the kitchen. 'You get a thin line right here,' she said, touching the corner of her mouth. 'Gives you away every time.'

Stacey tipped her head. 'Am I turning into a spoilt bitch?'

Devon smiled and kissed her lightly on the nose.

'No, my love, you thought you were hiding your feelings to protect mine. It was me that messed up and made a mistake. Maybe your boss is thinking the same thing. Maybe she wants to apologise,' Devon said, tapping her on the behind. 'So, you'd best head off and see what she's got to say.'

CHAPTER 47

'Right,' Kim said, facing her team. 'I make no apologies for what I'm about to tell you.'

She avoided looking directly at Stacey for whom the comment was intended.

'It appears our killer might be making his kills personal to me,' she said.

Stacey and Penn sat forward, and she felt the shared glance behind her back between Alison and Bryant.

'It would seem that he is trying to recreate traumatic events from my past. I'm not giving you the gory details but it's safe to say that significant points like handcuffs, radiator, location and the cracker packet are all relevant.'

She paused but no one spoke.

'Penn, Stace, there was another incident a couple of hours ago. A middle-aged couple in a burnt-out car parked outside the old speedway site in Cradley. All relevant,' she said.

They were getting no more detail than that. The vision of her foster parents burnt and blackened following the motorway crash was something she wouldn't, couldn't, dwell on.

'So, this person is trying to hurt you?' Stacey asked, wide-eyed.

'It appears so,' Kim answered.

'It's about pain not death,' Penn said. 'They want you to suffer.'

Kim nodded.

'Hang on, we don't know that for certain,' Alison said. 'This could all be a warm-up to something. The end game could be death.'

Kim turned. 'Thanks for talking about my potential murder without one ounce of emotion.'

'You're welcome,' she said. 'But if he hates you enough to do all this then it's pretty safe to assume he wants you dead.'

'Guys,' she said, turning back, 'I've decided it's okay for everyone to ignore what Alison has to say.'

No one laughed.

'That was a joke,' she explained. 'Although you should also know that Alison is here to watch me,' Kim said. 'She's here to observe my behaviour, monitor my performance and report back on any noticeable changes in my personality as a result of working this case.'

Alison didn't argue.

'She's gonna be a bit bored then?' Stacey observed.

Kim smiled at the vote of confidence.

'Well, let's make sure she's busy enough that she leaves me alone,' Kim answered.

'Sitting here,' Alison said, waving her hand.

Kim ignored her. 'But tomorrow she'll be looking at some potential suspects we've highlighted from previous cases and—'

'Symes on the list?' Stacey asked, demonstrating her eagerness to get cracking straight away. Her analytical brain relished any new information.

'Oh, yeah, he's on the list,' Bryant said. 'Along with Nina Croft, Dale Preece and—'

'It's not him,' Kim said, definitely.

'To be fair, boss, he does have reason, although Symes really does hate—'

'Thanks, Stace,' Kim said. She was fully aware of the level of that man's hatred.

'But surely there are more people than that who hate—'

'Cheers, Penn,' Kim said, folding her arms.

'Sorry, what I meant was, you've worked some pretty big cases and over time you've destroyed a lot of lives.'

'And are we even sure it's from a case you've worked?' Stacey asked. 'I mean there's your whole past to look at. I'm sure over the years we could come up with dozens of…' Stacey's words trailed away as she realised what she was saying.

The room was silent for a few seconds before Kim surprised them all by laughing out loud. She'd expected many things from her team but their ability to release some of the tension from her body had not been one of them.

'Well, thanks guys for being so enthusiastic and honest about the volume of people that could hate me,' she said, putting her hands in her pockets.

'And work colleagues,' Bryant piped up with a grin.

'Consultants,' Alison added.

'Neighbours,' Penn said.

'School kids,' Stacey said.

'Old friends… nah,' Bryant said, getting a chuckle from them all.

Kim rolled her eyes. 'Nice roasting, guys,' she said. 'Now bugger off home and we'll start fresh tomorrow.'

Stacey caught her eye and a silent conversation took place.

I'm sorry, I should have trusted you.

Forget it and move on.

Stacey grabbed her bag and headed out of the door behind Penn.

Alison clicked her briefcase shut. 'That was the right thing to do,' she said.

'Oh yeah, and your approval was tantamount in my decision-making process.'

Alison shook her head wearily.

'Hey, you okay?' Kim asked.

'Of course, why?'

'Cos, I swear to God you tried to make a joke just then when we—'

'Good night, Inspector,' she said, following the others out the door.

'Can't help it, can you?' Bryant asked, smiling.

She shrugged. 'She needs to loosen up a bit.'

'As all my responses to that are way too obvious I'll ask instead if you're okay?'

'It went well,' she said, moving towards The Bowl to get her jacket.

'Back to the future,' he said, suddenly.

'Huh?'

'This case is like the film. We have to go back to the past to find our killer and to predict the future.'

Kim understood and agreed with having to go backwards. 'But the future isn't important in this…'

'Yes it is. We have to think forward to what might happen if we don't catch him soon. Like, which traumatic event in your life is he gonna target next?'

CHAPTER 48

Alison immediately felt out of place as she entered the club, feeling overdressed in a pair of ripped jeans and a shirt. A quick assessment told her that many of the other patrons were dressed similarly except their ripped jeans weren't smart designer and their shirts weren't freshly washed and ironed.

Great, she had chosen the outfit to blend in, to look comfortable in her surroundings. Big fail.

Her decision to come here had been partly inspired by the detective inspector who had called them back to the station. Some of the woman's courage had rubbed off on her. She had watched as the police officer had admitted something to her team that she had really hoped to avoid. She'd appeared fearless even though the hands being thrust into the pockets had told her otherwise. So far she had realised that the woman tucked her short hair behind her ear when preparing for battle and hid her hands when she was feeling unsure. And yet her face gave nothing away.

Alison hoped she could do the same right now. One false move and her life could be in danger, especially if her suspicions were correct.

As she approached the bar she was struck by how the rules changed when you weren't looking.

She remembered being twenty-three years old and touring these pubs and clubs with her friends feeling totally at home and relevant.

Three years, just three short years she'd been absent with a boyfriend and when she'd returned after a disastrous break-up, she and her friends had spent the night with a glass of white wine and reminiscing about the 'remember whens'.

She checked herself as she found herself wondering if the majority of kids were carrying ID. They all looked so damn young.

There was no live music, instead a DJ blasted out trance music to an empty dance floor. She wasn't sure how long he'd been playing but even she could tell he had a grunge audience tonight. Although, he appeared to be in a world of his own bouncing up and down with one earphone clamped to his head.

She approached the bar and slipped in to a space left by a young couple who threw a filthy glance at the DJ before heading to the door.

She looked at the selection of drinks, unsure what most of them were.

'Hi, there, what can I get you?' asked the guy on the other side of the bar. He made no effort to hide his bemusement.

She fell silent for a second as she realised exactly what she was doing. She was sitting right in front of Tom Drury, her main suspect in the case of one murder and one attempted murder.

Every inch of her wanted to turn and run out the door.

'You lost?' he asked, raising one eyebrow.

Alison felt herself responding to the laughter in his eyes and smiled before she had time to check herself.

'Dry white wine,' she said, as he bent in closer to hear her.

She got a waft of pine coming from his smooth skin.

She watched as he moved along the bar almost colliding with a young female bartender. They both laughed and moved around each other with ease.

Alison took a moment to observe the athletic body clothed in dark jeans and a khaki rugby shirt sporting the name of the club. His arms were tanned and muscly, his only jewellery a sports watch.

He moved with the ease and confidence of someone who knew exactly what they were doing. His dark hair was cut tidily and smart at the back and just reached towards his collar line.

He turned and offered her a smile and for a second she almost forgot why she was here.

He placed the drink before her.

She took out her purse.

He shook his head. 'On the house.'

'No, no, I couldn't,' she protested.

'I'm the owner and I say you can,' he said, offering his hand. 'Tom Drury.'

Unsure what to do, she took his hand.

'Pleased to meet you, Tom. My name is—'

'Ali,' said a male voice from behind her. 'Sorry I'm late,' said Jamie Hart, taking a seat beside her.

Tom smiled at them both and moved back along the bar.

'Jamie, what the hell are you?…'

'I could ask you the same thing,' he hissed through gritted teeth. He grabbed his pint and her arm. 'Come with me.'

She followed him to a table in the corner.

The DJ seemed to have realised his market and was playing Nirvana but he'd lost his audience, who were slipping out one by one.

The last person she would have expected to bump into, or wished to, was Jamie Hart, the psychologist who had been assigned to the case before she'd been brought on board. He had spent more time than was necessary lecturing her about the junk food she ate while he nibbled on health bars and drank green tea. His health kick hadn't stopped there. The man was twenty-nine and had never owned a car, choosing to commute everywhere by public transport or bicycle. After one particular lecture on the joys of antioxidants she'd noticed he'd forgotten to remove his cycle clip from his trousers and had delighted in watching him walk around with one scrunched trouser leg all day.

'What the hell are you playing at?' he asked, once they were sitting.

'Just curious,' she said.

'About what?' he asked, shaking his head so that his fair hair fell over his blue eyes.

He pushed it away and took a sip of his drink. 'You know we got our guy and that you were wrong. Accept it and move on.'

They had clashed numerous times on the case but he'd never been quite so direct before.

'Look, I care about you,' he said, glancing away. 'I get it. You're young, ambitious. Believe me, I understand, but part of learning is knowing when you're wrong.'

He took a drink of his beer and then wiped at his mouth. 'You've got to let it go, Ali,' he said, touching her hand gently. 'I know it's hit you hard and you're probably bored but…'

She pulled away. She'd hated the shortening of her name when they'd worked together and she hated it even more now.

'It's Alison,' she growled. 'And what are you doing here anyway?' she challenged. 'Clearly you have some doubts too.'

He shook his head. 'I believe we got the right guy. There's no doubt in my mind that Curtis did it. But unlike you I'm here trying to strengthen the police case, not weaken it. Someone here must have seen him leave with Beverly.'

She tried to keep the frown from her face. 'Why are you still on it and I'm not?' she asked, taking a sip of her drink. She didn't really want it and pushed it away causing some of the liquid to splosh over the side. Jamie took out a tissue and wiped away the spillage.

'Because I didn't put my neck on the line. I listened to what was being said about the case, mixed that knowledge with my own experience of the human psyche and then offered my opinion.'

'But you said it was someone who had intimate knowledge of Jennifer and yet there's nothing to suggest Curtis had any intimate knowledge of Beverly who—'

'Is a known prostitute and has been intimate with hundreds if not thousands of men. I mean, given what she does…'

'Don't even think about saying she bears any blame because she's a sex worker,' Alison raged. 'Only one person is responsible and that's the bastard—'

'I wasn't saying that, now calm down. My point is that Beverly was putting her life on the line every time she got into the car of a stranger and you know that's true.'

Yes, she had to admit he was right.

Silence fell between them. 'And when I asked you to go out for a drink with me before you left this wasn't quite what I had in mind.'

Alison forced herself to calm down. He'd asked her a few times but she'd always been wrapped up in the case.

'Maybe another time we could meet and not argue about work,' he said, finishing his drink and standing.

'Maybe,' she answered.

'Well, at least I stopped you from whatever it was you were about to do that wouldn't have ended well.'

'Yeah, thanks,' she said as he brushed past her and headed towards the door.

In truth, she had no clue what she'd been hoping to achieve. This was not her world. She didn't meet witnesses or even interview suspects. Ironic that her work was based on people yet she met so few of them. Her subjects were abstract, not flesh and bone. She spent her days making composites like an identity artist only hers were psychological.

Like Jamie had said, she'd come here blindly, unprepared and ill-equipped, she thought, as she watched Tom Drury moving from one end of the bar, making drinks and chatting amiably.

Did she think that after a five-minute conversation he was going to confess all and prove her right, thereby reinstating the respect of her peers and an immediate thaw? Well she was surely disappointed because she'd barely exchanged two sentences with the man.

She kept her head down and left the bar quietly, relieved to be back out in the fresh air.

Having consumed no more than a half-hearted sip of white wine she felt confident to drive herself home.

It was only as she pulled out of the car park that a sudden thought occurred to her.

If West Mercia were so sure they'd got the right man, why was Jamie here trying to strengthen their case?

CHAPTER 49

Kim opened the single window and switched on the desk fan next to the printer. Despite a thunderstorm at 3 a.m. that had brought a terrified, shivering Barney onto her bed, the heat was still building towards the twenties and it wasn't even eight yet.

'Yay, chocolate muffins are my faves,' Stacey said from the general office. Clearly, she and Penn had met up on the way in and were discussing the contents of Penn's Tupperware box. Penn's brother had taken a shine to Stacey. Every day there was a specially decorated cake just for her and the detective constable was always eager to see what it was.

'Morning, boss,' they said, together, as they took their seats. Both had obviously seen the weather forecast and had not bothered with jackets.

Unlike the man who followed closely behind the pair in a navy suit, white shirt and sky blue tie.

'Guv,' he said, nodding in her direction.

'And that just leaves…'

'Am I late?' asked Alison, slipping into the chair at the spare desk.

Kim shook her head with the suspicion that the woman had never been late for anything in her life.

'Right guys, short briefing this morning as Bryant and I never got to meet with John Duggar, the ex-cellmate of Symes due to the car fire. So, here's what I want,' she said.

The whole team was poised for instruction, except for Alison who was slowly removing things from her briefcase.

'Penn, I want you following up on Jenks at the community centre. We know he's a sleaze and that Mark punched him. I want to know exactly what happened and I want to know everyone they came into contact with. I want to know who they were meeting on Sunday, cos if they were splurging what little money they had on flowers, it was to say thank you for something. So, who was giving them what?'

'Got it, boss,' he said.

'That's not all. I want you keeping up to date with developments on Rubik.'

He nodded his understanding.

She turned to the constable.

'Stace, I want you to work on finding the next of kin for Bill and Helen Phelps. Then I want you double-checking we haven't missed anyone that might want revenge against—'

'But, boss, I know we joked last night but how do I narrow it—'

'It's the level of hatred,' Alison cut in smoothly. 'For this depth of revenge, to kill innocent people, to go to the trouble of planning copycat events, we're talking life-altering incidents. This is major stuff.'

'Understood.'

'And anyone you identify, I want to know where they are and what they're doing now. And pass the name to Alison, who will start to build a psychological profile, just as soon as she's managed to find what she's looking for in that bloody briefcase.'

'Got it,' she said, holding up a battered KitKat.

Kim allowed the rest of the team to stare at her in disbelief while she continued.

'And Penn, when you've got a spare minute check on the junkyard to see if Dobbie has found his piece of paper detailing the car seller. Bryant and I will be attending the post-mortem of Bill and Helen Phelps later today.'

She shook away the images from the night before and the horrific manner of their death. 'Heavy workload, I know, but we need to crack on before this bastard strikes again.'

'Guv?' Bryant asked. 'You've given out all the work to these guys, we taking the day off?'

'You wish,' she said, taking a last swig of coffee.

'So, what we doing?'

'I'd have thought that was obvious, my good fellow,' she said, with a wry smile. 'We're gonna focus on the people that hate me the most.'

CHAPTER 50

Symes did his final bench press of the weight bar at 300 lbs. He prided himself at being able to lift almost 1.5 times his own body weight.

Dale Preece took one end, Kai Lord took the other and placed it into the rest.

Breakfast workout complete, Symes sat up, turned on the bench and wiped the sweat from his brow. It had been a tough workout but it was what he'd needed. His body ached from the exertion but it had clarified the situation in his mind. There was only one thing for it.

'I've gotta get the fuck outta here.'

'Huh?' they replied, together, as Screwball, a weedy kid in his late teens, started edging across the gym towards them.

Symes narrowed his eyes. 'Fuck off you piece of piss.'

Screwball backed off. Kid would do anything to try and listen in. Rumour had it he got extra smokes for telling old Gennard shit that was going around.

Symes felt safe speaking honestly to Lord and Preece. The hate club currently had seven members but few of them had as much reason to hate the bitch as these two.

Lord because he wouldn't see the light of day until he was drawing a pension and Preece cos the bitch had robbed him of his family.

'Can't hack it. Can't eat, can't sleep, can't wank because of that fucking cow. All I can see is her goddamn face and it's driving me insane.'

'Come on, Symes,' Preece said, shaking his head. 'We talked about this. Stick with the—'

'Fuck that,' he snarled. 'I know you like all your I's crossed and T's dotted, pal. You want all your fucking ducks in a row. Sensible and deliberate. Slowly, slowly, catchee monkey and all that shit but I'm fed up of waiting. I just want the whore dead. I want to put my hands around that cocky neck and squeeze...'

'Yeah, but you don't wanna be caught,' Preece insisted, tapping his head. 'You've got to use this.'

Symes wondered for a second if the man was being disrespectful, but only someone who felt the same rage as he did could take that kind of fucking liberty.

'Damn it, Symes, I hate that bitch as much as you do and if you want to do a poll let's pit losing two family members against robbing you of a good time. I win,' he spat as his eyes blazed.

Every instinct inside him wanted to knock this prick out for letting his mouth run, but the only thing that stopped him was the naked hatred he saw in the man's eyes every time he heard the slag's name.

My enemy's enemy is my friend, he said to calm himself down. Both Duggar and Preece had remained loyal to him. Sometimes he'd caught the two of them talking privately. He'd wondered if they were staging some kind of coup but his paranoia had been groundless and Duggar had been released.

Now Lord he wasn't so sure about. Too much standing back and watching for his liking. Happy to let folks fight it out and enjoy the entertainment. That's not how you treated comrades. You didn't have to like them but you needed to have their back.

'Look, Preece, don't get wound up cos I might get to the bitch before you do. You can have the carcass,' he said, with a smirk to lighten the air.

Screwball headed their way once more.

'Kid, you looking to get your fucking head?...'

'I know shit,' he whispered, wringing his hands.

'Not when to stay away,' Symes said, pushing himself to his feet. The rage at Preece had been stifled meaning he needed to punch something and this piece of shit looked good for it.

'He's coming back,' the kid said, looking around. 'Birdy's coming back.'

Looked like the kid's talent for listening worked both ways, which was the only thing that was gonna save him from a severe beating.

'Okay, now piss off,' he said as Screwball shuffled back towards the door.

Birdy was Paul Bird, a former member of the hate club who had not done what he was supposed to after being set free back into the wild.

'So, Birdy's coming back, is he? Well, I'm gonna punch every one of his teeth down his throat the second…'

His words trailed away as a light bulb illuminated in his head.

Preece and Lord waited expectantly.

'I think I just got myself a plan.'

CHAPTER 51

'So, this is The Civic?' Kim asked, remembering their conversation the previous day. From the front, the white, painted building looked small.

'Bigger than it looks,' he said, turning left in front of a single row of houses that looked like council dwellings.

'And I thought these were posh when they were first thrown up,' he said, driving slowly along the row.

'Really?' she asked, glancing at the identical, flat-faced properties as they passed by.

'New, shiny bricks,' he explained. 'Anything new was posh.'

'Well, I'm not sure they're so posh now,' she said, as a braless woman threw a black bag onto a pile that was building up beneath her front window.

'Is that?…'

'Next door,' Bryant clarified. 'His mother's old house. Died while he was inside.'

Kim stepped over the two piles of dog shit on the path and reached the door as a dog started barking at the rear of the property.

'Shut the fuck up, Mofo,' she heard, as she knocked the door.

'Who the hell is this guy?' she said to her colleague.

She had searched the database for any links between them and had found nothing. She'd studied his photo and no recollection at all had made itself known. But he'd been recruited by Symes, so they had to have some connection.

'Well, guv, we're about to find out.'

The shape that loomed up behind the door was not distorted by the patterned glass panel that opened to reveal a man-mountain with a bald head and a long ginger beard. ZZ Top reject immediately sprang to mind.

She knew he was about seven foot two and she'd guess him to be approximately twenty-five stone.

And she knew she had never seen him before in her life.

He was viewing her with the same level of confusion, which made no sense if he was in the hate club.

'If you're here about Mofo, he's just barking cos—'

'We're not here about the dog,' Bryant said, presenting his identification.

He took a good look.

He stepped back. 'Hey, you can fuck right off. I ain't done nothing since I got out. I'm keeping my nose—'

Kim silenced him by thrusting her own identification in his face.

He stopped speaking as his face broke into a wide and genuine grin.

'Hey, you is the bitch that killed my sister.'

CHAPTER 52

Alison knew with absolute certainty that she shouldn't be doing what she was about to do but she pushed open the door anyway.

She wasn't sure Stacey had believed her about an urgent errand but the detective constable had remained silent as she'd left the squad room. It had taken her no more than ten minutes to get to the small, unassuming dry cleaners in Romsley.

Her senses were immediately assaulted with the scent of fabric conditioner. Low rumbling sounded from the area behind the woman that greeted her with a functional but less than enthusiastic smile.

Alison guessed this was a woman who had accepted the fact that life had to go on; that no matter how much crying, pleading and praying she did, she couldn't undo the murder of her daughter.

'Mrs Townes?' Alison checked, not having met the woman during her time on the murder investigation.

She nodded warily and although her eyes narrowed the rest of her face relaxed as though she didn't have to keep up any pretence of trying to be normal.

The woman appraised her quickly. 'Are you a reporter?'

Alison shook her head and said what she'd been practising in her head.

'I was a consultant on the police case.'

'You're police?' she asked frowning.

'I work with the police,' she said and moved on quickly. 'It's just a follow-up call. Just to see if you were satisfied with the way the police handled…'

'You want me to review the police?'

Alison realised the pitfalls of starting out on a lie but there was no way she could tell this woman the truth. She'd been through enough.

She could either fess up or go deeper.

'It's not something we do all the time and it's confidential but we're always looking to improve the way we handle the family members of crime victims,' Alison explained, stepping deeper into the lie.

'Oh, okay,' she said, as the bell of the door sounded.

Alison stepped aside as a woman hurriedly produced a ticket, paid and took her dry-cleaned item without a word of thanks.

Something in Alison wanted to go after her, drag her back and make her apologise for her rudeness. She wanted to explain what this woman had suffered over the last four months and would continue to endure for the rest of her life. But ultimately to the oblivious customer she was the dry-cleaning lady without a life beyond that role.

'It's okay, I don't mind,' she said as though reading her thoughts.

'So, Mrs Townes, can—'

'Trisha, please,' she said. 'Have you noticed that you get called by your full name a lot when something very good or very bad is happening? Normally I'm just Trisha and I'd like to be Trisha again some day.'

'Okay, Trisha, how did you find the communication from the police officers during the case?'

She thought for a second. 'DCI Merton updated us a lot at the beginning. He made contact almost every day. I suppose it grew less as the weeks went on but Jamie helped us a lot in the early days. Helped us come to terms with it all… the horror… the…'

'It's okay, Trisha,' Alison said, reaching across to touch her hand.

The rape and murder of their daughter had been one of the most brutal acts Alison had ever seen. Jennifer's injuries had been so severe that Mr Townes had stumbled from the identification room and thrown up. That image would always play alongside any other memory of his daughter.

'And DCI Merton did come and let us know personally about Curtis's arrest.'

'Were you surprised at that result, Mrs… Trisha?'

A multitude of emotions passed over her face. 'Of course. I don't think either of us could believe it. The man had been in our home hundreds of times, cooked us meals, taken Lenny to hospital when he broke his arm, even filled in here when my husband couldn't work.'

'So, he and Jennifer had been happy?'

'For the most part. Jen would sometimes get frustrated with his lack of focus. Now and again she'd break up with him because he wouldn't find a proper job, but she'd always go back to him because she loved him and she loved his passion for what he did.'

'And were they broken up at the time of the murder?'

Trisha nodded and then regarded her seriously. 'Listen, I don't know why you're really here. You're not a good liar, but if it's got anything to do with any doubt then thank you. I know the police are convinced it was Curtis and I trust them, but I struggle to accept that someone we welcomed into our home, that was part of our family, did this to our daughter. I don't get to choose and I want justice, in the hope it will ease some of the rage and hopelessness I feel inside but I want the right justice. Do you understand?'

Alison understood perfectly. In her heart of hearts Trisha didn't feel Curtis was guilty.

'Thank you for your time, Trisha, and I'm so sorry for your loss.'

Trisha nodded, and Alison headed for the door.

'You know, just in case you're interested, there was one question that I asked DCI Merton that I never got an answer to.'

'Go on,' Alison urged.

'He never told me whether or not they found Jen's silver earring.'

CHAPTER 53

Penn removed the bandana and smoothed back the unruly curls. He closed every window that had been lowered to the max to get some air into the car for the fifteen-minute journey. He had no air con and the sunroof had been jammed for years. One of those jobs that he thought about a lot in the summer but not at all in the winter. He resolved to get it sorted as soon as this case was over, because the forecasters all agreed this heat was going nowhere soon.

He shrugged into the suit jacket that hung permanently in his car and instantly felt the discomfort of the extra layer. Unlike his colleague, Bryant, he could not truss himself up in a tie every day. If he had his way he'd turn up for work in Bermuda shorts, tee shirt and bare feet, mirroring the way he dressed at home, but he suspected his boss wouldn't like that very much.

After the revelations of the night before he'd been amused, but not surprised, that both he and Stacey had gone home to google. Once Jasper had gone to bed he'd pored over news reports about his boss. He'd been shocked, saddened and for some reason a bit angry and it had helped him understand her a little more. He didn't have the same history with her as the other two but he felt like he'd taken a crash course last night and had woken wanting to catch the bastard responsible with a passion.

He entered Stourbridge Community Centre and had two immediate emotional reactions.

The first was to the place. Tidy, efficient, well-equipped and nicely furnished. And completely unwelcoming to your average homeless person or someone down on their luck. In a weird way, it was how one would expect a community centre to look, but in reality, they were normally made up of mismatched, battle-scarred furniture, scuffed woodwork, stained carpet and old equipment. This place reminded him of a place ready to open. The before photo. Ready for a magazine article showing tax money at work. Not somewhere disadvantaged folks could come for help, advice and an occasional meal.

The second emotional response was to the man sitting behind the desk to the left. The right one was empty.

The snapshot that immediately clicked into his mind was of self-importance. The left desk was bigger. It had two chairs on the other side instead of one, the computer was newer, there was a small collection of metal toys, the chair was executive leather. This was a man who enjoyed his position.

'Mr Jenks?' Penn said, offering his hand.

The man nodded, stood and returned the greeting with a cool, firm grip.

DS Penn from West Mids Police, do you have a minute?'

'Of course,' he said, sitting. 'Is this about Mark and Amy?'

'It is. We just need to clear up something that's come to our attention,' he said, smiling.

Penn had learned long ago that he had a knack for putting people at ease. He knew that his long, unruly curls and inability to be at peace in a suit made him appear more casual, more open. Some people trusted the smart reassurance of a well-worn suit and some people did not. He had also learned how to hide his feelings well.

The man fussed with the tie knot at his throat.

'It's just a little misunderstanding I should think, Mr Jenks, but we've been informed there was some kind of altercation between yourself and Mark.'

The colour in his cheeks deepened.

'Did he hit you, Mr Jenks?' he pushed.

Hesitation. Headshake no. Head nod yes.

'Well. I suppose not really… I mean…'

'Sorry, Mr Jenks, you'll have to be a bit clearer,' he offered with a reassuring smile.

'We were just having words.'

'About what?' he asked, remembering what the boss had told him about this man's reputation.

'Disrespect, I would imagine,' he said, fiddling with his tie knot.

Penn didn't need Alison the behaviourist beside him to understand what that meant. Subconsciously, by messing with the tie Jenks was trying to reinforce that he was a stand up respectable kind of guy.

'Disrespect?'

Jenks nodded. 'That's what most trouble is about here. People disrespecting the services we provide.'

Penn idly wondered if any of the services had ever been used.

'Did the argument get physical?' he asked.

'Maybe a bit of pushing and shoving,' he said, getting more comfortable in what he was saying.

The best lies were based on truth, Penn knew.

'Only we heard that he punched you and gave you a black eye,' Penn said, without changing his tone.

Tie fiddle.

Headshake.

'Absolutely not, Sergeant. His hand may have caught the side of my face as he was gesturing but it was purely accidental, I'm sure.'

'Which is why you didn't report him?' Penn offered amiably.

'Of course, of course,' he said, eagerly, and Penn could see the man thought he had the upper hand with this conversation.

'Kids have got enough trouble without stuff like that. They live life on the edge, no home, no idea where the next meal is coming from, no security. Their emotions live very close to the surface and I didn't want to spoil things for them.'

Penn mumbled his understanding. 'Yes, so, it must be terrible when you start to hear there are rumours, especially when you're doing everything you can to—'

'Rumours about what, Sergeant?'

'Oh nothing, it's just something we heard about—'

'Well, if it concerns me then I'd certainly like to know what it is.'

The fact that the man couldn't let him finish a sentence in his eagerness to find out, and the forced tone of righteousness, gave away his nerves and knowledge of what was coming.

'I'm sure it comes with the territory but there are people that say you offer the women that come here extra help for sexual favours.'

Penn would have bet his car the man's right hand was going to touch the tie knot again. And he would have won.

'Oh, that is ridiculous,' he blustered with indignation. 'Why the devil…'

'Why indeed?' Penn agreed. 'But, obviously, we have no proof of—'

'Obviously,' he repeated. 'Because it's completely untrue.'

'So, what else can you tell me about the two of them?' Penn asked. The man would speak more freely if he did not feel under threat.

'Some saw the pair of them as ungrateful if you want the truth, myself included.'

'How so?'

'Amy was a perfect candidate for the sponsor a room project. She came off the drugs and she was placed in a studio above a Chinese takeaway in Lye, but she lost it.'

'Why?' Penn asked.

'She couldn't abide by the rules. She wasn't allowed male visitors, and of course she sneaked Mark in more than once. She got found out and had to leave.'

'Shame,' Penn observed.

'Thousands of other girls just waiting to take her place,' he offered coolly.

Penn couldn't help the jolt of sympathy inside. Sounded to him as though the kids had just wanted to be together.

Penn remembered something he'd said earlier. 'You said you didn't want to report Mark for fear of spoiling something for them. Spoil what?'

'They'd met some kind of outreach worker who was trying to help get them off the street. Not sure they deserved it but it looked like they were on their way to getting what they wanted.'

Penn thought about the behaviour of the pair around the supermarket; the flowers.

'Mr Jenks, in your opinion, what did Mark and Amy want more than anything?'

'If I had to pin it down I'd say the one thing they wanted beyond all else was a home.'

CHAPTER 54

'Hang on,' Kim said, frustrated, 'did I kill your sister, or not?'

They had followed a grinning giant through a poky hallway to a white Formica kitchen at the back. A can of cider was already open sitting between a pizza box and a tube of Pringles.

And now, Kim wanted answers.

'My sister wasn't murdered. I ain't even got no sister,' he said, taking a swig of cider.

Kim waited for an explanation.

'Look at me,' he said. 'Folks been wanting to fight me my whole life. School, pubs, clubs, chippy – always someone who wants to try it.'

'You can look after yourself, surely?' Bryant asked, voicing her thoughts.

'Duh, yeah,' he said. 'But who the fuck always gets the blame, eh? It ain't the fucking little squirt on a dare or the guy dumped by his missus with a point to prove. It's the angry big guy. And prison is full of dicks just wanting to prove themselves.'

'So, you joined the hate club?' Kim asked, as the dog, an Irish setter entered the kitchen and jumped up on the worktop.

'Down, Mofo,' he barked, rubbing the dirty spot on the counter with his tee shirt.

Kim wasn't sure of a man who named his dog Motherfucker but showed concern for dirty paws.

'Cos of Symes,' he continued. 'He is one nasty, sick puppy and no one in there will cross him, so if you're in his little hate club, you're safe.'

'Jesus,' Kim said.

'Oh yeah, and boy does he hate *you*,' Duggar said, grinning as though it was all some kind of joke.

'So, how'd it work?' Bryant asked. 'You put some kind of sign on your back to get picked?'

'Nah, I'm guessing you ain't never been inside, so I'll spell it out for yer,' he said, throwing away the empty can and reaching for another. 'You get in there and suss out the hard man. Not hard to do in this case cos even most of the guards are frightened of him. You ask who to steer clear of, you get a name and you know that's your guy. Then you watch for a bit to work out what you gotta do to get on his good side. Give 'em your dinner, batter a guard, rape a newbie.'

Kim was chilled by the cold, matter-of-fact way he reeled off the horrific acts needed to get protection.

'And all I had to do to get in was pretend I hated you. Easy. And two months later, guess what. I really did.'

'But we've never met,' Kim said.

He shrugged and swigged. 'Trust me, he's got a real powerful argument.'

'You got any names for me?' Kim asked.

He laughed out loud and she would swear it rocked the house.

'If you knew Symes, you wouldn't even ask that. Look, what that guy does is take your anger and turn it into hate. He massages it, feeds it, strokes it and makes it the object of every negative emotion you have. I was ready to kill you and you ain't even done anything to me.'

He paused and debated something for a second. 'Listen, you gotta get this so I'm gonna share something. Guy you put away for two armed robberies in Gornal. Stain or something…'

'Peter Staines,' Kim corrected.

'Yeah, him. He was recruited two days after he landed. Didn't read the memo about keeping your trap shut. Admitted he'd never considered hurting you and that he was just pissed at you for catching him.' He rolled his eyes. 'Fucking idiot.'

'And?'

'Safe to say his butt crack opened up like the Grand Canyon once Symes and his—'

'So, if I wanted to find out if he's behind something I need to look at all his cronies inside who I've helped put away.'

He observed her for a minute. 'You don't get it, do you? It's not only inside the prison. He gets quite the pile of fan mail, you know?'

'You're joking?' Bryant asked.

He swigged and shook his head. 'Even one-eyed monsters have their appeal. He gets plenty attention through the "email a prisoner" scheme.'

'All genuine nutcases?' she asked.

He shrugged.

Kim clicked. 'You saying he keeps in touch with people who have left through this system?'

He shrugged again and sighed. 'You gotta understand that his every waking thought is dedicated to you. He eats, sleeps and exercises to stay in shape for you. Everything is about aiming hatred towards you.'

'Got it,' Kim said, feeling that chill again despite the heat.

'But surely not everyone is manipulated by Symes?' she asked. 'I know you won't give me names but, say, someone like Dale Preece.'

Duggar hesitated before nodding. 'Yeah, he's in the club.'

She frowned not quite believing the man's admission.

'And make no mistake, Inspector, cos he hates you almost as much as Symes does.'

CHAPTER 55

By twelve thirty Stacey had had enough. Since returning from her urgent errand she'd seen the woman across the office chow down a breakfast bar, not bad. An apple, quite good. A bag of Maltesers, questionable, two cakes from Penn's Tupperware box and was now munching through a chicken and sweetcorn sandwich from the canteen.

Stacey had treated herself to her special cake from Jasper and then had a plain egg salad to compensate.

'Alison, are you part hobbit?' she asked.

'Sorry?'

'Well, from what I saw on the films they have breakfast, mid-morning snack, pre-lunch, lunch…'

'Oh, I get it,' she said, smiling. 'I'm just lucky, I suppose. I always get ravenous when I'm desk-bound.'

'You must spend hours at the gym,' Stacy said, hopefully.

Alison hesitated. 'If it makes you feel better, yes,' she answered.

Just one more reason not to like you, Stacey thought, turning back to her screen.

She'd started researching Bill and Helen Phelps, which was not rocking her world one little bit.

Google had turned up absolutely no results for anything. No social media activity, which wasn't too strange but not a lot of help at all.

He was a bank manager who retired at fifty-five, and Helen had managed a florist shop which she'd left when her husband had retired.

They'd spent a few years travelling on a boat but health problems with Bill had brought them back home. Stacey could find no good reason for their murder unless it was punishment for being too nice, too ordinary, too average. But surely too average didn't get you killed.

She followed her own protocols and put Bill's name into the system while laughing to herself. Yeah, like there was going to be anything from that.

And she got a hit.

She sat forward in her chair.

A neighbour dispute to which the police had been called. Mr Phelps had struck his neighbour over an ongoing issue with a wheelie bin.

Laughable as it was Stacey felt a stirring in her stomach at the possibility of conflict. And then she read further down where the two men had been encouraged to avoid charges, court and shake hands. And they'd agreed. Nothing further had occurred in the five years since.

Stacey read it again just in case she'd missed the involvement of anyone else in 'bingate' and her brain registered a sentence that she hadn't noticed before.

Mr Phelps was eventually restrained by his twenty-two-year-old son.

Which begged the question: where the hell was the Phelps' son?

CHAPTER 56

'Hey, wonder if Keats wants to join the fan club that Symes has got going,' Bryant said, as they got out of the car at Russells Hall.

'You think this is funny?' she asked, glancing at him sideways.

'No, I think it's tragic, creepy and frightening. I think you should be removed from the case and placed into protective custody under armed guard until this lunatic is caught, but seeing as neither you nor Woody agrees with me I'll just have to save my breath,' he said, as they entered the building.

'We don't agree because no one has threatened my life. No one is trying to actually kill—'

'Yet,' Bryant reminded her. 'We have no idea what this psycho is going to do next.'

Kim shook her head in disagreement and walked silently to the morgue, steeling herself for what she was about to see.

'Hey, Keats,' she said, keeping her eyes fixed firmly on his face as she entered.

He said nothing for a few seconds.

'I'm sorry but I was waiting for the witty rejoinder that normally accompanies a greeting from you. Scriptwriter on holiday?'

She ignored him and headed to stand beneath the air con unit. Keats kept it a constant 16 degrees which suited her just fine.

She watched the pathologist shoot a questioning glance at Bryant, who shrugged in response.

'You'll be pleased to know the burnt-out vehicle has been released to Forensics, who have their fire investigators on it right now.'

'Will they be able to identify the cause of the fire?' Bryant asked.

'Hard to say but I'm pretty sure they'll be able to rule out engine faults resulting in spontaneous combustion.'

Even though she had not yet looked directly at the forms on the metal dishes, she knew that unlike normal dead bodies the sheets did not cover the flat prostrate form. The covering was high, tented, as though there were kids playing underneath.

'Okay, let's begin,' Keats said, removing the first sheet.

Kim tried to swallow down the nausea as the burnt figure was revealed. The blackened form was resting on its side as though in the foetal position with knees bent but with a straight back. Kim knew that the heat caused the muscles to dry out and contract making the limbs move and adopt postures. Had the figure been upright it would have appeared to be still sitting on the car seat.

'What's that?' Kim asked, moving closer and pointing to the chest area at a piece of fabric unlike the strips of material that remained from the clothing.

Keats looked over his glasses. 'I'd guess it's a section of seat belt.'

'Welded to the skin?'

He nodded. 'I'll take a sample for analysis and confirm—'

'So, they were still wearing seat belts?' Kim asked, turning to her colleague, who looked as dumbfounded as she was.

'And still in a normal seated position?' she said, thinking aloud.

'Appears so,' Keats answered, although there was no need.

'Why?' Bryant asked, catching up with her thoughts.

'Why what?' Keats asked.

'If the car is on fire, don't you make some kind of effort to get out?' she asked. 'Surely there's time to move a bit, at the very least unbuckle your seat belt?'

'Not my job to work that one out, Inspector, but taking a closer look at this poor soul is,' he said, moving her away from the table.

'As you know, a human limb burns not unlike a tree branch,' Keats said. 'The outer layers of skin fry and begin to peel off as the flames work across the surface. After about five minutes, the thicker dermal layer of skin shrinks and begins to split, allowing the underlying yellow fat to leak out. Body fat can make a good fuel but needs clothing or charred wood to act as a wick. The wick absorbs the fat and pulls it into the flame where it is vaporised, enabling—'

'How long until they died?' Kim asked, licking her dry lips.

'Difficult to say exactly. The body can sustain its own fire for around seven hours…'

'I know that, Keats,' she snapped. 'I'm talking about these bodies and how long they suffered.'

She'd seen burnt bodies before but what she wanted to know was how long this poor couple withstood horrific pain.

'Minutes,' he answered. 'They would most certainly have died from smoke inhalation in such a confined space.' He paused to touch the body on the left. 'And this is the female, who we suspect to be Helen Phelps,' he said.

Kim switched from avoiding the sight to being unable to tear her eyes away.

A lock of blonde hair protruded from the blackened skull, over a space where the ear should have been and alongside the cheekbone supporting an expression of horror moulded permanently by the flames.

Erica's hair had been blonde.

Was this how her foster mother had looked after the car accident on the journey home from trying to adopt her?

She hadn't been allowed to attend the funeral; cut off by Erica's sister who had never been an aunt to her despite her three years with the couple.

But she couldn't comprehend sweet gentle Erica ever looking like this. She could only visualise the warm, tolerant, reassuring smile as she'd waited patiently for the first three months for Kim to even speak.

She could visualise that same lock of hair being tucked behind her ear as she leaned down to leave the hot chocolate on the bedside cabinet every night.

She could feel the emotion gathering in her throat and had to bring herself back to the present, which was no more an attractive place to be.

She knew that Keats was speaking and that Bryant was acknowledging those words but only one thing was filling her mind. She had avoided giving much thought to the way they had died, only that they had. Enduring the pain of their loss had been enough without visualising the agony of the event itself. She wasn't sure she could have borne it.

And this was how they had lost their lives. Trapped in a car, burnt beyond recognition. Hot flames lapping at their skin. Dear sweet and gentle Erica and Keith had suffered and died like this.

Kim turned and ran from the room.

CHAPTER 57

Penn arrived on the Hollytree estate around one fifteen and held no compunction of leaving his car unattended.

Nine-year-old Ford Fiestas didn't have a high street value, even for parts.

It wasn't that he didn't like fast showy cars. Yeah, he'd fantasised about a Lamborghini or a Ferrari or an Aston Martin and these days you could get one if you were prepared to give up your entire salary for the monthly payment and even that wasn't the reason he didn't hanker after one. He didn't want a car he had to worry about. He didn't want a car that he couldn't leave anywhere for fear of vandalism or theft. His Fiesta got him around fine and no one else wanted it.

He immediately saw that the Forensics cordon had been moved back, but he wasn't here for that. He knew any developments in that area would be communicated to the boss immediately.

He headed up to the fourth floor where the cordon was now only across the doorway of the property where Amy and Mark had been found.

A single officer manned it.

Penn nodded in his direction before moving along the hallway to the next property.

'Wasting your time there, mate,' said the officer, pointing to his temple. 'Nutty as a fruit bat.'

Penn gritted his teeth and knocked the door, glad to see the police diversity training at its best.

'Bet you a tenner she calls you Steve. Everyone's Steve,' he said, quietly.

'Who's Steve?' Penn asked.

He shrugged. 'Ain't no Steve,' he said, as the door began to open.

A lady he guessed to be late seventies, early eighties, assisted by a walking frame, opened the door.

Her wrinkled face broke into a grin.

'Steve, come on in,' she said, with a voice damaged by decades of smoking cigarettes.

He heard the police constable guffaw as he closed the door behind himself.

'Well, how are you?' he asked, following her slowly down the hallway, a strange clunking noise coming from her frame. She stopped before a wing back chair with a seat made higher with a mismatched square cushion. She used the frame to lower herself down to the chair.

'I'm fine, Steve,' she said, reaching over for a pack of Park Drive. His grandfather had smoked that brand for years. 'Did you bring the coupon?'

'I'll get it in a minute,' he said, pleasantly, with no clue what she was talking about.

'Bad bit of business next door,' he said, nodding towards the wall.

She sniffed. 'Don't care for them much to be honest. He thinks he's all that because he works at Bluebird, and she's been at Jonty's for years now.' She leaned forward conspiratorially. 'Stuck up to be honest.'

He had no idea what Jonty's was but he knew the Bluebird factory had closed down in 1998.

'Used to bring me those toffees but he doesn't any more, miserable bleeder.'

Penn hid his smile. She had some spirit.

'If he thinks I'm going to keep giving him my Green Shield Stamps, he can think again.'

'I'd keep them yourself,' he said, as an alarm sounded in the kitchen.

'Oh, that's my muffin done,' she said, making to get up.

He stood. 'Let me.'

'Oh, you're a good boy, Steve, and don't forget the coupon.'

'Okay,' he said, heading back down the hall.

He turned into the kitchen to see that it was indeed a muffin she'd been timing. The clock was set beside the grill. Except the muffin had been placed face down on top of the extractor fan.

He took it, blew it and placed it under the grill on low heat and found himself wondering at the safety of this woman living alone in this environment when she clearly suffered with dementia.

He could understand why other people had written her off in regard to learning anything about the incidents next door, but Penn wasn't as quick to walk away.

'Not quite done yet,' he said, retaking his seat on the sofa.

'Well, have you got it?' she asked, looking at his hand. 'The coupon.'

He slapped his own head. 'Oh, I've left it in the car.'

'Well, how am I gonna win if it's in the car?'

Of course, the football coupon. She thought he was the football coupon man.

'I'll go and fetch it in a minute,' he said. 'And I'll help you put the crosses in.'

She smiled her pleasure and he smiled back.

When Jasper was small he'd struggled to communicate and Penn had learned to just let him talk. Eventually the pieces had come together.

He glanced down at the walking frame and saw what had caused the clicking as she'd travelled down the hall.

He leaned down and lifted it up taking off the grey rubber foot. He wiped the inside and put it back on, firmer. Same thing happened on his mum's frame all the time.

'There you go,' he said, looking up into a face filled with suspicion. He immediately knew what had happened. She was back in the present.

'Who are you?' she barked.

'I'm here about that nasty business next door,' he said, wiping his hand on his jacket.

She narrowed her eyes. 'What, are you from some housing association too?'

CHAPTER 58

'Want anything from the canteen?' Alison asked, standing.

Stacey shook her head.

'I get a bit of a sugar low around this time each day,' Alison said, sitting back down. 'But, I've probably had enough for a bit.'

Stacey grunted in response. If the woman was fishing for compliments with the figure she had, they were not going to come from her, especially seeing as she'd had a bit of trouble fastening the button on her size 14 trousers this morning. Damn it, she loved to eat but maybe a trip to the gym now and again wouldn't kill her.

'So, did you research your boss last night?' Alison asked.

'Alison, I'm trying to work,' she said, without looking up. One because she didn't want the woman to see the lie in her eyes and two she didn't trust this woman's motivation in trying to talk to her.

Right now she was more interested in trying to locate the son of Bill and Helen Phelps. There was a young man out there who needed to know what had happened to his parents.

'It's not disloyal to try and find out everything you can,' she continued. 'It is an active case after all.'

'Hmm…' Stacey said, not really listening.

'I mean how could she not be affected by what she saw at that flat. An exact replica of one of the most traumatic events of her life. I mean the level of detail, the flat being just a few floors below. The radiator, the handcuffs, the cracker packet.'

Stacey looked up. Now she was listening as Alison bowed her head and began scribbling again.

Yes, she'd forgotten about the cracker packet in the throat of Mark Johnson.

How had she forgotten about that?

She'd read every newspaper report on the incident and yet she had forgotten about that.

As though sensing her stare, Alison raised her head. 'Sorry, was it something I said?' she asked.

Stacey returned her gaze to the computer screen and opened a new search tab.

'Yes, Alison, I think it was.'

CHAPTER 59

'Bryant, I'm fine,' Kim said for the twentieth time as she took a MentholLyptus sweet from the pack he offered. 'Just something I ate,' she continued, explaining why she'd just emptied the contents of her stomach in the toilet bowl.

'Yeah, if you ate,' he mumbled, popping a sweet in his own mouth.

She ignored him as he turned back towards the automatic doors.

'Ready to go back in?' he asked.

Was she ready to go back in the room and watch Keats violate those burnt and blackened bodies to seek answers she needed to find the bastard who'd done this? Could she watch the man do his job without visualising Erica and Keith behind those featureless faces?

She shook her head. 'You go back in. I'm gonna check on Rubik.'

He hesitated for just a second before hitting the button to re-enter.

Kim headed to the end of the corridor, knocked lightly on the incident room door and entered.

The room had been split into three clear areas. To the right was the remainder of the cube with Doctor A kneeling before it. From behind, her Doctor Martens protruded from the white coat she wore offering a comical appearance.

In her hand was the business end of an endoscope camera used to perform keyhole surgery. She pushed it into the wreckage and pictures flashed up onto the screen. Kim couldn't help the smile that began to form on her lips when she remembered the approaches and tools that had been considered by Keats and Mitch. Instead Doctor A had utilised the probing equipment used to work on flesh and organs to penetrate and interrogate the cube, to understand it before trying to separate the man from the machine.

The left side of the room contained a bright white sheet holding extracted pieces of metal. In the corner, closest to her, was a large clear plastic tub with evidence bags draped over the side and a metal detector against the wall. She guessed the instrument was to check any body parts for traces of metal before bagging the body bits and sending them next door to Keats.

'See, I told you, Mitchell, that the inspector had not forgetting about us,' Doctor A said, narrowing her eyes, and switching off the camera.

'Been a bit busy, Doc,' Kim said, returning her gaze.

Mitch nodded her way and returned his attention to the clipboard in his hands.

'Great progress, Doctor A,' Kim said, remembering the original size of the cube.

'Ahem,' Mitch said.

'Both of you,' she corrected, moving to stand behind the doctor.

'So far we have extracted one and a half legs, most of the arms parts, one hand and two feet. Still much middle to find,' she said, pointing to her stomach. 'We are assembling the parts on a stretcher in the cupboard,' she said, nodding towards the door.

Kim guessed she meant the room that held the bodies in the cooling drawers that were stacked from floor to ceiling.

'Tissue samples have been taken and sent to lab and if he was married he wore no ring.'

Kim remained silent and waited.

'What?' Doctor A demanded. 'I have no more at this time.'

'You're kidding?' Kim asked. Thirty-six hours and that was all they had? She'd been able to tell that from the hand sticking out.

'Oh, Inspector, your sense of humours appear to have gone AMOL. Our victim is male aged between forty-five and sixty. He is between five foot five and five foot eight and weighs around seventeen stone. He had two broken bones as a child, right arm and left leg but not at the same time. All weights and measurements are approximate and—'

'Doctor A, I love you,' Kim said, taking out her phone.

'Get in line, Inspector,' she said, tossing her long ponytail behind her.

'Can you send…'

'Emailed to you and your team ten minutes ago,' she said, returning her attention to the cube.

'Thanks, Doc,' Kim said. With that information, they could begin to build a detailed picture of their victim.

She sidled over to Mitch. 'Hard act to follow, eh?'

'Yep, nothing as sexy or progressive from me, I'm afraid,' he said, recording a measurement onto the clipboard.

To her it was a mass of numbers, arrows and mathematical signs.

'Interesting,' she said, unable to make head nor tail of what he was recording.

'This might make more sense,' he said, taking another sheet of paper from the back of the clipboard. He opened it out to A3 size.

She saw a collection of shapes in different colours with reference numbers attached.

'Red shapes are body parts recovered and blue are car parts.'

'Okay,' she said, taking his word for it. The body parts were labelled as numbers, so she had no way of knowing what was what.

'I've yet to feed all the data into a computer simulation back at the lab but I'm prepared to state that I think our victim was locked in the boot of the car.'

'Mitch…'

'I know,' he said, smiling.' You love me too.'

'Not as much as the doc,' she said. 'But you're on the Christmas card list.'

'Well, that's…'

His words trailed away as her phone began to ring.

'Stace,' she answered. 'You get the email from the doc?'

'Yeah, boss, gonna look at it in just a minute but need to run a couple of things by you. Still trying to find next of kin for our car victims, but there's something else.'

'Go on,' Kim said, moving back out to the corridor.

'The cracker wrapper in Mark Johnson's throat. I don't get it. I've been through every news report, twice, and I can't find mention of it anywhere.'

'Trust me, it's significant,' Kim said, quietly.

'Exactly. That's my point,' the constable argued.

'Stace, you're not—'

'If he didn't get the detail from the news reports then where did he get it from?'

Shit, she saw Stacey's point. Where else was there a wealth of information on her childhood?

Kim ended the call with a pretty good idea of where to go next.

CHAPTER 60

So far Penn had waited in the stuffy council office for twenty minutes for one of the two women behind the desk to become free.

The blonde, who seemed to be sorting two people to the brunette's one, occasionally glanced at him in a 'shouldn't be too long now' kind of way.

He had watched people pay their rent, report blocked pipes, shout about neighbours, collect keys and one woman had made an urgent request for money to buy sanitary towels. The blonde had taken a couple of pounds from her own purse and handed it over.

'Sorry to keep you,' she said as his turn finally came.

'No problem. I'd like to talk to you about a property on Hollytree.'

'Hollytree?' she asked with surprise. Obviously not that many people expressed an interest in moving to that particular estate.

He shook his head and held up his ID. 'I want to talk about the flat where the two—'

'I know the one,' she said in a lower voice as she looked behind him to the queue continuing to form. It appeared her colleague had only one speed and it wasn't in the higher numbers.

'It's yours, isn't it?' he asked.

She raised one eyebrow. 'As opposed to?'

'It's not housing association?'

Penn knew that most councils had sold off property to housing associations to fund other projects before finding themselves woefully short of social housing just a few years later.

She shook her head. 'There are no properties on Hollytree with a housing association. They're all still council owned,' she said. Penn could hear the silent 'lucky us' attached to the statement.

'So, what's the history with the place?' Penn asked. Few council properties remained empty for long. Even ones on Hollytree.

'Don't even ask,' she said, rolling her eyes. 'Last occupant was a fifty-six-year-old man on the sex register for kiddy porn. Got a lot of shi… trouble from the neighbours and played the 'I am innocent victim' card for all it was worth until a guy two floors below couldn't find his seven-year-old and broke down the guy's door.'

'And?' he asked.

'Kid was sitting on the sofa with his top off eating a bag of Haribos.'

'Jesus,' Penn said, feeling sick to his stomach.

'Dad rounded up some mates and gave him what for.'

'Dead?'

She shook her head. 'Not quite but it's safe to say he'll never live independently again.'

Understandably there was little sympathy in her voice.

He considered for a moment. He'd established there was no housing association linked to the property despite the brief lucid moment he'd shared with the neighbour. So, had he been wrong to listen to her, to trust that the police officer guarding the door had been wrong? To pursue something guided only by the ramblings of a seriously ill old lady.

He remembered a time when he was seventeen and Jasper was only two.

They had both been in the lounge, he watching telly and his brother staring around the room as usual. He had become very agitated pointing to a corner of the room above the dog's toy basket. Both his mother and father had searched the corner and had eventually given up and left the room.

Jasper had been distraught and had continued to point, until Penn had gone over to the corner himself and started to look. Like his parents he had found nothing but had figured the kid had to know something. One at a time he took the toys out of the dog's basket and showed them to his brother who had watched intently. The last but one item, a Kong toy designed to hold treats for their springer spaniel, had contained a trapped, angry wasp. Had the dog gone near, most likely it would have been stung. Penn had taken the toy to the window and had shaken the wasp free. His brother's smile had said it all.

So, no, he didn't think he was in the wrong for pursuing the woman's lead.

'Has anyone taken the keys to look around the property?' he asked.

'Oh, now that's a different story,' she said. 'No one wants to live there but there's a morbid fascination with going and having a look.'

'Can't I get a list?' he asked, hopefully.

She pointedly looked behind him to a queue that now stretched out the door.

'Just point me in the right direction,' he said, offering a smile as he stepped to the side.

She considered for a moment before pushing the chair away from the desk. He'd expected her to tap a few keys and for the printer to spur into action. Not the case.

Instead she reached for a lever arch file that appeared to have been relabelled a hundred times.

She placed it before him.

'They go in number order of the property,' she said, turning the file his way.

He thanked her but she was already listening to someone talk about rent arrears.

He opened the folder to find a good old-fashioned key register. Property, key number, name of key taker, signed out and signed back in. Simple and effective. This office was not going paperless any time soon.

He wet his finger and flicked through until he found the address he wanted.

The records dated back to the late Nineties but he moved forward to the period of seven years where the property had been occupied by the paedophile. The keys had been returned to the council five months ago and quite a few people had viewed it since.

He caught the eye of the blonde lady, who pointed to the photocopier.

He removed six pages from the folder and headed to the machine. And with roughly twenty-five entries per page he was looking at around 150 people who were on the list.

And any one of them could have copied the key to the murder scene.

CHAPTER 61

'Guv, I like the Cotswolds as much as the next person but is there no way we could have just called?' Bryant asked, as she put her phone back into her pocket. Her second message of the day from Frost who really wasn't getting that this time around she'd been gagged by her boss and that she could not talk to the press.

'I considered it,' she said, as Bryant negotiated the traffic lights in Stow-on-the-Wold. They were just five miles away from Bourton-on-the-Water, and the home of a man she'd never met, a man she knew nothing about but who had taken the time to find out an awful lot about her.

'Did he ever speak to you?' Bryant asked.

She shook her head. 'I knew nothing about the book until I was about fifteen and a social worker mentioned it.'

'You ever read it?'

'Why would I? I was there,' she answered.

'I meant for accuracy. Weren't you curious to know how much he'd got right?'

She shook her head. 'What would it have changed?'

All she'd known was that the man was a reporter trying to make money off everything bad that had happened in her life.

She hadn't thought about him for years until, three years ago, when Alexandra Thorne had tried to glean everything she could from the man to try and weaken her. She'd considered confronting him but had ultimately decided that any trips back to her past would do nothing to change the fact he'd exploited her story for money and that she'd been powerless to stop it.

'It's a left here,' Bryant said, turning into a single-track lane. Solitary properties were dotted on either side as they wound around a few tight bends that led to a row of stone cottages with a pull-in just beyond.

'Middle one,' Bryant said, as they got out of the car. A bicycle was propped up beneath the front window.

She took a deep breath before knocking.

The door was opened by a rotund man a couple of inches beneath her own five foot nine height, with a skirt of hair running around the back of his head from ear to ear.

He wasn't exactly what Kim had been expecting, and he didn't have the word opportunist tattooed across his forehead.

'Henry Reed?'

'May I help you?' he asked, pleasantly.

'Hopefully, my name is Kim Stone and you—'

She stopped speaking as he took a step back and all colour drained from his face.

Yes, as she'd suspected. He'd never expected this day of reckoning. He'd never expected to be confronted by the damaged child he'd exploited to make a few quid. And right now, he had a hell of a lot of explaining to do. Oh yes, he was right to look scared.

'Forgive me, my dear,' he said moving back towards her. 'But I've dreamt of this day for the last thirty years.'

CHAPTER 62

Alison returned to her notes, trying to make sense of what she'd learned.

Nowhere could she find any mention of a missing earring.

She had learned many years ago about criminals being so enamoured of their own crime they took souvenirs from their victims. Often a piece of clothing or jewellery, an item easily detached from the person. It wasn't always valuable or obvious items, but normally something the victim was wearing or had on them at the time.

Sometimes the trophies were more gruesome.

Ed Gein, a serial killer in the Fifties, had made furniture from human skin, bowls made of skulls, a corset made of a female torso, a belt made of nipples. Alex Mengel from New York kept the scalp of his victim. A Texas serial killer kept his victim's eyeballs. Yellowstone killer, Stanley Dean Baker, kept finger bones.

It didn't matter what was taken, the motivation was always the same: to prolong the fantasy of the crime, and between crimes – often while targeting future victims – a serial killer pulls out their trophies to relive the crime over and over.

The police had viewed the murder of Jennifer Townes as a crime of passion from the outset. A one-off attack by someone she knew. The taking of a trophy, a keepsake, went against that theory, but there was something else.

The murder of Jennifer could have been an escalation. No serial killer wakes up one day and starts killing just like that. There is always a history.

French serial killer, Michel Fourniret, only started killing after one of his rape victims reported him to the police.

Some start by breaking and entering for valuables, realise one night there is a woman living alone, rapes her and then targets homes of women living alone. Escalation. Another could strangle one of his victims because she fought back and he enjoys it. Escalation.

She knew from experience that an evolving serial killer is usually organised and demonstrates more maturity and confidence with each killing, learning and modifying his MO.

A devolving serial killer is normally unorganised and totally controlled by his fantasy and his impulses. His crimes would become more and more erratic, without real purpose, and usually loses complete control over reality and his own actions.

Her mind started to throw up possibilities, the most disturbing of which was that they had caught the killer as he was beginning to devolve: a dangerous time for any female crossing his path.

She compared the two crime scenes. Jennifer had disappeared from the bar at the end of her shift. The killer had subdued her successfully late at night and taken her to an abandoned warehouse two miles from the club, where he had been able to brutalise and rape her for hours before she'd even been identified as missing.

The abduction of Beverly had been around three hours earlier in the night. She had been dragged to an alley that ran behind a row of houses and was disturbed when a dog began to bark.

Was he already unravelling and making impulsive mistakes?

But given the fact she didn't believe this was the act of a rejected lover who had then gone on to attack another woman she had to consider the killer had escalated.

As a consultant for each police force she'd worked for she'd had no personal experience of the sharing database HOLMES and now HOLMES2 but she knew it was an information technology system for major incidents used by all UK forces.

And it could help her find out if any similar incidents had been logged before.

She had no access to the system, but she knew someone that did.

She lifted her head.

'Stacey, you got a minute, cos I really need your help?'

CHAPTER 63

Stunned by his admission, Kim followed Henry Reed into a light and airy space that was clearly a few walls short of its original build. The remaining walls were formed of exposed grey stone. The lounge blended into the kitchen before curling around into the dining area with one door that she presumed led to a bathroom.

The single chairs, small television and large bookcases told her everything she needed to know about how this man lived his life.

'May I get you something to drink, a snack?…'

'We're fine,' she said, still surprised at his admission upon answering the door.

'A glass of water,' Bryant said, shooting her a sideways glance.

'Please sit,' he said, pointing to a light beech table with a bench on either side.

He took a bottled water from the fridge and poured it into a glass and added two slices of lemon.

Kim hated her colleague right now.

'You have no idea how long I've waited—'

'Why did you write the book?' Kim asked, cutting him off. It was important to her. This man wasn't what she'd been expecting but it was a long time ago. Just because he didn't appear ruthless and cold now didn't mean he hadn't been a complete bastard back then.

'Did you write books on other damaged kids too?' she asked, bitterly.

He placed Bryant's drink down with a trembling hand, his face a mask of shock.

'Absolutely not,' he said.

'Then please explain why you chose to exploit me?'

His shock deepened. He shook his head. 'It wasn't like that.' He took a breath. 'Let me start from the beginning. I was there that day, at Hollytree. The day they found you both. I was twenty-eight and happened to be close by writing an article on the Halesowen cricket club. I was right behind the line. I saw your brother, that's to say I saw the tiny body bag holding your brother.'

Kim swallowed down the emotion that suddenly clogged her throat.

'There were people whispering about your mother, about your father or lack of and about the two of you. My heart was already breaking. And then I saw you.'

He shook his head and blinked rapidly.

'You were brought out of the tower block, and I'll never forget it. The silence. You were like a frail little rag doll. Thin and white with your black hair and dark eyes. The fear shone from you. You were six years old and you already knew you were completely alone. It was maybe four seconds until you disappeared from view into the ambulance but not one person spoke. Every gaze was on you. There were three photographers behind me that had jostled for position and you know something, not one of them took a photo.'

'Go on,' Kim said, eager to get past the memories they shared and onto his reasons for writing the book. She hadn't even known the press was there.

'We ran the story that night but it wasn't enough. I wanted someone to blame, to be held accountable. Unfortunately, my editor didn't feel the same way and before I knew it I had mounds of research, notes, interviews and no one who wanted to listen, but I couldn't let you go. That face, that expression when you were brought out of that building just wouldn't leave me. I couldn't give up on you. I just felt enough people had already done that.'

'So, you made money out of me instead?' she asked, although the question didn't feel right on her lips any more.

'Oh no, quite the contrary. I never wanted to make a penny from your heartache and pain. I wanted people to remember you, to learn from the mistakes. I wrote the book and self-published it. There was no Amazon KDP back then. I paid to have the book printed, and there's never been and never will be a penny profit from that book. As I said, it was designed to help people never forget.'

'And you think writing that book helped me?' she asked.

'I like to think I played my part in holding someone accountable.'

'But no one named in the book was ever…'

'Not the book, my dear. I told you I wanted someone to pay. Well I was a reporter, a journalist with investigative skills that were not being used covering the sports pages of the *Dudley Star*. So, I remembered everything I'd ever learned, used my sources and my own spare time and proved that I could do something tangible to help.'

'So, what did you do?' she asked, confused.

He met her gaze. 'I went out and found your mother.'

CHAPTER 64

If Symes was honest, he didn't mind prison life as much as most folks. He didn't much care about the loss of liberty or the structured day, being told what to do. Wasn't that different from the Army, except for one crucial thing. He didn't get to hurt people and call it a job.

His tours of Afghanistan had been the best years of his life. No one understood life out there, no one understood seeing comrades exploding right beside you from IEDs, the fear of stepping onto a mine if you just went to take a piss.

Frustrations built and grew, anger festered and poisoned until a village of unarmed civilians popped up like magic and served a purpose. An empathetic sergeant might look the other way as the soldiers did house-to-house checks. Rape had never been his thing. Now violence, causing physical harm, using his own hands to maim and damage was another thing entirely. And there'd always been someone he could find to use for that.

The real prize had been those two nine-year-old girls who had been promised to him, but that Stone bitch had taken it away. Months of planning, dreaming, fantasising about tearing them apart limb by limb had been ruined by one interfering cow who was too intelligent for her own good. Too intelligent for any woman to be. And now it wasn't their pain he dreamt about each night. It was hers. And that was his only issue with being inside. That it prevented him getting to her.

For the slammer this place was no different to the other places he'd been since leaving the forces. This one had ten accommodation units formed from a mixture of four landing wings radiating from a centre point. The more recent additions were residential house blocks.

He smirked as he remembered his first night inside. The guards had taken his fingerprints and personal details and then issued him with a pair of jeans, two tee shirts, two boxer shorts and a sweatshirt. Before his two-minute shower he'd been subjected to the naked body search. One officer in front and one behind as he'd bent over at the waist. Just to be sure he'd grabbed both arse cheeks and pulled so they got a good enough look. He'd been on A wing, most commonly known as Beirut, ever since. And that suited him fine. A lot of Stone's enemies lived on A wing, and he'd been able to recruit them all. But his most loyal two were Preece and Lord who had also learned to play the prison system like him. They'd all found something that got them through the day.

For him it was the gym he could access 365 days a year. His salvation and his church where he could spend hours building his strength all for one reason only.

Despite being an educated man, Preece had enrolled in every fucking course going, and Kai Lord had decided to find God, which was equally ironic.

'Here they come,' Symes said, as Gennard approached with three guys trailing behind.

'You the welcoming committee?' the guard asked, opening the gate.

'Yeah, got fucking bunting and everything,' he said, staring at Birdy.

'Well, play nice, fellas,' Gennard said, locking the gate behind them.

Symes nodded towards the two new guys. Lord ambled over and held out his hand. On admission prisoners had to choose between a smoking pack or a phone card. Didn't matter much cos they didn't hang on to either for long.

'Good to see you again, Birdy,' Symes said, placing his meaty palm on Birdy's elbow. 'Let's you and me go and have a nice chat, eh?' he said, guiding him into the third cell along.

Lord and Preece followed him in.

'Outside, boys. This is a private meeting.'

They closed the door as Birdy began to back away. The space was nine foot square. He had nowhere to go.

'You let me down, buddy,' he spat, cracking his knuckles.

Birdy ran his hand through his prematurely receding hairline. 'I got her, man. Fucked her up real good. Gave her a beating she won't forget in a—'

'Cos you hated her, yeah?'

'Yeah, man. You know I fucking did. What she did to me was—'

'She copped you for aggravated burglary and ABH, yeah? Your missus lost the house while you was inside? Your kids suffered. Your missus met someone else,' Symes said, taking a minute to remind Birdy why he'd hated the slag. 'Your bitch was sucking someone else's cock while you were banged up in here?'

'That's why I did what you asked and gave her—'

'When?'

The bastard had only been out for ten days.

Birdy started to relax. 'About a week ago.'

Symes tipped his head. 'Strange, cos she was here the other day without a fucking scratch on her,' Symes said.

'Nah, man, can't be. She—'

The first punch hit Birdy square on the nose and knocked him backwards. Symes enjoyed the rush of pleasure that travelled straight from his knuckles to the part of him crying out for satisfaction. The sound of cracking bone offered him satisfaction, as the blood exploded from his nose.

'You were welcomed into my club, you fuck. You enjoyed the benefits and only had to do one fucking thing. You let me down, brother.'

As he landed blow after blow, kick after kick, heard bones break and skin tear he wondered at some inmates' need for a weapon to cause a bit of bodily harm. Where was the fun in that? he thought as he looked down at the quivering bloody and broken mess on the ground.

Enough fun for now.

Now it was down to business.

And for that he did need a weapon.

CHAPTER 65

Kim envied the long slow drink Bryant took from the glass of water. It felt as though he was doing it on her behalf following that admission about her mother.

'Why you?' Kim asked.

'Because no one else seemed bothered. Once it came out your mother was mentally unwell everyone started worrying about covering their behinds to avoid being the reason for the breakdown in an inept system. Everyone was too busy trying to redirect the blame. Don't get me wrong – the police had a half-hearted search, asked the neighbours some questions, but were easily diverted onto other cases needing their attention.'

'But not you?' she asked.

He shook his head. 'I can't even explain to you what drove me,' he said, honestly. 'But your face as you were carried out of the building never left my mind.'

'So, how'd you find her?' Kim asked.

'Police didn't ask the right neighbours the right questions. They focussed on the ones that lived closest thinking they'd know her and her movements the best. I'd already learned that what you need are the nosey neighbours. Wherever they live. The nosey neighbours don't just observe and watch, they ask and talk, trying to find out everything about everyone. There was a man in his sixties, a widower, who made it his business to know everyone's habits. And he knew quite a bit about your mother.'

'Where was she?' Kim asked trying to visualise where her mother was while she'd been in hospital fighting for her life.

'She was drunk, off her meds in a squat in West Bromwich.'

'You spoke to her?' she asked.

He nodded. 'Asked her if she had any idea what she'd done to you and Mikey.'

'And?' Kim asked, wanting a drink of Bryant's water more than ever. The revelation that this man had actually spoken to her mother had dried every drop of saliva in her mouth. She had no doubt about what she was going to hear about her mother's reaction to news about her and Mikey but she felt compelled to hear it anyway, however hard it was to be reminded of her mother's disregard for the life of herself and her brother.

'You don't want to—'

'What did she say?' Kim asked, as her teeth clenched together.

'She asked me who you were.'

Bryant looked down into his glass.

'I called the police and waited until they got there. The whole conversation is recounted word for word in the book if you'd—'

'No, thank you,' she said, trying to keep her mind on the case. 'But in the book, did you mention about the cream crackers?'

He frowned and nodded. 'Of course.'

'Where did you learn of that?' Bryant asked.

'Police officer, I think, or may have been a paramedic but definitely someone who was there at the scene. They saw the packet.'

So, Stacey might have been right.

'Have you sold any books recently?' Kim asked.

He shook his head and stood.

'Please follow me,' he said.

Bryant finished the water and followed the man along the hall.

He opened a door into a small study which looked out onto a small but busy garden with low fences that showed the countryside beyond.

Her gaze immediately went to a box in the corner. She guessed there were about ten copies or so. The cover was the silhouette of a little girl beneath the words *The Lost Child*. She looked away as Henry Reed leafed through a folder.

'When you say recently, I sold one about four months ago. As he read his notes he began to nod his head. 'Yes, I remember now. The money came in a Jiffy bag with a stamped addressed envelope enclosed.'

Kim's heart quickened. 'So, you know where you sent it?'

'Oh yes, I remember it well. I sent it to Winson Green prison. I mean, I thought it was a bit strange but even prisoners like to read, I suppose.'

Kim glanced at Bryant to see if he was feeling the same level of surprise.

He was.

Kim realised she had gained far more from this visit than she'd expected.

'Thank you, Inspector,' he said, as though sensing the visit was coming to an end.

'For what?'

'Coming here. I feel that I can finally let go of the vision of that frightened little girl now that I've seen the strong, successful woman she's become.' He looked away as his eyes reddened. 'And how you've achieved that is a testament to your strength and determination, I'm sure.'

She had anticipated confronting this man and shaming him for trying to profit from her misery. Instead she had found a man who had done no such thing. In his own way, he'd been the only one fighting her corner while she had been fighting for her life.

The thought comforted her somehow. She hadn't been quite as alone as she'd thought.

'Henry, I'd like just two more things from you before I go,' she said.

'Of course,' he replied, closing the folder.

'Destroy those remaining books.'

He hesitated, glanced at the box and nodded.

'And?'

'I'd kill for a glass of water.'

CHAPTER 66

Penn prided himself on being a reasonable and patient kind of guy. But even he had his limits.

He parked the Fiesta well away from the entrance to the scrapyard for fear it would be mistaken and towed directly to the crusher.

He was pleased to see the site had been reopened for business.

'Hey, Dobbie,' he said, pleasantly, glancing around the office. Despite the down time of the guys on site, it hadn't been spent cleaning up.

'What the f… hell you want? Last van rolled out of here not ten minutes ago.'

And Penn could already hear the crusher going in the distance.

'Yeah, still waiting on that name, mate,' he said, leaning on the reception desk and then wishing he hadn't. The man had not taken an opportunity to refresh those armpits.

'Been busy, mate,' he said, without interest. As far as Dobbie was concerned he'd got his business back and could return to making money. 'And anyway, when do I get my metal back?'

Penn raised an eyebrow. 'You want it back, covered in skin, bone, blood and—'

'I paid for it, day I?'

'Yeah, I'll see what I can do,' he said. 'But I wouldn't hold your breath. It's all being logged as evidence. But yeah, you did pay for it, but to who is the question. Now, I'd like to think that you'd be as helpful as possible seeing as some poor sod got mangled in your crusher. And I'd hate to think you were withholding important information, like the owner of the car, because of your illegal way of doing business.'

'Hey now, just wait a fucking—'

'Every single transaction in this place should be logged with a registration number, purchase price and whether the seller was VAT registered. In another ledger you are required to record all sales, profits, VAT and tax so the Inland Revenue and VAT man can happen along and inspect at any time. Isn't that correct?'

Penn left no time for an answer.

'Now quite frankly, I don't give a shit how you operate your business, but I do care who sold you that car. I could be persuaded to care more about your bookwork, say, to call the VAT man with my concerns about—'

'Jesus, you coppers don't mind a bit of threatening behaviour yourselves, do yer?' he said, moving papers around on the desk.

Penn would swear there was a half-eaten burger under there somewhere even though he couldn't imagine this guy leaving half of anything.

'Here,' he said, thrusting a Post-it note towards him.

'And for your information I put the details into my purchase ledger this morning.'

Sure enough, the Post-it contained the date, the purchase price, the registration number and the name of the seller.

And it was a name he already knew.

CHAPTER 67

'Are we on lunch break yet, guv?' Bryant asked, half an hour after leaving the home of the journalist.

She checked her watch. 'It's almost three and you grabbed a sandwich from—'

'Yeah, but I'm still entitled to a lunch break,' he said, stubbornly, as they approached Redditch.

'Bryant, what the hell is wrong with you? We never take a proper lunch—'

Her words were cut off as he hit the brakes suddenly and pulled in to a service station. He brought the car to a stop in the area reserved for grocery shoppers.

'Guv, may I have my lunch break, please?' he asked, sharply.

'Of course, if you really want to.'

She expected him to rush out of the car to get something urgent or take out his phone to make some important call. Instead he unclipped his seat belt and turned towards her.

'I don't think you should be working this case.'

'Excuse me,' she said, sharply.

'I don't think it's healthy.'

Kim wondered where the hell this had come from.

'Is this because of what happened back at the morgue?'

'It's not one single thing,' he said, chewing his lip. 'I just don't think you ought to be putting yourself through this.'

For the life of her she couldn't understand his problem.

'I've not been overly emotional. I've not dwelled on the events of the past. I've not become hysterical or started crying while we've been questioning someone.'

'Yeah, that's what I'm worried about,' he said, quietly.

'Bryant, you're making no bloody sense.'

'There is no emotion. Even when Henry was recounting the meeting with your mother. I saw what you did, again. This was new information and yet your emotional reaction was stifled, suffocated and pushed down. This bastard is forcing you to face some of the most painful times of your life, dredge up the most horrific memories you have and there is no emotion. You're acting like it's happening to someone else. You're pushing your feelings so far down into yourself that—'

'That what, Bryant?' she asked.

'That you might never find them again. It's not normal and it's not healthy. Even your own body betrayed you earlier, at the morgue, but you just won't listen.'

'That was just a bug or something,' she lied. 'You gotta remember that I was there. These incidents are no surprise to me. I've experienced them already and I've lived with it all my life.'

'It's not like you're reliving a trip to the zoo or a good holiday that you remember fondly. These are traumatic events that you've chosen to box up in cold bloody storage. It's not even reaching you.'

'So, let me get this straight. You want me off this case because I'm handling it?' she asked to make sure she'd understood his warped logic.

'I want you off the case because you're handling it well. Too well for it to be normal. You're cutting off your emotions at the knees, crippling them and who knows if you'll ever—'

'Bryant, start the car,' she instructed. The long-term well-being of her emotions was not her greatest concern right now, and she would do whatever was needed to catch this bastard before he hurt anyone else.

'Guv, just listen to—'

'Start the car, Bryant, and take us back to the station. Cos lunch break is well and truly over.'

CHAPTER 68

Stacey couldn't help feeling bad for saying no to Alison. But interrogating HOLMES2 for incidents similar to those on her previous case was no simple task.

She had listened to Alison, who had thought it was a matter of entering a few key details, and it might have been had she been looking for cases of brutal rape and murder; but if Alison was right that the killing of Jennifer Townes was the result of escalation, they were looking at incidents of unsolved rape which numbered in the thousands and would take weeks of interrogation and analysis.

And if she was honest she really did think Alison was wasting time on a case where the West Mercia team had their man, and the behaviourist was just having trouble coming to terms with her own mistake.

She wasn't insensitive enough to say that but the air seemed to have cooled between them, and Stacey couldn't help her relief as familiar footsteps sounded in the general office.

'Hey, Stace,' Penn said, rushing into the office and casting off his man-bag.

He turned and nodded in Alison's direction as an afterthought, as though he'd forgotten she was there.

'Where's the boss?' he asked.

'Checking out a lead in the Cotswolds. Detail in the first crime scene our killer couldn't have got from the news. Haven't heard back from her yet,' Stacey said, thinking it strange. Boss normally checked in every couple of hours.

'Back up, what's in the Cotswolds?'

Stacey had almost forgotten how long he'd been gone.

'Guy who wrote a book about the boss's childhood, a journalist or something.'

'Bloody hell, there's a book?'

Stacey nodded. 'It's the cracker wrapper. Doesn't appear anywhere in the press so I got thinking…'

'Ahem,' Alison said, without looking up.

'With a little help from over there,' she acknowledged. 'That he had to have got it from somewhere. Boss has gone to see if he's sold any copies recently.'

'And she couldn't have phoned?' he asked, taking the last cake from the Tupperware box.

Alison offered him a hateful glance as he took a bite. Stacey didn't even want to try and count the daily calorie intake of the woman.

'Well, I've been…' Penn said.

'So, I've been…' Stacey said at the same time.

They both laughed.

'Yeah, well, you two can share your homework in a minute but first I'd like some information,' Alison said, peering over her rimless glasses.

Both she and Penn looked in her direction.

'I've been looking at the names you've given me and have been working up some character profiles. I've ruled a few out based on motivation. The loss they've suffered when weighed against the level of planning, energy, knowledge, tenacity rules. Many of them almost impossible.'

''Most?' Stacey questioned. 'So, do we rule them out, or not?'

'There will always be exceptions to the rule but in behaviourism and profiling we have to follow the rules and not the exceptions.'

Stacey wasn't sure that made her feel any better. She didn't feel comfortable with this woman ruling out people and dismissing them because they didn't fit neatly into her equation.

'I can see the doubt in your face, Stacey, but stay with me for now.'

Penn offered her a look as though they were two children being scolded by the teacher.

'Okay, look at it this way. In an investigation you look for motive, means and opportunity. You make links between the three prerequisites and a bit of forensic evidence doesn't hurt. It's no different for profiling but including personality traits. For example, is he angry but lazy? If so he's not going to be our killer. Is he energetic but not resourceful? Again, not going to be our killer if certain personality traits are present and in some cases dominant. Does someone suffer from severe rage but it's short-lived? If so, it's unlikely their anger will carry them through this level of planning and execution. Are they creative but not disciplined? Again, only someone disciplined could do this without confiding in someone else. There are all kinds of factors and considerations to—'

'What if there's more than one?' Stacey asked. 'Can't their strengths and weaknesses complement each other?'

'And destroy each other,' Alison answered.

'But with the kidnapping?...'

'It worked well, for a while, because both parties wanted something different out of it. One wanted money, the other wanted personal gratification. It's different with revenge. It's more personal and is unlikely to be shared.'

Okay, Stacey could see that for once the woman made sense.

'So, you got something?' Stacey asked.

Alison leafed back through pages of notes.

'I've looked at all the characteristics needed for these crimes and have definitely ruled many of them out, but there is still one name that I'm having trouble putting to bed at the minute.'

'So, what do you need?' Stacey asked.

Alison removed her glasses before speaking.

'I'd like you to tell me a little more about Nina Croft.'

CHAPTER 69

'Okay, recap,' Kim said, perching beside the printer at the top of the room. The slight breeze that had developed over the course of the day was blowing in through the open window, offering everyone some well-needed relief.

'So, we spoke with John Duggar first thing. He lied about hating me. We've never met and he joined the hate club for protection. Difficult to believe looking at him but, hey ho,' she said, catching a glance between Stacey and Penn.

'Post-mortem on Mr and Mrs Phelps has offered no obvious cause of death but tests are—'

'And how did that go?' Alison asked. But the woman wasn't looking at her. She was asking her colleague.

Kim too awaited the response with interest. And after their conversation in the car she had no clue what his answer would be. It was up to him now. She had given him no brief, had not asked him to lie on her behalf. He knew one wrong word would travel up the food chain quicker than a pat on the back and he would get his wish. She would be removed from the case.

Right now it was a matter of did he, or did he not trust her.

'The guv acted exactly as I would have expected,' he said, meeting her gaze. 'With professionalism and integrity.'

Okay, the last bit was a tad overboard but Alison seemed satisfied.

'We also established that our guy in the cube was most likely locked in the boot, and finally we learned that a copy of the book was posted to Winson Green prison about four months ago.'

'Jeez,' Stacey said. 'Don't suppose he?…'

'Couldn't remember the name of the guy that requested it,' Kim said, shaking her head.

'Rules out Nina Croft then?' Stacey asked, glancing at Alison.

'Huh, what am I missing?' Kim asked.

Alison flicked back a couple of pages in her notebook. 'I feel she's a likely candidate and after Stacey explained how she was aware of her husband's actions regarding the murder of those young girls, I'm even more suspicious. And is it true that she paid the nanny to sleep with her own husband?'

Kim nodded. 'Oh yeah, didn't want to sleep with him herself but also wanted control on the germs he was bringing around their boys.'

Alison made a note. 'I really think—'

'It's not her,' Stacey argued, but Kim caught her eye and shook her head. Kim's gut wasn't feeling it either, but while Alison was focussed in that direction she wasn't looking elsewhere, specifically, at her.

'So, what you got Stace?' Kim asked.

'Been looking at past cases with Alison, as instructed, and doing some digging. Mr and Mrs Phelps have a son.'

Kim frowned. 'Well, where the hell is he?'

Stacey shook her head. 'Not a clue. Travelling abroad say the neighbours of the Phelpses. That's what they were told when he disappeared about a year ago. Not a popular chap to be honest, and no one particularly missed him.'

'Keep on that, Stace,' Kim said. Missing children of dead parents did not give her a warm and fuzzy feeling.

'Penn?' Kim asked.

'Well, boss, I met with Jenks, who said the thing Amy and Mark wanted the most was a home. One of the neighbours in the tower block mentioned something about a person from the housing association hanging around.'

'The flats on Hollytree?…'

'Are council owned,' he continued. 'I know, so I went to the council and got a list of everyone who had taken the key to view the property.'

'Good work.'

'And on the way back I dropped in on Dobbie and got the name of the person who sold him the car and the registration number.'

'Jesus, Penn,' Kim exclaimed. 'Will somebody give the man a plant.'

'He's already got it, boss,' Stacey said, wearily.

'Oh, right, good.'

'Registration doesn't help us. Car was stolen ten days ago from a nineteen-year-old painter's mate and reported straight away. No link to anyone involved or connected—'

'From where?' Kim asked.

Penn rechecked the address. 'Taken from Fairview Road in—'

'I know it,' she said. Fairview Road. The location of Fairview Children's Home. The place she'd spent the majority of her childhood. There was the link. There was the jab like an elbow right into her ribs.

'But there's more,' Penn said. 'The person who sold the car to Dobbie is also on the list of people who viewed the flat.'

'You're kidding?' she asked, as Bryant also sat forward. This was huge.

'Yeah, but you're not gonna like it cos it's someone you've already written off. It's our very own John Duggar, who has no reason to hate you at all.'

CHAPTER 70

'Hmmm… interesting,' Alison said, appearing beside Kim at the bottom of the stairs.

She and Bryant were heading over to Duggar's but Bryant had detoured to powder his nose first.

Kim agreed with her about what Penn had just uncovered. 'Yeah, strange that Duggar's hands appear—'

'Not that,' Alison said, following her through the key-coded door. 'What's interesting to me is Bryant's response to my question about your behaviour at the post-mortem.'

Oh, that, Kim thought, hoping the woman had accepted his reply at face value.

'I mean I wouldn't exactly call him a liar but…'

'Excuse me?' Kim said, turning to face her.

'Well, if Bryant was being truthful about your reaction to the burnt bodies at the post-mortem then your feelings for Keith and Erica are nowhere near—'

'Alison, I strongly suggest you shut the fuck up,' Kim said, striding towards the car.

'And there you prove my point without even trying,' Alison said, following her. 'To have no reaction at all to the similarities between the two is just not normal, even for you, especially when those clenched fists show me the level of emotion you have towards the couple.'

Kim unclenched her fists, felt in her pockets and realised Bryant had the keys. Getting into the vehicle and reversing over the woman was no longer an option.

She turned. 'Surprisingly, I am able to remain professional and do my job…'

'I don't doubt that,' Alison said, shaking her head. 'What interests me more is the phraseology of Bryant's response. That you "acted exactly as he would have expected you to".'

'Bryant didn't lie so don't you dare…'

'I will dare because I can and that's what I'm here to do. If you think I expect you to have no emotional reaction to these events and that that is the best way to try and deceive me then you're out of your mind. Your lack of transparency just makes me doubt your ability to handle this all the more, so you're doing yourself no favours trying to pretend this is just like any other case.

'And secondly I dare because you are not my boss. I'm attached to your team but—'

'Yeah, cos if I was you wouldn't be leaving after half a day's work,' Kim said, glancing up to the window where the rest of her team were still hard at work. It had barely passed five o'clock.

'I have a relative in hospital,' Alison answered vaguely.

'For a behaviourist you're a shit liar, you know,' Kim observed. 'But unlike you I'll accept your answer because clearly you don't want to tell me the whole truth. I'll respect your wish to—'

'Listen, I'm not your enemy here,' Alison said, tipping her head. 'You know yourself and I know people. I understand behaviour and whether you like it or not you're going to be betrayed. No matter how hard you try and manage all your physical and psychological functions, something is going to let you down.'

Kim thought about the moment she'd been staring down the toilet pan after running out of the morgue. 'Alison, I don't need—'

'Hear me out. I don't know how you manage your past, whether it's separation, ignorance, denial or a mixture of them all, but I can tell you that your normal techniques, your way of getting through an average day, are no match for the stress of having all your demons thrown into your face.'

Kim took a deep breath and looked away, hating again that everyone knew it was her demons they were fighting.

'See, the problem isn't so much being forced to remember all the bad shit, it's the analysis of it that's the real issue. You can't glance at it like a billboard and look away, allowing the memory to drift safely back to the place you've stored it. To solve this case, to find out who is behind it you're being forced to analyse, inspect and dissect it all for clues and leads.'

Kim met her gaze and was surprised to see empathy and understanding in the woman's eyes.

'Basically, you're being forced to relive every horrific event, and I swear that at some time in the future it's going to make you do something you later regret.'

CHAPTER 71

Alison had just about thrown off her irritation with the detective inspector when she entered the hospital foyer. Trying to get the woman to understand that she wasn't the enemy was turning out to be a complete waste of time. Her words and advice were going nowhere and she had the feeling she was watching a high-speed car travel towards a wall with no way to stop it.

She had offered as much warning as she could, she resolved, as she said her name into the loudspeaker and was buzzed through.

Valerie was sorting papers at the desk.

'How is she?' Alison asked.

'Same, I'm afraid. Not responsive yet but we've not given up hope.'

Alison was glad to hear it.

She thanked the nurse and headed away from the desk.

'Good to see that your mother finally arrived,' Valerie said, quietly.

Alison's step faltered. 'Wh… what?'

'Your mother is with her now. I assumed you'd want to know. It could have been quite the shock for you seeing as you told me she was dead.'

Alison felt the heat surge into her cheeks. She tried to think of a way around the lie.

'Don't bother,' Valerie said. 'You're a terrible liar. Has anyone ever told you that?'

Recently, a few people, she thought.

'I'm sorry for lying. I should—'

'I knew the first time you came, but no one else had been to see her. She'd been completely alone.'

'So, you just let me in?'

Valerie shrugged and half smiled. 'You looked smart enough and I read that the guy who attacked her was in custody. You weren't a risk to her.'

Alison couldn't believe that she, as a total stranger, had been allowed to sit beside the bed of an attack victim for hours on end.

'You seemed so sad, so sorry and lost that—'

'You let me in because I was sad?' Alison asked.

Valerie smile. 'No, I let you in because I have this,' she said, pointing beneath the rising of the desk.

Alison looked over. A single screen displayed four screens.

'CCTV?'

'I was watching you the whole time.'

Alison hadn't even known there was CCTV.

'Look, I don't know what your deal is but her family is with her now. There's nothing more you can do for her.'

Suddenly Alison realised there was someone she could apologise to that might help relieve the burden that was like a chain attached to her body, being dragged wherever she walked.

'Can I just go and speak to her mother?'

'Depends,' Valerie said. 'Do you have anything to give her? Any comfort? Any reassurance? Anything that will make looking at her daughter in that state any easier to bear?'

Alison thought and then shook her head.

'Then no, I'd rather you left them alone.'

Alison understood that there was nothing more she could do. Except one thing.

'Do you have her belongings?' Alison asked.

'I'm not sure I want to know why you're asking me that but no, everything was taken away by the police once she was taken into surgery.'

Damn, of course. It was painfully clear that she was no detective.

'But of course, we removed everything from her and listed it. When a victim is alive their personal safety comes before the preservation of evidence and I was not about to let those officers or crime scene guys touch her.'

Alison couldn't hide her smile.

'And obviously we log it all for chain of evidence and to cover ourselves,' she said, reaching behind for a lever arch file.

She licked her finger and leafed past the first couple of sheets before turning it towards her.

Alison saw Valerie's signature next to DCI Merton's to agree the items handed over.

Alison read down the list:

Trousers
Tee shirt
Bra
Pants
Sandal x 2
Handbag – brown
Purse – brown (unopened)
Casio watch
Ankle bracelet

Alison's heart began to hammer as she reached the bottom.
She pointed. 'Are you sure?'
Valerie nodded. 'Removed it myself.'
The entry read,

Plastic earring – pink flamingo x 1

CHAPTER 72

'Hey, Bryant, knock like you bloody mean it,' Kim said, banging harder on the front door.

It had taken less than fifteen minutes to get from the station in Halesowen to Duggar's house behind The Civic.

The journey had been frenetic but not so much for Bryant who'd had his eyes closed. He'd asked what she and Alison had been discussing and one look had told him she wasn't in the mood to share.

'Let's try around the back,' Kim said, jogging to the end of the row. Behind the houses was a narrow gulley filled with old kids' toys and garden rubbish.

Kim negotiated her way to the third one along, and stopped dead.

The six foot fencing was finished off with a trellis that ran the length of the wooden panels, adding another foot to the height. That wasn't the problem. The issue was the barbed wire wrapped all the way around it.

'Bloody hell, home from home or what?' she said.

'Don't even think about it,' Bryant warned. 'Even Bear Grylls ain't getting over that.'

'Hey, Bryant, what costs more, a glass panel or a fence panel?' she asked, thoughtfully.

'Well, fence panels are pretty cheap these—'

'Yeah, my thoughts exactly,' she said, raising her leg and kicking the fence panel.

'Jesus, guv, we don't even know—'

'Shut up and help,' she instructed. When he hesitated she rolled her eyes. 'Look, Woody will be overjoyed I considered his budget restraints, and I have reason to believe the man is in danger, satisfied?'

'Well, not really cos he's built like a brick shithouse as my nan used to—'

'Who doesn't like conflict,' she reminded him, as his second kick made the hole bigger. Two more and they were through to the row of laburnum trees that hid the barbed wire from the house.

Kim pushed through aware of the cobwebs attaching themselves to every piece of her clothing.

She headed towards the patio door but could already tell the kitchen was empty.

She tried the door.

It opened as the sound of dog barking began.

Bryant looked at her questioningly. She knew what he was thinking. *Would a man who had barbed wire around his garden leave a door open when he left the house?*

She stepped into the kitchen and stood beside the door to the utility room.

'It's all right, Mofo,' she called out. The dog gave one last bark, a growl and then quietened down, as though his job of keeping people away had failed, so there was no point carrying on.

Bryant stepped into the lounge so that both exits were covered.

'Police,' he shouted. No answer and no sound of movement.

'Police,' he repeated. 'I'm coming up,' he called heading to the stairs.

Kim could see that Bryant was not going to find anything upstairs.

A cup of coffee sat in the middle of the kitchen work surface. It was still lukewarm to the touch.

John Duggar had left the house some time in the last half hour, and by the looks of it, he'd been in a bit of a hurry.

CHAPTER 73

Despite the boss's instruction to go home Stacey found herself standing outside the home of Mr and Mrs Phelps.

There was something incomplete about this whole situation. Two respectable, unassuming people had burned alive in a car fire and there'd been no one to tell.

She had established they had a son who was away travelling and she hoped there was some kind of clue here as to where he'd gone. A postcard, a letter, a computer she could check for emails.

The neighbour had given her the name of Joel and her searches for 'Joel Phelps' had turned up nothing on her normal searches: no police record, no social media, so wherever he was travelling he appeared to have checked out of civilisation; but surely, he was in touch with his parents.

She showed her ID and slipped under the cordon tape. A few onlookers were hanging around in small groups but there was no spectacle. Looking around at the tidy, unremarkable semis in the street she guessed the folks here didn't really do spectacle, but there was little to see. There were no bodies being brought out, no scandalous secrets being broadcast on the news. Their home was being combed for clues.

'Hey, Mitch,' Stacey said, stepping into the hallway. 'You having a break from Doctor A?' she asked, remembering what the boss had said.

He rolled his eyes. 'I swear, if the woman calls me an idiot one more time…'

His words trailed away as he shook his head.

'Anything interesting?'

'Nothing to indicate any kind of struggle. All rooms are in order, stuff put away. What brings you here, anyway?' he asked removing the mask from the top of his head.

'Just wanna get a feel for them. You see any computer or iPad?'

He shook his head again. 'Folks didn't even have Sky or cable. Freeview and a normal landline.' He checked his watch and looked around. 'And we'll be sealing the property in about half an hour.'

Stacey nodded and began to walk around. The first thing she noticed were the books. Everywhere, on shelves, on occasional tables, small piles beside chairs. This couple had liked to read, a lot, which explained their lack of interest in television channels.

She ventured upstairs and counted three bedrooms. The biggest held a double bed, fitted wardrobes, a dressing table and more books. The second double bedroom had been turned into a library-cum-reading room and the smallest was being used as storage.

Looked like the son wasn't coming home anytime soon.

She returned to the master bedroom and sat on the right side of the bed.

She pulled open the single drawer in the bedside cabinet and almost jumped back.

'Jesus,' she whispered as her eyes took in the colourful assortment of sex toys and lubricants. Stacey closed the drawer and smiled. The couple had clearly enjoyed more than a good book. And fair play to them, she thought.

She moved to the other side of the bed and hesitated before opening the drawer, unsure what she might find.

She sighed with relief. No more sex toys, instead she found a few hair grips, a couple of items of jewellery and a clutch of receipts, and underneath everything was a small lockable diary that reminded Stacey of the one she'd had as a teenager. The tiny key dangled from the strap, but the diary clicked open.

Stacey wondered how many different ways she could invade this couple's privacy as she leafed through it.

The latest entry had been made the night before they died. The handwriting was tidy but the words brief, Stacey noticed, as she read what appeared to be short notes as a form of record rather than an outpouring of feelings.

The day before their murder they had attended a doctor's appointment for Bill's blood pressure, visited the post office to buy stamps and nipped into the library.

Stacey leafed backwards seeing similar entries throughout until she reached a date two weeks earlier.

Saw Joel. Didn't know what to say. Left early.

Stacey frowned. Where had Helen Phelps seen her son? The neighbour had given her the impression that Joel had been travelling for a while.

And why had she struggled for conversation?

This was no longer making sense, she realised, as she leafed to the back of the diary and found a single piece of paper, battered and marked by time.

She opened the piece of paper to find it was a birth certificate.

Her eyes took in the detail a few times.

The birth certificate was for Joel and his last name wasn't Phelps at all.

No wonder she'd been unable to find any trace of him.

She'd been looking for the wrong man.

CHAPTER 74

'Look, guv, there's just nothing else we can do right now,' Bryant said as they pulled back into the station. 'We've put out a description of Duggar. If he turns up anywhere we'll be the first to know. It's almost eight so…'

His words trailed away as her phone began to ring.

'Working late, Keats,' she answered.

'Only for my favourite detective,' he answered.

'Yeah, he's right beside me,' she said, putting the phone on loudspeaker.

'Hey, Keats,' Bryant said.

'Sorry for the late call but had to get some results checked and thought you'd want to know the results—'

'Yep,' she interrupted.

'Toxicology came back on Amy Wilde and Mark Johnson. As expected there were substantial amounts of heroin in their system and most certainly enough to cause an overdose. But there's something else. Also present were high levels of a drug called Baclofen, a muscle relaxant used to treat spasticity and musculoskeletal conditions.'

'Bloody hell,' she said. 'So, you're saying our killer most likely relaxed them enough to be able to shoot them full of heroin?'

'I'd say so,' Keats replied.

'Thanks for—'

'That's not all, Inspector,' Keats said, stopping her from ending the call.

'Same drug was found in the soft tissue of Mr and Mrs Phelps.'

Silence fell for just a few seconds but it was long enough.

'So, they were paralysed?' she asked, quietly.

'Yes,' he answered. 'Most likely semi-conscious but unable to move.'

'Shit,' Bryant said, shaking his head.

She was guessing they were all imagining the couple forced to sit still as the flames engulfed them and licked at their flesh, searing it away from the bone. She just hoped the smoke inhalation had got them quick.

Kim swallowed and shook the image away.

'Thanks, Keats,' she said, ending the call.

Kim got out of the car shaking her head. Was there any worse way to die?

Bryant rested his arms on the roof of the car. 'Guv, we're gonna catch this bastard,' he said as the doors to the station were thrown open.

Three officers headed for the squad car beside them. The driver accidentally barged into her side.

'Hey, watch…'

'Sorry, Marm, didn't mean…'

The others were already in the car.

'What's the bloody rush?'

'Rape at Linley Park, Marm… gotta…'

'Wh-what?' Kim asked, as her blood turned to ice.

He repeated the words and slid into the car.

Kim all but fell back into the passenger seat of Bryant's car.

'Guv, what's up?' her partner asked, getting back into the car.

'I-I'm not… I mean…'

'Guv, talk to me,' Bryant ordered.

She nodded and pulled herself together.

'Bryant, follow those officers. Now.'

CHAPTER 75

Linley Park was a much grander name than the place deserved.

It was a patch of land with a swing set, a see-saw and a space where a spider's web roundabout once stood. Beyond the park was a playing field and at the far end was a clutch of trees about thirty metres square.

The entire space was nestled between two small housing estates of private terraced dwellings.

And one of those houses had belonged to foster family number five.

'Why are we here, guv?' Bryant asked quietly as he parked behind the squad car that was behind the ambulance.

Kim said nothing as she got out of the car.

'Where is?…'

'In the trees,' Kim said, unable to look his way.

Her gaze was fixed on the direction of the officers running across the field. As they reached the treeline the two males slowed and allowed the WPC to enter first.

'Guv…'

'Bryant, please stop talking to me,' she said, quietly.

Right now, she had nothing to give.

Her brain was a kaleidoscope of images. She saw herself sitting on the see-saw as dusk fell and the kids disappeared back into their homes, parents at the top of the park just shouting out their child's name. Some shouting a five-minute warning as the light began to disappear.

Kim waited and waited hoping that it would be Mrs Lampitt that called her tonight. And not him.

She walked across the field focussing on putting one foot in front of the other. It was as though her brain had forgotten how to do it automatically.

She tried not to look around, at the two goalposts at either end of the field. Even the grass around her feet felt familiar. Only her feet had been smaller, encased in plain black plimsolls and he had been holding her hand.

She shuddered and tried to push the memories away. She couldn't remember this right now. She couldn't be back in that place. She couldn't revisit the events that happened in the family she never spoke of. The family right after Keith and Erica.

She stepped past the PCs and into the woods. The aroma of lilac overwhelmed her. The smell travelled right to her memory bank, and she stumbled. Bryant was right beside her and put a steadying hand in the small of her back.

She moved forward to where the WPC was kneeling on the ground. A paramedic knelt either side.

'It's okay, sweetie, we've got you,' said the WPC gently.

Kim couldn't see the girl, and the WPC waved them back.

Kim understood and respected her call. No one knew exactly what she'd been through and the police officer was trying to establish trust. Too many faces and the girl wouldn't know who to listen to.

Kim took a few steps to the right and saw a mound of blood-soaked tissue beside one of the paramedics. They were both focussed heavily on her mid area. Both were sweating profusely, and one was shaking his head.

Oh Jesus, what had the bastard done to her? she wondered, as her heart began to race.

Kim could see past one of them to bare feet with painted toenails. The slim legs were bare and as her gaze travelled up Kim could see lines of dried blood travelling down her thighs.

A second paramedic team rushed past her with a stretcher.

'Thank God,' said one of the guys on the ground. 'Not sure how long she's gonna last with this level of blood loss.' He turned to the uniformed officer. 'We gotta move her now. We can't stop the bleeding.'

The WPC nodded. 'I'm going in the ambulance with her.'

Even more bodies suddenly crowded around the girl, who, to Kim's recollection, had not yet made a sound.

She wanted to step forward hold her hand, reassure her that everything was going to be okay, but she couldn't, because somehow this was all her fault.

On the count of three the girl was hauled on to the stretcher, and Kim would swear she heard a groan. The WPC continued to whisper while holding her hand.

The team began moving towards the clearing to get out, and still Kim couldn't see the girl.

'Nature of the injury?' Kim asked, as the paramedics passed her.

'Pop bottle wedged right up inside her.'

Kim swallowed down the nausea, stepped aside and let them go. Any doubt she'd had about this assault being linked to their current case had been extinguished.

She followed the stretcher out although the sickly lilac smell seemed to have attached itself to her skin. Just as it had back then and no amount of showering had managed to remove it from her nostrils.

She walked between the two male police officers as one called out over her head.

'Gives new meaning to being on the bottle, eh?'

Kim stopped moving, falling completely level with the constable. She turned her head. 'Are you fucking kidding me?'

His face was bewildered. 'Crime scene humour, Marm, we—'

His words were cut off as she grabbed the front of his stab vest and pulled him towards her. She raised her clenched fist into the air.

'Okey dokey,' Bryant said, grabbing her arm and pushing her towards the open field.

'Bad taste, mate. Real, bad taste,' Bryant said with disgust. 'Just be glad it isn't your fucking sister.'

The rage burning through her body begged her to break free of her colleague and head right back to the heartless bastard behind.

'Let me go,' she snapped. 'I'll wring his…'

'Oh no you don't,' Bryant said, keeping a hand on her elbow.

'For fuck's sake,' she growled.

'Yeah, scream, shout and swear at me all you like. Hit me if it'll make you feel better. I won't report you for it. Probably,' he said.

'You think he should get away with saying that about a young, innocent kid who…'

'Punching him and losing your job is not gonna put the words back on the other side of his lips and help us catch the bastard that did this.'

Bryant only let her arm go once they'd reached the car.

For the second time that day he looked at her over the roof of the Astra.

'Am I allowed to ask the significance of what we just saw in the woods back there?'

Kim shook her head and forced down the emotion building in her throat. Her reply was little more than a whisper.

'No, Bryant, you are not.'

Bryant did her the favour of staying quiet as they followed the ambulance at speed through the evening traffic.

It was what she'd asked him to do, but was it really what she wanted: more time to think?

She stared at the rear ambulance doors, picturing the girl within. Violated, hurting, scared, confused, angry. She had a police officer holding her hand.

She wanted to be beside her, to apologise, to explain that this was all her fault; that these things were happening because of her, that she herself had done nothing wrong. But most of all she wanted to tell her that she was going to catch the bastard who had done this and they were going to make him pay.

'Guv, I'm not sure how this links…'

'It was foster family number five, and Mr Lampitt worked at the pop bottling plant, and if you ask me any more questions I'm gonna jump out of this moving car, got it?'

'Well, the kiddie locks are on but you're welcome to try the sunroof,' he said, deadpan.

Kim felt a smile touch her lips despite the emotion churning around her veins.

'Bryant, sometimes you—'

'Yeah, yeah. So, you going to try and talk to this girl at the hospital?'

'Hope to,' she answered. 'Not sure she's in any fit state to offer us anything at the minute but I'm happy to wait. Maybe I can speak to the WPC in the meantime, get a name or something.'

'Could be quite a wait,' he observed, pushing on the brakes as an idiot in an MR2 pulled in between them and the ambulance. 'I wish she'd been noisier,' he said, echoing her thoughts at the scene.

Her phone began to ring. She took it out to see Woody's name at the top of the screen.

She considered not answering it until she'd received some kind of update from inside the hospital.

'Evening, sir,' she answered, realising she hadn't updated him in a while.

'Stone, where are you and what are you doing?'

There was an edge to his voice that she assumed was due to the time of night.

'We're following a sexual assault victim in an ambulance to the hospital to try and speak with her about—'

'Put me on loudspeaker right now,' he bellowed.

She glanced at Bryant as she did so, but his focus was on keeping pace with the ambulance as they headed down the Pedmore Road.

'You're on, sir,' she said.

'Do not go to the hospital. Do not attempt to question that victim and get back to the station right now. And Bryant, unless you want to risk both of you losing your jobs you'll do exactly what I say.'

The line went dead in her hand.

Bryant slowed the car as the ambulance sped away from them.

And then he took a left.

CHAPTER 77

'Sit down, Stone,' Woody said as she knocked and entered.

Silently she did as he asked. His brusque phone call had been followed up with a brief text message that had read.

'Just you.'

She'd told Bryant to head off home to his wife and pasta bake but she knew he was sitting downstairs in the squad room.

'The incident this evening?' he said, giving her a hard stare.

Kim really had no clue why he was bordering on hostile but she'd learned that when he was like this it was best she just did what he said.

'We'd just arrived back at the station, sir. I was on my way to give you a briefing,' she said, hoping to appease him. Perhaps she wasn't keeping him in the loop enough. 'And we became aware of a situation at Linley Park. We followed the officers to the scene and—'

'Stone, it may surprise you to know that I keep a radio on my desk and am well aware of the incident at Linley Park and your reasons for attending. But what I didn't hear over the radio, and what reached me via a phone call from Sergeant Wilkins, is that you assaulted a police constable at the scene.'

Oh shit, she'd forgotten about that.

'May I have a chance to explain?'

'Did you grab the man by the vest and raise your fist?' he asked, nostrils flaring.

'Yes, I did, but…'

'There is no but, Stone. You know full well that is unacceptable behaviour.'

'I absolutely do, sir, but I was provoked,' she protested.

He sat back in his chair and listened as she relayed in detail what she had seen and the constable's comment.

He appeared unmoved.

'Is this your first crime scene?'

She shook her head.

'Is this the first crime scene you've attended where something was said in poor taste by either yourself, your team or another person present?'

'No, but—'

'Don't say anything, Stone. I'm no longer confident about your involvement on this case despite Alison's favourable reports.'

'Really?' she asked, surprised.

'She assured me that you were handling it well, up until now. This is behaviour I can't condone regardless of the opinions of anyone else.'

Real fear settled in her stomach. Fear that this bastard would never be caught and that more innocent people would suffer.

'Sir, let me speak to the constable concerned. I'll apologise and smooth—'

'You'll do no such thing, Stone.'

'But if you just let me—'

'You'll keep well away for the time being. As of this minute you are no longer assigned to this case until I say otherwise. So, I suggest you take a couple of days leave to cool down and put some distance—'

'Sir, you can't do—'

'I can and I have, now with all due respect, Inspector, get yourself out of my sight.'

CHAPTER 78

Bryant headed up the stairs to the third floor, which wasn't a trip he made often.

He had no idea what had been said to the boss but her face had been filled with rage as she'd stormed past the squad room door and barked that it was his turn.

He knocked and waited for the instruction to enter. That was normally the guv's job and he was happy for her to do it.

Not that he didn't respect the man sitting behind the desk before him. Over the years DCI Woodward had straddled the position perfectly. He had managed to maintain the respect of his team and the trust of his superiors. It had not always been easy. He knew that but Woody had always found a way to do what was right.

'Inspector Stone is off the case,' he stated.

Until now, Bryant thought.

'May I ask why, sir?'

'Because she's not handling it,' Woody snapped. 'You saw how she acted with that constable. Was that not out of character?'

He nodded. 'Extremely out of character but it was an exceptionally horrific crime scene.'

'Which does not excuse that she would have struck that officer had you not intervened.'

'Sir, I don't think she—'

'You grabbed her arm in mid-air, Bryant, so I beg to differ on that. Luckily, you were there to save her bacon and her job again;

however, she is not out of the woods and I have no choice but to remove her from this case. I have one very pissed off sergeant who already hates CID biting at my heels.'

'What about the officer?' Bryant asked.

'Makes no difference. It's the sergeant making all the noise about how CID think they can treat his constables any way they like.'

'To be honest, sir, I wanted to punch him myself. What he said—'

'Was crude, unfeeling, foul, and repulsive. I have no argument. Believe me when I say that I sit in meetings with suits bartering budgets for public safety and I could quite happily get an Uzi and take them all out. But it's about control and your boss showed none when dealing with that constable, so I can no longer trust her to run this case.'

Bryant thought for a moment before speaking.

'Sir, you're making a mistake,' he said, politely but definitely.

'DS Bryant, do you know how many complaints land on my desk each week because —'

'And do you know how many people don't die because of those complaints?' he asked, sombrely. 'Don't get me wrong, there are many days I question her methods, her directness but I never question her passion or her drive to catch the bad guy.'

'Agreed but this case isn't good for her. She's losing perspective, control. Her emotions are either too close to the surface or being buried too far down that they're fighting to be let out, but either way it's not good for her and it's not good for the case.'

Bryant was not surprised that Woody had voiced the exact same concerns he had earlier that day. The man was astute, even from a distance. And even though some small part agreed with him he also knew that there was no one better to run this case.

'But by the same token no one is as close to these events as she is. If she can't provide insight to catch this bastard before he kills anyone else then the rest of us have no chance.'

Woody shook his head. 'I'm not budging on this one, Bryant. You're it until I find a replacement DI to head the case.'

Bryant groaned inwardly. His day was not getting any better.

'Sir, you know I'll do my best but I repeat that you are making a mistake. I know that you're angry with her and part of you feels she's let you down by losing control, but just think about what she's had to face this week. Almost hitting someone doesn't even come close to being equal with the emotional rollercoaster. I know you're in a difficult position but without her on this case I fear that many more people will lose their lives.'

Woody shook his head. 'Sorry, Bryant, but it's out of my hands.'

CHAPTER 79

Alison entered the club feeling less out of place than she had the night before.

A pair of scissors and a cheese grater had scruffed up her Victoria Beckham jeans and her blouse had been replaced with a V-neck tee shirt. Her hair had been shaken out and hung loosely around her shoulders.

Surprisingly it was a whole different animal this time around. Although the place wasn't heaving with people, there were just a few free tables and the others seemed to be occupied by couples enjoying a quiet drink to a Coldplay track in the background.

Tom looked up from the till, hesitated and then smiled.

'Back again?' he asked.

She nodded as she took a seat. 'Although it's much quieter tonight.'

He looked around. 'Yes, my usual Wednesday night entertainment is otherwise indisposed.'

She frowned and then pretended to put two and two together.

'Aaah, that musician who attacked—'

'Yes,' he interrupted. 'But, please keep your voice down.'

'Sorry,' she said, realising the people at the table behind probably heard.

Damn it. She wasn't here to get herself noticed. She was here to observe Tom.

Unlike police officers she had no experience of gut instinct or that special feeling for the truth. All she did was analyse actions, behaviour. She didn't interview, interrogate or speak to many people directly. She had used all of her knowledge and experience to develop a profile for the killer of Jennifer Townes and she needed to see how closely this man came to fitting it.

'Dry white wine?' he asked.

'Please,' she answered, reaching for her handbag and she was pleased that this time he didn't try to stop her. 'And a bag of chicken crisps.'

He placed the drink and packet on the bar and took her money.

She noted his clean fingernails, remembered the pleasant smell of pine from the night before.

Clean and well groomed.

Check.

He glanced towards the other end of the bar as a couple had just entered, but Tilly miraculously appeared and began to serve them. Alison had read the statements of the bar owner and his staff member numerous times.

She opened the pack of crisps and turned slightly to the side. She took a couple, but one fell from her fingers before it reached her mouth.

'Oops,' she said, watching it fall to the ground.

'So, that guy last night,' he said, leaning forward, resting his forearms on the bar. 'Your boyfriend?'

'Oh no,' she said.

'Seemed like you were having a bit of a tiff over there.'

Observant.

Check.

'He's a colleague. Just a difference of opinion.'

'And what is it that you do, Alison?' he asked.

How did he know her name?

'Your colleague said your name last night before he whisked you away and I never forget the name of a beautiful woman.'

She felt the heat flush into her cheeks.

Charming.

Check.

She ate another crisp and dropped one.

'Teacher,' she lied. 'Maths,' she added. It would have been her second career choice.

'Hey, Tom,' Tilly said, sidling over. 'Stock requisition forms done and—'

'Filed?' he asked.

She smiled. 'Of course. I know how you get.'

'Okay, can you give Freda a call and see if she's feeling better? If not, we need to get her covered.'

Tilly nodded and moved away.

Efficient and organised.

Check.

She ate a crisp and dropped one.

'How about you?' she asked. 'How long have you owned this place?'

'Three years,' he answered proudly.

'Since…' she started to say, 'you were twenty-six,' but realised he hadn't told her his age. 'Since it went into liquidation from the previous owners?'

He nodded, giving no reaction to her slip-up.

She ate a crisp and dropped one.

'Luckily for me they just wanted shot of it. I managed to do some decent deals with suppliers, made use of that business degree and managed to get the place into the black in two years.'

Educated.

Check.

Alison saw her opportunity.

'I suppose having live entertainment has helped?'

He nodded. 'As long as it's the right kind.'

'Like that guy, Curtis something?' she asked dropping a few bits of crisp and then scrunching up the packet.

He took it from her and put it behind the bar. He nodded towards the corner. 'Let's talk over there.'

She stood as he came around to her side of the bar.

'Really sorry to have made a bit of a mess round here,' she said.

He shrugged. 'Let's hope Freda is back from sick leave tomorrow. Whole place needs a good clean.'

She couldn't help feeling a little disappointed with his response as she picked up her glass and followed.

'You a reporter or something?' he asked, frowning.

'Goodness, no. Why'd you ask?' she asked, taking a seat opposite.

'You seem overly interested in Curtis.'

Alison stroked the stem of the wine glass. 'That's not really what I'm interested in,' she said, looking away. 'It's just something to talk about but if you'd rather I left…'

'No, it's fine,' he said, shaking his head. 'It's just like, I know the guy so…'

'Yeah, that must be so weird. Any clues he was capable of something like this?' she asked.

He rubbed at his forehead. 'I've asked myself that a hundred times. I mean… some people thought he was a bit strange. Introverted, intense, but I just thought he was a creative type. He was a good guy who played his set with the same enthusiasm to a roomful or a handful. It was just about the music, I thought.'

'Has it affected business?'

'Not so much as you'd notice. Folks haven't really put together that Jennifer worked here and that Beverly was here the last night too. Obviously the police know but…'

'They been around much?' she asked.

He shook his head. 'They were here the morning after Beverly was attacked. Wanted to know if we'd seen anything but Tilly and I were cashing up out back when Curtis left, so there was nothing else to add.'

Alison swallowed down her rage at DCI Merton. Yeah, sounded like intense questioning for someone who completely fitted her profile.

She took another sip of her drink and moved in her chair. 'Well, thanks for the chat but I must be—'

'So soon?' he asked, with a crooked smile. 'I was hoping we could talk more, maybe grab a bite?…'

'Perhaps another time,' she said, trying to keep her tone even.

She walked away from the table feeling his gaze upon her as she left. Oh, like she was going to leave this well-populated area with a man she suspected of rape and murder.

Again, she'd barely touched her drink and felt able to drive.

She knew as she headed to the car that she was going to have to do something but she didn't know what. Who did she complain to? How were these things done? She didn't want to get anyone into trouble, but this investigation had gone—

A hand on her shoulder startled her. 'Wh-what?…'

Tom turned her to face him. 'Are you sure you wouldn't like to get that bite?' he asked, the interest burning in his eyes.

The saliva had dried in her mouth, her heart hammered against her chest. His gaze was intense and dark.

She shook her head and glanced to his hand still gripping her arm.

'I h-have to go,' she said, pulling away.

He looked as though he wanted to challenge her more, but turned and returned to the bar. For just a second she had seen beyond the friendly, affable bar owner and now she wanted to get as far away from this place as she could.

Her thoughts came to an abrupt stop as something on the ground caught her eye.

She stopped walking and bent down as her heart thudded in her chest.

No way. It couldn't be.

With trembling fingers, she took out her phone and found the contact she was after.

'Alison, what the hell is it now?' asked DCI Merton making no effort to hide his hostility.

'Please, just give me a minute,' she begged. 'I'm at Elite and—'

'Alison, I swear I just misheard you when you said where you were, because if I heard you right I'd be filling out a formal complaint to your superiors right now concerning your attempt to derail an ongoing investigation. Am I being clear?' he hissed.

She couldn't answer even though her mouth had fallen open. Would he really do that?

'Do not call this number again,' he said, ending the call.

Damn, damn, damn. Now what was she supposed to do?

She really needed help and there was only one person she could think of to call.

CHAPTER 80

Bryant headed out on to the rugby field as the rest of the team were finishing warm-ups. The opposing team from Hereford stood to the right and the two team captains stood somewhere in the middle.

He looked to Lenny for his position in the match and was given his answer in a finger sign.

Bryant knew the twenty-six-year-old captain wasn't sure where to stick him in the team any more and sheer obstinacy on his part prevented him from bowing out gracefully and allowing a younger player to take his place.

Back in the day he'd played position of a three-quarter, normally reserved for the fastest players whose aim was to use the ball won by the forwards to motor through and score. The forwards were the heavier guys who set up and formed the base of the attacks by securing possession.

Tonight he was in the back row of the forwards called the flankers.

Damage limitation, Bryant realised and a good decision considering this was a game that would decide if they were to move up the league.

He nodded to his team mates as he began a couple of stretching exercises. There were still a couple of guys on the team from when he'd first started but he could tell their hearts weren't in it so much any more. The bruises and cuts healed slower in your late forties, the aches and pains from a tough match lingered longer, but the guys still hung on having not yet found anything to replace this golden snatch of man time.

And he had his reasons, too. While he was running up and down the field trying to keep up with players half his age he was thinking of nothing but the game. The physical exertion and focus left no room for thoughts of the job, his family, his worries. Everything stayed in the dressing room with his clothes.

He groaned as he saw a player he recognised. A rough kid named Beasley in his late twenties with some kind of point to prove. At six foot three and shoulders across which you could run an A road, he wasn't known for playing nice.

Bryant appraised the red-haired man wondering if he'd been hardened by the shit he'd taken at being one letter away from his doppelganger in the Harry Potter films.

Come get me, dickhead, Bryant thought. Cos I am just in the mood for you.

He took his position and waited for the whistle.

Immediately he could feel the rhythm of the game. There was a tension being passed around with the ball.

Within a few minutes he narrowly escaped a kicking in a maul, got a smack to the back of the head in a rolling maul and a kick to the shins in a ruck.

Oh yeah, a rough game was just what he needed right now, he thought, as Lenny called him forward.

A scrum was being formed following an accidental offside. He took his place in the front row ready to push against the other team to win the ball.

The scrum half fed the ball into the scrum and the hooker turned his foot to get possession. His team had the ball.

As he was released from the scrum an elbow caught him just above the right eye. The pain shot around the whole of his face as the skin split and he felt the coolness of the blood oozing down his cheek.

He wasn't surprised to see Beasley's grinning face as he followed the direction of the elbow.

'What the fuck was?…'

That hadn't been fair play. The damn scrum had finished.

'Get off the field, old man,' said Beasley.

Bryant lunged with his fist raised as the blood began to drip into his eye. 'Say that again, you—'

'Hey, hey, hey,' said Lenny, stepping in front of him.

Beasley's coach took the opportunity to guide him away.

'What the hell, man?' Lenny asked, blocking his view. 'It was a fair—'

'You're joking. He's a thug with a bloody shirt…'

'Calm it, mate. This ain't you. Yeah, he's a shit but that was just rough play. You had a bad day or something?'

'I'm fine,' he snapped, wiping the blood away from his eye with the back of his hand.

'Yeah, well go and be fine in the block. You're playing no more tonight.'

'Jesus, Lenny,' he protested.

Lenny shook his head. 'You're off or I end the game. You ain't right. Now go.'

'Fuck, fuck, fuck,' he spat as he stormed across the field to the changing room. He took off his shirt and used it to wipe the blood from his eye.

'Had a bad day?' he raged, throwing the shirt to the ground. Nah, he'd only spent the week watching the private life and past of his boss and friend being used as a knife to stab her with. He'd watched her bury her emotions to get the job done, to catch the sick bastard who was killing innocent people to prove a point. He'd watched her continue to lead a team and analyse evidence and facts, sifting and sorting clues, while quietly detaching herself in the midst of losing the thing that meant most to her. Privacy. And then he'd had to watch as she'd been removed from the case.

Yeah, it had been a bad fucking day at work. Was there really any other kind? Every single day he was forced to look at and analyse the despicable depths of humanity, see things that he couldn't unsee, images that wedged in his brain and played over and over in his mind's eye, torturing him and sickening him repeatedly, only to return late at night in his dreams.

He kicked his kit bag across the floor with force.

'Fuck it, fuck it, fuck it,' he screamed, as his teeth ground together.

He paced the changing room floor, his hands clenching into fists at his sides. He needed a target. He needed an outlet, somewhere to expel the rage that was surging like molten lava around his veins.

The knowledge.

The thoughts.

The images.

'Nooooo,' he cried out as his right fist hit the wall.

The pain was immediate and welcome but it didn't clear his mind. Somewhere in there, mashed up with everything else he'd witnessed this week was the image of Billie Styles, viciously and brutally assaulted. Left for dead in the woods, subjected to unspeakable horror that would change her life for ever.

But that wasn't the image that tortured him. That wasn't the image that had followed him onto the rugby field. This one was more personal and closer to home and filled him with a rage that burned like a wildfire all the way to his soul.

A thirteen-year-old girl, abandoned by everyone, loved by no one, unprotected, frightened but trying not to be, taken into the woods and raped.

That was the image that would never leave him.

He dropped down to the bench, lowered his head. And cried.

CHAPTER 81

It was almost nine when Kim parked outside the yellow front door.

The rage was still surging around her body, ingrained in her blood, being kick-started by her heart every time it passed through.

'You gonna behave yourself?' she asked Barney as she knocked on the door she knew so well.

He looked up and looked back at the door, which she took for a yes.

Ted Morgan opened the door and smiled, just as he'd been doing since she was six years old and she'd first been sent to him for counselling.

'You're late,' he said.

'I'm sorry about the…'

'I meant, I expected you earlier in the week,' he said, standing aside. She stepped in, Barney followed and Ted closed the door behind them.

'Where are we sitting?' he asked.

'Kitchen,' she answered.

'Aah, I see,' he said.

'See what?' Kim asked, taking a seat at the dining table.

'It's that kind of chat,' he said, filling the kettle. 'It'll be instant tonight,' he said. 'I'm not wasting Colombian Gold on a drink you're probably not going to finish.'

'Ted, have you finally lost it?'

He chuckled. 'Oh, my dear, I'll explain it to you later. First, tell me why you're here,' he said turning towards her.

'You've seen the news?'

'Of course.'

'And you know what the deaths mean?'

'Obviously. The first one was a copycat of you and Mikey, the second was reliving the death of Keith and Erica, which is why I expected you sooner. How are your memory boxes holding up?'

'Intact,' she said, and missed off the word, barely.

'There was a third incident this evening.'

'The girl in the park?'

Kim nodded, unaware it had made the news already.

'There was little detail. Is this one linked to you?'

Kim nodded. 'Foster family number five.'

He turned, frowning. 'The one you've never talked about and the one I always remember.'

She nodded. 'Why do you always remember it?'

He placed the cups on the table as Barney lapped greedily at the plastic water bowl he'd put on the floor.

'When you came to me after foster family five you were different to all the other times. There was a hardness in you that hadn't been there before. Despite everything that had happened to you it was like family five taught you how to hate.'

'Go on,' Kim said.

'Up until that point I'd always had hope that I could help you; that somehow we'd make a breakthrough and I could help you heal.'

Kim felt pieces of her anger break away in the company of this man whose only aim had been to try and help her.

'But when you came to see me after that family, I felt that you had stepped beyond my reach. That I couldn't get to you any more.'

She guessed his assessment was probably right.

'I almost hit someone at the crime scene,' she admitted. 'A constable.'

'But you didn't, so surely that?…'

'Only because Bryant stopped me. I would have hit him, Ted.'

'I'm tempted to ask what the constable did but it's not his actions that matter, is it?'

She shook her head. 'Well, it puts Bryant's theory to bed,' she said.

'Which is?'

'That I'm repressing my feelings about it all and acting like it's happening to someone else.'

'Hmm… not necessarily. Has there ever been a time when you've used that technique as a coping mechanism? Pretended that something that's happening to you is actually happening to someone else?'

She swallowed and nodded.

'So, if it got you through before there's no reason why you wouldn't use that technique again. Disassociation is the correct term and people often use it in childhood in cases of sexual—'

'Move on, Ted.'

'But there's no easy answer for this one, I'm afraid. If you allow your emotions out, your memory boxes will collapse and engulf you. We're not talking one or even two traumatic memories to deal with; we're talking all of them at the same time because you can't pick and choose. You can't open one memory box and ignore the others. Not when you're being faced with recreations of the incidents themselves, because it's kind of in your face.

'So, the only way for you to behave is to stifle your emotions, block the memories and swallow them down.'

'So, that's okay?' she asked, feeling vindicated.

'Not really,' he said, sipping his drink.

'Oh,' she said, reaching down to stroke Barney's head.

'Because you're compounding hurt on top of hurt on top of anger. Imagine a cupboard door full of clothes and yet you just keep buying new ones. You open the cupboard door and just throw the garment in without looking and then slam the door closed. Eventually, what's going to happen?'

'I buy a bigger cupboard.'

'Ha, funny. Now answer the question.'

'Eventually I'm going to open the cupboard door to throw in a garment and the whole lot is going to collapse on top of me.'

'Exactly that.'

'So, you're saying that I'm only delaying the feelings, that they're going to get me eventually?'

'Every cupboard has its limits, Kim.'

She took a deep breath. 'Woody's taken me off the case.'

Ted didn't seem surprised. 'Because of the constable?'

She nodded.

He sipped his drink.

'You have some kind of madman recreating every traumatic point in your life. They are doing this to make you suffer, to make you hurt. They are going to a great deal of trouble to cause you pain from which, given that level of hate, the only possible end game can be death. Your death. It's the only final outcome that makes sense.

'And now I'll explain the significance of the room. You choose where we sit when you come here. If you want to be alone to reflect or you want me to sit close by silently, you head out into the garden. If you want an in-depth conversation with an equal amount of give and take, where you're happy to accept my thoughts and opinions, you choose the living room. If, however, you just want me to agree with whatever you've got to say, you choose the kitchen.'

'Really?'

He nodded. 'That's why you got instant coffee. Because I very rarely agree with you. And, I'm afraid this time is no exception. Given the circumstances, your emotional state and your actions, not to mention your physical safety, I think Woody was absolutely right to take you off the case.'

Kim felt the pieces of anger reattach themselves to the whole that lay heavy at the base of her stomach.

And whether or not she was acting true to form, she got up and stormed from the house.

CHAPTER 82

Alison saw the taxi pull on to the car park and breathed a sigh of relief.

She got out of the car. 'Stacey, thank you for—'

'What the hell is going on, Alison?' she asked, looking around her. 'Jesus, are you drunk?'

Alison shook her head.

'Then why are you parked diagonally taking up three spaces? And if it's a lift home you want, I'm the only one who doesn't—'

'I don't need a lift,' she said. 'And I don't need a breathalyser. What I need is a police officer I can trust.'

Stacey groaned and indicated to the taxi driver to go.

'I swear, my partner wants your guts for garters. Popcorn, Baileys, Melissa McCarthy film and actually, thinking about it, I could bloody well kill you. Now what the?…'

'Stacey, I'm sorry,' Alison said, genuinely. Sometimes she did forget that people she worked with had lives outside the job. 'Sit in the car and I'll explain.'

Stacey narrowed her eyes but did as she'd been asked.

Alison got in, took a deep breath and told her the whole story.

She watched as Stacey's expression and posture went from disinterested to curious to shocked to angry to disbelief.

Alison came to a stop after revealing her conversation earlier with Tom.

'And you think he did it?' Stacey asked.

'I'd bet my next meal on him before Curtis,' she answered.
'So why call me?'

'Because it's here,' Alison said. 'Beverly's missing earring, the pink flamingo, it's here.'

Stacey looked around and then looked her way. 'It's underneath us, isn't it? You're parked over it?'

Alison nodded. 'I didn't want it to get even more contaminated. The killer's DNA could be on it.'

'Novel idea for preserving the evidence, Alison, but if Beverly was attacked over a week ago that earring could have hundreds of people's DNA on it,' she said.

'So, it's useless?' Alison asked.

'I'm not saying that. I'm saying that from an evidential point of view it's problematic but still a bloody good find,' Stacey said, taking an evidence bag from her pocket.

'Shall I back up so you can?…'

'No, no, no,' Stacey said, quickly. 'We don't want to risk anything else happening to it. I'll crawl under and retrieve it.'

Alison got out of the car and suddenly felt bad as the detective dropped to her knees.

She had pulled this woman away from her partner during some much-needed downtime. She had burdened her with the whole story and now the constable was scrabbling underneath her car for evidence on a case that she had nothing to do with.

Alison briefly wondered how many police forces could be pissed off with her at any one time.

And all because she believed in her profile.

'Okay, got it,' Stacey said, crawling away from the car and dusting herself down.

'Thanks, so much, Stacey. I'm so sorry to have called you out. It's my problem not yours, so if you hand it over I'll just have a think and work out what I'm gonna do with it.'

Stacey rolled her eyes. 'Unfortunately, Alison, I can't unsee or un-hear everything I've learned, so whether we like it or not I'm involved; so the more pertinent question is, what are WE gonna do with it?'

CHAPTER 83

It was almost eleven when Kim's key slid into the lock of her front door.

She'd driven straight from Ted's to the Clent Hills just as dusk had fallen. Normally, she loved catching that period between sunset and night and used it to walk the events of the day out of her system.

She remembered once when Bryant had tried to explain the difference between civil, nautical and astronomical dusk. Her interest had waned after ten seconds. For her it was when she liked to walk the dog.

Except tonight the negative feelings had not made it through the soles of her boots and had remained firmly in her body.

She refreshed Barney's water bowl and filled the percolator for herself. A pot of coffee at this time of night was not conducive to a restful night's sleep but it wasn't like she'd got work in the morning.

She paused and looked down at the dog slurping greedily and splashing droplets onto the stone floor.

'Yeah, you're right, boy, that was pathetic.'

She'd never been one to succumb to self-pity, she mused, as she sat on the sofa.

'But, just this once, eh?' she said, as the dog materialised beside her and nudged her hand to the top of his head.

She smiled as he leaned into her side and slid so that his back was against her hip and his head resting on her thigh.

He'd trained her very well, she realised, as her hand stroked the top of his head and down his back.

It was hard not to feel the effects of the day wash over her now that she was sitting still.

It felt like days had passed since she'd stormed out of the post-mortem, unable to bear the sight of the charred, blackened bodies and trying desperately not to let the vision overlay the picture of her foster parents, smiling and joking as they had been the last time she'd seen them. She squeezed her eyes shut tightly as though it would block the snapshot from entering her mind.

She kept her eyes closed and rested her head back against the sofa as she recalled the kindness in the eyes of the man who had written about her life. The anger towards him had dissipated when she had understood his motivation for writing the book and exposing the truth.

Harder to bear had been Bryant questioning her ability to run the case.

Suddenly Barney shifted beside her and rubbed his chin against her leg.

'Yeah, okay, he didn't exactly say that,' she admitted. But that's what it had felt like even though she knew his concerns were only for her well-being.

And then Alison's assessment of her mental state outside the police station. Which she had disagreed with vehemently right before assaulting a fellow officer at a crime scene. Go me, she thought, shaking her head.

And yet she struggled not to feel justified in her actions on that score even though it had prompted her removal from the case.

But just seeing that girl, lying there, sexually assaulted, violated in the worst possible way, had brought back feelings she'd spent her whole life fighting away: helplessness, fear, loathing, disgust, rage.

She felt her hand tense on Barney's head as emotions began to engulf her.

'Oh no, oh no, oh no,' she said, moving the dog aside and standing. She headed over to the coffee machine and poured a tall mug of Colombian Gold.

She would never allow those emotions to torment her again. She wasn't thirteen any more. But just for a few minutes…

And the final insult had come from Ted; the man who knew more about her than anyone and still thought Woody had been right to take her off the case. She could have understood the others being unable to see the truth but not Ted. She'd felt sure he'd understand.

But none of them could comprehend that the memories had to stay in their boxes. She couldn't take them out, examine them and then blow the cobwebs away into the wind. Everyone around her insisted that the emotions that were attached to the memories were being pushed down, somewhere deep inside, where they would ferment, bubble and explode, but they were wrong.

It was like a magic trick, an illusion, maybe sleight of hand. Look over there while I do this over here. She could just about manage to disassociate herself from the events unfolding before her eyes as long as she could distract her mind with solving the case, sifting the clues, following leads and searching for evidence.

What Woody, Bryant, Alison and even Ted seemed unable to understand was that it was the focus of catching the bastard that was keeping the demons away.

CHAPTER 84

Bryant took a deep breath as he mounted the stairs to the squad room. How the hell was he supposed to explain this to the team? How was he supposed to even begin to move this investigation forward without the guv? His mind didn't work in the same way hers did.

He viewed her brain like a cyborg with tentacles, reaching out in all directions and bringing back minute pieces of data, inputting them and coming up with answers. There were times he kept quiet because he couldn't actually keep up with her. So, how was he supposed to lead this investigation never mind manage a team?

'Hey, Bryant, was it you?' Sergeant Devlin asked with a smirk as they passed on the stairs.

'What?' he asked.

'Err… nothing,' Devlin said, without stopping, although his shoulder movement told Bryant he was still chuckling.

What the hell was all that about? Whatever it was he wasn't responsible. He'd only just got here, but thinking about it, Jack on the desk had given him a knowing smile when he'd entered the building. He reached the top of the stairs and gave himself the once-over. No, his shirt was definitely tucked into his trousers, he wasn't wearing odd shoes and there was no sign on his back.

The cut from the night before was obscured by his eyebrow and these folks were used to his occasional war wounds from the pitch. They were becoming more frequent with time.

'Idiots,' he whispered to himself as he wandered through the general office to the squad room.

A few chuckles followed him and then he saw why.

The door to the squad room was closed and hazard tape had been pulled across in the shape of an X.

'What the?…' he said, reading the sign.

No Entry Do Not Open

Great, just what he needed. Some idiot playing practical jokes was not going to start this day well.

'Who did this?' he asked, as everyone looked away and returned to their business.

He shook his head and ripped at the hazard tape.

'Can't read, Bryant?' said a deep voice from behind.

He turned to find Woody frowning at him.

'Sir, some dickhead's been putting stupid signs on—'

'I'm the dickhead that put the sign on the door, Bryant, and with very good reason.'

Great, he'd just called the boss a dickhead.

'Sir?'

'Fleas, Sergeant. The office appears to be infested. Went in last night for a copy statement and got bit to death around the ankles.'

Bryant was confused. They'd all been in there yesterday with no issue.

'But?…'

'You can't work in there until the fumigators have been out.'

'So where the hell?…'

'You're a big boy, Bryant. You're in charge for now, so providing you follow procedure and maintain efficiency, where you choose to run the investigation is your concern not mine,' he said, before turning away.

Bryant hid his smile. He knew he wasn't the fastest car in the race but he always managed to get there in the end.

CHAPTER 85

Kim tipped the fourth cup of coffee down the sink and switched off the pot. Each sip was now sending a jolt of electricity through her veins and wiring her emotions.

Jesus, she was angry at so many things, and even offering herself balanced rational answers was not helping.

She was pissed at Woody for taking her off the case but could understand his position. She was mad at Bryant for taking over her role, but unsure what else she expected him to do. She was raging at Ted for not agreeing with her but accepted she went to him for an honest point of view.

And yet the one thing she couldn't resolve in her head was that not one member of her team had called or texted to see if she was okay.

Obviously there had been the twenty text messages from Bryant the night before, but they didn't count, and what about the rest of the team this morning? They'd arrived at work to be told she was off the case yet not one message.

She hopped off the bar stool and wandered towards the door that led into the garage, for the third time. Barney was right beside her, looking up questioningly.

'Yeah, I know, boy,' she said. 'I'm doing my own head in too.'

Normally, with any spare time she was straight into the garage, iPod on full, being soothed by Brahms or Beethoven as she worked on her current restoration project, but not today. This wasn't spare time. Today she'd been displaced. She wasn't supposed to be on a day off. Her brain was in work mode and she couldn't switch it off.

She sighed and took out her phone as Barney headed back to the sofa.

No calls, no messages, no consideration for—

Her self-pitying thoughts were disturbed by a banging on the front door.

Oh, go on, she thought, someone just try and sell me double glazing today. I dare you.

She threw open the door to find a grinning Bryant before her.

'What the?…'

'Yeah, we're commandeering your home as our temporary headquarters,' he said. 'Now get out the way, this stuff is heavy,' he said, barging past with cases of equipment.

'Hey, boss,' Stacey said, entering her home.

'We have fleas,' Penn said, crossing the threshold.

'You have?…'

'Excuse me,' said Alison, bringing in another case.

'You as well?' she asked, as her living room became over-crowded.

'I'm attached to the team, so, wherever they go, I go,' she said, edging cautiously around the dog.

'Okay, so how are we gonna do this?' Bryant asked, standing with the rest of her team in the middle of the room.

For some inexplicable reason the emotion gathered in her throat.

She pushed it away.

'Hey, don't go getting comfortable. Not, until you've told me more about these fleas.'

CHAPTER 86

By 9 a.m. Bryant had found the extra leaves and opened up the dining table that had never been used. Who knew it expanded like that? She'd noticed the cut above his eye and guessed he'd been on the rugby field the night before but he didn't much like being reminded that he wasn't as fit as he used to be.

'So, Woody shut down the office?' she asked, curiously.

Bryant nodded. 'Yep, and told me to find somewhere to camp out for the day.'

Kim couldn't help the smile that pulled at her lips. She understood the pressure her boss was under because of her performance at the crime scene of Billie Styles. He'd reacted appropriately for the sake of appearance but ultimately had found a way to reunite her with her team. Unofficially.

Penn and Stacey were taking the lion's share of the table with their computer equipment, leaving a small space for Bryant at the end.

Alison had perched on a bar stool at the breakfast bar with her laptop open before her.

She'd been amused to see Penn unpacking the Tupperware box and Betty the plant which now sat in the middle of the table.

'I snuck back in,' he said, catching her gaze. 'Couldn't leave her behind.'

Kim didn't feel that Penn had been in any real danger from fleas.

There was just one more thing before they got started.

'You okay up there, Alison?' she asked.

'He keeps looking at me,' she answered without turning.

And she was right. Barney had quickly dispensed with the attentions of Bryant, Penn and Stacey and was now focussing all his attention on Alison.

'Don't like dogs?' Kim asked.

'Scared of them,' she said, staring straight ahead.

Okay, this needed resolving, Kim realised. Barney was not being shut out for anyone.

She made her way to the other side of the breakfast bar and cut a carrot in half.

'He's never bitten a soul in his life but I know that doesn't help. He must be more interested in you because he can sense your fear. So, without looking at him, lower your hand and allow him to take the carrot.'

Her face filled with panic.

'I swear, he won't hurt you,' Kim said. 'Give him the carrot and he'll get bored and leave you alone. Trust me.'

Alison took the carrot and held it to the side. She dropped it before he had chance to take it but the sudden crunching confirmed he was now otherwise distracted and would leave her alone.

'Okay, guys, if it's okay with Bryant, I suggest we do a round robin of where we're at with—'

'He's back,' Alison whispered across the breakfast bar.

Kim peered over the breakfast bar to see Barney staring up intently. It was most unusual, unless…

'Alison, do you have food in that briefcase?'

'Ha, I'd think so,' Stacey said.

Alison nodded and opened the case.

Kim smiled. 'Are you emotionally attached to that apple? It's his favourite thing in the world. That's why he won't leave you alone.'

Alison shook her head and took the apple from the briefcase. This time she lowered it and gave a little squeal as his nose touched her hand.

Barney took his booty to the other end of the living room.

'Okay, so,' Kim repeated, now she had everyone's full attention, 'if Bryant agrees…'

'Let's just say I agree with everything ahead of time, okay?'

'Right, Penn, can you try tracking down Duggar and also find out a bit more about the drug Baclofen, as it was found in the systems of all four dead victims. It's a lead worth pursuing, but Duggar is the priority. Having his name attached to both Amy and Mark and also Rubik is more than coincidental.'

He made a note and lifted his head. 'Boss, just want to follow up on something from Jenks yesterday. He mentioned Amy and Mark were getting help from an outreach worker of some kind. Just wanna see if I can nail anything down.'

She considered. 'Okay but not too long. You've got the main charities like Crisis and Shelter…'

'The Big Issue Foundation,' Stacey added.

'Centrepoint,' Bryant piped up.

'And the Salvation Army,' she said. 'You've got a lot of volunteers there that don't necessarily record or remember everyone they offered a blanket.'

'Got it.'

'Stacey I want you focussing on identifying Rubik. He's part of this somehow and we need to know more.'

'Boss, there's something else,' Stacey said. 'Went to the Phelps' home last night as Mitch was finishing up. This son of theirs, Joel, it doesn't look like Dad was the real father. He's supposed to be away travelling, but I'm not so sure after something I read in Mrs Phelps's diary. Now I've got his real name I'd like to try and track him down. He needs to know about his parents.'

'If Bryant ag—'

'He does,' Bryant said.

'Okay, Stace, you just bagged yourself another job.'

Stacey seemed happy with that fact.

Kim glanced to the breakfast bar. 'And Alison you just keep on doing whatever it is you're doing.'

'And I know Bryant has updated you on the incident last night,' she said, grateful that she didn't have to.

'Bryant and I will be keeping abreast of that one,' she said, turning towards her colleague. 'As long as the Acting Detective Inspector agrees.'

CHAPTER 87

'So, how exactly are we gonna work this?' Bryant asked, as they got in the car.

'I'm riding alongside you in a purely advisory capacity, Bryant, and the rest we'll figure out as we go.'

'Does that mean I get to tell you to shut up when I—'

'You could always try it,' she said.

'Hmmm… you're mauling me now, aren't you?'

'A little bit,' she admitted.

'So, we off to Winson Green seeing as everything keeps leading back there?' he asked.

'You're in charge, but if it was me, I'd probably want to head to the hospital first and see how Billie Styles is doing.'

'Guv, I gotta say that deference does not become you, so please cut it out,' he said, pulling off the car park. 'In fact, no, that's an order,' he said, smirking.

She glanced out of the window at the pedestrians already weary from the heat and it wasn't even ten. The promised night-time storms had not arrived and the clammy heat was continuing to build.

'You know, extreme weather can drive people to do some real crazy things,' Bryant observed.

'Which you should bear in mind when you keep giving me instructions,' she said.

'Oh yeah, meant to ask. You lose your phone last night?'

'Didn't want to talk,' she said, honestly.

'Well, if you'd replied to just one of my twenty messages I'd have—'

'I'd have thought my lack of response to the first ten might have given you a clue.' She turned towards him. 'So, what did you say to Woody about me being taken off the case?'

He shrugged. 'Told him I supported his decision and I was looking forward to a bloody rest.'

She smiled. 'And how's that working out for you?'

'Damn fleas,' he said.

*

'Are you sure you should be doing this?' Bryant asked, as they headed towards the ward.

'I'm not here to question her, Bryant, I'm here to see how she is, which is something I would have done if my home hadn't been commandeered,' she said, walking ahead and entering the ward.

She approached the desk but waited for Bryant to show his ID.

'A young girl… never mind,' Kim said, as she saw the WPC from the night before step out into the hallway.

Kim walked towards her. The woman had shed her stab vest but was still wearing her black trousers and tee shirt from the previous night.

'Not been home?' Kim asked.

She shook her head. 'No, Marm. Got some kip while she was in surgery.'

'Name?'

'Billie Styles… we already confirmed…'

'I meant yours,' Kim clarified.

She smiled wearily. 'Sorry, I'm Annie.'

'You wanna go take a break while?…'

'No, thank you, Marm. I want to be here when she wakes up. I'm hoping she knows my voice and I want to be able to try and get any info from her. Rape kit was pretty pointless given the mess.'

Kim nodded her understanding as she glanced into the room.

The girl was dressed in a hospital gown that was showing bare shoulder and a purple bruise. Her straw blonde hair had been pushed back from a face drained of colour.

'How old?' Kim asked.

'Twenty-one,' Annie replied, rubbing at her tired eyes. 'I've been trying all night to understand what kind of person would do this to another human being.'

'A monster,' Kim said, dragging her eyes away. 'Possessions?' she asked.

'Bagged, tagged and with Forensics,' she answered.

'Thank you,' Kim said. This WPC had had a very long night and still managed to follow procedure.

'Marm, may I ask if you really did punch Twonk?'

Kim shook her head. 'But almost,' she said, glancing at Bryant. 'His name is Twonk?'

Annie shook her head. 'It's a nickname. He's a bit of an idiot who tries too hard to fit in.'

If that was the nickname he'd earned it would be a hard one to shift.

'Okay, Annie. Well, thanks for everything and try to get some—'

'Just one thing, Marm,' she said, scratching her head. 'In the girl's belongings there was her driving licence in a wallet in the back pocket of her jeans with about forty pounds in cash, but in the front pocket of her jeans there was something else.'

'What?' Kim asked, trying to keep her face neutral.

'A five pound note. A ripped-up five pound note. Not sure if it means anything.'

Kim nodded her thanks.

Oh yes, it definitely meant something.

CHAPTER 88

Alison stretched her back at the breakfast bar and read over the notes she'd made about John Duggar, preparing to start work on his profile, but try as she might to concentrate she just couldn't rid herself of the feeling she'd seen or heard something the previous night that had jarred somewhere in her brain. The more she tried to capture it the more elusive it became.

'What are you frowning about?' Stacey asked. 'On second thoughts, I don't wanna know. I'm still in the doghouse with Devon because of you. Didn't help that I had to leave early this morning to get that earring over to Mitch.'

'Stacey, I've said…'

'Jeez, woman, loosen up,' Stacey said, winking at her. 'I'm only joking and, if it helps, my mum always tells me to retrace my steps,' Stacey advised, turning back to her computer.

Alison wasn't sure what use that advice was to her. It wasn't as though she'd lost something.

But actually she had, she realised, thinking again about Stacey's advice.

She clicked on the folder holding scanned copies of the statements.

She read through Curtis's vague recollection of finishing his set and getting his stuff together on the night Beverly had been attacked. He'd smoked a few joints and couldn't remember what he'd done next. Nope that wasn't it.

She read through Tom's account of the evening. He'd served Beverly with two drinks, gin and tonic. She'd been no trouble and had sat alone sometimes, closing her eyes to the music. He hadn't seen her leave but she'd still been there while Curtis was packing up and he had gone to cash up with Tilly. Exactly as he had told her the night before. There was nothing different to what she already knew.

She moved on to Tilly's statement who reiterated Tom's account that she'd seen no interaction between Curtis and Beverly. Curtis was no different to usual. He took no alcohol, just a pint of lime and lemon to sip on while he played.

She also hadn't seen either Beverly or Curtis leave as she and Tom had gone to start a deep clean on the restrooms.

That was it.

That's what had stuck in her mind. Tom said cashing up and Tilly said cleaning. They had said they'd been together but where: office or toilets? It couldn't be both.

So, effectively they had alibied each other. The question now paramount in her mind was: for whose benefit had it been?

CHAPTER 89

It wasn't until they'd reached the hospital reception that Bryant spoke.

'I want to ask the significance of the ripped-up money but I don't want to lose my head in the process.'

'It's what he gave… the girls to keep quiet,' she said.

'The girls?'

'Yes, the girls,' she said with finality and remembered what Ted had said.

Disassociation

Disassociation

Disassociation

'So, we gonna head off to the prison now, or what?' he asked, as a text message dinged to her phone.

'Apparently not,' she said, turning around. 'Keats wants to see us.'

'And he obviously doesn't know you're "officially" off the case,' Bryant said, glancing at her phone. 'Is it a good idea for you to come with me to see him when?…'

'I absolutely promise not to get in your way of running this investigation,' she said. 'And I'll make it clear to Keats that you're in charge.'

'Well, if I'm in charge I say that we really need to get over to the prison. Need to know who got that bloody book and shake them all up. That's where we're going to find our answers.'

'Agreed,' she said, taking the steps down to the morgue. 'But, we're right here.'

He followed her through the double doors mumbling something about empty gestures.

'Wow, it's an ambush,' she said, seeing Keats, Mitch and Doctor A in the same room.

'We are almost completed,' said Doctor A. 'Our man is untangled from the wreckage but I have no more detail than I have told you.'

Kim held up her hand. 'I must tell you that I am here in no professional capacity whatsoever, so please direct your comments to my colleague,' she said, jumping up onto the stainless steel work surface.

Doctor A turned to Bryant. 'As I told your boss the other—'

'Got it, Doctor A, thanks,' he said.

'So, Bryant,' Keats said, stepping in front of her, 'how do you keep your sanity on a daily basis?'

'Oi, I've still got ears,' she said.

'I shall return to my cell along the hall to sort the debris,' Doctor A said.

'Debris?' Kim asked.

'Bits and pieces I think you say. Not man nor machine. I shall bring them tomorrow for your puzzlement.'

'Thanks, Doctor A,' Kim called after her.

The other two scientists just watched her leave.

'God save us from brilliant women who are so much more intelligent than we are,' said Keats once she'd gone.

'We forgive you,' Kim said.

'You're not even here,' he said, moving to the other side of the room. 'I'm not sure why you're not here but I'm sure the accusation is correct, and you're totally guilty of the crime.'

'Jeez, Keats, thanks…'

'So, Bryant, the reason I called you down here. The toxicology results are back on the first tissue samples we retrieved for our man in the car.'

'And?' Bryant asked.

'Just like the other four victims, he too had been pumped full of Baclofen.'

'I'll just add this name to my list, then,' Stacey said, writing down the name 'Billie Styles'.

Right now, she was trying to track down Joel Greene abroad, and searching missing persons to identify the man in the cube. So far, she'd gone back eighteen months and there was no match.

'Anyone want it?' Stacey asked. 'Penn?'

'Sorry, boss said priority was in finding Duggar, so you're on your own,' he said.

'Alison?'

'No,' she said, simply.

'You still working on Duggar and Nina Croft?' Stacey asked.

'Yes, and I think—'

'You're wasting your time on Nina Croft,' Stacey said. 'It's not her.'

Alison turned towards her. 'And what makes you so sure?'

'Instinct,' Stacey answered. 'We've all got it. It's hard to define but every copper relies on it.'

'And it's never wrong?'

'Well, sometimes, I mean…'

'So, this woman is pretty mean, manipulative, conniving, clever, resourceful and hates your boss with a passion. She fits the profile perfectly but we ignore her because it doesn't feel right?'

'Something like that.'

'Okay, got it. Except what if she also volunteers her legal services at Stourbridge Community Centre. What do you say to that?'

'Oh shit,' Stacey said, reaching for the phone.

CHAPTER 91

'Bryant, I know you want to get over to the prison, but after what Stacey just told us we need to see Nina Croft first. I get that everyone has their doubts about her involvement, as do I, but we can't ignore that she may well have had contact with our first two victims,' she said.

'What about the Phelpses? There's no connection to them or to Rubik.'

'That we know of yet. Leave Alison on it and who knows what she'll find.'

Bryant glanced her way as he headed towards Cradley Heath.

'She's growing on you, isn't she, Alison?' Bryant asked.

'Like some kind of fungus, you mean?'

'You're warming to her. I can tell.'

'Whatever, Bryant,' she said, turning away.

She wasn't sure warming was the correct word but she definitely admired the woman's tenacity. Against all of their better judgement, Alison had felt there was something not quite right and she had found a link.

'And what are your thoughts about Rubik?'

'I'm thinking we need to find Duggar as soon as possible. His paws seem to be on everything.'

'I know we ruled him out initially but right now he's looking good for it.'

'And could you sound any more like an American cop show?' she asked as he parked behind the carpet shop.

'Watched *Law & Order* last night,' he said, smiling.

'Well, don't do it again,' she said as they exited the car and headed along the high street.

'Reckon she'll offer us coffee this time?' Kim asked as they mounted the stairs to Nina Croft's office.

'Unlikely,' Bryant said, reaching her at the office door.

Kim held up her hand to knock and then decided against it. This woman needed no time to prepare.

'Good morning, Mrs Croft, we—'

Kim stopped speaking as her gaze rested on the figure of Nina Croft behind her desk.

And the person who was sitting on the other side.

CHAPTER 92

'This kid is a real contradiction,' Stacey said out loud.

No one answered but she continued anyway. The silence was driving her mad.

She'd been looking into Billie Styles for the last half an hour and felt she knew her very well. She was present on every social media platform and her accounts were open and accessible.

'It's like she used each platform differently. She took to Twitter to voice her political beliefs, Instagram to post photos of meals and kittens and Facebook to socially interact with friends.'

'Not unusual,' Alison said, turning. 'Social media isn't a reliable mirror or interpretation as it doesn't catch everything about us. It's only a snapshot of how we perceive ourselves.'

'Say what?' Stacey asked.

Penn had removed one headphone, which was now resting on the back of his head.

'Give me three words to describe yourself,' Alison asked her.

'Hard-working, passionate…'

'Not work, your personality.'

'Fun, geeky, caring.'

Alison nodded. 'I'd agree with that,' she said, pressing keys on her phone.

Stacey's phone dinged. She looked at Alison. 'You want to be friends on Facebook?'

'To demonstrate something.'

Stacey accepted and Alison grew quiet. As she read a brief smile touched her lips.

'What?' Stacey asked.

'One minute.'

Stacey glanced at Penn who was now watching with interest.

'Right, so over the last week you've shared some Aunty Acid jokes, very funny. You've commented on posts about data protection and GDPR, explaining how it works and you've shared a public appeal for a missing dog.'

'Yeah,' she said. She knew what she'd posted on Facebook.

'Funny, geeky and caring. All three of your perceptions are covered and the more I scroll I find more of the same.'

'And?'

'You're also moody sometimes. You sulk. Occasionally you're envious and often you're insecure about your weight.'

Stacey could feel the heat flooding into her face.

'All perfectly normal feelings,' Alison said. 'But what I'm trying to say is that we only show on social media what we want people to see. Billie obviously felt comfortable showing different parts of herself but not all in the same place.'

'But it's so clearly defined,' Stacey said, glad the focus of the conversation was off her. 'Just look here. Just a few weeks ago on the very same day she's causing a Twitter storm voicing her thoughts on abortion she's posting photos of her pasta meal at the Park Lane Tavern.'

'Where?' Penn asked, snapping to attention.

'Park Lane Tavern, Colley Gate. Why?'

'Because that's where John Duggar used to work.'

CHAPTER 93

'Fuck's sake, King,' Symes spat. 'You gotta do better than that,' he said, rubbing his jaw. The punch to the mouth had stung but gone no way to what he was really after.

'Preece, you do it,' he instructed. He'd asked King to oblige thinking his previous gang leader background would have meant he could throw a decent punch, but maybe the bookworm had been the better choice after all.

Preece stepped forward and rubbed his knuckles.

'Here,' he said. 'This fucker's a bit loose and you know what or who to think of when you're doing it.'

Symes saw the rage fill his eyes and braced himself for impact.

The fist hit him exactly where he'd indicated with a force he'd not been expecting. Just give folks the right motivation, he thought, as the taste of blood filled his mouth. His acknowledgment of the pain came secondary.

He nodded approvingly as he held on to his jaw. 'More fucking like it.'

He strode out of the cell and called out. 'Gennard…'

'What the?…' Gennard called, seeing the trail of blood oozing from his mouth. 'What the bloody hell happened?' he asked, opening the gate. His glance towards King and Preece was met with shrugs.

'Fell over,' he said. 'Clumsy bastard.'

He opened his mouth wide for the guard to take a look.

'Jesus Christ.'

Symes's tongue had already told him part of the tooth had been knocked out but not all of it. Perfect.

Symes watched the guard perform a rapid risk assessment. 'Come on, Symes. That needs sorting.'

Symes held his jaw dramatically and groaned as he followed the guard to the health centre. Two inmates were sitting outside the dentist suite. The door opened as they approached.

'Emergency,' Gennard called out as the next in line had begun to stand.

'Oh my goodness,' exclaimed the young, male dentist ushering him inside.

'Sit down, sit down,' he instructed, as Gennard closed the door behind him. He knew the officer was just praying the tooth could be fixed, preventing an outside trip. Generated a lot of paperwork. Which was fine. Today.

Symes opened his mouth. The dentist with the name badge 'Dennis' placed some gauze into his mouth while he took a seat and pumped them both into position. He switched on the overhead light, removed the gauze and added the suction tube.

Symes groaned for effect.

'Open wide,' he instructed.

Symes obliged and tried to stop himself from smiling. The plan was going perfectly. Get punched on Marcia's day off. Having worked at the prison for over ten years Marcia was experienced and knew all the tricks in the book. Despite being five foot nothing in socks, in her forties and a few stone overweight, Marcia was the subject of many an inmate fantasy. No one messed with Marcia.

But the 'fill-ins' as they called Marcia's relief staff were nowhere near as canny and made mistakes. The main one being forgetting who they were dealing with and not seeing the bigger picture.

'Mandibular right first molar requires extraction,' Dennis said to Gennard.

Why was he talking to the guard? It wasn't his fucking mouth.

Gennard nodded.

Dennis turned away and reached for a syringe. 'I'm going to inject local anaesthetic to numb the pain. You'll feel a sting.'

Symes said nothing and had no reaction as Dennis injected his gum in three different places. Immediately he felt the numbing effect.

Gennard shuffled from one foot to the other as Dennis lined up the tools he needed for the job. Now they were getting somewhere.

Dennis stood up, moved to his left side in front of Gennard and towered over him, opening his mouth and placing the pliers ready to pull. He reached out his right hand and felt around the instrument tray. His hand retracted slowly and went into his pocket.

He felt the pressure from the pull of the tooth. Perfect.

He bolted upright, screaming with pain, sending the dentist and all his instruments crashing to the ground.

Gennard took a second to recover and instantly bent down to assist the dentist. It was all the time he needed to put his booty down inside his jeans.

'What the hell was that?'

'Fucking butcher,' he cried out, cradling his jaw. 'He's no fucking dentist. You're not touching me again,' he said, swinging his legs off the seat.

'Don't be ridiculous, Symes. Get back in the chair and let him finish…'

'He touches me again I'll sue; you hear me?' Symes said. 'I'll wait until Marcia's back tomorrow. My fucking choice.'

Symes headed for the door while the dentist leaned down to start collecting his tools.

Gennard hesitated for a moment, opened the door and then shook his head. 'Okay, have it your own way but don't go changing your mind when the anaesthetic wears off, cos that tooth is gonna hurt like hell.'

Symes stepped through the open door.

It was fine. He'd got what he'd come for.

CHAPTER 94

'What the hell was Harry Jenks doing here?' Kim asked, once he had beaten a hasty retreat from the office.

'I don't have to discuss that with you,' Nina said, loftily.

'So, it was business?' Kim pushed, sitting down.

'None of your business,' she retorted.

'Although, I could understand if it was pleasure; Nina, if I recall you like them slimy and—'

'What do you want, Inspector Stone?' Nina asked, covering over a piece of paper.

'Ah, so it was business?' Kim said. 'Seeking your advice on sexual harassment, I shouldn't wonder. Has someone had the courage to report him, finally?'

Nina coloured, telling Kim she was close enough to the mark.

'As I said, it's none of your business. Now you didn't come here to talk to me about Harry Jenks so…'

'Actually, we did in a way, Nina. How do you know the man?'

'We've worked together in the past.'

'Distant or near?' she asked.

'Near, I suppose.'

'Your volunteer work at Stourbridge Community Centre?'

Nina nodded.

Boy, this woman knew how to keep her cards close to her chest.

'And how did that come about?'

'Sorry but I don't see what this has to do with you.'

'You don't strike me as the charitable type,' Kim said, honestly.

'You don't know me as well as you think you do.'

'I know that the downtrodden, disadvantaged, poor and homeless hold no appeal for you.'

'Think what you like,' Nina said, seeming to enjoy her confusion.

'Only some folks from the Community Centre have turned up dead.'

Shock registered on her face. Real or manufactured Kim couldn't tell.

'Who?'

'A young couple, Amy and Mark—'

'The druggies?' she asked with distaste.

'What a very charitable response, which is kind of proving my point there, Nina, that you did not offer your services there for nothing.'

'I have little patience for those unwilling to help—'

'You have little patience for anyone who can't pay you for your services, so what exactly do you gain from volunteering your very expensive legal services to the downtrodden?'

'Gained, Inspector. Past tense. Your research should have told you that. I no longer offer my services.'

Kim felt the frustration growing inside her. Just one straight answer would be nice.

'So, how long were you involved?'

'A couple of months.'

'Nina, I swear I'll charge you with evading—'

'Calm down, Inspector. It really is quite simple. You are correct that I have no interest in them or their pathetic sob stories. I couldn't care less if they all drop dead tomorrow. I volunteered because I wanted something. They had a purpose and once they had served their purpose, I left.'

'So, what am I supposed to do?' Alison asked, once Penn had left the room, offering to go and speak to the relatives of Billie Styles.

Alison knew she was draining Stacey's time but she didn't know where else to turn.

Stacey folded her arms. 'Well, clearly one of them is lying, and you spoke to Tom last night and he was consistent, so perhaps it's time to talk to her,' Stacey advised.

'How can I? I can't impersonate a police officer.'

'Ask Penn to do it, he's been impersonating a police officer for years. Boom, boom.'

'That would have been funny if he'd been sitting there,' Alison said, glancing at the empty dining chair.

'And anyway,' Stacey advised. 'You're only impersonating a police officer if you actually state you are one. Be creative.'

With Stacey's encouragement, she dialled the home number for Tilly Neale. A gruff male voice answered, unnerving her. Stacey nodded encouragement.

'May I speak to Tilly, please?'

'Who is it?'

'My name is Jane Lowe,' she answered, using her middle name.

'Til, phone,' he called out.

She heard feet on the stairs.

'Thanks, hun, see you later,' and then a door closed.

'Hello?'

'Tilly Neale? My name is Jane Lowe and I'm just signing off some statements regarding the Beverly Wright case. May I just go through your recollection quickly? I won't keep you long.'

'Of course,' she replied.

Helpful. Wary.

Alison read out key sentences and then waited for sounds of affirmation.

'And then yourself and Tom Drury went to deep clean the toilets?'

'That's right.'

'Okay, oh, hang on a second. I'm just reading Mr Drury's statement and he said you went to the office to cash up.'

Silence. Brain churning.

'He must… I must… one of us must have made a mistake but I'm sure we went to clean the toilets.'

'Only Curtis said—'

'Curtis said what? Have you spoken to him? Has he remembered anything?'

The panic in her voice set off all her alarm bells.

'You weren't in the toilets or the office, were you, Tilly.'

Silence.

'I'm not a police officer but you have to tell me the truth.'

'Oh God, I can't. If he finds… oh no, my husband… he'll kill…'

'Just say it, Tilly,' Alison urged, feeling the beads of sweat forming on her brow.

'Okay, Curtis Swayne was with me. We were together having sex in my car.'

Alison wanted to shout it from the rooftops. She hadn't been wrong about Curtis.

He now had an alibi for the attack on Beverly Wright.

And now Tom Drury did not.

CHAPTER 96

'Do you believe her?' Bryant asked once they were back in the car. 'That Nina wanted the volunteering on her CV to get back into a decent practice?'

Kim shrugged. 'I can kind of see it in a way. Nina Croft works better with the prestige of a law practice behind her. She likes the structure, the belonging, having a bigger name behind her. It doesn't suit her to be out here alone. Why else would she stay with Richard Croft after all she'd learned about him?'

'But still…'

'Look, if we can tie her to the car fire involving the Phelpses we'll go bring her in right now.'

'Give Alison time, she'll probably find something,' he said, only half-joking. 'And now can we please start heading towards the bloody prison?' he asked as her phone began to ring.

Kim smiled as she held the ringing phone up in front of her face, unanswered. 'Oh Frost, I'd love to answer you but I can't. Boss says I can't talk to the press and I was gonna give you an exclusive on this one but—'

'Guv, you've lost it,' Bryant chuckled as the ringing stopped.

As she returned the phone to her pocket it began to ring again.

'Jesus, she's persistent… aah, Stacey,' she said, pressing the answer button. 'Whatever it is we can't do it,' Kim said, glancing at her colleague. 'The acting boss here is insisting we head over to Winson Green.'

'Yeah,' Stacey said breathlessly. 'That's exactly where I want you to go. I've found the Phelps' son, Joel Greene. He hasn't been travelling at all. He's been in prison for just over a year.'

CHAPTER 97

Penn knocked on the door of the end terrace in Colley Gate.

As the two strands of what both he and Stacey were investigating had come together, they'd agreed that he would come and speak to Billie's family and she would continue trying to trace Duggar's whereabouts. He had to admit he was beginning to get a very bad feeling in his gut about John Duggar.

The door was opened by a frail-looking man with reddened eyes.

'Mr Styles?' he asked.

The man nodded and stood aside.

Penn entered. 'I'm here about Billie,' he said. Her father was much older than he'd imagined.

'The nice police constable told me someone would come,' he said, shuffling down the hall. From his own experience with his mother Penn guessed the man needed a new hip.

Penn followed him into a small lounge that, although old fashioned, looked clean and comfortable.

He eased himself down into the single chair, slowly.

Penn sat on the two-seater sofa.

'How is she?' he asked.

'You haven't been to see her?' Penn asked, before he could help himself.

The man shook his head sadly, and Penn wondered if it was a mobility issue.

'She's stable,' Penn offered. 'Not out of the woods yet but she's alive and given the nature and extent of her—'

Mr Styles held up his hand and shook his head. 'I'm sorry, I can't hear that again.'

'Sir, may I ask if Billie is?…'

'My granddaughter,' he said, staring at the carpet. 'My daughter died of breast cancer at the age of forty-five. Billie was nine and came to us. There was no one else.'

'Her father?'

'Never met him. It was only Sylvia and Billie until…' His words trailed away as he wiped at his eyes again.

'And your wife?' Penn asked, gently, feeling the silence of the house.

'Died five years later. Massive stroke, so we've kind of muddled through, Billie and me.'

Penn had a sudden rush of sympathy for this man who had endured too much tragedy already.

'Mr Styles, if you need someone to take you to see…'

'Thank you but no,' he said, shaking his head.' I just can't face her, knowing what was… I'm sorry but…'

'It's okay, Mr Styles,' Penn said; although his heart went out to the young woman, barely conscious, lying alone in a hospital bed, he felt the misery emanating from this elderly man.

'Is there someone I could call to come and sit with you?'

He shook his head. 'I'm fine, son. What can I help you with?'

'I'd like to talk to you about a friend of hers. Do you know a man named John Duggar?'

The watery blue eyes sharpened showing Penn the man's brain was not ageing at the same rate as his body.

'You don't think?…'

'Let's just say the man is on our radar.'

'I suppose it would… oh my goodness.'

'Did they know each other well?'

He nodded. 'They were together off and on for a couple of years. They met at the pub where he worked. She'd always liked tall men and this one had the added attraction of being an ex-criminal. Except he wasn't so ex. He was still up to no good even though he'd been given the chance of a decent job. One of the reasons I didn't like him.

'I tried to warn her about him but she insisted he'd changed and put his past behind him. She wouldn't listen and she was earning her own money as a dental assistant, had her own place.'

'Sounds like she's a very sensible girl,' Penn noted, bringing her back into the present. She wasn't dead.

'That's what made it all the stranger at first. It's like she was blinded by his bad boy image or whatever it is they call it. And then she started to see sense.'

'Was he ever violent with her?'

He shook his head. 'Not that I know. He liked to try and scare her but…'

'Sorry, but I'm not sure…'

'Let me explain. The first time John got caught for fencing stolen goods she forgave him. Visited him in prison, stood by him and accepted he'd made a mistake. He did his time and got out. Second time he got caught she wasn't quite so forgiving and started to see what life could be like with a career criminal. She waited until he was out and told him it was over.'

'And how'd he take it?'

'Well, it seemed, until Billie started hearing noises late at night and lots of hang-up phone calls.'

'Did she report it?' he asked, although they'd found nothing on the system.

'She had no proof it was him and she thought if she ignored it, he'd get bored and just stop.'

'And did he?'

'I don't think so. She was still getting the hang ups when we spoke a few days ago.'

Penn sat for a moment and considered what he'd just learned. The man was not given to violence. Strange given the level of death in the case they were investigating, but more interesting to him was one simple truth that stood out.

That when John Duggar was focussed on something in particular, he was not prepared to let go.

CHAPTER 98

'Storm's on its way,' Bryant said, as they parked outside Winson Green. There'd been a few rumbles of thunder and the clouds were gathering. Every other person was looking to the sky expectantly.

'It'll probably pass,' Kim said, heading towards the entrance.

They repeated the process imposed a couple of days earlier and cleared security. They were shown to the visitor's centre by a sullen officer who offered no conversation en route.

The hall was more crowded than before but her gaze swept the room and easily found one man sitting alone with his head down. She didn't need the surly guard to point him out and headed through the crowds towards the back. She kept her head held high ignoring the curious glances that never ceased to amaze her, like some kind of sixth sense that there were police officers in the building.

'Joel Greene?' Kim asked, sitting.

He raised his head and nodded.

'You're not the easiest man to find,' she said.

'Well, I ain't been hiding,' he said, looking around.

'I'm assuming you know about your parents?' she asked.

'He wasn't my dad. And yeah, I saw it on the news.'

Kim felt a sadness steel over her.

'I'm really sorry you had to find out like that,' Kim said.

'Yeah, it was shit but I let Gennard know and he sent me to sort some books.'

Kim thought for a minute and then understood what he was saying. This wasn't a place where you wore your emotions on your sleeve. Gennard had offered him a period of privacy.

'Your last name complicated matters along with the fact that everyone told us you were away travelling,' Kim explained.

He smiled sadly. 'Yeah, my parents used that line every time I got stuck in here.'

Kim found herself having a strange reaction to this man. He was almost thirty yet there was a sense of hopelessness about him that she couldn't fathom.

'How many times you been inside?' Bryant asked.

'Six, seven and I'll be back again,' he said, honestly.

'Were you not close with your parents?' she asked.

He shrugged. 'Not really. Don't get me wrong. I loved them but we didn't understand each other. They couldn't understand why I was always in trouble and I didn't get why they were so happy to toe everyone else's line. They loved me but I wasn't exactly what my mother hoped for.'

Kim found herself wanting to know more.

'Go on,' she urged.

'Well they worked their whole lives at average paid jobs, living in an average house with average friends and neighbours. Nothing wrong with that. It's clean, tidy, respectable. Everything I don't want to be. I want to be rich and I'm happy to try and get there by breaking the law. It's how I live my life, how I want to live my life. I'll get released and I'll reoffend. I know that. I may get caught or I may not but that's what they couldn't accept about me, that I actually didn't want to change.'

Kim admired his honesty even though she now wanted to follow him on release day and nab him when he did reoffend.

'So, can you think of anyone who would want to hurt them?' Bryant asked.

He looked at them incredulously. 'Now I know you're joking. Neither of them ever offended anyone in their lives. I bloody wish they had but they were the most inoffensive people on the planet. You can ask most of these guys. When they came to visit they spent more time buying sandwiches and coffee and chatting with other visitors; it was easier for them than sitting here talking to me.'

Kim sensed she was getting nothing further. Their lives had been worlds apart.

'We'll release the bodies as soon as we can and you can apply for a day pass.'

'I won't be going to the funeral,' he said, quietly, turning his head away. He swallowed deeply, twice, before turning a face with reddened eyes back towards them. 'Imagine if I turned up attached at the wrist to Egor over there. It would give their friends and neighbours gossip fodder for months and they'd hate that. I wouldn't do that to them. I'll say my own goodbyes.'

Kim wondered if Joel Greene understood the core of decency that ran through him.

Kim thanked him for his time and stood.

She saw that team leader Gennard had joined Officer Surly next to the vending machine.

His eyes were sweeping the room efficiently, assessing the situation, ensuring all was as it should be.

'Just the man we're looking for,' Kim said to Bryant.

It wasn't until she reached the other side of the room that she realised Dale Preece and Symes were nowhere to be seen.

CHAPTER 99

Stacey closed the front door behind Charlie and Barney. The neighbour had come to collect the dog for an afternoon walk.

'It's okay, Alison, you can come down from the bar stool now. He's gone,' she said.

'I'm fine up here,' she said, stubbornly. 'Although I do need a quick pee,' she admitted.

Stacey chuckled. The woman had been up on that stool for almost six hours without venturing into the shark-infested waters occupied by the saft as tuppence dog.

'Where is it?' she asked.

'Door next to the garage.'

Having found it herself earlier, Stacey had been unable to resist a sneak peek into the garage. The boss's Ninja had gleamed at her from the furthest point, right by the roller shutter door. Between her and the bike was a sheet covering the concrete filled with what looked like scrap metal.

Stacey had known her boss restored classic motorcycles in her spare time but she'd assumed they came in kit form with glue, fixings and instructions, like the Airfix aeroplanes her dad had spent hours on when she was young. She hadn't thought the garage would resemble the back of a scrap man's van.

'Oh for goodness' sake,' she said as the doorbell rang again. 'Boss needs a flipping butler. Oh, it's you,' she said, opening the door to Penn.

'Yeah, sorry about that,' he said, rushing past her. He removed his jacket, sat and looked around. 'Err… we lost a dog and a profiler?'

'Both gone wee wee,' she said, taking her seat opposite.

'So, what did you find out?' she asked.

'Duggar and Billie were definitely a couple, as we thought, but she broke it off months ago. Had enough of being a prison wife. He didn't take it too well. Harassed her a fair bit.'

'Violence?'

Penn shook his head. 'Strangely not. Looks like Duggar was telling the truth when he said he didn't like fighting.'

'Yeah, but given the brutality of the attack on Billie…'

'I know. I mean Duggar's all over this but he never laid a hand on his girlfriend and none of his crimes are violent. Never been in possession of a knife or any other weapon.'

'What do you think about Duggar, Alison?' Penn asked, as she retook her place on the stool.

'We have a situation where the evidence says yes. He viewed the flat where Amy and Mark were killed, so he had access to the key. He was the person who took the car into the scrapyard and could have met the Phelpses at the prison. We know he's linked to Billie Styles. But, and it's a really big but, he doesn't even come close to fitting the profile. And we've all agreed that whoever is doing this must hate your boss very much. He was pleasant, co-operative and honest, so, quite frankly, my opinion is… I have no clue.'

Stacey couldn't help the chuckle that broke free at Alison's admission. It made her more human, somehow.

'Well, the boss'll be on her way back from Birmingham soon and I'm pretty sure she's gonna expect a bit more than that.'

CHAPTER 100

Alison waited for Penn to close the door as he left for a snack run. She counted to three and then went for it.

'Stace, you got a minute?'

The constable turned to her. 'Did I miss the memo on being assigned to?—'

'I'm sorry,' she said, meaning it. After the call-out last night the woman was demonstrating great patience, but Alison knew she was out of her depth. Stacey had already told her that she'd passed the earring along to someone named Mitch to maintain the chain of evidence, and now she was asking for even more help.

Many times she'd considered asking Penn for help but she had no idea if he'd worked with Merton and therefore had a connection. If they were friends Penn might drop her in it.

'I just don't know what to do. I know that Merton won't even take my call. I can't pass all this on as the entire team at West Mercia thinks I'm useless.'

'Is there no one involved in the investigation you can trust?' Stacey asked, turning back to her computer.

She considered Jamie, but he was so far up Merton's behind he'd probably drop her in it without even realising it.

She shook her head. 'I just feel as though I should be doing something. I mean, what if he is still out there? What if they have got the wrong guy and the real killer is out there. He could be targeting somebody right this very—'

'Sorry, but I need to—'

'Will someone just bloody listen to me,' Alison raged, banging her fist off the table. 'My whole career has been trashed, my reputation all but destroyed. It's unlikely I'll ever be asked to consult again but, most importantly, they have the wrong man and I'm sick and fucking tired of—'

'You're shouting and swearing at me?' Stacey asked, wide-eyed.

'Put yourself in my position,' she said, trying not to take out her frustration on the one person who had tried to help. 'I'm about to lose everything and I know I'm right. An innocent man is going to prison for the rest of his life and the real killer is going to walk free. As a police officer that—'

'Alison, are you trying to use your powers on me?' Stacey asked.

'I don't have—'

'Joking, Alison.'

Alison wondered how these people managed to keep their sanity. There was no way she could make jokes while both her stomach and her head were in turmoil and her nerves were shot to bits.

Lives were at risk and these people did this every day.

Stacey gave her a long look. 'Okay, so what do you actually have? You've found an earring at the location that Beverly was taken from and you've got the barmaid now saying the singer was with her.'

'And the fact I just know Curtis didn't do it.'

'Yeah, we'll leave that aside for now,' Stacey offered. 'So, given that you have absolutely no access to any of the evidence—'

'I have statements.'

'CCTV?'

Alison shook her head. She'd never viewed the CCTV images.

'Damn. We're going to need more than that to divert this investigation. You don't even know if that woman will repeat her confession officially, so if you can't disprove Curtis, you're going to have to try and establish the real killer.'

'But how?'

'Shush, I'm thinking,' Stacey said, opening a new tab and Google Earth.

Alison watched as she enlarged, clicked and navigated with speed and accuracy.

'Hang on one…'

'What?'

'Shush,' Stacey snapped.

Alison realised that she really had to get a handle on when people were speaking to her and when they weren't.

She watched as Stacey moved around the screen, putting the blue figure onto roads and looking around.

'Just give me two…'

Alison said nothing.

'Jackson Little,' Stacey said, reaching for the phone.

'Who's?…'

Stacey held up her hand. Alison listened in awe as Stacey gave the nature of the call. She quoted dates and times and gave her email address.

'I don't understand,' Alison said.

Stacey went back to the map. 'Okay, you said that the club CCTV turned up nothing and the local council CCTV search was focussed on Curtis's van, assuming they left the club together. We now know they didn't, so did Beverly leave alone? Again, I'm sure all registration numbers of vehicles on the car park were checked, so we have nothing to gain there.'

'Okay,' Alison agreed.

'So, what if she left on foot and the killer followed her. She was found less than a mile from the club, so it's possible she never got into a car at all.'

Stacey put the map back onto the screen.

'So, if you look at the route from the pub to the crime scene, Lissett Road runs for a quarter mile of it and the only industrial premises that takes up one side of the road is a fastener manu-facturing company called Jackson Little who have an entrance gate for the delivery vehicles right about here.' She switched to the satellite view. 'See?'

Alison nodded, dumbfounded at the speed of both Stacey's mind and actions.

'And if we're lucky that ding we just heard is a collection of the footage from their external cameras and we can see if Beverly walked past and, more importantly, if she was alone.'

'Is this legal?'

'No, Alison, as a police officer I feel that I can commit any kind of crime,' Stacey answered. 'Of course it's legal. This is private CCTV footage, which is their prerogative to share especially with the police and we got a helpful security officer.'

'Stacey, I think I might have a girl crush on you right now.'

'I'm taken, but thanks anyway. Now let's have a look.'

Stacey loaded up the first of the two disc icons.

'What was she wearing?'

'Yellow jeans and trainers.'

'Not usual attire for a night worker,' Stacey observed.

'She wasn't working,' Alison explained. 'Just went to the club for a drink and some music.'

'The footage is on time-lapse but we should spot her if she goes by,' Stacey said as Alison pulled up a chair.

The half-hour window Stacey had given passed by in silence as they both stared at the screen.

'Nothing,' Alison said as the screen went blank.

'Let's try the other one.'

'Oh,' Alison said, seeing that the view was a downward view of the pavement, trained on a small hole in the fencing.

'Yeah, that's not great,' Stacey said. 'All we're going to get is a look at some lower legs as they—'

'Stop,' Alison cried out.

'Bloody hell, woman, I'm only here,' Stacey said.

'That's her,' Alison said, barely able to get the words out. 'That's Beverly, look, yellow jeans and trainers.'

Stacey rewound and played it again. They watched silently as the legs entered the shot and left it again.

Alison had the urge to scream at the camera to turn, to follow her, to protect her from the horror that was to come.

Stacey sighed heavily. 'Sorry, Alison, but she was definitely on her own.'

Alison felt the deflation as she continued to watch the screen. For a while there she'd had real hope of proving herself right and showing that Curtis had been innocent all along.

As Stacey's arrow headed towards the red cross, Alison grabbed at her arm.

'Wait,' she whispered, as her mouth dried up. 'Play those last few seconds again.'

'Thank you for taking the time to speak to us this afternoon, Mr Gennard,' Kim said as they crammed into the tiny office reserved for the shift manager. In the absence of a proper noticeboard rosters and memos had been taped to the white painted breeze block wall.

'We understand you keep intelligence on most of the inmates, like who is speaking to who and that kind of thing. We'd like to know more about Symes, Dale Preece, John Duggar and Joel Greene.'

'Well, I can tell you that Joel Greene is not in the same league as the others. He comes in, does his time, keeps his nose clean, doesn't get into the factions and there's nothing linking him to the other three.'

Kim was strangely relieved to hear that.

'The others are all part of your fan club and—'

'You know about that?'

He frowned. 'Our intel would be pretty shit if we didn't.'

'And you allow it?' Bryant asked.

'Hang on, it ain't like we give 'em a room and supplies to make a voodoo doll. We control every aspect of their day: when they wake, sleep, eat, piss, see family. We can't control what they think or talk about.'

'So, how do you stop something like this getting out of control?' Bryant asked.

'We have methods and that's all I'm going to say.'

'You have someone in the group, don't you?' Kim asked. Her immediate thoughts went to Duggar, the man who had pretended to have a beef with her.

'I'm really not going to say more.'

What better way of monitoring the group than having someone inside it that would flag up if things were getting out of hand?

'How would we find out if any of these three had had a book sent here?'

'Post records, we log everything that comes in or out of the prison.'

He tapped into the computer in the corner after removing a couple of Post-it notes stuck to the screen.

He accessed the system and they waited while he tapped and scrolled. He moved along the columns and scrolled again.

'Okay, fan mail for Symes. Seventeen letters since he's been here all from different women.'

'Really?'

'No accounting for taste, is there?' Gennard asked.

The man had neither looks, charm or personality. He was cruel, mean and lived only to inflict violence. What type of woman would be attracted to that?

'Dale Preece has had a couple of fan letters. Not on the level of Symes.'

She could at least understand that. There was no denying the man was handsome.

'And the rest are care packages from his mum. So, no record of any books coming in to either of them.'

'You only checked two,' she said. 'What about John Duggar?'

'No need to check on him. Duggar wouldn't have ordered a book. That guy couldn't read or write.'

CHAPTER 102

'So, what do you think?' Bryant asked, as they exited the building.

'Not being able to read or write doesn't stop the man ordering a book but at least Gennard still checked.'

'He didn't react too kindly to your suggestion that one of the guards ordered it and passed it along,' Bryant observed.

'Yeah and despite his bluster he couldn't completely rule it out. I mean, come on, we know guards have been persuaded, cajoled and threatened into bringing in mobile phones, smokes, drugs, weapons. If someone got forced to bring in a book, I'd imagine they'd not lose too much sleep.'

'My guards are trustworthy and have integrity…' Bryant said, lowering his voice and impersonating Gennard.

Kim laughed, allowing some of the tension to seep out of her body.

For someone officially not working it had turned into a very long day, and they still had evening rush hour to contend with.

'Okay, Bryant, let's head back and…' her words trailed away as a silver BMW pulled onto the car park two rows behind.

She watched as Mallory Preece stepped out with a carrier bag.

'Give me one sec, Bryant,' Kim said, getting out of the car.

Mallory shook her head as Kim headed towards her. 'Leave me alone, Inspector, I have nothing to say to you and neither does my son.'

'I wasn't here to see Dale,' Kim said, falling into step with the woman who hadn't even paused. 'But out of interest, do you know if your son ordered a book?'

'How would I know what my?—'

'The book is about me.'

Mallory stopped walking and looked at her. 'You're not all that, Stone. Why the hell would there be a book about you?'

'I'm not going into that but you must be aware of how much he hates me,' Kim said.

'Do you blame him?' Mallory asked. 'Because of you he lost his grandfather and his brother and now he's locked up in here. He was very close to both of them but especially his grandfather who—'

'Mallory, your father was a cold-hearted despicable bastard who—'

'I'm not going to listen to—'

'Okay, but Mallory, I need to know if he ordered that book. There's a hate club for me in there and your son seems to be a huge part of it. If you find out about the book would you let me know?'

'Of course, Inspector. Right after I burn in hell.'

Kim sighed heavily. 'Jesus, you do know that innocent people are losing—'

'I couldn't care less about anyone else,' Mallory said, coldly. 'I care only about my son and if you want the truth if there's a book about you he probably did get it. You seem to occupy his thoughts more than you should do,' she said, bitterly. 'And much as I love him, I'll never be at peace with what he did.'

'I'm not—'

'He had a choice, Inspector, to save his own brother or you. And I'll never understand why he chose you.'

CHAPTER 103

'Guys, I hope you've got something good,' Kim said, as she and Bryant entered her home.

'Getting there, boss,' Stacey said, rolling her head to release the tension in her neck.

'No fix on Duggar's location,' Penn said, eating the last finger of a KitKat. 'Last sighting I've got for definite is a meeting with his probation officer yesterday morning and…'

'Stace, we need to meet this—'

'You have an appointment with her first thing in the morning.'

Kim smiled and removed her jacket and headed for the percolator in the kitchen. The overindulgence of caffeine first thing had long since been absorbed into her system. Her nerves needed a swift top up.

She updated them on their afternoon at the prison as she prepared the coffee machine.

'So, pretty sure Joel Greene isn't involved in any of this, but his parents could have come into contact with John Duggar.'

'Learned a lot about the guy,' Stacey said, scrolling back through her notes. 'Born in 1986 to an alcoholic mother who left him and his two sisters when he was three. Grandmother managed for a few years until Duggar was seven and she gave him and one of his sisters to the state. She kept the oldest girl and never saw the other two again.'

'Rough,' Bryant said.

Stacey nodded. 'Didn't have a good time at school, got targeted for his height and written off as stupid. Spent more time in trouble for skiving and was expelled from three different schools. Eventually at fourteen he just disappeared from the education system.

'His sister fared better and after a long-term fostering stint with a good family left school with some half-decent qualifications. Works in business admin and moved to the Isle of Wight with her husband eight years ago. Trying to make contact to see what she knows but no response yet. And now over to Penn while I just finish off this last check.'

'Good work, Stace,' Kim said, even though there was little there to help them. It did help to confirm what Gennard had said about the man being illiterate.

'Inevitably,' Penn continued, 'he drifted into petty crime and did his first stint in prison aged nineteen. At times tried to reach out to his grandmother, who refused to see him.'

'Jesus,' Bryant said. 'Great bloody life he's had.'

'And yet none of this dictates he'll become a violent individual,' Alison interjected. 'In fact, in many cases such experiences would have instilled in him a need to belong, to be a part of something bigger where he blended. People who stand out physically don't always want that singular attention. They've been isolated for their differences all their lives.'

'You're saying that's why he joined the hate club?' Kim asked.

Alison shrugged. 'Could be and could also explain his refusal to go straight. Prison life would have been familiar to him. Along with the punishment there is an element of being taken care of, meals prepared and available, somewhere to sleep, a routine.'

'Bloody hell, Alison, Winson Green is no weekend spa,' she said.

'Tell that to the guy sleeping in Gregg's shop doorway when it's minus two degrees. See if he wants the bed and the meal. What I'm trying to explain is that we have certain needs as children:

protection, boundaries, safety, love, encouragement, nurturing and if we don't get them we continue to look. A kid who got no pats on the back is likely to develop into a people pleaser.'

Kim couldn't quite marry the conflicting images of John Duggar.

Penn cut in. 'A few years ago, he met Billie Styles on one of his trying to go straight phases. They got together and—'

'Hang on,' Kim said. 'The two of them were a couple?'

'Not recently. He didn't change his ways and she got fed up of visiting him in prison and binned him. Only he didn't go quietly.'

'He's been harassing her?' Bryant asked.

Penn nodded.

'Guys, this isn't making any sense,' Kim said. 'He has no record for violence and people have died horrific deaths. We agree that the killer has to hate me passionately and yet Duggar has absolutely no—'

'Aww, shit, boss I think I just found something.'

They all waited as Stacey began to read. That she was licking her lower lip as she did so, gave Kim cause for concern.

'Six years ago, boss,' Stacey said quietly. 'House fire on Sutton Road. Two kids were saved by two detectives who heard the radio call.'

Kim nodded. She remembered the incident well. Travis had grabbed the boy and she had carried the girl.

'By the time we got them out the fire service were there. Wouldn't let anyone back in.'

'The mother died,' Stacey said.

Kim swallowed and nodded. She had crawled under the bed in the master bedroom. They hadn't known.

'Her name was—'

'Abigail Turner,' Kim offered, having no trouble recalling the woman's name.

'But before that she was called Abigail Duggar, so regardless of what John Duggar said, indirectly, I suppose, you really did kill his sister.'

It was almost seven when Kim realised it was time to throw the team out of her house.

She likely would have continued working for a while longer but Stacey's neck stretches and Penn's not-so-secret glances at his watch told her the working day had already been long enough.

The speed with which bags and jackets were gathered confirmed it was time to call it a night.

'Except you, Alison,' she said, as the woman walked a wide berth around Barney.

She caught the glance that passed between the behaviourist and Stacey before Bryant ushered them out of the front door.

'Relative still sick?' Kim asked as Alison retook her seat.

'Yeah, that's it,' Alison replied vaguely.

Kim knew that Alison was lying and her lies had somehow involved her detective constable.

'You wanna share what's going on with you and Stacey?'

Alison shook her head. 'It's nothing. She's just been helping me with something.'

Kim folded her arms. 'Connected to this case?'

'No.'

Kim realised she was getting nothing more than that and resolved to call Stacey later.

'You wanted something from me?' Alison prompted.

Kim dropped her arms and hid her smile. Directness was a quality she both liked and admired.

'Your opinion,' Kim answered.

Alison laughed out loud. 'You're joking, right? You've spent the whole week decidedly not wanting, or ignoring, my opinion.'

Kim rolled her eyes. 'Give me a break, woman. It's been a tough week and right now I want to know what your opinion is before I ignore it.'

She offered a smile to demonstrate she was joking. In her case it wasn't always clear.

'What's your gut saying about John Duggar and this new information?'

Alison raised one eyebrow. 'My gut is not what inspires my professional opinion. I tend to use my education and my degree in—'

'Why do you do that?' Kim asked, pouring two coffees from the pot.

'What?'

'Recite your education and qualifications whenever we talk?' she said, pushing one mug towards the woman. 'You spend a lot of time quoting your CV when all I want is a bloody conversation.'

'You don't trust me,' Alison blurted out, coloured and looked away.

'I do,' Kim protested. 'Well, as much as I trust anyone… actually… okay… you got me.'

To her surprise Alison laughed out loud but it wasn't the derisive sound of a few moments earlier. This was hearty and came from her stomach.

'Okay, look, it's not that I distrust you completely. It's just that I object to the assumptions that are a staple of your profession. Works well for TV shows like *Cracker* but not so much in the real world.' Kim held up her hand as Alison opened her mouth to protest. 'However, on this occasion you've been involved in the case for almost as long as the rest of us. You've built up a knowledge of the people we're dealing with and the crimes committed. Putting that information together with your expertise is something I can live with; so now will you answer my question?'

'Did we just bond?' Alison asked with amusement dancing in her eyes.

Kim narrowed her gaze.

Alison took a breath. 'Okay, this new information does change things but also doesn't change a thing.'

Kim threw her hands in the air as Alison took a sip of her drink.

'I'll explain. You didn't kill Duggar's sister but you didn't save her either. They were not close and hadn't grown up together strengthening that sibling bond. He didn't know her. We think that the person behind these crimes hates you because you irrevocably changed their life. You didn't change Duggar's life by not saving his sister.'

'So you don't think it's him?'

'I didn't say that. If Duggar is a fantasist and had invested a great deal of emotion into the life he might have if he connected with his sister then he could still hate you enough for having taken that option away from him.'

'I sense a *but* in your voice.'

'We need to know more about his dominant personality traits to put it all together, which I hope we'll be able to do after you've talked with his probation officer tomorrow. We have no evidence of prior violence against Billie but her injuries were—'

'Horrific,' Kim finished for her.

'Exactly.'

'But doesn't his lack of violence rule him out completely?' Kim asked, trying to get her head around it all.

Alison considered. 'I'm afraid not. Traumatic events or triggers can incite different behaviours and inspire people to act against type.'

'To this extent and over a prolonged period of time?'

'Absolutely.'

'So basically, you're saying that…'

'I can't give you the answer you want. I can't say for certain whether Duggar is or is not your man, but with each new piece of evidence or information it becomes easier to suppose one way or the other.'

Kim felt as though an awful lot of words had been used to tell her nothing at all.

'Okay, Alison, thanks for your time…'

'But you've been no help at all,' she finished, raising herself to a standing position.

Kim returned her smile. 'I appreciate the insight you've given me.'

'Okay, I'll take that,' she said, heading towards the hall. 'And on that note, I'll see you tomorrow.'

Kim shouted good night as she disappeared out of the house.

'Yeah, sorry, boy, it's just you and me again,' she said to Barney who was still staring at the front door. It appeared he liked Alison more than she liked him, and despite her chat with Alison she still didn't know how she felt about John Duggar. The revelation from Stacey about his sister being the victim of the Sutton Road house fire had been a complete shock to her. She could still remember the guilt both she and her old partner Travis had felt upon learning that the children's mother had perished in the fire, despite the fact it had not been possible for either of them to re-enter the property.

But John Duggar had been open, friendly and apparently helpful when they'd spoken to him and he'd known this all along. It made no sense to her.

And then she thought about what Alison had said earlier in the week about the end game: that it was the only thing left for him to do. Was he watching her right now? Was his disappearance linked to his preparation for her death?

'Jesus,' she cried as her phone rang, startling her.

'Evening, sir,' she said to her boss.

'Bryant's just updated me. You really think it's this John Duggar?'

'Everything is pointing that way,' she admitted.

'Well, you'll be pleased to know that the insect problem in the office has been resolved and the team is free to return to the squad room in the morning.'

'The team, sir?' she asked.

'The whole team, Stone. Seems it was a whole lot of fuss about nothing, but I trust your day away from the case has given you time to cool down and reassess your actions.'

Kim felt relief that she was being let out of the naughty corner.

'Of course, sir.'

'One more thing. Alison's daily report focusses on the end game, as she calls it, where she feels the threat of violence will inevitably turn away from replicating events and will turn towards you directly.'

'It's a guess, sir,' she said, wondering why she hadn't known there was a daily report.

'I would prefer to be safe, so given the level of threat against you, you will ensure that you remain with a colleague at all times.'

'Yes, sir,' she said.

Poor Bryant, she thought.

'And there will be a car outside your house all night. It'll be there in fifteen minutes.'

She opened her mouth to argue and then closed it again.

'Thank you, sir.'

'Fifteen minutes, Stone,' he said, ending the call.

She appreciated the gesture of protection from her boss.

But she needed to leave her home and she didn't have fifteen minutes to wait.

CHAPTER 105

Alison paused and took a breath outside Elite, aware she was doing this without the support of West Mercia Police.

Not that she hadn't tried. Her first three calls to Merton had been cut off and the fourth had been answered curtly.

She'd only got as far as saying that Curtis was innocent before being interrupted with the statement that he was now lodging an official complaint against her. And then he'd ended the call. She hadn't tried again.

She had made one other call and had known there was only one person who could help her now.

The car park was half full and the majority of those customers appeared to have brought their drinks outside to the canopied entrance to enjoy the air as it cooled back to the low twenties.

She entered the club and saw Jamie Hart sitting in the corner. She waved as she glanced at the bar and swallowed. Tom looked her way, a smile forming on his lips. He glanced in the direction she was headed. The smile disappeared and he returned to what he was doing.

Good, she didn't want his attention on her. Not yet.

'Th… thanks for coming,' she said, slipping into the seat opposite.

'You okay?' he said, pushing a glass towards her. 'Dry and white and it looks like you need it. What's wrong?'

She followed his instruction and took a sip. Just one.

'I tried to talk to Merton but he wouldn't listen. He's reporting me instead. Says I've obstructed the investigation.'

Jamie took a sip of his drink to hide his smile. 'From his point of view, you have been a bit of a nuisance.'

'Yeah, I suppose so,' she said, looking over his head. 'But I didn't know who else to call and you hinted the other night that there're cracks in the investigation, so I knew I could trust—'

'I didn't so much say cracks but—'

'He didn't do it, Jamie,' she blurted out. 'Curtis has an alibi. He was with Tilly from behind the bar.'

He frowned and looked behind her disbelievingly. 'So, why wouldn't he say?'

'He probably doesn't remember, but she does. Don't you recall that Tom and Tilly effectively provided alibis for each other?'

He nodded. 'In the office or something?'

'Said Tom, but Tilly said something else just a bit different. Enough to get her to admit that she lied to protect her marriage.'

'Bloody hell, are you sure?' he asked, rubbing at his chin.

'Oh yeah, she's got a lot to lose in coming clean.'

'But hang on,' he said, catching up with her. 'That means Tom Drury no longer has an alibi for Beverly's attack.'

'Exactly,' she said. 'Now can you see why I called you?'

'Ali, you've got to speak to Merton; however you do it, you've got to make him listen to your suspicions about Drury.'

Alison shook her head. 'He won't believe me, but he might believe you.'

Jamie considered her words while looking over her shoulder towards the bar.

'So, you were right all along. Your profile was spot on. He's young, good-looking, successful, organised, probably academic…'

'Business degree,' she confirmed.

'Lives local and—'

'And you know he didn't do it, don't you, Jamie?' she asked, turning back to face him. 'Because you did.'

His face registered shock before being covered by a grin. 'Have you lost your mind?'

Alison forced down the nerves inside and forged ahead. 'You blocked me every step of the investigation, argued my profile, made cases for people who couldn't possibly have done it all because my profile fitted you too. You murdered Jennifer and then got yourself involved in the case. You pushed the investigation towards Curtis, but the team were listening to me. You couldn't help yourself. You had to do it again. Had the thrill of Jennifer's earring worn off? You could no longer imagine her begging for her life. And you chose someone who had some contact with Curtis knowing the police would have to consider him more seriously after that. And Curtis played right into your hands when he couldn't remember a damn thing.'

'This is fabulous, please continue,' he said, with amusement.

'You see, Tom is a good fit for my profile but he's not perfect,' she said sloshing her drink, deliberately.

Immediately his hand rose from his lap to wipe away the drips.

'I also said fastidiously tidy,' she observed.

'That means nothing. I just don't like messy tables,' he said, frowning.

'Admirable quality,' she said, sarcastically.

'And Jennifer's mother sends her best regards, you bastard,' she spat. 'Says you were very helpful in helping them come to terms with their loss. You were feeding off their fucking misery, reliving the event, prolonging the ecstasy, power tripping over your own knowledge of—'

'Is that the best you've got, Ali?' he asked with a sneer, and suddenly she knew beyond a shadow of a doubt that she was right.

'Absolutely not,' she said, gaining strength from his derision. 'I have the earring that you came here to plant the other night.'

A small amount of colour left his face but he said nothing.

'You knew that the case against Curtis was falling apart, so you planned to use my profile to focus attention towards Tom Drury. You thought that earring would be found quickly, but it wasn't because the cleaner has been off sick, so it got kicked around by patrons and ended up on the car park, where I found it, bagged it and began the chain of evidence.'

He wasn't smiling any more.

'If you even touched that piece of jewellery with your bare hands there'll be DNA all over it, and if they have something to match it to with a suspect you are in some shit.'

'Easily refutable,' he said, trying to gain composure. 'Of course I was here and my DNA could have got on it a hundred different ways.'

An admission that his DNA could be on the trophy he'd taken.

'And that's not even the best bit,' she said, taking another sip of her drink and then a deep breath. 'You chose Beverly as a single unaccompanied female leaving the club. You followed her along Lissett Road past the fastener company on the left-hand side of the street.'

'How could you know that? There's no—'

Realising what he'd said, he stopped speaking.

'In your haste, you forgot to take off the cycle clip clasped around your right trouser leg. You followed five paces behind. I'm betting a decent forensic CCTV tech will be able to identify both the trousers and the bike clip and find the exact same ones in your home.'

His expression turned from rage to tentative amusement.

'Well done, Ali, you're better at this than I gave you credit for. But I see that you have no police support, no backup. You're completely on your own and no one is going to believe—'

'I believe her,' said Stacey, standing up behind him. 'I'm Detective Constable Wood and I just heard every word.'

CHAPTER 106

Kim stopped off at the hospital shop before heading up to the ward. She had been saddened when Penn had explained about Billie's grandfather, but she also understood that male relatives sometimes reacted this way to sexual assault, often finding themselves unable to face their wife, daughter, grandchild.

Kim smiled at the ward sister she'd seen the previous night. Concern shaped her features.

'Don't tire her, she's very fragile.'

Kim nodded her understanding unsure why she was receiving a warning. She stepped into the room and got it. There was someone already sitting beside the bed.

'Hey…' she said, unable to use the only name she knew for him.

The officer she had almost punched got to his feet.

'Marm…'

His face filled with colour and he looked to the ground.

'How is she?' Kim asked, moving to the other side of the bed.

'In and out. Not saying a lot. Has a little cry and then fades away again.'

'Have you tried to ask her…'

'No, Marm, I'm not on shift,' he said, quietly, as he sat back down. 'I just came to apologise for what I…' He shook his head. 'You were right to…'

'No, I wasn't,' Kim admitted. 'I shouldn't have grabbed you and I am sorry but… hang on, what's your name?'

'Twonk.'

'Not your nickname.'

Whatever he'd done wrong she wouldn't call him Twonk.

'Calvin, Marm,' he said.

'If I can give you one piece of advice to take through your police career, it's to never forget the individual behind the victim. It's always someone's sister, brother, mother and they deserve your respect.'

'Got it, Marm, but I don't think I'm cut out for this career.'

'Why'd you say that?'

He shrugged. 'Just not working out how I thought. I'm not suited…'

'I'd disagree,' Kim said, shrugging.

'But you don't know—'

'You're here,' she said. 'In your own time to apologise to someone who didn't even hear what you said. That tells me enough,' she said as Annie entered the room carrying a large coffee.

'Sorry I wasn't…'

Kim waved away her apology. The officer was dressed in jeans and a tee shirt and Kim could only wonder when she'd found the time to go home and change.

Calvin stood. 'I'll be getting off now,' he said taking one last look at Billie. He nodded at them both before leaving the room.

Kim watched him leave and turned to Annie.

'Do me a favour, eh? Put it around that he came.'

Annie smiled. 'Will do.'

The guys who were calling him Twonk deserved to know there was a decent guy in there somewhere.

'J… John…' said a small voice from the bed.

Annie placed her coffee on the side, sat down and took the girl's hand.

'Hey, Billie, it's me, Annie,' she said, quietly.

'W… was… th… that John?'

'No, sweetheart, it was a police officer come to check on you.'

Billie's eyes fluttered open. She looked around the room as though seeking proof for herself. Her eyes rested on Kim. She frowned before looking back to Annie whose presence seemed to reassure her.

'This lady is a detective, Billie. She's going to find out who did this to you.'

Her eyes closed again and a single tear fell from her eye.

'Is John your boyfriend, Billie?' Annie asked.

She shook her head and then nodded and swallowed.

'Used to...'

Kim guessed she was retreating again. She stepped forward and touched Billie's arm.

'Billie, did John do this to you?' she asked, gently.

Billie shook her head, then nodded as another tear forced itself from beneath her eyelid.

'M... met him... b... but...'

'You met him at the park?'

She nodded.

'B... but... he's not v... violent,' she said, and then sighed with the effort.

Kim exchanged a confused glance with Annie. 'I can't get a straight answer either. The doctors are reducing the drugs tomorrow, so I'm hoping she'll be a bit more...'

Annie's words trailed away as a figure appeared in the doorway. It was an elderly man who only had eyes for the figure in the bed.

'Billie,' he whispered, as he moved forward.

Kim was surprised to see Penn right behind him.

She sidled over as Annie stood to let the man sit down beside his granddaughter.

'You brought him?' she asked her colleague.

He nodded. 'Had to give him another try, boss. Poor girl needs her family.'

The man touched Billie's arm, the tears streaming down his face. 'Billie, it's me. It's granddad.'

Her eyes fluttered open. She stared for just a second until her own tears matched his.

'Granddad,' she said, as the man gathered her into his arms.

'I'm here, love, I'm here,' he said, holding her tight.

Kim swallowed the emotion in her throat.

'Good job, Penn, bloody good job.'

'Thanks, boss.'

Kim made eye contact with Annie and indicated she was leaving.

'I'll walk you down, boss. I'll grab a bite and then take him home.'

Now she understood why he'd been paying close attention to his watch. At this rate he wouldn't be home before ten.

'She say anything?' Penn asked, once they stepped out of the lift.

'Said she met Duggar but that he wasn't violent…'

'Which makes no sense,' he said, 'seeing as we have five dead people and we can link him to most of them.'

She nodded her agreement.

'So, you going straight home, boss?'

Normally she would have offered a suitably terse response but she understood why he was asking.

'Yes, Penn, I'm going straight home,' she said, rolling her eyes.

She left him at the café and headed out the door, with one thing troubling her above all else.

Everyone they spoke to claimed John Duggar was not violent. So, either he wasn't responsible for these murders or he was saving it all up for her.

CHAPTER 107

'Morning, guys,' Kim said, as her team assembled at 7 a.m. for the briefing. 'Firstly, I'd like to thank Stacey for popping round last night to brief me on a situation with Alison and her previous case and that someone I've never heard of has been arrested for double murder. Not sure it needed to take almost two hours, but thanks for that, Stace. And then as if by magic Bryant appeared the second she left to pack away and remove all the computer equipment, very very slowly, and then once I threw him out I received ten or more text messages from you, Penn. Not like you planned this, eh, folks, to make sure I was safe?'

'Coincidence,' they all said together.

'Well, I'm sure you're all relieved to know that I had a squad car escort into work this morning but I'd like to assure you all that I'm perfectly capable of looking after myself.'

Amused glances passed between the three of them.

She rolled her eyes. 'Right, someone get the board.'

'Shouldn't we wait for Alison, boss?' Stacey asked, standing. Having taken the desk of Kevin Dawson after his death, she was now the closest.

'I'd imagine she's going to be busy assisting West Mercia now they've got the real killer. I'm sure we'll get official notification from Woody that she's been re-reassigned, if you know what I mean.'

'Missing her already,' Bryant said, glancing at the spare desk.

Yeah, Kim had kind of got used to her presence too.

'Knocker knocker,' she heard from the doorway.

Kim smiled in the direction of Doctor A, who was carrying a white Perspex tray. She waved her into the room.

'Good morning,' Kim greeted.

Doctor A frowned. 'Are you here today or are you not here like yesterday when you were but weren't…' she shook her head. 'You English are strangers.'

'I'm here,' Kim confirmed.

She lay the tray down on the empty desk and moved to the top-right corner holding out her hand.

'Nice to meet you, Penny,' she said, shaking the hand of the newest member of the team. 'And Bryan,' she said, nodding to the other sergeant. 'And the lovely Stacey,' she added, causing Kim to wonder for the hundredth time how many of the woman's misspoken words were mistakes and how many were uttered for her own amusement.

The detective constable positively beamed from the compliment while Bryant simply shook his head and Penn looked around bemused.

'I bring you the puzzlement I spoke of yesterday,' she said, standing beside the empty desk. 'These are the unidentifiables and are neither flesh nor machine. All photographed, examined and tested for DNA. Maybe they help, maybe not but I wouldn't care less as I am tired and my work here is done.'

'Thank you for assisting at short notice, Doctor A,' Kim said.

'You are welcome and now I shall leave you in pieces. Must get back to the university as my students are revolting.'

Kim understood her real meaning and thanked her again for her help as she headed out the door.

They all huddled around the tray and took a look.

'Oh,' Kim said, feeling slightly underwhelmed.

She could make out a few bits of plastic no more than a centimetre wide, a clip that had been flattened and a few pieces of blue fabric.

She pushed the tray to her left. 'Here you go, Penn. I know how much you like a puzzle,' she said. He had been the person to find the missing letters in a paper puzzle that had ultimately led to the team saving the life of Stacey Wood.

'Cheers, boss,' he said, taking the tray back to his desk.

'Anyway, questions I want answered. Number them, Stace.'

Stacey put the number 1 at the top of the board.

'How did Duggar know or tempt Amy and Mark to the flat on Hollytree?'

Kim waited until Stacey was halfway before continuing.

'What's the significance of the drug injected into Amy, Mark, the Phelpses and Rubik?'

'Next question. Where did the book go once it reached the prison? Four, did Duggar meet the Phelps at Winson Green and is that how he chose them? Joel Greene, their son, said they spent a lot of time chatting with other people. Next, why was Duggar so violent with Billie? And finally, who the hell is Rubik?'

'Could Duggar have turned violent because Billie refused to take him back?' Stacey asked, tapping the marker pen against the board.

'Not sure,' Kim said. 'He hadn't been violent to date and what little Billie did say would indicate he wasn't violent with her, although he was with her at the time of the attack.'

Kim shrugged in response to their questioning glances. 'Yeah, exactly. Annie is going to try and get something more from her this morning.'

'That it, boss?' Stacey asked, having caught up.

'Another couple of things bothering me,' she admitted. 'I'm not comfortable with the relationship between Jenks and Nina. It smells off to me.'

'That a question, boss?'

Kim shook her head. 'Just note it on the board.'

'But we're not changing direction, are we, guv?' Bryant asked. 'I mean, Duggar's definitely our guy, right?'

Kim glanced at all the questions on the board.

She nodded. 'Oh yeah, Duggar's definitely our guy.'

CHAPTER 108

Stacey stared at the board for a good few minutes after the boss and Bryant had left the room.

'Do you ever think about it, Penn?' Stacey asked.

'About what?'

'The crimes and the boss. Putting the two together.'

He shook his head. 'Really try not to.'

'I mean there was a book written about her childhood. The physical and mental abuse at the hands of her mother while trying to protect her brother. Being chained to that bloody radiator.'

'I said I try not to think about it,' he said.

'And then there's Keith and Erica who took her in for three years and loved her, broke down her walls and—'

'You did hear me say I try not to—'

'And the vicious sexual assault on Billie Styles that—'

'Yeah, I'm really not gonna think about that one, Stace,' he said, firmly.

'What I'm trying to say is that this vicious bastard is laying out her entire life for everyone to see. Everything she's tried to keep secret and hidden from…'

Her words trailed off as she stared at the board.

Penn followed her gaze. 'Yeah, which of those questions you wanna make a start on?'

Stacey frowned as she grabbed her satchel.

'I'll leave you to get cracking,' she said.

Because suddenly Stacey had a few questions of her own.

CHAPTER 109

Kim had had many reasons to visit the National Probation Service based at Hope House at Castlegate Way in Dudley and today she found herself sitting across the table from a plump woman with owls dangling from her earlobes. Her salt-and-pepper hair cut was short and severe so that the ear embellishments took centre stage.

'John Duggar,' Kim said. 'Can you tell me when you last saw him?'

'Two days ago,' she answered, and then checked her diary. 'Around lunchtime.'

'And, how was he?' she asked.

'Agitated, not quite himself.'

'You know him well?' Bryant asked.

She smiled. 'It's getting harder,' she admitted. 'We have many more to look after than the old days, and I've been at this for twenty-six years but yes I know John reasonably well.'

'So, when did you first meet him?'

'About nine years ago. After his second or third spell inside. Gentle giant, I like to call him. Never hurt a fly.'

Kim pictured Billie in the hospital bed and wasn't sure she would agree.

'Tell us about him,' she urged.

'His story isn't unique; abandoned by his mother and then surrendered to the care system by a grandmother who couldn't cope with three kids but found enough energy to get to the off-licence for cider.'

'She kept the oldest child,' Bryant noted.

'Took less looking after than the younger two. And she could help out around the house.'

'She died, you know, the eldest. In a house fire, a few—'

'We know,' Kim said. 'And how did John take that?'

'Not well,' she said, shaking her head. 'He'd lost touch with his other sister with whom he was placed into care. She was a much calmer kid: quiet, took instruction and got fostered long-term, I believe, but John not so much. He was bullied for a number of reasons, his size, struggled to read and write. The kid was lonely. He wanted someone, anyone. He'd tried to reach out to his eldest sister even though they didn't know each other and she'd agreed to see him. But she died before they met up.'

'Shit,' Bryant whispered.

She offered him a sideways look. Even for her it was difficult enough to remember this was the man trying to kill her. She could do without her colleague losing that focus as well.

'So, when he lost his sister?…'

'It was like he lost hope for anything better. Like everything he'd been chasing was out of reach. He stopped expecting anything good. Until he met Billie.'

Kim said nothing and waited for her to continue.

'Happiest I've ever seen him. It was his first serious relationship and it was like he'd just discovered the secret that everyone else had been keeping. It didn't last of course, but—'

'But, why didn't it?' Kim asked. 'If he was so happy.'

'He's in the vacuum, Inspector. His life of petty crime has trapped him into more crime. He's on a cycle that he's unlikely to escape.'

Kim couldn't work out if this woman was a pessimist or a realist, but she didn't support to the 'No hope' theory that she prayed wasn't being ascribed to the fresher, younger batches of criminals.

'Despite meeting Billie, he was destined to reoffend. It was only a case of when and for how long Billie would put up with it.'

'So, you'd written them off as a couple before their second date?' Kim asked, tightly.

She shrugged. 'Over twenty years' experience and I was right, wasn't I?'

Kim tried not to react to the triumph in her voice.

Yes, this man they were discussing hated her with a passion and yes, he was trying to kill her but bloody hell, was there anyone who hadn't given up on him over the years?

'And even that break-up didn't make him violent?' Bryant asked.

'I'm not sure anything would have, officer. He's not built that way. He's a bit like the local, loveable village idiot,' she said. 'And before you react I'll explain what I mean. John is a people pleaser. He's driven by other people's opinions. He's easily led and manipulated.'

Kim's interest was piqued, remembering what Alison said about his eagerness to belong.

'So, he could be persuaded to act against his nature given the right set of circumstances.'

The woman thought. 'John Duggar does not expect to be liked. Not many people have liked him all that much, so I'd say John Duggar could be persuaded to do just about anything by someone who was being nice to him.'

CHAPTER 110

Penn finished the email he was typing and glanced over to the Perspex box on the spare desk.

The boss had delegated the puzzle to him and he was guessing she'd meant when he had nothing better to do, but considering the list of questions on the whiteboard that time wasn't coming any time soon.

And yet, there was something about it that demanded his attention. Not least because he was in awe that the mangled cube of man and metal he'd seen just a couple of days ago had been reduced to this. For that, the woman responsible could call him anything she liked.

Almost against his will he pushed back his chair and moved over to the spare desk.

He took a moment to assess the contents and pushed aside items he felt could not help him, which were three short pieces of wire, a couple of bent coins that must have been in the victim's pocket, four buttons and a zip.

That left three pieces of card, approximately two centimetres square, a clip and three pieces of blue fabric.

He took these items from the tub and lay them on the desk. He used a pencil to push them around for a better look.

The blue fabric pieces were slivers approximately 10 cm long and 1 cm wide and ribbed, the fibres woven tightly for strength. He moved them around to see if the frayed edges matched each other like bin bags ripped from a roll. They did not, meaning that pieces of the fabric were missing and therefore the whole had been longer than the 30 cm he had in front of him.

He pushed them aside and turned his attention to the flattened clip. The mechanism for opening the clip had been broken and the little pincer teeth were jagged and worn. He pushed it aside towards the blue fabric and pulled the three pieces of card closer. He moved them around with his pencil as he had done with the fabric to see if any of the pieces fitted together, but couldn't find a match.

All three pieces were plain on one side.

He looked more closely at each piece individually. The first had a snatch of grey at the top left. To the right he could make out three letters. He grabbed a notepad and wrote down the letters 'REN'. He put it back and reached for the second. This too had a couple of letters between the tears in the card. He wrote down the letters 'IC' and went for the third. On the last piece there were no letters but what looked like part of a white arc that grew thicker as it travelled up and across the paper. It reminded him of an artistic dab of sauce at a fancy restaurant.

He sat back and looked at what he had. It wasn't much but it was something and now it was up to him to make it count.

CHAPTER 111

Stacey approached the glass partition. 'Excuse me, you said it might be a while until someone could speak to me but it's been almost half an hour since…'

'Officer, when I said a while I meant you might have to come back tomorrow and the next day. This is Children's Services and we don't sit around eating pasta salad all day.'

'What if I wanted to report a child in danger?' Stacey asked, unable to believe getting a quick meeting was so difficult.

'Do you?' she asked.

Stacey shook her head.

'Then rest assured that the people you're here to see are either taking new reports or dealing with existing cases.'

'Who deals with all the old cases?' Stacey asked. 'Say from thirty years ago.'

'Well no one,' she said frowning. 'Because they wouldn't be children any more, would they?'

'I mean who looks after the records for old cases,' Stacey clarified while trying to keep the impatience out of her voice.

'They're kept in a central archive. All social workers would have access.'

'Would there be a record of who had recently accessed a file?'

'From thirty years ago?'

Stacey nodded.

'Wouldn't be electronic, not that old, but personnel have to swipe into the archive room, so there's a record of who accessed the room but not which records they looked at while they were in there.'

Damn, Stacey thought, biting her lip.

As she'd looked at the board with Penn, Stacey had been struck by the level of detail Duggar had gone to in recreating these events. The exact location of the assault, the reference to the pop bottle, the ripped-up five pound note. None of these things had made it into the book because the author hadn't known. His account had covered the past, the death of Mikey and the couple of years following the boss's entrance into the care system.

She doubted very much that these were details the boss would have chosen to share with anyone. Ever. So, she suspected they could only have come from the file.

She had hoped that someone would be able to log into their mainframe and tell her who had accessed any electronic record for the boss in the last few months and give her a lead she could follow.

'And if that's what you want to talk to one of the social workers about I'd bring a packed lunch tomorrow. You could be waiting weeks.'

'Yeah, I know. They're busy, we're all busy but we don't keep banging on about it,' Stacey said, turning away. Her time would definitely be better spent back at the station, answering the boss's questions on the board.

'Thanks for your time,' she said, heading to the door. She paused as her phone began to ring.

'Wood,' she answered.

'Stace, you still in Dudley?' asked Penn.

'Just leaving. Getting nothing…'

'Can you see a staff member?'

She turned. The woman was back on the phone. 'Errr… yeah.'

'Is her identification card white and grey?'

Stacey moved back towards the glass partition and took a look.

'Yes,' she answered.

The woman looked at her questioningly as she continued to speak into the phone.

'Blue lanyard?' Penn continued.

'Yes.'

'With the words "Children's Services" on it?'

'Yes.'

'And the Dudley Council logo with the arc of white line on—'

'Penn, all yeses now what the?…'

Her words trailed away as she remembered the contents of the tray brought in by Doctor A.

'Oh shit, you don't think?…'

'Yep,' Penn answered.

'I'll call you back,' she said, ending the call.

She knocked on the glass.

The woman gave her a filthy look before putting down the phone.

'I think it's time for you—'

'Do you have a staff member off sick or absent?' Stacey asked as her heart began beating in her chest.

She hesitated before nodding. 'Yes, one of our case workers, Ernest Beckett, been absent for a few days. Can't get hold of him—'

'Sorry to interrupt, but can you give me a description?' Stacey asked, taking out her mobile phone.

It looked like Rubik was about to get a new name.

CHAPTER 112

'Bryant, I gotta be honest, there's something about this guy not sitting right in my gut.'

'You know, guv, never do I want a cigarette more than when you say things like that.'

'Almost four years, Bryant, remember that,' she said of his abstinence from the thirty-a-day habit he'd kicked.

'But we're all agreed that Duggar is our guy. His fingers are in every pie. You think we should ignore that?'

'We can't ignore anything,' she said. 'Even the stuff that points away from him.'

'But nothing has actually pointed away from him. Yeah, he had a shit life and if you like I can show you another hundred or more guys in Winson Green with the same history and background. He's not unique and I don't understand the change in your gut—'

He stopped speaking as her phone rang. They would continue this conversation later.

'Stace?' she answered

'Boss, I'm at Children's Services in Dudley.'

'Err… why?' Kim asked. She wasn't sure of any link from her questions on the board to that particular building.

'The detail, boss,' Stacey explained.

Kim listened to her explanation and found herself surprised she hadn't realised that herself.

And her colleague wouldn't be calling if she hadn't found something.

'Go on,' she said.

'There's a social worker. Early fifties, exact description we got from Doctor A for Rubik. He's been absent from work for a few days and could easily have had access to your records.'

'You think he passed some detail on to Duggar.'

'I do, boss,' Stacey said.

'Okay, Stace, try and get me an address for—'

'His name is Ernest Beckett. It's 17 Wilmslow Avenue in Norton, Stourbridge,' Stacey answered.

'Stace…'

'Gotta go, I'm being called through. Somebody here wants to talk to me.'

'Okay, but do me one favour when you get back to the office.'

'Yeah, boss.'

'Take the plant from Penn.'

'Will do,' she said, ending the call with a chuckle.

'Right, Bryant,' Kim said, with renewed energy. 'Let's go see if Ernest Beckett is at home.'

CHAPTER 113

Stacey followed the lanky, thin man through a general office to a room at the back. The space wasn't personalised and she guessed it was a meeting room used by all.

'May I know of your interest in Mr Beckett?' he asked gravely.

Stacey hesitated before answering. In the short space of half an hour she'd gone from waiting in the outer office in Siberia for the scrap of someone's time to find out about the protocols of accessing information in an old file, to being escorted into the nucleus of the operation by Mr Tweedy, Team Leader. But only once she'd hinted at a link to Ernest Beckett.

This man wanted something from her and he wanted it quick. She was in no rush.

'Mr Tweedy, I need to know if Mr Beckett accessed a particular file I told your receptionist about. The one concerning a girl called Kimberly Stone. Until I have that information I'm unable to share any knowledge that—'

'Yes, officer, we have reason to believe he accessed it. He entered the archive room two months ago.'

'Is there any way of knowing what he went in there for?'

'Only two people have been in since. And one of them was me. It's not a room we use often. The files in there are very old.'

'So, why are you so sure he accessed the record that I mentioned?' she asked, confused. They were talking thousands of files, surely.

'Because the records are no longer there,' he said, quietly.

'He took the whole file?' she asked.

He nodded. Oh, she could not count the levels of shit this man was in and about that she couldn't give a flying fig. Her boss's entire childhood was in that file and it was no longer contained in a safe environment. Away from prying eyes and hungry gossipmongers. If that file got into the wrong hands...

Okay, she needed to leave right now.

She pushed back her chair and stood.

'Wait a minute,' Tweedy protested. 'You haven't told me what link you have to Ernest Beckett.'

'I'm sorry, but as it's part of an active investigation, I'm unable to share the details.'

He sighed heavily. 'Can you at least tell me if you have him in custody?'

Stacey considered his question and nodded. They had most of him in custody.

'Can you give me any idea of the nature of the charges against him?'

Why was the man assuming that he was a suspect in something?

'You seem awfully nervous about our dealings with Mr Beckett,' she observed.

'I just need to know something, officer. I need to know if your business is linked to a complaint received about Mr Beckett this week. A very serious complaint indeed.'

CHAPTER 114

'There's a definite smell,' Kim said, raising her head from the letterbox. 'I don't think it's a body but it's not Chanel N°5 either.'

'You reckon he's our guy in the cube?' Bryant asked, looking around.

Kim knew what he was doing and followed. They both smiled at the row of three plant pots beneath the front window.

'Which one?' Bryant asked.

'Far right,' she said, without hesitation.

'I say middle,' he smirked.

She crossed her arms while he did the honours. First, he lifted the left. Nothing. He lifted the middle and groaned. He lifted the far right and the metal sparkled up at him.

'How do you do that?' he asked, shaking his head and retrieving the key.

'The middle is too obvious. Everyone would try that first.'

'Thanks,' Bryant mumbled.

'The left is too close to the actual door, which is too close for the subconscious, so the only one remaining is the one on the right. Simples,' she said as he opened the door.

'Jeez, you're right about the smell,' he said, pulling a face.

She leaned down and picked up the small pile of post on the floor as her phone began to ring.

She took out her phone and groaned. 'Frost, get the message. I can't speak to you. Boss's instructions,' she shouted at the screen before cutting off the call.

'You being the guv, I'll let you check out the kitchen and I'll do the lounge.'

'Cheers,' she said, pretty sure that's where the smell was coming from.

'Jesus,' she said to herself as she entered the space.

Ernest Beckett was clearly a man who cleaned and tidied only when he'd run out of things to use.

The sink and surrounding area was awash with plates, bowls, cups and glasses still containing leftover food and drink. A few flies rose from the carnage as she approached. They hovered frantically before heading towards an area of the work surface where the man had clearly been preparing himself a snack. A block of cheese had been left out in the path of direct sunlight next to the kettle that was spottled with grease stains.

A tub of margarine sat beside a dirty knife.

To leave everything out had to mean the guy had left in a rush but there were no signs of a struggle. The door had been locked and a spare key in its normal place.

'Never gonna win cleaner of the year,' Bryant said, joining her.

He glanced at the mess by the sink as he swatted away a fly from in front of his face.

'And there's more of that upstairs on his bedside cabinet.'

'Ugh,' Kim said.

'Wife won't even let me take a slice of toast to bed,' he moaned.

'Surprising what some men get up to when left to their own devices.'

'You know, I did it once,' Bryant said, opening and closing cupboard doors. 'Wife went with her sister to a weekend spa in Cheshire. Remember the film *Home Alone* where Macaulay Culkin is tearing round the house doing whatever he wants? That was me that was. Spent all day Saturday in my pyjamas, ate what I wanted, drank what I wanted, downloaded every mindless action movie I could find.'

'Turned into a ten-year-old boy,' she observed.

'Exactly that, but by the next morning I was over it and spent Sunday cleaning up the evidence. She still knew I'd had toast in the bed, though.'

'Your missus sounds like a better detective than—'

'And I'm gonna stop you saying something right there that you can't unsay, guv.'

'So, what's this tell us about the man?'

'Tells us he either didn't care or had stopped seeing the mess around him,' Bryant answered. 'Also tells us he probably wasn't expecting any visitors.'

'Doesn't tell us if he's the man in the car,' Kim grumbled.

'No, but the computer in the lounge might.'

'Bryant, we could have been working on…'

'Relax,' he said, smirking at her. 'Stacey and Mitch are already on their way, so don't even think of touching it until they get here.'

CHAPTER 115

'Really, boss?' Stacey asked, looking at her, then at Mitch and Bryant and then back at the table.

The laptop had been logged and bagged by Mitch but he'd expertly done it so that the computer was on, open and the keys could be seen through the plastic.

'Come on, Stace, you've worked in tougher conditions than this,' Kim said, standing behind her.

'Yeah, working through a giant condom is not my normal working day,' she said, turning to the three of them looking over her shoulder. 'And a little space, please.'

They all backed away as Stacey began to type.

'I think I know what I'm going to find,' Stacey said, as Kim saw the screen flash from one back-end menu to another. Kim was constantly amazed at Stacey's ability to know exactly what she was looking at. It reminded her of the back corridors at an arena. Service areas and dark passageways that operated behind the scenes. Only the people that knew it well could find their way around.

'You wanna share?' Bryant asked.

'If I did I would've,' she said. 'What I'm really interested in is how they—'

Stacey stopped speaking and Kim knew better than to push her. She wasn't really talking to them but more to herself.

'I'm gonna head off,' Mitch said, collecting up his things. 'Let me know what you want doing with the rest of this place.'

'Will do,' Kim said. She'd already explained they had no positive identification on whether this guy was the man in the car.

For all they knew the homeowner could walk in any minute with a perfectly reasonable explanation for his absence from work and from his home.

Although after what Stacey had told her about the missing file she doubted that scenario very much.

'Wanna take a good look for it?' Bryant asked, thinking the same as her.

She shook her head. 'No point. If Ernest Beckett took my file it wasn't for some late-night reading. He could have read it at work without risking his job and career. I reckon he got it for someone.'

'I'd agree with that,' Stacey said.

They both ignored her.

'Yeah, I am actually talking to you guys, now,' Stacey said, with amusement.

They both moved closer to the dining table.

'Okay, as I thought. This file here is full of kiddie porn. Over three thousand images to be exact.'

'Bastard,' Bryant said. And Kim hoped that if it was Ernest Beckett mangled in the metal that he'd been alive at the time.

'Not so fast,' Stacey said, hovering her mouse over one short line of data amongst the thousands.

'That is the only image that's been viewed.'

'Why?' Kim asked, surprised. 'Not normal behaviour for a paedophile.'

'To check, I think,' Stacey said. 'Because I don't think he downloaded them. Not intentionally anyway. They all landed on his computer on the same day. Nothing before and nothing since. He accessed one single image as though making sure that's what they were.'

'Blackmail?' Kim asked.

'Looks like it. I've got the email the attachment was embedded in. It came as a chance to win a holiday. Pretty poor and amateurish but to the naked eye convincing enough; but as soon as he pressed on the link to enter the images downloaded.'

'I'm thinking there must have been some kind of follow-up message somewhere to tell him what to do, so I'll carry on going through his emails and stuff.'

'And you say there was a complaint at work?'

Stacey nodded. 'An anonymous letter stating he'd acted inappropriately with one of his cases.'

'But if he'd done everything they wanted, why do that anyway?' Bryant asked. 'He got them the file, handed it over so…'

'Unless he said no. Maybe he had some sudden rush of conscience and said he was going to the police,' Bryant said.

'Could be,' Kim agreed, taking out her phone.

She took the card from her pocket that she'd grabbed earlier and called the number.

The probation officer for John Duggar answered on the second ring.

Kim offered her a brief outline of what they'd found and then asked the all-important question. There was no hesitation from the woman in answering.

'Absolutely not,' she said. 'John Duggar would not be remotely capable of executing anything near what you've described.'

Yes, that was exactly what she'd thought.

'But I think he'd know a man who could.'

Bryant ended the call and turned to her.

'Yep, Officer Gennard confirmed that Duggar's cellmate for five months was one Derek Lowry who was inside for cyber theft and selling on stolen identities. Could easily have cooked up the message with the images imbedded.'

'Great, you get an address?'

Bryant nodded. 'As of three days ago he was residing at HMP Bristol after breaking his parole.'

'But that's for young adult and…'

'The kid is seventeen years old.'

'Got it,' Stacey said, causing them both to turn.

'Email came the day after the download message. Here it is.'

Kim read it over her shoulder.

Mr Beckett.

Please read this carefully. This is not junk mail and your reputation and career rely on you taking this message seriously and following the instructions below to the letter.

At 10.05 a.m. yesterday you downloaded thousands of images containing child pornography to your computer. You will find them in the photographs folder on your directory in a subfolder called Childs Play. If you try to delete them they will still leave a trace.

The police and your employers will be contacted if you do not do the following:

1. *Obtain the file of Kimberly Stone who entered the care system on 15 June 1988*
2. *Deposit the file in the yellow grit bin on Llewellyn Avenue, Lower Gornal at 11 p.m. on Friday night.*
3. *Return home and delete this message.*

Any variation on these instructions will prompt an immediate complaint and call to the police.

'Jesus,' Kim said. 'If only he'd contacted us we could have stopped this. We could have had them right there and then.'

'Should we go and check out the location stated?'

'Don't need to,' Kim said. 'It was the street of foster family number one.'

'But why?…'

'Because he knew, Bryant. He knew we'd follow this trail. It's just one more slap in the face for me,' she snarled, pacing the room. 'I swear to God, just one more fucking—'

She stopped speaking as her phone began to ring.

'Keats,' she snapped into the phone, catching the exchange of expression between her two colleagues.

'Well, if you were pissed off before I called,' he said, 'you're going to be even more irate by the time I've finished. Come meet me at the entrance to Netherton Tunnel and I'll show you why.'

CHAPTER 117

Netherton Tunnel opened in August 1858 and was the last major canal tunnel to be built in Britain during the canal age. Built with a width of 27 feet it allowed two-way working of narrowboats with towpaths running through it.

Kim remembered Keith bringing her for a walk through the tunnel on a bright Sunday afternoon, guiding her into the darkness and then pointing out the speck of light that signalled the other end over 9,000 feet away.

As they travelled towards it, he would point out the chainage markers on the eastern wall of the tunnel and talk to her of horse-drawn narrowboats. She would try to ignore the drips that fell from the vents called 'pepper pots' on the roof of the tunnel and focus on how exciting he made it sound.

Kim pulled herself back to the present. There were many emotions she should be feeling, but her first emotion as she looked down at the body of John Duggar was sadness.

This guy had not had the best start in life and fate seemed to have just dealt him one blow after another. His height, background and illiteracy had all made him a target to the insecure and cruel. She knew at times there'd been hope. His job, his relationship with Billie had all been opportunities for him to change his life.

'You been looking for this guy, Inspector?' Keats asked, standing up.

She nodded. 'Yeah, suspect in a lot of what's happened this week.'

'Well, if it's anything that's happened since Wednesday night it wasn't him because he's been dead for approximately thirty-six hours.'

'And he's only just been found?' Kim asked.

'He was back there,' Keats nodded towards the side of the tunnel mouth. 'Covered in foliage but some guy's retriever came back with one of his shoes and the body was spotted. Single stab wound to the heart by the looks of it.'

Kim stepped back and took a good look. Whether or not he liked to fight this would have been a hard man to fell and yet she could see no defensive wounds on his hands or arms.

'Got any more for me, Keats?' she asked.

'Judging by the blood loss back there he hasn't been moved.'

Yeah, cos that would have taken a small army, she thought.

Keats continued. 'Small knife, well placed, judging by the wound so he wouldn't have suffered. I can give you more when I get him back.'

'Okay, thanks,' she said, turning away.

Three steps later.

'Um… Inspector, aren't you forgetting something?'

She turned. 'Like what?'

'A disrespectful attitude, a request for me to meet unrealistic timescales, annoying jibes, poor attempts at humour. All of the above?'

She offered him a brief smile before continuing her journey to the car.

'It could be over, you know,' Bryant said, falling into step beside her. 'There have been no incidents since Duggar's death. We know he was with Billie and then disappeared. This could be some totally unconnected incident. It's unlikely this guy is without enemies. Maybe one of them just got to him in the nick of time and did us a favour.'

'Hmmm…'

'You don't sound convinced.'

'Hmmm…' she repeated.

'I'm lost,' he said, scratching his head. 'If you didn't think Duggar was our guy and that this was the end of it, why didn't you ask Keats more questions?'

Kim remained silent as she got into the car.

Bryant didn't understand that just the sight of John Duggar lying dead on the ground had told her everything she needed to know.

Yes, there was no doubt that John Duggar had hated her.

But someone else hated her more.

CHAPTER 118

'So, where was the blood?' Kim asked, as Bryant tried again to convince her that Duggar was their man.

A quick call to Keats had confirmed that he detected no traces of blood on the man's clothing or shoes that were not consistent with the man's own injury.

Penn and Stacey continued to watch the exchange as though at a tennis match.

Bryant rubbed at his head in frustration. 'I don't—'

'If Duggar assaulted Billie with that bottle there'd be some of her blood on him.'

He made a face. 'Keats might have made a mistake. How the hell could he tell there was only the man's own blood on—'

Kim held out her phone. 'About ten years of training and thirty years of experience but feel free to call and question his judgement. Not sure you'd still be his favourite detective but knock yourself out.'

Bryant ignored the gesture. 'Duggar could have had time to change and—'

'Where?' she asked, with growing frustration. 'We were at his house. Blood-soaked clothing might have caught our attention, don't you think?'

'We didn't do a full search, guv,' he replied patiently.

'And what about all this, Bryant?' she asked, standing next to the board and the questions she'd posed.

'How did Duggar tempt Amy and Mark to the flat?'

'How did Duggar get hold of the drug found in most of our victims?'

'Who ordered the book and where is it now?'

'Did Duggar meet the Phelpses at prison?'

'Why was Duggar suddenly violent with Billie? And now we have even more questions. What's Ernest Beckett's role in this?'

The room fell silent in response to her words.

'Damn it, guys,' she growled, smacking the desk in frustration. 'Are we really going to accept Duggar's death as serendipity and leave those questions unanswered while we pat ourselves on the fucking back?'

Everyone looked away until eventually Penn braved the silence. 'But, boss, we can tie Duggar to at least—'

'At least isn't good enough, Penn,' she said, shaking her head. 'And Bryant, just because you want it to be over doesn't mean it is. Now I'm going to brief Woody, so if you can answer all these questions by the time I get back, we'll close the case, head down the pub to celebrate and the first round is on me.'

CHAPTER 119

'You ready?' Symes asked Lord and Preece.

They both nodded and he could feel the excitement building in his loins. Not long now and he'd be out of here and on his way to give that bitch exactly what she needed. After which he'd probably hand himself in. Could even be back by bedtime.

'Just a couple of minutes down there will do it, okay?'

'Got it,' they said as Lord approached the table least receptive to the presence of a black man.

He sat down. 'Hey, blud.'

The group of skinheads looked from one to the other and then at Lord. 'You on some kind of bet, blud?' one of them asked with emphasis on the last word.

'Just taking the weight off, ya get me?'

'Mate, for your own sake…'

'Free country,' said Preece, moving in. 'Man can sit where—'

Seven skinheads stood at the same time as the attention of the whole wing focussed on that middle table.

Symes moved towards the hostility and got himself into position. 'Come on, let the man…'

His words trailed away as chief skinhead threw a punch at Lord. Lord grabbed his arm, easily and twisted him around, pushing him back into his gang. The eruption came as onlookers surged forward at the same second the gang retaliated. Symes started counting as he lowered himself to the ground just a foot away from the scrabble.

He could hear the guards shouting from the gate but they wouldn't enter the space without riot gear.

He took the instrument he'd stolen from the dentist suite and dug into his scalp with the hook that was normally reserved for being pushed up into teeth and dragged it across. Immediately blood gushed from the wound.

He had chosen to injure his own head, which would bleed profusely due to the number of tiny veins and arteries that lay just below the surface of the skin. Head wounds were rarely as serious as they appeared but had to be dealt with seriously for fear of concussion and brain damage.

The screaming around him had reached fever pitch as inmates pushed, shoved and punched each other with no idea why – but a fight was a fight.

A pair of legs fell against him as he made the second cut across his scalp. The blood began to gush over his forehead and into his eyes. Perfect.

He heard the gates open and the deafening sound of a herd of officers in full gear.

Inmates began to move aside, realising they didn't even know what it was all about. The scenery opened up around him as he lay his head down on the ground and closed his eyes.

He sensed someone tower above him.

'Shit, over here, quickly,' Lord shouted. 'This man needs an ambulance.'

CHAPTER 120

'You don't look like you've walked in here with that Friday afternoon feeling, Stone,' Woody said, with the hint of a smile. 'And I hear that congratulations are—'

'No, sir, they're not,' she said, sitting down before she'd been invited, which prompted an immediate expression of concern from her boss.

'But I heard your main suspect had been found dead and—'

'Sir, do you have a direct line to Bryant that I don't know?'

'I saw it on the system, Stone,' he corrected. 'I'm just now confused as to why this is not a good thing.'

'There are too many loose ends, too many connections we can't make between Duggar and events,' she said, trying to temper her frustration.

'Like what?' he asked, lacing his fingers beneath his chin.

'I can't find a definite link from Duggar to Amy and Mark.'

'Didn't he view the flat they were found in?'

She nodded. 'I'm not saying he didn't get the key cut, but if he called to get them to the flat, why'd they take him flowers?'

'Did they arrive with the flowers?' he asked.

'Don't know,' she answered honestly.

'So, they could have been for someone else. It's not beyond the realms of possibility that they were dropped off en route and had no link to their murder.'

Kim had never been keen on eliminating facts for the purpose of trying to make something fit, but he did have a point.

'I don't know how Duggar would have come by the drug that—'

'An ex-prisoner able to get his hands on drugs. Yes, that's a stretch.'

'But, why did Duggar get so violent with Billie? He loved her.'

'It wasn't about Billie Styles though, was it? It was about his hatred for you.'

'Sir, my stomach is positively growling at you right now. We're making too many concessions, too many what ifs or could haves. My jaw is tightening at the route we're taking. Where is the solid evidence?'

'So, nothing I've said is plausible?' he asked.

'Plausible but not solid. I mean, do you remember us ever having a conversation like this before?' she asked.

Right now, it felt to her they were doing a jigsaw and trying to force similar-shaped pieces into the available holes just to get it finished.

'Not every case weaves neatly into the plait at the end, Stone, but that's not why you're objecting to the facts and the possibilities. What's really driving the motor in your gut?'

'The end game, sir. There isn't one. Right at the beginning of this case it was clear that the motive was to hurt me as much as possible, to cause me the maximum psychological pain. There's no point to all these murders to leave me alive at the end of it. Someone with this much hate needs to see me dead. It's the only thing that makes sense. With Duggar gone there's no end game and no signs of there being one. What was his plan? What was he going to do with me? We all knew that was the aim once Alison actually—'

'And what's her take on this? Does she think Duggar's your man?'

'Nice one, sir. I'd have liked to ask her that one myself, so great time to release her back to West Mercia.'

Kim frowned as his eyebrows moved towards each other.

'Stone, I'm not sure what you're talking about but Alison Lowe has not been reassigned.'

'Try her again, Stace,' Kim said, pacing the office. 'And Penn, see if the squad car got to her home yet?'

'Will do, boss,' they said together and looked at each other before reaching for their phones.

'Yes, I know it's only been a few minutes but every second counts, right?'

'Nothing, boss,' Stacey said. 'Straight to voicemail.'

'And DCI Merton said she left them last night at?'

'About half an hour after me,' Stacey answered. 'Around midnight. She gave a statement and a squad car took her straight home. Merton told her he'd be in touch if he needed anything further during questioning of Jamie Hart, but he's not spoken to her since.'

'Okay, start looking at CCTV for the times she arrived and left this week. I want to know if she came in any vehicle other than her own.'

Stacey nodded and started tapping away to access the station cameras.

'Penn?' she said, as he ended the call.

He shook his head. 'Still a few minutes out. They'll call as soon as they get there.'

'Okay, where else can we look? What do we know about her?' Kim asked.

'She eats a lot,' Stacey offered while Penn just shrugged.

'So, this woman has been working alongside us all week and the best we've got is she's not keen on dogs and has a healthy appetite?'

Her colleagues said nothing. Kim wasn't only angry at them; she was just as angry at herself.

'I don't think it matters,' Bryant said, staring at the board.

'Bryant, I swear if you're gonna try and tell me this is all some weird coincidence, that Duggar is our man and Alison is off at an all-you-can-eat buffet, I'm gonna…'

'I'm not saying that, guv,' he said. 'I'm saying that I'm not sure it matters where she's been or what she's been doing up until this point. All that matters if we're right, and I mean we, is where she is now and the only person who can tell us that is you.'

All the tapping in the room stopped.

'Me?' she asked.

He nodded. 'The first crime was Amy and Mark, staged to look like you and Mikey in a place identical to where you used to live. The second murder was a middle-aged couple designed to replicate the death of Keith and Erica outside a place that was special to you. The assault on Billie Styles…'

'Make your point, Bryant,' she snapped but she had a rough idea where he was going.

'If this goes true to form we're looking at a traumatic event that involved one of your colleagues.'

'Dawson,' she whispered.

Stacey swallowed, and Penn looked to the ground.

The sound of Penn's phone ringing startled them all.

He grabbed it quickly and listened.

'Nothing, boss,' he said. 'Her car's in the drive but no answer from the house.'

'Give them my authority to force entry,' Kim said.

Penn relayed the message as she turned to Bryant.

'Throw us your keys. This I want to see for myself and this time it's my turn to drive.'

CHAPTER 122

Kim said nothing as she negotiated the traffic at speed while Bryant hung on and prayed for his life. Not once had he told her to slow down.

She pulled up almost kissing the rear bumper of the squad car.

'Thanks for that, guv. The not smashing us into an oncoming vehicles bit,' Bryant said getting out of the car.

The front door was open and two constables stood in the doorway.

'No one here, Marm,' said one.

'No sign of a struggle,' said the other.

'Thanks, guys,' Kim said, walking past them.

She glanced into the living room as she passed and did a double take.

She always headed for the kitchen as it was the best indicator of recent activity, as they'd seen with Ernest Beckett who had been in the throes of preparing a snack and had evidently rushed from the premises.

The lounge often indicated the personality of the owner and boy did this room have personality. The room was a chic tribute to the Sixties. Plush carpet with orange swirls that reminded Kim of a kaleidoscope. A gramophone and cabinet occupied the furthest corner with vinyl albums stacked beside it, but the wall-mounted TV was state-of-the-art curved with a speaker cut into the wall and a subwoofer at the back of the room. A long square sofa with two cushions placed on four thin, spindly legs faced the TV, with a single chair statement piece shaped like half an egg sat to the side. Kim just knew that chair was going to twist and tilt.

The fact that she could not place Alison for one second in this room brought a smile to her face. The woman had surprised her and she liked it. This one room told Kim that Alison lived for herself and no one else. She wanted retro furniture but high-tech viewing. She hadn't tried to fit a style, she simply liked what she liked. Her own home was furnished sparsely and was clutter free but that's how she liked it and she wasn't into buying ornaments and trinkets to make other people feel at home.

She headed to the kitchen which was dominated by a bubble-gum pink American-style fridge freezer.

Without room for a table, kitchen units had been removed from beneath the marble countertop and two stools completed the self-made seating area.

The unit to the right was an integrated dishwasher containing glasses, cups and a dozen small plates. Stacey was right, looked like this woman was a grazer living on snacks but with few proper meals.

'Nothing upstairs except for a few weird furnishings,' said Bryant. 'Which I can see is a recurring theme down here.'

Kim nodded her agreement as her phone signalled the receipt of a text message.

She took it out and saw it was from a number she didn't recognise.

She opened it and read the words as her blood ran cold.

Bryant was opening cupboard doors as she turned away and read it again.

'What's up?' Bryant asked, noticing her silence.

She had to make a quick decision.

'Update from Keats,' she said, placing her phone back in her pocket.

'Saying?'

'Nothing much,' she hedged, her mind already forming a plan.

He gave her an odd look.

'Nothing that's gonna help us find Alison,' she said, trying not to make the lie worse; but right now she felt like every second mattered.

'Bryant, I'm gonna go check her bathroom for any clues. Wanna head out and check that shed in the back garden?'

He didn't know that she already knew it was a complete waste of time. The text message said so.

He reached the back door and turned.

'You okay, guv, you look a bit?…'

'I'm fine, Bryant, now go check so we can get moving.'

He opened the back door and stepped out just as she turned and left the house.

CHAPTER 123

Bryant opened the shed door with an uneasy feeling that was not caused by what he might find. He was as convinced as his boss that Alison was not at home, either dead or alive.

No, it was the look on her face when she'd told him the text message was from Keats.

He was sure she was lying and had they been at her house, drinking coffee and she was Kim, he'd have said so. But while she was Guv it wasn't a great idea.

What she didn't realise, and he wasn't going to mention it, was that although she was a good liar she was a reluctant one. Everything about her was direct and truthful, so he'd learned to read her eyes. And they held regret.

He cast his eyes over the normal assortment of shed guts. A battered barbecue, ripped parasol and an assortment of cobwebbed hand tools. Nothing of interest. He took a cursory glance around the perimeter in the name of thoroughness.

He headed back to the house. If he asked her again who had sent the text message, he wasn't exactly calling her a liar but just giving her a second opportunity to tell the truth.

'Hey, guv, who'd you say?…'

It didn't take him long to realise he was talking to an empty room.

He moved to the hallway and glanced into the lounge.

Of course, she was heading upstairs to check Alison's bathroom.

'Hey, guv,' he called, from the bottom of the stairs.

'She ain't up there, mate… sorry… I mean…'

'So, where is she?' he asked, turning to one of the constables who had broken into the house.

'Tore off in an Astra Estate just a few—'

Bryant swore and headed back to the kitchen, taking out his phone.

He dialled her number and quietly seethed as it rang and rang before depositing him at voicemail. He ended the call and tried again. Same.

'Damn it,' he growled, calling Stacey. What the hell was she playing at?

'Hey Stace, the guv call in?'

'Err, no… aren't you?…'

'Did you call her for anything?'

'Nope, not a—'

'Stace, we had anything through recently from Keats?'

'Hang on… nope nothing. I can—'

'Fuck,' he said, looking around.

The squad car already here had to stay to keep the premises safe until they could get it re-secured.

'Stace, send a squad car out to fetch me.'

'Okay, Bryant, but what the hell is?…'

'It's the guv, Stace. The guv has gone AWOL.'

CHAPTER 124

Kim ignored the seventh call to her mobile and pulled over.

She knew some of those calls would be from Bryant and some probably from Stacey.

Yes, she felt bad running out on her colleague like that and not least because she'd taken his car but the text message had been specific.

She took out her phone and read it again.

> *'You know who I have and you know who I want. Come alone or she dies. You know where I am.'*

Enough people had died this week because of one person's sick vendetta against her. She couldn't risk one more person getting hurt.

And the person who had sent the text message was right.

She did know where Alison would be.

She just didn't know who she was with.

CHAPTER 125

Alison tried to stem the feeling of panic rising within her, but the fear inside her body wanted to get out.

She knew that she was outside; she could feel wisps of her hair blowing in the breeze and the freshness of the air around her.

She knew that she was lying on her back and that storm clouds were passing overhead.

She could feel brick biting into the bare skin of her arms and her scalp.

She knew she was on some kind of ledge because her right arm had fallen over the side and hung limply, uselessly, against the brick.

She didn't know how long she'd been here, but none of these things were causing the terror to surge around her veins.

That was coming from the fact that she couldn't move.

Not one muscle in her body was responding to the commands in her brain.

Her mind was clear, sharp, focussed. But no matter how forcefully she told it to send messages along her nerves, communication had been severed.

She had no clue of the time and her last memory had been early morning.

She remembered getting out of bed, drinking a green tea, heading upstairs and changing into her running gear. It was enough to ease the guilt for her constant grazing habit while desk-bound and her adrenaline had still been high from the night before. She'd needed the exercise to expel it from her system.

She'd left the house just before 7 a.m., turned left to the end of the street, shortcut through the trading estate to the park. Joined other morning joggers, taken a rest at the halfway point close to the bins and then…

Her thoughts came to a standstill. It was what she did every morning, knowing the circuit was approximately two miles. And she could remember it from that morning.

She closed her eyes and thought harder, trying to get past the brick wall of the bin rest.

Leave house
Turn left
Cross Road
Trading Estate
Enter Park
Man with poodle
Joggers
People sitting on benches
Lady on bike
Stop at bins
Bend over, catch breath
Ouch

There it was, the brick wall again but there was something else first. A pinprick, like a sting to her back as she'd bent forward hands on knees, breathing heavily.

And then nothing.

She had no recollection after that.

Had she been assaulted, raped? What the hell was going on?

Knowing she'd been drugged did nothing to calm the fear because now she understood why she couldn't move and she also understood there wasn't a thing she could do about it.

CHAPTER 126

'Come on, guys, talk to me,' Bryant urged from the top of the room. 'What the hell do we think is going on?'

'The text message must have been from the killer,' Penn said, more to fill the silence, he thought.

'But why no contact?' Bryant asked in frustration.

Stacey put down the phone. 'Nothing. I reckon the battery is out,' she said.

Damn, they were trying to track someone who did not want to be found.

'I've got nothing on CCTV,' Penn offered. 'It's a mile to the first camera and three traffic islands in between. She could be anywhere.'

He hadn't yet informed Woody that the guv was MIA but he had no clue how long he could cover. She was a phone call away from a whole heap of shit which, right now, was the least of his worries, but if they didn't have some kind of breakthrough soon it was a phone call he was going to have to make.

What was she walking into and against whom?

'Maybe the killer told her to come alone? That'd explain why she legged it,' Penn said.

Bryant knew he had a point. If the guv thought she was putting anyone else in danger she would have gone it alone.

'Should we have listened to Alison?' Stacey asked, quietly. 'She urged us to consider other potential suspects but we've been stuck on Duggar this whole time. Maybe we should have—'

'Doesn't matter, Stace,' Bryant said, staring at the board. 'Knowing who it is doesn't help us at all. Just like earlier, all that matters is following the crumbs, the logic of the killer. It's the only thing that will tell us where she is.'

All three of them fell silent and stared at the board for a few minutes.

Penn broke the heavy silence. 'Everything about these incidents is as close as it could possibly be to the actual event. The young kids in the identical flat, just a few floors below. The handcuffs, the radiator, the cracker packet. All accurate.'

'The middle-aged couple, respectable, likeable, burned alive in front of the place that was important to them all,' Stacey said.

'And the assault,' Bryant added. 'In the exact same place that the bastard used to take… the girls to abuse them. The five pound note, ripped in her pocket. So, what does that tell us?' Bryant asked, frowning.

'That it's all in the detail,' Stacey said. 'Our killer has to remain as close as possible to actual events to cause the maximum amount of pain.'

'So, Dawson's death,' Penn said. 'He's using Alison as the work colleague who fell—'

'So, it has to be somewhere high,' Stacey finished. 'Alison has to fall from a great height.'

'And the place has to mean something to the boss,' Penn said.

A memory from earlier in the week clicked in to Bryant's brain. Something the guv had said.

'Come on guys,' he said, grabbing his jacket. 'I think I know where we have to go.'

Kim parked the car, looked up to the sky and shuddered. It was a long way to fall. No one would survive.

She tried to push away the night-time eeriness of the place as she began to climb the stairs to the top.

She knew without a doubt that this was where Alison had been taken. It was the only place that made sense.

Every fibre of her being urged her to go faster, to take the stairs two at a time, but she had to pace herself. It was a long climb and despite her beating heart she had to force herself to remember that the floor show would not start without her. The floor show was for her.

The killer wanted her to witness the death of her colleague and then meet her own end, as that had been her most recent torture and one where the wound was still open.

But how the hell could she hope to save Alison or herself when she didn't even know who she was fighting?

Her opponent knew everything about her and she knew nothing about them.

She could feel her own momentum growing faster. Her feet trying to keep up with her thoughts.

She had to go back to the beginning. She had to know who she was dealing with, who she was up against so both she and Alison were not going to wind up dead.

Her gut had told her Duggar wasn't behind the killings despite the evidence. Both her meeting with him and everything she'd learned since had confirmed that feeling despite the presence of his footprint all over the case.

As she climbed, Kim thought about Amy and Mark, young and addicted to drugs, without family support and desperate for somewhere to belong. A home of their own.

The Phelps family had been good people, forced to visit their son in a place that was completely alien to them, uncomfortable in an unfamiliar landscape.

John Duggar acting against type, simply doing what he was told by someone who had probably been nice to him.

Billie Styles lured to a place by her ex-boyfriend who probably had no clue how she was going to be assaulted.

Ernest Beckett, blackmailed and threatened with ruin of his life and reputation.

Symes and his hate club with a reach far beyond the prison walls.

And still Kim didn't know who had ordered the book. Her gut told her that one single fact was important.

But from what she had seen she knew this person hated her with a blind passion. She knew they were ruthless, cunning and had ice running in their veins. They were able to murder without a second thought yet charm to get what they wanted.

'Oh shit,' Kim said out loud as lines began to appear between the dots in her mind.

'Oh shit,' she repeated as her pace up the steps quickened.

She finally knew who she was going to meet.

CHAPTER 128

'How many steps to the top?' Bryant asked, as the three of them tried to remain together as they climbed the watch tower of Dudley Castle.

The space was narrow and claustrophobic, forcing them into single file for the ascent as all of them shone their torches on the ground.

'Around two hundred, I think,' Penn said from behind. Stacey was sandwiched in between.

'Good job getting us in, Penn,' Bryant whispered.

'Everyone round here knows about the shortcut.'

They had parked on the car park just down from the main entrance to the site.

'I used to do the Ghost Walks in my teens,' he said. 'I was a skeleton but had to get back down to the pub to be the Grey Lady too,' he whispered back.

Penn had guided them through the darkness, up the hill and past the cannon on the north side of the castle.

'You really think she's here?' Stacey asked as Bryant felt some air from the top. They were getting close.

'Guv mentioned it earlier in the week. Keith and Erica used to bring her to the zoo and castle all the time. The place is significant for her. The killer has to know that. And it's bloody high,' he added.

Besides which, he thought to himself, she has to be here because otherwise she'd be dead.

CHAPTER 129

Kim took the last step which led to the top of the building.

She took a deep breath, back where it all began.

She pushed open the door to the roof of the tower block called Chaucer House.

Her eyes quickly adjusted to the altered light as her gaze rested on the figure who was waiting.

Kim stepped onto the roof.

'Good evening, Mallory, and, how are you?'

'All the better for seeing you, Stone,' she said with a coldness that chilled Kim's blood.

'Where's Alison?' she asked, trying to keep her voice even. 'You have me now, so it's time to let her go.'

A light laugh came from her lip. 'Oh, you really don't want me to do that?' Mallory asked, looking to the ground.

Kim followed her gaze and saw a rope, a fucking bell rope, like the one that had given way on Dawson.

For a second she was right back there, on the ground, crawling across gravel, screaming warnings when the frayed rope snapped and sent her colleague plunging to his death.

She caught her breath and focussed on the woman before her who had taken out a knife.

'I'll let her go when I'm ready.'

Kim followed the trail of the rope across the flat roof from where it was double tied around the fixings of a heating unit, coiled in the middle of the roof like a discarded fire hose and then trailed to the edge of the building where Alison lay, unmoving, on her back.

Kim knew the width of that edging and one false move would send her tumbling over the edge and to certain death. Kim had no idea how securely the woman was tied to the rope.

All she knew was that she had to stop this final outcome. If Mallory wanted to remain true to form, then she would push Alison over the edge to torture her before killing her. Another life lost because of her.

She had to find a way to trade Alison's life for hers.

'I'm the one you want,' Kim said, taking a small step forward.

Mallory did the same, towards Alison.

'If you try to come near me, I'll push her,' she warned. 'You should know that I'm the one in control here and I will get what I want.'

Kim stood still. 'You know, Mallory, if you wanted my attention that badly you could have called. We could have done lunch. Did you really have to kill all those people?' she asked, trying to keep her voice calm and even. Right now, Mallory held all the cards. She was only a few steps away from Alison.

She had done exactly what Mallory had asked of her, in an effort to save Alison's life, but now she was here she honestly didn't know if she could, and no one knew where she was.

Mallory was right about two things: she was in control and Kim was very much on her own.

The woman smiled at her in a sickly sweet way as she took two steps backwards. The evil glinted at her; the menace stilled the breath in her chest.

Mallory reached out one delicate, manicured hand and pushed Alison over the edge.

CHAPTER 130

'What's the time?' Bryant asked, as they hurried towards the car.

'Ten to eight,' Stacey answered.

'And Dawson died at?…'

'About three minutes past the hour,' Stacey answered.

Bryant cursed himself for having called it wrong. If anything happened to either Alison or the guv he would never be able to forgive himself.

'So, we're agreed?' he said, as they got back into Penn's car. 'The flats where the guv lived at Hollytree.'

'It's the only place left,' Stacey said, breathlessly, as his phone began to ring.

'Damn it,' he said, seeing Woody's name flashing on the screen. He had the feeling of being out of time in more ways than one.

'Sir…'

'Bryant, please tell me that an incident on the roof of Chaucer House has nothing to do with your boss, yourself or the current investigation into—'

'What type of incident?' he asked.

'No detail as yet. Officers are en route now what the hell?…'

'Thank you, sir,' Bryant said, ending the call and switching off his phone.

Bryant did a quick calculation of the time and distance that stood between them and the guv.

'Okay, Penn, let's see how you can make this thing go,' he said, putting on his seat belt.

As his colleague tore out of the car park Bryant had that feeling of rushing and speeding to work when the clock was telling you that you were already too late.

CHAPTER 131

'All those people died because of how much you hated me?' Kim asked, as they stood facing each other. Her eyes were now focussed on the taut rope that strained against the heating equipment, saving Alison from certain death.

'Don't try and distract me, Stone. I'm sure you've put it all together.'

'By my reckoning, if you want to do this right we've got a few minutes to kill. What the hell am I going to do to stop you?' Kim asked, throwing out her arms. 'I have nothing to fight you with and Dawson fell at three minutes past the hour, so talk to me. Why so many people?' she asked, trying desperately to think. She had nothing. No weapon. No way to distract her opponent to gain the upper hand.

All she could do was play for time.

Time… she realised, suddenly.

She deliberately looked down towards the straining rope. Mallory watched her every move. She took a step closer to the heater knowing that the woman would do the same.

'You were the outreach worker,' Kim said. 'You offered Amy and Mark blankets, a meal. You gained their trust. Told them you could help them with a flat. You called and lured them there with the key Duggar had cut when he viewed the flat?'

'Ah, yes, John, a lovely boy.'

'You met him at the prison, didn't you?' Kim asked, taking another step towards the straining rope.

Mallory did the same.

Timing, Kim reminded herself. It was all in the timing.

'You saw a tall strong man who could be easily manipulated with a few gentle words. The guy only ever wanted someone to be nice to him. To treat him like a human being.'

'And I did that,' she answered. 'It paid dividends.'

'He had no clue what he was doing, did he? You told him what to do and he just did it. He got his ex-cellmate to send the blackmail email to Beckett. He had no idea what you were going to do to Billie but he lured her to those woods so you could assault her so brutally.'

Mallory shrugged without one ounce of emotion.

'He ran away like a stupid little girl,' Mallory said, sounding uncomfortably like her father. 'He'd served his purpose, so I dispatched him. It was the kindest thing to do,' she said as though he was an injured animal beyond repair.

Kim worked hard to hide her disgust but she knew she had to fight the emotion back down if she had any hope of saving Alison's life. She had to concentrate and keep Mallory focussed.

She took another step forward.

Mallory followed and held out the knife. 'Stone, I'm warning you…'

'And the Phelpses were an absolute gift, weren't they?' she asked. 'A respectable couple out of their depth visiting their son in prison. I bet they just loved the reassurance of someone like you; so similar, so knowledgeable about the system. Joel told me they spent more time chatting with other visitors. They were the innocent trusting couple that you could easily subdue with the quick injection and then set fire to the car.'

'The higher the dose the quicker it works,' Mallory offered. 'From the back seat of their car it was easy enough to give them a quick prick and then cover the seat belt buttons for a few seconds.'

Kim thought about the two of them, imprisoned by a mechanism that was designed to keep them safe.

'You started the blaze inside the car so you had enough time to get out and drive away, while they sat there paralysed as the flames leapt up around them.'

'Ingenious, I thought,' she said, pleasantly.

Oh, how Kim wanted to rush across the space that separated them and smash that expression from her face, but she had to stay focussed. She knew the time was getting close.

'But why kill Ernest Beckett?' Kim asked. 'You'd already blackmailed him into giving you the file so?…'

'Because he was a weak, pathetic specimen of a man who would have gone to the police eventually. He was a loose end.'

'So, you drugged him too and then killed him? Just another body on the pile?' Kim spat, unable to keep her feelings out of her voice, but the woman's disregard for human life revealed just how much she was like her father.

'And that's where you got the drugs from. It's what you used to inject your father to keep his muscles…'

Kim's words trailed away as something suddenly occurred to her. The drug used was a muscle relaxant.

'Oh my god, he wasn't paralysed, was he?' Kim asked, only now wondering why someone who had no feeling would need a muscle relaxant. 'You *kept* him in that chair?'

'Made him easier to handle,' she said as a distasteful look fell over her face. 'For the first time in my life, I had control. I could treat him just as he'd treated me for so many years.'

It occurred to Kim that during the hate crimes investigation they had uncovered many of the Preeces' family secrets. But maybe not all of them.

Kim took another step.

Mallory followed.

'What the hell did he do to you, Mallory?'

'Nothing I didn't repay him for tenfold once I had the chance,' she said with steel in her voice. 'And then I had a son who was just like him. Bart was cut from the same cloth and it was like looking at the old man all over again.'

Kim couldn't help the irony that struck her that she was exactly like them both.

'But my Dale made everything better,' she said. 'He was the son I wanted, the one I really cared about. The others never mattered to me.'

Kim couldn't stop the confusion that formed on her face.

'But that's what all this was for,' she said. 'You hate me because of your father and your son. Indirectly I took them away from you.'

Mallory's eyes widened in surprise. 'That's what you think? You think I did all this for those two bastards? You think that's at the core of my rage?'

'Of course.'

The woman laughed out loud.

'I don't hate you for what you've done to them. They're both dead and I hated them. I hate you for what you've done to the one that's still alive.'

CHAPTER 132

'Time?' Bryant asked as Penn brought the car to a screeching halt in front of Chaucer House.

'Two minutes to eight,' Penn said, as he appraised the scene.

Groups of people were pointing up to the roof, some laughing as though the sight was being provided as night-time entertainment.

'Fuck,' Bryant said, as the others followed his gaze.

'It's her,' Stacey whispered. 'It's Alison.'

The woman was hanging by a rope tied to her feet. It didn't take Bryant long to realise that she wasn't struggling or moving at all.

A squad car pulled up behind them.

'Get everyone away,' Bryant instructed, as the three of them rushed into the building.

Bryant had spotted his own car parked further along the row and once again cursed himself for making the wrong call.

'Fucking lifts,' Bryant growled at the OUT OF ORDER sign on one and the other clearly resting below ground level.

'Stairs,' they all said at the same time, rushing through the heavy fire doors.

A dark figure appeared in front of them.

'Where yer going, blud?'

'Out the way,' Bryant said.

He held out his hand. 'There's a toll…'

Bryant reached out and closed his hand around the young man's throat and hauled him out of the way.

'Okay, who's the fastest?…'

Penn didn't even bother to answer as he started to run up thirteen flights of stairs.

CHAPTER 133

'What the hell are you talking about?' Kim asked, taking one more step towards the woman, who had clearly lost her mind.

'You don't get it, do you?' she hissed. 'He's obsessed with you. He thinks about you all the time. He killed his own brother to save you and even in prison—'

'He hates me,' Kim said, trying to make the woman understand.

'Damn well wish he did. I've been trying for long enough to make him. He's the only one I ever cared about. My dad, Bart, I couldn't care less. Dale is the only one of them I ever loved and all he can think about is you. You're right there in the prison with him and you'll be with him when he gets out. That's why I hate you and that's why you have to die.

'Because then I'll get him back. Then he'll be all mine again.'

'Mallory, you've lost your damn mind,' Kim said, taking another step, her mind's eye picturing Alison hanging over the side of the building.

Mallory followed and held the knife aloft.

'I told you, now one more time and I'm gonna…'

Kim stepped forward one more time, praying she'd timed it right.

CHAPTER 134

'We'll never catch him,' Stacey puffed as the two of them raced up what felt like the tenth flight of steps but had probably been less.

He agreed. Penn had headed off like a whippet. But the roof was not where they were going.

'This one,' he said, exiting the stairway. He stood for a second, getting his bearings. He turned left, ran to the window and then headed for the first door.

He banged his fist against it and shouted at the same time.

'Bryant, what the?...' Stacey's words trailed away as her thoughts caught up with his. 'Got it,' she said, bending her head and opening the letterbox while Bryant continued to thump.

'Let us in,' she shouted. 'Police, let us in. Come to the door.'

The door opened next to it and a kid with low-slung jeans and a ponytail answered. 'Hey, wassup?'

'Who lives here? We need to get in,' Stacey said, as Bryant continued to bang.

'Old Mrs Thomas but Friday night, innit? Bingo till ten.'

'Shit,' Bryant said, looking around. He grabbed the fire extinguisher. He knew this was the flat from where they could try and reach her.

'Stace, go in there, find a window and just call out to her. Tell her we're gonna get her down.'

Stacey ushered the lad inside as he took a swing at the door. It left a decent dent but no movement on the door.

He swung back and then forward again with all his might and aimed right for the door handle throwing in the loudest cry of persuasion.

The door crashed open.

Even from the front door he could see through to the lounge and Alison's torso hanging in front of the window.

He wiped the sweat from his brow as he sprinted along the hall, almost falling over a metal walking frame.

The whole window stretched from floor to ceiling and was formed of three parts: the bottom part that came up to his waist was by far the biggest – the panel behind which was Alison's head and shoulders. The other two panels above were half the size and only one had a window handle.

Immediately he could see that it wasn't big enough to be able to grab the rope and pull her inside.

'Shit, shit, shit,' he said, rubbing at his forehead again.

His only option was to try and smash the biggest panel of glass. He knew to do so was to risk showering her with shards, injuring, blinding or possibly killing her.

Or she could potentially fall to her death, said a small voice inside his head.

He ran back for the fire extinguisher and launched it towards the glass.

It bounced right back at him.

CHAPTER 135

Mallory took the final step towards the straining rope and leaned down.

The knife flicked across the taut strands as the heating system burst into life right beside her, bang on time at 8 p.m.

Kim lurched forward, only needing that element of surprise to distract the woman for one second.

Mallory managed to get one more cut across the rope before Kim knocked her backwards.

The taut rope had been sliced not severed but Alison's weight on the other end hanging over the side of the building was adding strain.

'Get… off…'

Kim rolled around on the floor atop Mallory who still had possession of the knife.

Mallory struggled to get back towards the rope to give it one more slice.

'Have to… kill…'

'You're killing no one else, you fucking bitch,' Kim barked, finally able to let her true emotions out.

Kim knew that her colleague was currently dangling over the edge of the building secured only by a rope that was suffering under the strain but she couldn't let this woman free while she still had the knife.

'It's getting weaker,' Mallory said, breathlessly, looking at the straining threads.

Kim felt underneath the woman and found one hand and then the other.

Nothing. No knife.

Kim lifted Mallory's head up and then banged it off the ground but she wouldn't stop squirming and Kim had no clue where the knife was now. But Mallory did. If she gave her even a second of freedom she could reach over and sever the rope.

'Where is it you fucking bitch?' Kim screamed, rolling her slightly to the right.

Nothing.

'Aaarrrgghhhhh…' Kim cried out as she rolled her to the left and her injured thigh got caught between them.

But there it was, resting beneath her hip bone.

Kim grabbed for it giving Mallory the opportunity to swing her arm back and strike Kim on the side of the head.

Her vision clouded for a second, which was all Mallory needed to buck Kim off her, but Kim still had the knife clutched firmly in her palm.

Mallory squirmed and scooted out from beneath her delivering another elbow blow to her head.

Kim rocked sideways as Mallory got to her feet and took a step towards the rope. The woman didn't have the knife but she could untie the knot.

'Oh no you don't,' Kim screamed, lurching forward. She aimed the knife and thrust it into the back of the woman's knee.

Mallory cried out in agony as she fell to the ground.

Kim instantly reached down to re-secure the rope. It snapped in her hand.

Kim grabbed onto it with both hands as the momentum of Alison's weight falling pulled her and the rope across the rooftop. She managed to secure both palms around the rope and was slammed against the wall.

'I'm not letting go,' she screamed out as the rope burned into the skin on the palms of her hand. Every muscle in her arms and shoulders felt like it was being ripped from her bones.

'I'm not fucking letting go,' she cried out again and prayed that Alison could hear her.

She would allow the rope to pull her over the edge before she let it go.

She screamed out in pain as she felt as though her shoulders were leaving their sockets.

'I'm not. I'm not… I'm not,' she said to herself as Mallory managed to stagger back to her feet.

The woman reached down and pulled the knife from her knee and limped forward, crying out with every movement.

'Stay back, Mallory,' Kim cried, knowing there was nothing she could do.

She couldn't defend herself and hold onto the rope that held Alison.

Blood was oozing from the wound in her knee but Mallory barely seemed to notice as she advanced on Kim.

'And now I'm going to finish it,' Mallory said, just three paces away from her.

Kim held tight to the rope.

She would not let go of Alison.

She met Mallory's hate-filled gaze defiantly.

'I'm not letting her—'

Kim's words were cut off as the roof door burst open.

The noise distracted Mallory for as long as Penn needed to sprint towards them and throw her back across the roof.

Never had Kim been so pleased to see anyone in her life.

'I'm not losing her, Penn,' she said, as the rope bit into the cuts on her hands. 'I swear I'm not letting her go. I've got her.'

Penn placed his hands on the rope above hers.

'I know, boss, and now I've got her too.'

CHAPTER 136

Even by Hollytree's standards they were providing quite the floor show.

Six squad cars, four ambulances and a fire engine that had been called when Alison was spotted dangling over the edge of the building. Thankfully, Bryant's second attempt to break the window had been successful and he, Stacey and a kid named Brad had hauled her to safety.

'You okay?' Bryant said, as they watched the first ambulance containing Mallory Preece leave the scene.

Two squad cars followed and Penn was close behind, insisting on attending the hospital to ensure the woman was properly guarded during emergency medical treatment to her knee.

'I look ridiculous,' she said, holding up her bandaged hands. A local injection had numbed the pain for now but had done nothing for the agony in her shoulders. Thank God Penn had arrived when he had, helping her to hold on to Alison until Bryant pulled her in.

'You stole my car,' he observed, drily.

'Borrowed,' she corrected. 'I always intended to give it back. I mean if I was gonna nick something I'd go for—'

'Hey, leave her alone, she does okay.' He narrowed his eyes. 'Seriously, though, you couldn't give us some kind of clue?'

She shook her head. 'The message said come alone and I couldn't risk Alison's life. Enough people have died this week.'

'Guv, how many more times are we going to have this conversation?'

She smiled. 'Oh, lots, I should think,' she said, pushing herself up from the rear of the ambulance.

'I swear, one of these days…'

'Yeah, yeah, where is she?' Kim asked.

'Ambo on the left,' he said, following her.

'Hey,' she said, opening the ambulance door. She wasn't surprised to see Stacey sitting beside the behaviourist.

Alison's face had regained some colour but a sheen of terror remained in her eyes.

'Getting any feeling back?'

A slight nod confirmed that she was. 'A lot of tingling,' she said in a husky voice. She swallowed and a tear formed. 'If you hadn't come…'

'But we did, Alison,' Kim said, reaching over and taking a glass shard from her hair. 'We all did.'

The tear slid over her cheek as the female paramedic leaned over.

'We're taking her in to get her checked over but should be okay in a few hours.'

'I'm going with her, boss,' Stacey said.

Kim was not surprised.

'Inspector…'

Kim moved closer.

'I don't know what… there are no…'

'Save your energy,' Kim said.

Kim couldn't imagine the terror she'd experienced in the clutches of Mallory, having full control of her brain but no control of her body. It would take a while until she felt normal again.

'Okay, go and get checked now and, for God's sake, Stace, as soon as you can, get her something to eat.'

She was rewarded with a chuckle from both as she stepped back on to the gravel.

'Hey, Stone,' she heard and didn't need to turn to know it's source.

She groaned. 'Bryant, have I not done enough good in my life to—'

'Just one fucking minute, Stone,' Frost called louder.

Kim grudgingly changed direction and headed towards the journalist.

'What is it, Frost?' she asked, reaching the cordon.

'Your voicemail broken?'

'My voicemail is perfectly fine, thank you. I was under strict instructions from my boss to stay away from the press and no matter how many messages you leave I'm not gonna call back and discuss the finer details of an ongoing—'

'Oh, how I'd love to let you continue your lecture and allow you to look even more ridiculous,' she said, folding her arms and tipping her head so that her long blonde ponytail swished across her back. 'But I think I'll just shut you up right now by telling you there's a big, thick file in the back of Bryant's car.'

A file? Her file?

'Yeah,' Frost continued. 'Stupid bitch sent it to me thinking I'd publish it.'

And the hits from Mallory Preece just kept on coming.

'You weren't tempted?' Kim asked.

'You ain't all that, Stone. Much more interesting stuff to report this week.'

'But you read it?' Kim asked, knowingly. The woman was a reporter after all.

She shook her head. 'Like I said, you ain't all that.'

Kim offered her a smile and turned away realising she could still be surprised by people after all.

CHAPTER 137

Kim rubbed her right palm against her hip as she waited to be shown into the visitor's centre.

In the days since the confrontation with Mallory on the roof her thick dressings had been reduced to a thin bandage and had begun to heal. And itch.

Mallory Preece had been charged with the murder of Amy Wilde and Mark Johnson, John Duggar and the Phelpses. CPS were dubious about the murder of Ernest Beckett as the only tangible link was the use of the drug Baclofen but with no proof of who had injected it. They hadn't given up yet and her team would continue to work towards a conviction. The one they had to let go was the horrific assault of Billie Styles who had not seen or heard her attacker and had only responded to a message to meet John Duggar at the park.

Mallory was saying nothing and had chosen to hide behind a very expensive lawyer. Kim wasn't sure what she was hoping to achieve but CPS were confident that she'd never see freedom again.

Amy's mother had been truly mortified that her suspicions about her daughter's involvement had been groundless. After a little digging had confirmed it to be the same MO as seven other attacks traced back to a travelling gang from Lincolnshire, Kim had been able to reassure her that Amy had had nothing to do with her attack and mugging. Kim had felt as though she was piling guilt on top of guilt when speaking to the woman, but once the horror faded she hoped her memories of her child would be a bit more positive. Amy deserved that much. Sadly, she had been unable to find anyone who cared about Mark's demise.

But Kim consoled herself that wherever Mark and Amy were, they were together, which was clearly what they had wanted. Other than some petty theft neither of them had ever hurt a soul. There was no doubt in her mind that they had loved each other very much.

Ernest's colleagues at Children's Services had been genuinely sorry about his death. He'd been a hard-working, genial man with a kind word at the ready for everyone. She was pleased they'd been able to quash the rumours following the bogus complaint and could leave his memory and reputation intact.

Alison was on the mend and had ventured on her first run earlier that morning, accompanied by Stacey who had insisted on needing to shift a few pounds. Kim was interested to see how long that would last. Not because the constable lacked determination but because, whether or not Stacey realised it, she was actually completely content with herself.

Jamie Hart had been questioned and charged with one count of murder and one of attempted murder due to Alison's tenacity and Stacey's assistance. A partial fingerprint had been found on the flamingo earring that had belonged to Beverly and a search of his home had turned up Jennifer's missing silver earring at the bottom of the toilet bowl. Curtis had been released, and Jennifer's parents had been there to greet him.

All the loose ends had been tied up. Except one.

She had known since her time on the roof with Mallory that this was a conversation she had to have and she didn't relish it.

The guard gave her the nod.

She entered the visitor's hall and spotted him straight away. The anxiety shone from his eyes.

'Dale,' she said, taking the seat opposite.

'Inspector…'

'Kim,' she corrected.

For a few seconds their eyes held across the silence.

He rubbed at his forehead. 'I don't even know what to say to you. How can any kind of apology from me help what?…'

'It can't,' Kim said, honestly. 'But that doesn't make it your fault.'

'How could I not have known? She's my mother.'

Kim could hear the bewilderment in his voice, and the last sentence was filled with so many emotions she couldn't even begin to pick them apart.

'She's very much like your grandfather, Dale. There's a ruthless streak that she got from him.'

'And then passed on to Bart. So, how the hell did I get so lucky?'

Kim looked around. 'Lucky?'

'I'd rather this than live with so much hatred.' He closed his eyes and shook his head. 'How many deaths are my family going to be responsible for?' he asked, not really seeking an answer. 'And how many of them have tried to kill you?'

She smiled. 'I attract it.'

He didn't smile back. 'All those poor people. They lost their lives because my—'

'You can't change it, Dale, and you can't hold on to the guilt. That's great advice coming from me but you weren't the one to kill them. Your mother has to live with what she's done.'

Kim knew her words were going nowhere. Dale Preece was the only decent human being to come out of that family and he would assume the guilt of his mother's actions just as he had with his brother and grandfather, thinking it would help the victims or their families in some way.

'I saw the news report. The roof of that building. Did you talk to her?'

The question she'd been waiting for.

She nodded.

'And did she offer any explanation. Did she admit she'd done all this because she holds you responsible for the deaths of my brother and grandfather?'

No, Dale, she did it because of you. She killed all of those people because she didn't have your full attention. She only ever loved you and got caught in some sick and twisted jealous rage because you looked my way. So, indirectly, the death of six innocent people really does come right back to you. Now, eat that guilt for your supper… is what she should have said if she was being truthful.

She raised her gaze and met his. 'Yes, that's exactly what she admitted to me,' she lied easily. This man had saved her life, and she would not saddle him with even more guilt for his mother's actions. That she had done it all for him.

'I still can't fathom…'

'Why did you buy the book?' she asked, crossing her arms.

'Curious,' he answered, honestly.

'And?' she asked, pushing out her chin.

'I didn't read it,' he said. 'Got to the end of page one and it felt too invasive. It's not a book you wrote yourself. You had no control over the contents and I didn't like that feeling.'

Kim appreciated his honesty.

'So, your mum took it?'

He nodded and Kim could picture Mallory gobbling up every detail of the book imagining ways she could use the information to cause as much pain as possible.

And now for the last piece of the puzzle.

'You were the mole in Symes's hate club?'

All along they'd thought it was John Duggar.

He nodded. 'Symes approached me within hours. Green as I was I mentioned it to Officer Gennard, who asked me about my acting skills, and I've been pretending to hate you ever since.'

'And you probably should, you know: hate me.'

He shrugged. 'But I don't.'

'So, what happens for you now?' she asked. It hadn't taken long for the prison grapevine to find out that it was Dale who had alerted Gennard to Symes's plan. He had known that once beyond the confines of the prison walls Symes had many opportunities of reduced security to find a way to break free. And come looking for her.

Symes had still been transferred to the hospital but with double the security presence and two armed police officers.

'I'm being transferred to Featherstone this afternoon. I'm not safe here now but you should know that Symes won't stop trying to get you. If he ever does manage to get out of here he's coming right for you. He uses every day to stroke his hatred of you. It's all he talks about, all he thinks about.'

'I know,' she said as a shudder worked through her.

Silence fell and Kim realised there was nothing left for either of them to say.

She stood, unable to offer her hand across the table.

'I'd shake your hand if I was allowed to,' she said, honestly.

'And I'd have been honoured to shake yours.'

'Take care, Dale, and don't feed the guilt.'

She turned and walked away, feeling his eyes on her back as she went.

She glanced at the clock on the wall as she left.

Now to her real reason for coming.

CHAPTER 138

Kim parked the car opposite the entrance to the crematorium giving herself a good view of the entrance.

She watched silently as the two hearses made their slow approach along the main roadway towards the group of friends and neighbours who had congregated outside the door.

Kim tried to ignore the irony that the Phelpses had both wished to be cremated. The furnace would have less work to do than normal.

The cars pulled to a stop and the black-clad team focussed respectfully on the first coffin, removing it and wheeling it into the building seamlessly, practised hundreds of times, before moving the first car forward to remove the second coffin.

She couldn't help but wonder if this was how Keith and Erica's funeral had been. The one she hadn't been allowed to attend, cut off by Erica's sister because she wasn't 'real' family. She was a foster kid, a social conscience act. But not to Kim and not to them. They had loved her and she had been their daughter. She wasn't sure just how much 'real' family meant anyway. Despite her daughter's excitement, Gemma's mother had once again managed to get in trouble just hours before her impending release from prison and another bunch of flowers had landed in the bin. Kim took no pleasure in having called it correctly at the beginning of the week.

A week that had brought many emotions, all to be buried. Too many memories to be avoided and ignored and in some cases simply denied. Mallory Preece had violated her entire life and chosen the most traumatic events, picked at the closed boxes in her mind to destroy her. And it could have had she not chosen to push the emotions down and bury them all over again.

In truth she had wanted to curl up in a ball beneath heavy blankets when she'd first seen Mark and Amy chained together in the flat. Her arms had felt the familiar sensation of Mikey's body within her embrace. She had remembered his smile, his laugh, his pain, his death.

When she'd seen the burnt-out car outside the old speedway site she'd been rushed by memories of the three years she'd spent with the loving couple and the safety she'd felt in their home. But also the terror when they had both lost their lives.

There were no words to describe the emotions that had coursed through her when she'd seen the brutalised figure of Billie Styles in the woods.

She understood Bryant's concern about her refusal to deal with issues from her past and maybe she had swallowed a ticking time bomb that would explode at some time in the future, but it wasn't now and no more people would die because of someone's twisted jealousy towards her.

But throughout it all the one thing, the one emotion, that had refused to be silenced was regret. Regret that she hadn't fought her corner or asked someone to fight it for her. She should have been allowed to say goodbye to the only parents she'd ever known.

She had visited the graveyard afterwards to say her own goodbye but their ashes had been scattered at the rose garden and the small plaque bearing their names had not yet been made. It hadn't been a suitable farewell and that final missing piece had haunted her always.

She watched as the final mourner entered the building and reached into the glovebox for the last remaining copy of *The Lost Child*, the book about her life. Something to read while she waited.

She turned in her seat to Joel Greene, suited, grateful and without handcuffs.

'Go on, Joel,' she whispered, emotionally. 'Go in and say goodbye to your parents.'

A LETTER FROM ANGELA

First of all, I want to say a huge thank you for choosing to read *Dead Memories,* the tenth instalment of the Kim Stone series.

This book is the perfect example of how characters can suddenly dictate a different direction of travel. My mind is always a couple of books ahead with regard to what I want to explore at what stage of the journey. So I knew the theme I wanted to study in book 10, however that was not meant to be and as I began working on book 10 another idea kept interrupting my thoughts.

I made a note of the idea thinking this would quiet it for a while but it had the opposite effect and more and more ideas, plot lines and characters flew into my mind. I fought it for weeks before eventually giving up the battle and starting book 10 again.

The idea that refused to go away was about a killer that wanted to recreate traumatic events of Kim's life causing her to re-examine both her own past and previous cases worked by the team. Even I was eager to know how she would handle such a situation and I hope you enjoyed the result.

If you did enjoy it, I would be forever grateful if you'd write a review. I'd love to hear what you think, and it can also help other readers discover one of my books for the first time. Or maybe you can recommend it to your friends and family…

I'd love to hear from you – so please get in touch on my Facebook or Goodreads page, twitter or through my website.

And if you'd like to keep up-to-date with all my latest releases, just sign up at the website link below. I promise to only contact you when I have a new book out and I'll never share your email with anyone else.

www.bookouture.com/angela-marsons

If you haven't read any of the previous books in the DI Kim Stone series, you can find them here:

Silent Scream
Evil Games
Lost Girls
Play Dead
Blood Lines
Dead Souls
Broken Bones
Dying Truth
Fatal Promise

Thank you so much for your support, it is hugely appreciated.

Angela Marsons

www.angelamarsons-books.com

angelamarsonsauthor

@WriteAngie

ACKNOWLEDGEMENTS

Without fail I must first acknowledge the contribution to these books from my partner, Julie. Along with me she treats each book as the first journey and attacks the process with enthusiasm and often more confidence than me. Her patience and faith in me never wanes and neither does her willingness to help me through every part of the process. It must be said that although brutally honest at times she knows my capabilities better than I do and always finds a way to reach in and understand the vision in my mind and help me find the best way to get there. She is and will always be my partner in crime.

Thank you to my Mum and Dad who continue to spread the word proudly to anyone who will listen. And to my sister Lyn, her husband Clive and my nephews Matthew and Christopher for their support too.

Thank you to Amanda and Steve Nicol who support us in so many ways and to Kyle Nicol for book-spotting my books everywhere he goes.

I would like to thank the team at Bookouture for their continued enthusiasm for Kim Stone and her stories and especially to Oliver Rhodes who gave Kim Stone an opportunity to exist.

Special thanks to my editor, Claire Bord, whose patience and understanding was truly appreciated and her response to the book both delighted and reassured me. I think we did okay, lady, and I look forward to working on the next.

To Kim Nash (Mama Bear) who works tirelessly to promote our books and protect us from the world. To Noelle Holten who has limitless enthusiasm and passion for our work.

Thank you to the fantastic Kim Slater who has been an incredible support and friend to me for many years now and to the fabulous Caroline Mitchell, Renita D'Silva and Sue Watson without whom this journey would be impossible. Huge thanks to the growing family of Bookouture authors who continue to amuse, encourage and inspire me on a daily basis.

My eternal gratitude goes to all the wonderful bloggers and reviewers who have taken the time to get to know Kim Stone and follow her story. These wonderful people shout loudly and share generously not because it is their job but because it is their passion. I will never tire of thanking this community for their support of both myself and my books. Thank you all so much.

Massive thanks to all my fabulous readers, especially the ones that have taken time out of their busy day to visit me on my website, Facebook page, Goodreads or Twitter.

Lightning Source UK Ltd.
Milton Keynes UK
UKHW021813100519
342479UK00013B/187/P